Praise for the Allison Campbell Mystery Series

KILLER IMAGE

"An edgy page-turner that pulls the reader into a world where image is everything and murder is all about image. Great start to a new series!"

— Erika Chase,
Author of The Ashton Corners Book Club Mysteries

"Wit, charm, and deliciously clever plot twists abound...the author has a knack for creating characters with heart, while keeping us guessing as to their secrets until the end."

— Mary Hart Perry,
Author of *Seducing the Princess*

"This cleverly revealing psychological thriller will keep you guessing...as the smart and savvy Allison Campbell (love her!) delves into the deadly motives, twisted emotions and secret intrigues of Philadelphia's Main Line."

— Hank Phillippi Ryan,
Mary Higgins Clark, Agatha, Anthony and Macavity Award-Winning Author of *The Wrong Girl*

"Nancy Drew gets a fierce makeover in Wendy Tyson's daringly dark, yet ever fashion-conscious mystery series, beginning with *Killer Image*. Tyson imbues her characters with emotional depth amidst wit, ever maintaining the pulse rate."

— Deborah Cloyed,
Author of *What Tears Us Apart* and *The Summer We Came to Life*

"An intriguing psychological thriller. The book reminded me of Jonathan Kellerman's Alex Delaware series...I loved the book, it's dark and hopeful at the same time. Five stars out of five."

— Lynn Farris,
Mystery Books Examiner for Examiner.com

KILLER
IMAGE

KILLER IMAGE

An Allison Campbell Mystery

WENDY TYSON

HENERY PRESS

KILLER IMAGE
An Allison Campbell Mystery
Part of the Henery Press Mystery Collection

First Edition
Trade paperback edition | October 2013

Henery Press
www.henerypress.com

ISBN-13: 978-1-938383-60-1

Printed in the United States of America

This book is dedicated to my parents, Gary and Angela Tyson.
Together they taught me the importance of hard work,
the value of faith, and the incredible beauty and power of love.

ACKNOWLEDGMENTS

They say it takes a village to raise a child; I'd say it also takes a village to inspire a novel and bring it to completion. So many people have played a role in supporting or inspiring my writing life. I am so very grateful.

First, I'd like to thank my family, especially my husband, Ben, who has shown endless patience. Compromised vacations, writers' groups, writing classes, conferences, night time ramblings about plot and character and, of course, the self-pity party that comes with rejection, are but a few of the things you've lovingly endured over the years. So thank you, Ben! And thanks to my boys, Ian, Matthew and Jonathan, whose love and endless encouragement are incredible gifts.

I'd like to thank my talented agents, Frances Black and Jennifer Mishler of Literary Counsel. Fran, you've entertained my five a.m. emails—and written right back! You and Jenn have been a constant source of support, wisdom and encouragement and I love working with you.

Thank you to Henery Press, especially my fabulous editor, Kendel Flaum. Kendel, I appreciate your keen eye and sharp pencil. You have a gift for writing and editing, and I have learned so much simply from watching you work.

A great big thanks to Rowena Copeland. You have helped me navigate the very new waters of publishing with patience, creativity and vision. I love your passion for books.

I am forever grateful to my early readers, especially Mark Anderson, Virginia Lofft, Toni Lopopolo, Greg Smith, Jennifer Brown, Marnie Mai, Suzanne Norbury, Carolyn Sweeney, Ann Jordan,

Michelle Rosenstein Sofield, Stephanie Wollman and Carol Lizell. Your thoughtful feedback made this a better book. And Toni Lopopolo—a special thanks for seeing potential in an impatient writer. You are an incredible teacher, editor and mentor.

Love and gratitude to my uncle, Greg Marincola. All those philosophical discussions growing up sparked my love of reading and learning and probably had the biggest direct impact on my desire to write. Thanks U.G.!

A huge thank you to my parents, Gary and Angela Tyson, who always encouraged my reading habit. Dad, I know you would be so proud (but practical) if you were still with us today. And Mom, you have been the best cheerleader ever. A big thanks to my brother, Gary Tyson, and my extended family, too. What a blessing to grow up in the midst of so much love.

And, of course, I'm grateful to mystery readers, who share my passion for the genre. Thank you for making this possible.

ONE

Arnie Feldman needed a drink, a bath, and a screw, in that order. But no one was home, except Sasha's dog. Stupid beast. Arnie picked up the Chihuahua, tossed him in the study and slammed the door. Then he took off his shoes, careful not to scuff the newly polished leather, and placed them next to the foyer closet. Sasha could put them away later. Where was she, anyway? And where was Ethan? He glanced at his watch: 7:18. Too late for shopping. Who was he kidding? For his wife, it was never too late to shop.

Arnie walked through the hall and into the kitchen. Like a showroom kitchen, he thought. Damn. Might as well be a showroom kitchen for all the use it gets. Something seemed out of place, but what?

He headed for the bar. Scotch. Straight up. He was too tired for ice. It was the Bremburg case. That little girl with her sad eyes and lopsided pigtails. That mother with her pleas and allegations of Jack Bremburg's sexual perversions. But *Jack* was his client. Arnie was paid to advocate, and advocate he would. The allegations were false. He was sure of it.

They had to be.

Arnie poured three fingers of scotch. Four. What the hell? Why was he plagued with a conscience? A good divorce attorney should never be swayed by crap the other side made up. Never. And he *was* a good divorce attorney. The best. He smiled, tipped the glass into his mouth, and swallowed, savoring the slow burn that would lead to oblivion. He poured another glass. Where was Sasha?

He heard a noise coming from upstairs. Ethan. Sasha must have left him home while she went to the mall. Shopping. Was that all she did these days, shop? And have her hair done. And exercise with that idiotic personal trainer. Damn, he worked hard so his wife could spend money at Neiman Marcus and his kid could act like a spoiled prick. Teenagers. Should have let Brenda keep the kid. He lived for the day he and Sasha would have an empty nest. No mess, more privacy. They could do it whenever and wherever he damn well pleased.

He threw back the second glass.

He wanted Sasha now. Wanted her to wear that little black number he'd bought online, wanted her face down on the bed...

Crash.

What was that boy doing? "Ethan?" Arnie slammed down his glass. His head was starting to throb.

Crash.

"Ethan!"

Arnie made his way up the stairs. The scotch was working its magic, and his feet felt lighter. Jack Bremburg no longer felt like a noose was around his neck. Jack was innocent. Of course he was innocent. How could a man so rich, so successful, let a little character flaw get in his way? He wouldn't be so stupid. Arnie tried not to think of other people, equally rich and powerful, who *were* that stupid.

Crash.

"Ethan! Knock it the hell off!"

Three more steps to the top of the stairs.

Crash.

It was coming from his bedroom—noises like dressers being thrown to the floor. What was Ethan doing in his bedroom? If he had that little hussy up there using the Jacuzzi, his ass would be toast tonight. That little witch he'd forbidden Ethan to see? Grounded. For a week. No, a month.

Crash.

The bedroom door was closed.

Crash.

Arnie braced himself for a confrontation with his son, then flung open the door and stepped inside. It took a moment for his eyes to adjust to the darkness. Shadows on the walls, paint on the hardwood. That smell. What was that smell?

An object hissed through air. Arnie felt a blow to the side of his skull and then, for a moment, everything went black. When he came to, a deep throbbing filled his head. Something covered his mouth and bound his hands. He couldn't scream, couldn't move.

Suddenly, unseen hands tore open his shirt. Arnie flinched as nails bit into tender skin. He heard the snap of the match before he smelled the sharp scent of sulfur. With horror, he caught a glimpse of a shadowy face. Eyes like the devil. He thought of the Bremburg girl's pigtails, brown and glossy and uncentered. Only one red bow.

Then came the pain.

And it didn't stop.

TWO

Allison Campbell may have spent the last eight hours teaching people how to project confidence, class, and charisma, but by three o'clock Wednesday afternoon, she was feeling uncharacteristically drained.

It was nearly the end of March, the time of year early-rising daffodils should begin stretching their way from a long sleep, but winter held on with the tenacity of a stubborn two-year-old. Clouds shifted and sulked in the sky, their brooding manner warning of even more snow and sleet. Allison tried to keep her focus on work, but her mind drifted to the weather, her sore feet, what she would have for dinner...anything but the paper in front of her.

She looked again at the pink slip crumpled next to her, at Vaughn's tight, slanted handwriting. *Call your sister. Important.* With Faye, it was always important. Allison didn't have the stomach for it. Not now. Still, she felt that familiar knot in her belly at just the thought of Faye. She'd call her back later.

Allison took off blue-framed eyeglasses and rubbed her temples before focusing her attention back on the woman across the desk. Neck swathed in a maroon-print scarf, short, wavy black hair perfectly coiffed, Midge Majors was picking at the edges of her scarf with elegantly manicured fingers. Allison had spent the last eleven months convincing Midge that she could reinvent herself, that the world had need of women like her, even after the family life she had carefully cultivated had fallen apart. And Midge had risen to the challenge.

This Midge looked almost the same as the Midge she had met a year ago: pillbox hats and coordinating scarves in colors that matched her array of shirt dresses, sensible one-inch pumps in neutral colors, little circles of red rouge on her heavy cheeks. But the changes were deeper. She no longer apologized after every other sentence. She maintained eye contact for long periods of time. And now, most important of all, she could laugh about her divorce.

When seventy-one-year-old Midge caught her husband cheating with the neighbor's adult son, in a burst of rage, she tried to kill him with an antique Remington-Ingersoll Life Line gun. Luckily she was even less skilled with the gun than she'd been at expressing her feelings. The ex-husband was fine, but Midge suffered a breakdown. Over the last year, all that had changed.

"I can't do it," Midge had said.

"You can, Midge—and you will."

"I'm too darn old."

Allison smiled. "It's never too late for a new adventure."

"Who's going to take me seriously? I haven't worked in forty years. My son says why bother."

"Your son doesn't always know what's best for you, Midge." Allison placed her hands down on the desk between them for emphasis. Midge's deference to the family that abandoned her when she most needed them had been maddening at first. But as sessions with Allison wore on, Midge seemed to like the person she saw in the mirror and her dependence on her sons' opinions had lessened. Today's self-doubt, Allison knew, was simply a case of the nerves. And who could blame her?

"Your sons are not part of this equation. This is about you and the school's musical director. And *you*," Allison said with a smile, "are going to be fantastic."

Allison watched a theater of emotions flicker across Midge's face: disbelief, fear, anger, and, finally, determination. It was the determination Allison wanted, for Midge and all of her clients. The determination to fight against a world that wanted to dismiss her as frivolous or unworthy. The determination to create something better for herself.

Midge nodded, the helplessness in her expression replaced by a slow-burning fire in her eyes. "One more time? Just to be sure I have everything covered?"

And so Allison went through it all again: the protocol, the interview outfit they'd agreed on—charcoal gray dress, soft cream scarf, silver beads, black pumps, rose-colored lipstick—and the reminders to have good posture, make eye contact, and project her voice. "Quiet confidence," Allison said, "is your number-one asset."

"I was a darn good pianist once upon a time."

"You're a damn good musician *now*."

Midge rose to leave, her grin sincere. Allison felt hopeful that Midge would get this job and, with it, a new start on life. Hopeful, but...well, sometimes life could pull a fast one.

When Midge was gone, Allison sat back down at her desk and pulled out another file. Inside were the details of another woman whose story was similar—years of family devotion followed by divorce and a frustrating reentry into a very changed world. Allison started to feel a well of anger and sadness at the injustice of it all.

She thought: Don't go there, Al.

Adding her own emotions to the mix wasn't going to help anyone. Besides, often having an advocate, someone who believed in them even when it felt like no one else did, was the magic that made the difference for her clients. It was her job to be that person, and she could think of no better way to spend her days. Even when the circumstances weighed heavily on her heart and mind. Like now.

"You have a visitor, Allison."

Allison looked up to see her business manager, Vaughn, standing in the doorway. He had a mug of coffee in his hand, which he placed on her desk. Two creamers, one sugar, just the way she liked it. Allison smiled her gratitude.

"Don't be so quick with a grin. You haven't seen who your visitor is yet."

Oy. She thought of the note from Faye. It wasn't exactly shaping up to be a great day, so luck was probably not on her side. Maybe Faye could wait until tomorrow. Doubtful. Allison tugged a stray blond hair away from her face and tucked it behind her ear. She looked up at Vaughn and noticed, not for the first time, the signs that something bigger than this business, First Impressions, was happening in his life. Vaughn's hair was beginning to gray around the edges, his eyes held a tired glaze, and his near-black skin looked ashy and dry. Clearly he wasn't sleeping. Concerned, she wanted to ask what was going on, but something in Vaughn's manner held her back.

Instead, she said, "Who is it?"

"Hank McBride. And his wife."

"*Congressman* Hank McBride?"

"One and the same."

Allison's mind spun. What was Hank McBride doing here? "Do they have an appointment?"

"No." Vaughn frowned. "I told them you couldn't be disturbed, but the congressman was quite insistent."

Allison could tell by the look of distaste on Vaughn's face that insistent meant rude. She glanced again at the pink slip on her desk. She didn't know Hank McBride, didn't know much about him, either, other than a rumor that he had his eye on the White House. But at least his presence would distract her from other things. Things she couldn't control.

"I'll see them in the conference room."

Vaughn's eyebrows shot up in a questioning arc.

"I know, I know. I have other appointments." Allison sighed. "Tell them they have fifteen minutes, tops."

Vaughn nodded, but the look on his face said he thought she was making a mistake.

The first thing that struck Allison about Hank McBride was his smile. There was something about the twist of his lips that set off Allison's lie detector, the way the edges pulled up too high on his face. It didn't match the insolence in his eyes. Before she even shook his hand, Allison knew this was a man who wasn't faithful to the truth.

"Congressman McBride."

"Ms. Campbell." That smile again. "This is my wife, Sunny."

Sunny was the last name she would have picked for the dark goddess standing before her. At five foot seven, Allison had to wrestle Nautilus machines for a penciled-in hour every other day to keep her curves in the right places. But this woman had curves everywhere. She was at least Allison's height, if not taller. Long, wavy black hair that cascaded down her back and flowed alongside sculptured cheekbones. If Hank looked like an Irish longshoreman in his Sunday best, with his reddened nose and bulky build and scrubbed Anglo skin, Sunny resembled a Gypsy Madonna.

"Sunny, lovely to meet you. Please. Sit." Allison motioned toward the loveseat and waited until the couple settled before sitting opposite them in a chair. Hank sat rigid, limbs and hands to himself. Sunny pressed against her husband's side as though siphoning strength.

He said, "We'll get right to the point, Ms. Campbell."

"Please, call me Allison."

"Allison, our daughter Maggie is in need of your—" Hank waved his hand as though searching for the right word, "expertise."

Allison noticed a twitch in his left eye. Every few seconds, he rubbed at the corner of that eye like he could smooth the twitch away.

"I don't want to waste your time or mine," Allison said. "So before we go any further, I don't work with children."

Hank said, "She's fifteen, not a child, really. And we're not looking for a therapist. She's had enough of those. We need someone to help her become more polished."

"I'm sure there are finishing schools, somewhere to send a young lady—"

Hank snorted. Allison caught the subtle movement of Sunny's arm sinking into Hank's side. She wondered about the balance of power in this relationship.

For the first time, Sunny spoke. Her voice was as sultry as her appearance, husky and melodic with the faintest undertones of a Southern accent. "Ms. Campbell...Allison...you have to understand. Maggie is special. She's very smart, but she's, well, eccentric. A bit awkward. She would never, ever go for a finishing school. She requires tender handling."

"And someone who is used to working with misfits," Hank said. "I'll be honest, Allison." He turned to look at Sunny before continuing and gave her a quick stare that said, *This is the truth, file it away for future reference.* Sunny lowered her head, her mouth set in a resigned frown. Hank continued, "Maggie is headstrong. She's had a few minor incidents along the way that keep her from a more prestigious school program. Kid stuff. Shoplifting, peer issues. I get away with a daughter like Maggie because I'm a congressional incumbent. But once the Senate race starts, there will be photo ops and interviews. I cannot have my daughter's appearance or behavior become the sticking point. Frankly, she needs a little refining before she's ready for her public debut."

Sunny touched his arm. He brushed her hand away, leaned in, and said, "I can't put Maggie in front of the camera, Ms. Campbell. I need you. And I'm willing to pay a large sum for your services. A very, very large sum."

Allison took her time responding. Hank's gaze never wavered; his body language—hands on his knees, torso tilted forward—suggested a man who felt tense but confident. And although his words offered incentive, the arrogant look on his face told Allison money was only one side of the coin.

"What makes you think Maggie will work with me?"

"She probably won't," Sunny said. And this time Allison heard the despair in her voice. Hank made a move to interrupt her, but Sunny waved him away. "Allison, please. Our Maggie's got issues. She's a typical teen trying to find herself. I care about Hank's career, I really do, but I care about Maggie more." Sunny looked down at her hands. Her long fingers dug into the tiny bit of flesh on her thighs. Once again, Allison wondered what they weren't telling her.

Sunny looked up. "I read your book, *From the Outside In,* and I thought, wow, that's what Maggie needs. Maybe if she changes the way she dresses and acts, her self-esteem will follow. She has none, esteem that is. Oh, she wears those clothes like she doesn't care what anyone thinks about her, but I know it's an act. Inside, she's a frightened little girl."

Sunny looked at her husband for confirmation. Met with only a stony stare, she said quickly, "I saw your ad in the back of *Philadelphia* magazine. Our older daughter, Catherine, is getting married next year. First Impressions was in the bridal section. It was a sign, Ms. Campbell, I just know it, seeing your ad like that when I wasn't even looking for it. In the bridal section of all places." She looked into Allison's eyes. "Please?"

Allison saw tears clinging to Sunny's lashes, and something told her that this was no act, that Sunny's words were the only honest ones spoken by the McBrides all morning. And that Hank McBride didn't really want to be there. He came solely to appease his wife.

Hank was staring at Allison with a look that said he'd been playing nice, but he could try the asshole route if he wanted to. She wasn't afraid of him. But Sunny...the way she slumped in her seat reminded Allison of her own mother when she found out she had Alzheimer's.

"I'll meet her," Allison said softly.

The tension in the room evaporated. Sunny sat straight and clapped her hands together.

"Wonderful." Hank grinned. "I knew you'd come around."

Allison put her hands up to hold back their enthusiasm. "That's all I'm agreeing to. If I believe Maggie's receptive, I'll take the job. Otherwise—"

"Thank you," Sunny said. "Maggie needs help. You're the person to give it to her."

Another face flashed in Allison's mind. Young, beautiful, haunted. Violet Swann. Someone she couldn't help.

Allison shook her head, as much to ward off unwelcome feelings as to push aside Sunny's gratitude. "Don't thank me yet, Mrs. McBride. I'm only agreeing to meet her."

THREE

After escorting the McBrides out, Allison wandered to Vaughn's office. She wanted some company. She felt restless, annoyed with herself for giving in to the McBrides and breaking her no children policy. But then...poor Maggie. True, she hadn't met the girl yet, but how could a father talk that way about his own daughter? No wonder the kid had issues.

She found Vaughn reading a newspaper, a tight look of concentration on his face. He glanced up when Allison entered and flashed a sympathetic smile.

"You don't look so happy. Meeting not go well?"

"You could say that."

"Don't say I didn't give you an out."

Allison sighed. "He would have gotten to me eventually. Politicians like McBride aren't used to being told no."

Vaughn nodded. "True enough. What was he after?"

"He wants me to work with his daughter, Maggie."

"You don't work with kids."

"No, I don't." Allison stretched her legs out in front of her and felt the pull of tight muscles. "And I probably won't now, either. I only agreed to meet Maggie." She shrugged. "What can I say? I feel sorry for her. And that mother." She shook her head. "So heartbroken."

"Family can do that." When she didn't respond, he said, "So what else is on your mind? You've seemed distracted ever since I told you your sister called."

"My sister's calls never portend anything positive."

"Your mom?"

"Who knows what it is this time? Our mom, the neighbors, the way I fold towels. Could be anything."

Vaughn held Allison's gaze for a long moment before looking down at the newspaper in front of him. "Look at this."

He pushed the paper across the desk to Allison. It was folded, one article prominently framed on the first page. Allison stared at the headline for a moment, its meaning gradually sinking in.

Main Line's "Custody King" Found Dead at 54.

Allison looked up. "The 'Custody King'? Arnie Feldman?"

Vaughn nodded. "Just read the first paragraph."

Allison started reading and the opening shoved all other thoughts aside.

> *Arnie Feldman, well-known divorce attorney and self-proclaimed "Custody King," was found dead at his Villano-va estate yesterday evening. Lieutenant Mark Helms says the police have not ruled out foul play. An anonymous source close to the family told us that Mr. Feldman's widow, Sasha Feldman, was being questioned by the police. An attorney for Mrs. Feldman refused to comment.*

Allison read the article again before looking up. "Murder?"

"Maybe," Vaughn said. "Although murder in these parts doesn't happen too often."

True, Allison thought. Tax evasion. Extortion. Insider trading, perhaps. Rich people's crimes. But not murder. Here amongst the manicured lawns, new money McMansions, and old-money estates of the Philadelphia Main Line, people prided themselves on having class. Murder was far too base.

Allison said, "Right in my neighborhood. Explains all the sirens I heard last night." And then it hit Allison. "Oh, no. Mia."

Vaughn nodded. "I thought of her, too. From what you've told me, Arnie was a bastard toward her during the divorce. I can't imagine she'll be broken up over the news."

"No, she won't shed too many tears for Arnie Feldman. Edward wanted the most ruthless divorce attorney he could find. Arnie fit the bill. Still..." Allison shook her head. "Just the mention of his name will bring it all back for her."

For all of us, Allison thought. Four years ago, Allison had started her own downward spiral. It began when Mia, her mentor and former mother-in-law, lost her daughter Bridget in a tragic car accident. Mia's husband Edward had been at the wheel with a blood alcohol level of .23. Soon afterward, Mia divorced Edward in a bitter, drawn-out battle. Allison's then-husband Jason, Mia and Edwards' son, was bereft at the loss of his sister and undone by his parents' constant battling. He changed. As a result, Allison's own marriage crumbled, and although her divorce hadn't quite sparked the fireworks that Mia's had, she and Jason drifted apart in a way that left an aching hole in Allison's heart. An ache that lived on to this very day.

Allison took a sip of her coffee. She thought about calling Jason to check on Mia. She wanted to call Mia directly, but she knew any attempt to reconnect would be rebuffed. They hadn't spoken since Allison and Jason divorced, nearly two years ago.

As though reading her thoughts, Vaughn said, "You were close to Mia once."

"Once, yes." Allison stood and walked to the window. The small parking lot reserved for her First Impressions clients remained empty except for her own Volvo and Vaughn's spotless BMW. She knew she needed to call Faye back, but the dreary day outside echoed her own feelings of hopelessness when she thought of her parents. Of her childhood home.

Allison turned back to Vaughn. He'd folded the newspaper neatly on the edge of the desk, and now stared intently at a spreadsheet. Vaughn, her jack-of-all-trades. He managed the money, negotiated contracts, handled appointments and did some minor detective work—cheating spouses and the like—on the side, when required. He was intelligent, kind, handsome and, most importantly, loyal. But there was a reserve about him that Allison had never been able to break.

Still focused on that spreadsheet, Vaughn said, "Well, maybe Mia won't learn about Arnie. She doesn't live on the Main Line anymore."

True. After the divorce, Mia had moved from the image-conscience world of the Philadelphia Main Line to a small farm, miles away, on the outskirts of suburbia. A different world, Allison thought—although she supposed that was the point.

Allison said, "Someone will tell her. Or she'll see it on the news. And then it will be her daughter Bridget all over again."

Allison knew from Jason that Mia was still fragile, that her daughter's death was as fresh as if it had happened yesterday. The murder of her ex-husband's divorce attorney would not speed the healing of those wounds. And if it was a murder, it would be a major headline. Allison wished there was something she could do to soften the impact, but it was hard to help someone who wouldn't even speak to you.

"Besides, maybe it wasn't murder," Allison said. "Maybe Arnie had a good, old-fashioned heart attack or a stroke. Or maybe he tumbled off his ivory tower and cracked his head open."

Vaughn smiled. "Unlikely, from the sound of it."

Allison shrugged. Despite her curiosity, she had other things to worry about. She tried not to consider the fact that Arnie had died so close to her own house. That a killer was out there, lurking between the stately homes of her supposedly safe neighborhood. With optimism she didn't feel, she said, "Even if it was murder, at least it has nothing to do with Mia—or any of us, for that matter."

It was after six o'clock before Allison finally got around to calling her sister. Vaughn was still in the office and Allison could hear the comforting *click, click, click* of his fingers tapping against the keyboard.

Faye answered on the second ring. "It's about time," she said instead of hello.

"Sorry. When you didn't call my cell, I knew it wasn't an emergency. This is the first chance I've had to call you back."

"Yeah, well...it's a little late. I don't need you now." Accusation in her tone, weariness in her voice.

"What happened?"

"Mom. She disappeared earlier."

Allison's stomach clenched. "She's back?"

"Yes." *No thanks to you*, was the message in her voice.

"Is she okay?"

"Mom will *never* be okay, Allison. When will you come to terms with that?"

Allison held back a sharp retort. An argument now would only fuel the tension. "I meant did she get hurt?"

"No, other than being cold and confused, she wasn't hurt. The police picked her up a mile from the house."

Oh, God. What if...no, Allison couldn't allow herself to even think that way. "I'm coming over."

"Don't bother. It's all under control now."

Allison glanced at the clock on her wall. She could be there in an hour. Ignoring her sister's last statement, she said, "I'll be there as soon as I can, Faye."

"Whatever."

It started to drizzle. Cold, steely drops that threatened to morph into sleet. The rain hit Allison's windshield, slithered in rivulets to the corners, and turned to ice, so that she had to scrunch down and squint to see the road. She fingered the envelope that sat on the seat next to her. Her head ached.

Home. She turned the word around on her tongue, flipped it backward and forward, and swirled it around until the nausea passed. At home lived a different Allison. Fat ankles. Uneven bangs. A preference for peanut butter right from the jar.

"Self-reinvention is the key to survival," Mia had told her when she was first hired by her mentor's image-consulting firm. "In this line of work and in life."

"Yeah, right. There's no escaping the past," Allison had wanted to say in response. But she'd been twenty-five, poor, and disillusioned. Funny how an empty bank account can make one into a believer.

And so she'd Jennifer Aniston-ed her hair and painted her lips and learned the difference between Gucci and Prada, first for herself and then for her clients. She traded her third-floor studio in Ardmore for a two-story townhouse in Wayne and learned to navigate ten courses worth of silverware. Eventually she married Jason, her mentor's son, a man with a nice, normal American surname and then divorced him, keeping the name as a booby prize. Chalupowski would have looked awful on a book jacket.

At times, she missed the old Allison. She missed the energy of idealism and the ease with which someone who has nothing can move through the world. She knew this new life was based on the perpetuation of a lie, of a million little daily lies. But the lies, if told often enough and with enough enthusiasm, could become truth.

Just look at her.

Allison kept one hand still on the steering wheel and used the other to peel back the flap of the envelope. Wedged between the stiff edges of her mother's official documents sat the sickly yellow of an old newspaper clipping. She knew without touching it, without reading the bold-lettered headline, what it said. *Man Drives over Embankment in Apparent Homicide/Suicide Attempt.* Her father. Her mother. And over twenty years later, the pain still blanketed her like a low-lying fog.

She pushed the article back into the packet. Miraculously, her parents had lived through the ordeal with few serious injuries, but the emotional wounds had never really healed. *Your mother has Alzheimer's, Allison,* her father had said back then, as though that simple fact explained everything. *It'll be uphill from here.* So the years before that, the mom-has-a-migraine-and-is-in-her-bedroom-make-us-some-dinner-watch-your-sister-Allison years, were the easy ones?

Allison shook her head. The contents of that envelope didn't tell the full story any more than a pile of individual timbers resembled a finished house. Where were the court hearings, the social workers with their shopworn empathy and mind-fuck questions, the belt beatings, the experimental drugs and doctors' visits and furtive glances when the electricity went off because no one had paid the bill?

The rain stopped.

Allison flicked off her wipers and made a left onto her parents' street. Tiny ranch house after tiny ranch house, all with tiny yards and chain-link fences. She pulled up to their home, behind a grit-sprayed Ford. From the outside, nothing much had changed. Same peach-colored stucco, same white stone-filled flower beds, same crumbling walkway. Though it was nearly spring, a woven-wicker doe and fawn, leftover Christmas decorations, remained in the front yard. The doe lay on her side. The fawn stood over her, as though in mourning.

FOUR

"Get out of the damn barn, Buddy, and leave those chickens alone!"
Mia raised the broom over her head and lunged for the mutt. He
glanced up from the melee in the chicken house just long enough to
give her the dog version of the finger and then dove in for another
round of chase-the-hens. O'Connor, Mia's favorite bird, squawked
indignantly and scurried across the dirt floor, head up and tail
feathers wagging. She hid behind Mia's legs. "Buddy! Now!"

Mia dropped the broom and ran toward the dog, but not before
he cornered two more chickens against the back wall of the building. Scalia puffed his chest in normal rooster fashion, but Mia knew
he lacked the *cajones* to attack. As the only cock in this hen house,
he'd gotten too used to a sure thing and had gone soft. Sure enough,
he turned his back to the dog and let Kennedy handle the intruder.

"Buddy! You little pest, come here." Mia grabbed Buddy by the
collar and dragged him to the door, kicked the gate open with one
foot, and pushed the dog into the yard. Then she turned back to the
chickens. Scalia still stood with his back to the room, shifting his
weight from one foot to the other nervously, but Kennedy had wad-
dled back toward the middle of the small enclosure. Ginsburg and
Thomas were already pecking at the leftover feed on the floor.

"Come here Kennedy. Poor baby. Mommy's here." Mia knelt
down and took the shaking chicken into her arms. She stroked back
the bird's black and white crest and let her peck gently at the flesh
on Mia's palm. "There, there. Your little heart is beating so loudly.
Calm down, Kennedy, that bad Buddy is gone now."

"I always knew you had some granola in you, but this is ridiculous."

Mia froze. She hadn't heard a car come down the long driveway. Buddy hadn't barked. And the sound of that voice felt like ice water in her veins.

"Edward." Mia stood, slowly, and faced him, the bird still in her arms. She forced her features into a neutral mask. She wasn't prepared, though, for the changes four years had wreaked on her ex-husband. The skin on his face, once tan and glowing from hours of tennis and golf, was lined and gray. Deep wrinkles were etched around his mouth and nose and on his forehead. Where once he'd had a head of thick blond hair, thin strands of white stuck out from under a Phillies cap. Serves him right, she thought. Time had turned this demon into an old man.

Mia placed the bird on the ground. Her hands strayed upward, and she pushed her long hair away from her face. She saw in his eyes that he too was taken aback by the changes the years since their divorce had caused. Mia knew any aging had less to do with the breakup of their marriage and more to do with her daughter Bridget's death, but she didn't have to tell that to Edward.

"I came with some news, Mia. Do you have time?"

Mia stared at him, suspicious. He was the last person she wanted to see. Then, in an effort to collect herself and hide just how shaken she felt by his presence, she said, "Where are my manners? Come in the house."

Edward backed out of the chicken coop and into the gloom cast by thick clouds and the setting sun. Mia followed and closed the half-door that secured the enclosure. She watched Edward's form—the arrogant broad shoulders, the cocky athlete's gait—make its way from the lower yard that housed the chickens and goats, up through the stone path that meandered through the flower gardens toward the house. Like the cock of the walk, she thought. Some things never change.

She wondered what news he could be bringing. And why did it need to be said in person? Apprehension coursed through her. Calm down already, she told herself.

Mia found him waiting by the porch door that led into the back of her house. "Go ahead," she said and watched his face adjust to the sight. The bungalow she now called home was a far cry from the five-bedroom Tudor in which they'd raised Jason and Bridget. She looked around, trying to see the property through his eyes. The hand-split cedar shingles she treasured looked jagged and rustic, the stone paths and small patio, built with flagstones dug from her field, seemed uneven and amateurish. She followed him inside and absorbed his reaction to the Spartan porch, the table made of saw horses, and an old barn door, on which flower pots and gardening tools waited patiently. She saw the plain screen door that led into the kitchen, its frame in need of a fresh coat of paint. The expanse of brick floor, unswept, the cranky old AGA stove, the farmhouse sink, its white porcelain basin stained from years of honest use.

Stop. Mia took a deep breath. She caught her reflection in the window—recognized the thinker's crease in her forehead and the anxiety in her eyes. He's not doing this to you, she thought. You are doing it to yourself.

She said, "Tea or coffee?"

"Tea."

Without waiting for an invitation, Edward took a seat at the small Formica table she'd pushed up against the far wall. Mia picked up the blue-enameled teapot and turned on the faucet. The place *was* small. A kitchen, bedroom, and living room downstairs and a small bedroom upstairs. The upstairs lacked heat, and, in the winter, she closed it off with a heavy tarp placed at the bottom of the steps. She could see that tarp now from her vantage point by the sink. Gray and utilitarian.

Mia had bought this house after the accident that had killed their only daughter. Edward had been drunk. Bridget had been nineteen. Edward's drinking had been out of control for a long time, but after the crash, Mia could no longer make excuses for the man. When he refused to get help, she filed for divorce. But she supposed she was as angry at herself as she was at Edward—for letting his problem go for so long. Bridget's blood was on her hands, too.

"Mia?"

She looked down and saw the water had overflowed the pot and was running down her fingers. *Damn it, Mia, focus.* She turned off the faucet, poured out the excess water, and placed the teapot on the stove.

"Mia—"

She reached for two mugs on the same overhead shelf and fished two teabags out of a porcelain jar. She placed a teabag in each cup. Edward's presence stirred up memories Mia hadn't been prepared to face. She and Bridget had been close. Impossibly close for a teenage child and a parent. Bridget had been a freshman at Yale. She wanted to be a doctor. She had everything going for her. She was smart and kind and gentle—

"Mia."

—and her future had been snatched away from her because this man could not say no when it came to gin. Witnesses said Bridget had argued for the keys, but Edward insisted on driving. And then the head-on collision. Maybe if his reaction timing hadn't been impaired, the accident would have turned out differently. But instead, in the face of her loss and his obstinate refusal to accept blame, Mia left. And when she did, she left everything: her business, her house, her life. And eventually she'd come here to the rundown farmhouse, away from anyone who used to matter.

"Mia!"

Mia jumped. She knocked one cup to the ground. It broke. Ceramic shards shot across the floor. She looked down. Edward rose to pick up the pieces.

"I don't need your help." Mia said.

He grabbed her arm and led her to the table. "Sit. You'll cut yourself."

She sat, the venom draining, suddenly feeling every one of her fifty-six years. She watched him throw away the ceramic pieces and wipe down the floor with a damp paper towel to catch any small slivers. He took another cup from the shelf and finished making tea for both of them. He placed the cups on the table and sat back down.

He looked around. After a pause he said, "What the hell are you doing, Mia?"

"What does it look like, Edward? I was making tea."

"I meant with your life. This house, your reclusiveness. It all looks like a lot of escapee nonsense."

His voice was not unkind, but that made it worse. She felt off-balance. He didn't deserve an explanation. And, anyway, how to explain that here, with the quiet and the animals, she felt some semblance of peace? The expectations were clear and largely unchanging. But Edward would never understand that. Wasn't it the very thing he'd tried to twist during the divorce? To make her look crazy and unstable. No, explaining was pointless, the divide between them, too vast to bridge.

"This is my life now."

"It's been four years since Bridget died, Mia." He reached across the table, but Mia pulled her hand away before he could touch her.

He winced as though she'd slapped him. "Fine." His tone turned brusque. "I just came to tell you that Arnie Feldman is dead."

She looked at him blankly. "Arnie? Arnie Feldman?" She repeated the name until it dawned on her. Edward's divorce attorney. In a flash, she saw a small man, big nose, ingratiating smile. Tiny pointed teeth. She shook her head. "I'm sorry, Edward, but I don't understand. Why are you telling me?"

Edward met her gaze with a harshness that startled her. "Because he was murdered, Mia. And a murder means an investigation."

"So?"

"So the police are looking at anyone who's had a conflict with Arnie. Anyone with motive."

She swallowed, sudden comprehension tearing through the layers of denial she'd so carefully stacked, layer upon layer, like bricks. "No."

"Yes." He stood and turned toward the door, his tea untouched. "And this,"—he motioned around the room—"will not look normal to the police. Normal people don't get off the grid, give up a marriage and a career because of one accident."

"You know I didn't do it, Edward."

"You may want to call your son, Mia. Jason won't speak to me, or I'd ask him myself. But you just may need a lawyer. The police have already visited me. They wanted to talk about you."

"Oh, for goodness sake, I didn't kill anybody. Bridget's gone. Nothing can bring her back. I made those threats against Arnie during the divorce because I was angry. Hurt. You and Arnie tried to make me look like a paranoid lunatic. I would never kill someone. You know me better than that."

"I *knew* you, Mia. Before. But this Mia," he said, gesturing toward the window, at the barn and fields beyond. "This Mia, I don't know at all."

Fear and anger closed in on Mia. The result was rage. "Leave, Edward. Now."

Edward opened the door to the porch. "Just call that son of yours and tell him to get his head out of his ass long enough to recommend an attorney." He slammed the screen door closed but turned back before leaving. "Just in case."

Allison stood at her parents' door for what felt like eons, unable to act.

The rain had turned to a biting sleet that pummeled the walkway behind her and landed at an angle, so that even standing under the small vestibule, the pellets struck her back. She barely noticed. Instead, she felt the same twisting anxiety she always felt when she returned here.

She turned the knob. Locked. She put her head against the doorframe and knocked. Nothing.

She knocked again, harder. Eventually, the door opened and Faye's angular face peered around the edge.

"Can I come in?"

Faye stepped back to let her inside, but not before she gave Allison a disapproving once over. "Suit yourself."

Over her sister's shoulder, Allison caught a glimpse of the darkened living room. A sagging floral sofa perched against the far wall, between mismatched coffee tables. A large bronze crucifix hung over an ancient television set, which had two knobs missing and a pair of pliers affixed to the dial. A smaller, newer television sat on top of the old one. The curtains were drawn, shutting out any remaining daylight and the world beyond these walls. Smells of onions and cooking oil and Lysol wafted from within.

Her father sat slumped in a chair in the corner, a caricature of the man who haunted her childhood. He raised his head to look at her. Allison saw no warmth in his expression. His thin legs were propped on a ragged beige ottoman. She noticed socks worn threadbare at his heels, and ankles that looked too skinny and too frail to support his weight.

"It's them spics across the street, Ally," her father said, as though continuing a conversation he'd had with her just yesterday instead of years ago. "They're the ones taking our stones. Every morning I notice some missing. They're storing 'em up to make their own rock garden. Bit by bit, I tell you." He shook his head. "When them foreigners move into a neighborhood, it goes downhill fast."

He raised a fist for emphasis, but the energy needed to project his anger at this bit of fantasy was too much, and he sank back against the cushion and closed his eyes.

Allison was at a loss for words. How do you respond to a man whose last real words to you were, "Get your fat, lazy ass out there and make your own damn living"? Her mind tug-o-warred between revulsion and pity.

Shaken, she let her eyes travel from her father to her mother, who sat on the old Queen Anne chair next to him. Allison knelt beside her. She took her mother's hand in her own, ran her fingers across skin that felt dry and papery, and squeezed gently. Her mother didn't squeeze back.

"Was this what you expected?" Faye said.

"I didn't know what to expect."

"That's because you don't see it every day like I do."

"Yes, Faye, I know. And you take every opportunity to remind me what an awful daughter I am."

Faye looked away. "I didn't mean that, Allison."

"Yes, you did." Unwilling to rehash old hurts, Allison changed the topic. "Did she go to the hospital?"

"No. The medics were here. Physically, she's not in any immediate danger."

Allison nodded, unable to escape the feeling she was moving through a dream. For most of her childhood, her mother had been like a ghost, lurking upstairs in the shadows. Even before the Alzheimer's, her mother suffered debilitating migraines that kept her in bed for days, sometimes weeks, at a time. Allison's memories of her younger years were a patchwork quilt of bright spots, marked by her mother's warmth and laughter, and large, dark squares shaded by sickness and her father's poor attempts to parent Allison and her two sisters. And now even the bright spots were dulled by this awful disease that stole the few memories the sisters shared.

"They want to bring in social services," Faye said. "The medics say she's malnourished."

Allison stood up and looked again at her mother. The blanket had slipped from her shoulders, and Allison saw the tips of her mother's collar bones peaking from beneath her sweater. Her eyes were sunken, her cheeks hollow. Her hair, once the color of fresh straw, lay matted in gray strands around her face.

Allison turned back to Faye. Her older sister, once the family beauty, wore the Purple Heart of martyrdom in the frown lines around her mouth and the burdened curvature of her spine.

"What happened today?"

"I left Mom with Daddy when I ran to the store. Just for a half hour, that was all. He dozed off, and she left."

"I was awake!" Her father shouted. "I didn't hear the door. I wasn't wearing my hearing aid."

Faye looked at him sharply. "You said you were asleep."

"I was awake!"

Allison turned to Faye. "Can I talk to you in the kitchen?"

Faye looked at her sideways. "Why?"

Allison tipped her head in the direction of their father.

In the kitchen and safely out of earshot, Allison said, "We've known for a while that dad's showing signs of dementia, and Mom needs to be watched. I think it's time to hire a nurse. Someone to help you out."

Faye's gaze hardened. "It's a waste of money we may need later."

"We have to do something."

"We? Since when is it 'we,' Allison?"

"It's always been 'we,' Faye. I'm still here, aren't I? Despite everything."

"Like Katie, you're there in a way that's convenient for you."

Allison's younger sister Katie had married an enlisted man when she was eighteen. She sent flowers every Mother's Day. Other than the flowers and sporadic Christmas cards, no one had seen Katie or her kids in years. Allison resented the comparison. She said, "That's not true. Daddy—"

"Daddy *nothing*." Faye gave her a withering stare.

Daddy everything. Although Allison and her father had never gotten along, it was when Allison had left graduate school—after losing a young patient named Violet to the streets of Philadelphia—that she really needed him, needed a place to heal and recover. And with a cruelty she hadn't expected, he'd turned her away. Allison shuddered at the memory, still fresh and stinging as a razor slash.

"Look, Faye," Allison said, forcing herself away from the past and on to the practical. "Social services may insist on bringing someone in."

"I don't want governmental interference. We don't need help."

"You're blaming me for not being here, yet you're insistent that things are fine." Allison motioned toward the living room. "But what happened today makes it pretty clear that things are not fine."

Faye's hands balled at her side. "What do you expect me to do, given our current circumstances? They refuse to leave. Won't budge. And anyway, Daddy has mortgaged the house to the hilt. They have nothing, Allison. *Nothing.* Aside from what you give them. And I'm too busy with *them* to get a job."

Allison met her sister's angry glare. Faye was right. Her parents had no savings—and plenty of debt. They subsisted on social security and the money Allison sent home every month. And while Allison might be able to afford full-time nursing care, it would eat up her savings quickly. Then what? If her father got worse, they would have fewer options, some of them unpalatable.

Faye put her head against the wall and folded her thin arms across her bony chest. "Today won't happen again. I'll ask Carmen from next door to watch Mom when I go out."

Allison nodded. It would have to do for now. "Make sure Mom eats. She's so thin. I'll arrange for a nutritionist to come to the house." She paused, looked around the spotless but well-worn kitchen. "In the meantime, we'll have to think of something."

Allison walked back into the living room, where the shadows sucked the little light that flowed from the table lamps. Faye followed a moment later. She thrust a Tupperware container into Allison's hands.

"Take this, please," Faye said. "For all your trouble."

Allison wanted to say, *We're sisters, dimwit. We're in this together*, but the words wouldn't come. Instead she glanced around one more time before leaving. Her mother sat limp, eyes staring at nothing in particular. Her father had nodded off. His snores echoed like roars across the cramped space.

The hour-long drive home took nearly two. The roads loomed slick with black ice. A gloomy mist clung to the ground, swirled around Allison's headlights and enveloped the silver Volvo in gray. Allison felt numb. She tried to push away the image of her mother huddled under the blanket. What if they hadn't found her? And her father— the family despot now turned into a child: helpless, whiny, and demanding. If the dementia progressed, soon he would need care, too. Faye was struggling as it was. *Two* infirm parents would break her.

A few miles from her home, Allison checked her voicemail. A few referrals, an insurance salesman, her client Midge Majors, her literary agent. And Congressman McBride.

Allison pulled into her driveway. The Colonial, with its stone façade, three dormers, and landscaped lot, was a welcome sight. Unlike the cramped and gloomy interior of her parents' house, here she had room to breathe. She pushed away thoughts of Arnie Feldman's murderer and poked at the buttons on her cell, trying to recall the number the congressman had provided when they met about his troubled daughter. *Any time, Ms. Campbell.* One ring, two, five...she thought maybe she'd luck out and get voice mail when Hank McBride answered.

"Finally," he said. "Sunny and I have arranged for you to visit tomorrow."

"I don't know what my schedule—"

"I spoke to your assistant, Vaughn. He said you're free at ten o'clock. Sharp."

"Fine." Firmly, she said, "I don't need to remind you that I don't work with teenagers, Congressman. I am only agreeing to meet with her."

"Maggie needs help. Once you meet her, I'm sure your heart will see to it that you say yes. Your heart...and your purse."

Allison swallowed. A face flashed before her, pale and pretty and haunted. Violet. It was a night for painful memories, it seemed. Allison shoved the image away. She thought of her mother—ill, lost, in need of more care than she was getting now.

"You understand that First Impressions is an image-consulting firm?"

"Yes. And I also understand that you have a background in psychology. A PhD."

"I'm not a practicing psychologist, Congressman. With all due respect, if you need a therapist, you should look elsewhere—"

"I told you earlier, I don't. Please. Just meet her tomorrow."

Allison felt a strange urgency to get him off the phone and out of her life. If she'd been more superstitious, she would have called it a premonition. Instead, she chalked it up to her mother's ordeal and the unrelenting exhaustion that had a hold on her body.

Allison gripped the container of pierogies Faye had handed her. Her knuckles glowed white from the pressure.

"Okay," Allison said finally. "Tomorrow at ten."

"Thank you. You have no idea what this means to us."

She said good-bye, clicked off the phone, and stormed inside. Determined to put the day out of her mind, Allison tossed her pumps and purse down in the foyer, then pulled off her hose and threw them on the steps to bring upstairs later. She walked through the short hallway that led from the foyer to the kitchen and unbuttoned her pencil skirt. She used the kitchen doorframe to support her weight and pulled the skirt down over her hips, then slipped her Donna Karan blouse off her shoulders and let it fall down to the floor in a crumpled heap.

Freedom.

In the kitchen, she pried open the food container, grabbed a fork out of the dishwasher, and ate cold pierogies over the sink. With each mouthful, that looming sense of foreboding slipped further into the distance.

"Crazy is as crazy does. It's arrogant to think otherwise." The words echoed through Allison's head. *Crazy, crazy, crazy.* The clock flashed 2:28 a.m. She pulled the pillow over her face, took a deep breath, and squeezed her eyes tight against the memories, just like she used to do as a kid. Squeezed until she saw random flashes of light and color in her eyelids, and her forehead hurt from the effort. Squeezed until the bad thoughts went away.

It was no use. *Violet Swann.* The name still came to her, unbidden and resonating with an overwhelming sadness that threatened to drown out the years of carefully cultivated success that had followed. But she knew no number of valued clients, no celebrity dinners, no large paychecks, could wipe out the consequences of a few bad choices.

The worst of which was choosing to care.

Allison tried not to think about the flat storage container under her bed that held proof of her own incompetence. She tried not to remember the teen, Violet, whose short life was documented in its cold plastic walls. She tried not to consider the reasons she kept that container after all these years. Hope? Or a reminder that things could come crumbling down, especially when they looked most promising.

Margaret McBride. Fifteen. Just like Violet.

"You should reconsider your vocation, Allison. There's no room here for poor judgment." At the end of her tenure at the Meadows, a home for troubled teens, kindly Doc had been replaced by an irate Dr. Nutzbaum, his usually placid eyes and swarthy complexion colored by fear and embarrassment. *"We have rules for a reason, Allison. And now look at the mess you've caused. There will be an inquiry. There will be accusations. Whether or not they have any credibility doesn't matter. The damage is done."*

The finger-pointing, the politics, the pressing worry not about her own future but about the future of someone far more vulnerable. How old had she been then? Twenty-four? Almost ten years older than her young patient, Violet, an abused runaway who'd looked to Allison for safety and who'd ultimately been exploited once again.

Because Allison hadn't kept her safe.

It all seemed like a lifetime ago, carefully removed from First Impressions and the world she'd created for herself here. Allison turned over in bed and burrowed deeper into the covers, willing her mind to stop whirling, twirling memories around like a mini cyclone. All Hank McBride's fault. The man was already stirring up trouble.

Allison punched the mattress, flopped over on her back and stared at the ceiling. No, I can't take on Maggie McBride. I have enough demons in my life. She pulled a pillow over her face. There wasn't room for any more.

FIVE

Allison rang the McBrides' doorbell at ten o'clock, on the dot. It was another chilly day, with just a sliver of sun attempting to break through the relentless cloud cover. As much as she liked her pin-striped Dolce & Gabbana skirt, Allison wished she'd traded it for a nice, warm wool pants suit. She pulled her coat tighter and waited for someone to answer.

The old house loomed over her like something out of a Gothic novel. The main structure, a hulking stone rectangle shrouded in ivy, was flanked on either side by one-story additions. A driveway stopped just feet before the main entrance and then wound around the side of the house, coming to a halt at the entrance of a three-car garage. Stone lions guarded the double front doors, which were painted black. Oversized brass knockers, each emblazoned with a lion's head, perched on the doors' centers. The overall effect was elegant, in a haunting, antiquated way.

Allison glanced around. The entire street was lined with these estates, separated by acres and enough stylistic differences to make each one unique. But make no bones about it, Allison thought, this home in this neighborhood was not purchased on a congressman's salary. Someone in the McBride family was bleeding money.

A stout, pasty-faced woman in her sixties opened the door. She wore a perfectly-starched gray and white maid's uniform that covered a thick body and rigid shoulders. Her iron-colored hair had been pulled into a tight bun. Not one hair escaped. Her mouth was pursed in a wrinkled frown.

Allison introduced herself. "I'm here to meet Maggie."

The woman cocked her head to the side. "Please, come in."

Allison stepped through the door into a large center hall. The room was lined with paintings, one after the other, only inches apart. Colorful abstracts, watery impressionists. It reminded Allison of the display at the Barnes Museum, where paintings were grouped by theme or color rather than era or artist. Allison didn't have time to ponder the incongruity of these modern paintings—or the unusual presentation—in an otherwise staunchly traditional home before Sunny walked in.

"Thank you, Udele," Sunny said to the iron-haired lady. "Ms. Campbell, the congressman and I are so happy you came. He couldn't be here today, he's on his way to Washington for government business, but I'll introduce you to Maggie. This way, please."

Allison followed Sunny through the center hall and up a set of stairs. Sunny wore jeans today, faded and low-slung, with a red sweater that set off the highlights in her hair. No makeup, but even without it she was stunning. Allison found herself wondering what it would be like to have her for a mother. Could you ever measure up? Halfway up the steps, Sunny turned suddenly and asked if Allison would like coffee. It seemed an afterthought and Allison declined. They continued toward the second level.

More paintings lined the upstairs hallway. One, an abstract portrait of a nude woman, her arms and legs swirling off into magenta obsolescence, struck Allison as particularly sad and sensual. It was then that she noticed the "SM" painted in the corner of the canvas.

"Did you paint these, Sunny?

Sunny took a moment before responding. When she did, her voice was hoarse. "I was an art major, once upon a time. Before the girls came along."

"They're lovely."

Sunny mumbled a thank you and continued her trek toward Maggie's room. Allison stole another glance at the nude. It was a self-portrait. She had no concrete reason to think that—there were no identifying marks, and the only thing that made it apparent the painting was of a woman at all was the milky hourglass of the torso. But somehow Allison knew. And in that moment she also knew that Sunny McBride, Gypsy wife of a rich and powerful congressman, was a very unhappy woman.

Sunny rapped on the door three times. "Maggie, let us in. Ms. Campbell is here to meet you."

Allison tensed. Sunny seemed too tentative, like a hand-shy dog who'd endured one too many swats with the newspaper. Allison had no current experience with children, but she knew this much anxiety on a parent's face meant Maggie was no Laura Ingalls.

Sunny knocked again. "Maggie, come on. Daddy's not here. It's just Allison Campbell and me. Open up." Sunny turned to Allison with an apologetic smile and said, "Maggie had a fight with Hank last night before he left. They don't always see eye-to-eye."

Understatement of the year? The Cleavers were looking more and more like the Munsters.

Sunny pulled a key out of her pocket. "Last chance, Maggie."

Allison started to protest, to tell Sunny this was a mistake, when the door swung open into blackness.

Sunny leaned toward Allison and said, "I'll leave you two to get acquainted. It's better that way. There's a buzzer at the top of the steps, on the wall. When you're finished, press it and Udele will find me." She touched Allison's arm hesitantly. "She's a nice girl, really. She's just misunderstood. And has no self-esteem. You'll see, Allison." That desperation in her eyes again. "I think you're just what she needs."

Sunny disappeared down the hall, and Allison squinted into the room. Once her eyes adjusted to the dimness, she saw the reason for the darkness. All the windows were covered with black curtains, and the walls were painted black. Even the bedspread was black. And there, on the bed, was a tiny figure dressed entirely in black.

"Margaret?"

"Maggie."

"Mind if I come in?"

"Yes."

"Have it your way." Allison turned to leave and, out of the corner of her eye, saw Maggie stand up.

"Fine. Come in."

Allison stepped inside. She looked around for a place to sit. A chair, painted black, sat next to a desk, painted black, but books and papers were stacked on its seat. The room looked surprisingly neat. It was smaller than Allison would have expected, but other than the stack of books, orderly. A black dresser sat against the wall between two windows. On its surface stood candles, a dozen or so bottles of various sizes, and an incense holder. A computer had been placed on the desk amid neat piles of books and papers and what looked like a strobe light, its silvery fish scales reflecting the narrow slices of light that seeped around black curtains. Another stack of books tilted precariously next to the bed.

Allison took this all in during the space of a second. Then her eyes were drawn to Maggie. A tiny pudge ball of a girl, Maggie sat on her bed with her arms wrapped around her knees. Allison saw black-stockinged legs, the ruffle of a black skirt, a black shirt with a torn collar, spiky black hair. All she could see of Maggie's face were her eyes, which looked to be encircled in black crayon. Everything was the flat black of matte paint or cheap hair color: no texture, no highlights, no depth. Allison sighed. If I take this job, she thought, I'll certainly have my work cut out for me.

"Maggie?"

No response.

"Maggie, can I sit?"

Still no answer.

"No games, Maggie."

"No games, Allison. I don't want you here."

Touché, sweetheart, I'm not so sure I want to be here. "I just want to talk."

"I don't need another shrink."

"I'm not a shrink, Maggie."

"A therapist."

"Nope, I'm not a therapist."

She sat a little straighter. "Then what are you?"

"I'm an image consultant. Your parents want to hire me to help you get yourself together."

For a second the girl on the bed didn't speak or move. Then she let out a laugh like a witch's cackle, long and loud and mean.

It took Allison a second to regain her composure. "Something funny, Maggie?"

Maggie rolled around on her bed for a second, clutching her gut as though she couldn't contain the guffaws. "This is...the best...yet. Daddy...is...such an...idiot."

"Maggie!"

She stopped laughing. "Don't 'Maggie' me. He is an idiot. An image consultant? Know how many people they've made me see? There was Dr. Schuman, the bald-headed pedophile, Dr. Turner, the three-hundred-year-old psychologist who smelled like moth balls and said I was developmentally delayed, Dr. Lee, the neuro-acupuncturist, whatever the hell that is. Oh, yeah, there was also the hypnotist, two psychiatrists, and the dude in New York who decided I needed a blood-letting. With leeches. I said no way to that one. Want me to keep going?"

Maggie stood up and flicked on the strobe light. A pulsating glow reflected bands of color across the black walls. Allison watched stripes dance their way across Maggie's features. A pretty child lay under the sneer and the hideous makeup. Maggie had a round face and pale skin, but also her mother's wild eyes and soft, full mouth. Someday, Allison thought, with a dash of luck and a few ounces of guidance, Maggie could be a beauty.

"Well, I'm not here to psychoanalyze you. And I promise—no blood-letting." When Maggie didn't respond, Allison said, "What do you say, Maggie? Shall we at least give it a go?"

"No effing way."

Allison turned to leave.

"Wow, you quit with the least resistance," Maggie said.

"I told you. No games."

"Fine, leave." She slumped a little. "Tell my mother I'm oppositional. Go ahead." The high pitch of her voice betrayed her brave front. Allison heard fear.

"What do you get out of this, Maggie? Do you just enjoy making your folks angry?"

"I'll never do what they want."

"Because you disagree with them?"

"Because I'm not so easily controlled."

Allison met her angry glare. "Don't you think automatically doing the opposite of what people want you to do is just as pathetic?"

Maggie jutted a round chin up defiantly. "How so?"

"Think about it, Maggie. When you follow everyone's command, you don't have to think, right? You become a sheep. When you automatically do the opposite of what they tell you, you don't have to think either. You end up in the same place."

She shook her head. "Nice try."

"Hey, look, I have no idea what this little routine between you and your folks is. You don't want to cooperate? Fine by me. I wish you the best."

Allison reached for the doorknob.

Maggie ran to block her exit. "Wait."

This close, Maggie smelled of strawberry shampoo and patchouli. A strange mix, Allison thought, the trappings of a teen caught between childhood and the need to assert her independence. Not so atypical, no matter how Hank had painted her.

Allison said, "Tell me why I should stay."

"Because if you leave, they'll lock me up. Daddy already told me the next step is boarding school. Somewhere far away."

"So they *did* tell you about me."

Maggie looked down at her black combat boots and shuffled her feet like a schoolgirl waiting in the cafeteria line. "Not exactly. My mother said my last chance was on her way over."

Great. Allison leaned against the door. She didn't want to be this kid's last chance. She didn't want to be anyone's last chance.

She took another look at Maggie. This was not an abused teen, like Violet. This was not a girl who had no one else to turn to. This was a spoiled, alienated teenager in need of a firm hand and some self-esteem. And that's what Allison did well. Her mind flashed to Hank McBride at their first meeting, at the cold way he'd referred to his own daughter as a misfit. Allison swore under her breath. Get a grip, Al, she thought. You've dealt with the worst the Main Line has to offer. You can handle this kid.

When Maggie refused to look at her, Allison touched her chin, gently, and pulled it forward so Maggie would meet her eyes. "Seems each of us has something at stake. Shall we give it a go? What do you say, Maggie?"

Maggie's momentary panic seemed to have evaporated, replaced with cocky defiance. She gave Allison an appraising glance, head to toe and back up again, one that echoed Hank's mannerisms the day before.

"I say you're stuck-up and in it for yourself. But because I have no other choice, I'll do it. You should know now, though, that I'll never be like you. I like who I am and I won't let my father change that."

"Fair enough." Allison could feel the tension in her shoulders snake down her spine. She thought of Hank's smile, the way he dominated his wife, not so different from the way her own father had ruled their household. "Clearly we both have a challenge ahead of us."

Udele met Allison at the top of the stairs, appearing just seconds after Allison pushed the antique brass buzzer.

Allison said, "You startled me."

Udele seemed unfazed. "Mrs. McBride would like to see you before you leave." Udele's words were crisp, separated by hard edges. Allison wondered whether she always looked like she'd just swallowed a spider or if she actually cracked a smile now and again. Was it this household? Despite the perfect furnishings and the decorator's fingerprint everywhere, the house felt empty and cold. Only Sunny's paintings and Maggie's bedroom showed any sign of vibrancy or creative flair, even if it was morose in Maggie's case. Perhaps the atmosphere had gotten to Udele.

Allison followed the aging housekeeper to a parlor on the first floor. The entire room was done in navy blue toile. Even the ceiling was papered. Allison glanced around the room and tried to get a sense of this family from the photos and bric-à-brac. Not a lot to go on: several pieces of heavy walnut furniture, a wood-carved elephant on the writing desk, a crystal bud vase on an end table, an engraved silver-plated letter opener by the phone. A framed portrait of a young and impish Maggie hung next to the fireplace. Allison saw freshness in her eyes that seemed gone now, but Allison also recognized the glint of devil that must have rooted and thrived until it grew into the opposition witnessed in Maggie's room.

Next to Maggie's painting hung a portrait of another young girl, as fair and striking as Maggie was dark and brooding. Allison stood staring at that second painting, trying to reconcile how two sisters could be so different, when she heard Sunny enter the room, a young woman beside her. The second woman was tall and slender, with Sunny's long, graceful neck and Hank's light coloring. Her hair was twisted in a neat chignon. Fine-boned limbs. Tiny, neat breasts. The fairer daughter, no doubt.

"Allison, this is my older daughter, Catherine."

Allison stood. She accepted Catherine's outstretched hand. "Very nice to meet you, Catherine." Catherine's handshake was cool and limp. She looked at Allison with a rather calculating stare of her own. With such a beautiful mother and thoroughbred sister, Allison felt for Maggie. It had to be hard to carve out a niche for herself in this family. Perhaps that explained the defiant attitude, the Goth clothes and makeup. If you know you can't join 'em, don't even try.

Sunny said, "How did it go?"

"It went fine." Allison forced a smile.

"Will you take the job?"

Against her better judgment, Allison nodded.

Sunny grinned. "Thank you! I was so worried. You saw her...she's not an easy child and, well, she doesn't take to everyone immediately."

Immediately? Allison doubted she ever took to anyone.

Sunny held out an unmarked manila envelope.

"What's this?"

"The contract. There's a confidentiality addendum enclosed. And your retainer. The congressman's idea. He wants you to know we will keep our end of the bargain."

Allison opened the flap and looked inside. A bundle of paper-clipped documents and a check. Allison shook her head and handed the envelope back to Sunny.

"I don't sign contracts. You'll have to trust my professionalism, Sunny. And as for the retainer, I'd prefer to be paid as we go. Tell Hank I'm certain he's good for it. Besides, I know where to find him."

Allison's attempt at humor was met with a polite laugh from Sunny and a cold glower from Catherine. Tough audience. "I'll see Maggie this Friday? After school. Say four o'clock?"

Sunny nodded. "I think this will work out fine."

SIX

On the drive home, Allison couldn't shake a creeping sense of shame. It was that mother. Sunny. With her colorful paintings and colorless home and sullen housekeeper and manipulative husband. Allison knew the whole McBride show was aimed at conning her into taking on Maggie: the absent father, the warning that this was Maggie's last chance. The money. She had a price and they knew it.

And she couldn't shake the comparison to Violet. The two girls couldn't have been more dissimilar. One deprived, sad and poetic. The other bratty, spoiled and rude. But they were both oppositional and, she knew, too intelligent for their own adolescent good.

Allison's gut said she should have told the McBrides to find another consultant for their daughter. But, she had to admit, her willingness to work with Maggie went beyond the money. A piece of her looked forward to the challenge.

It was high noon. Allison drove north on Route 30 toward her office, past strip malls and banks and restaurants whose parking lots were quickly filling. Allison felt antsy again. She checked her phone to see who Vaughn had scheduled next. Another session in forty minutes. On impulse, Allison dialed her ex-husband Jason's number.

"Nice to hear from you," Jason said. He sounded genuinely pleased. "The occasion?"

Allison hesitated. What *was* the occasion? Thinking quickly, she said, "Clogged sink. Any chance you can swing by and give me a hand with it?"

"Sure," Jason said.

Allison thought she detected disappointment in his voice. Wishful thinking, Al, she mused. You made your bed.

At four-thirty that afternoon, Vaughn interrupted a session with Allison's client, Kit Carson. Allison excused herself and followed him into her office.

"There's a detective on the line for you. Lieutenant Mark Helms."

"What does he want?"

Vaughn frowned. "He wouldn't say. Insisted on speaking with you immediately."

The only thing Allison could think of was the Main Line Murder, as the papers had dubbed it. But what did that have to do with First Impressions?

"I'll take it," she said.

As soon as she got on the line, a man said, "Ms. Campbell? Lieutenant Mark Helms. I'd like to arrange some time to meet with you tomorrow. When would be convenient? I can come to your office."

Helms had a pleasant baritone voice. And while his words were respectful, his tone left "no" off the table.

"What do you want to talk about, Lieutenant?" she said.

"Arnie Feldman."

"I didn't know Arnie Feldman well."

Helms sighed. "This is an ongoing investigation. We're looking at all angles. And your connection to his widow is what we're interested in."

"Sasha Feldman? I don't know Sasha at all, Lieutenant."

"Perhaps you remember her as Sally Ann Reilly."

"*Sally Ann* was Arnie's wife?"

"That's correct."

Allison remembered a skinny woman with buck teeth and a bad attitude. Sally Ann Reilly had been Allison's client for all of five sessions, sent to First Impressions by an employer trying to help

Sally Ann overcome something they described as a lack of gravitas. A euphemism for immaturity and abrasiveness. Before they could make much progress, Sally Ann had quit her job and the sessions ended.

"I haven't spoken with Sally Ann—Sasha—in almost five years."

"I understand, Ms. Campbell, but we'd still like to talk to you. We're just looking for information. And in addition to Sasha, you're also acquainted with Mia Campbell."

Alarmed, Allison said, "What does Mia have to do with anything?" But even as the words escaped her, Allison knew exactly what Mia had to do with the investigation. During their divorce proceedings, Arnie had done everything in his power to make sure Mia's accusations of criminal recklessness fell on deaf ears. The only way to do that was to discredit Mia. She reacted by threatening Arnie's life. The threats did little to improve her image back then— and they were clearly hurting her now. "Is Mia a suspect?"

Another tired sigh from Helms. "No one is a suspect at this time. But *everyone* is a person of interest."

"That should do it." From her vantage point behind the closet door, Allison watched Jason pull himself out from under her bathroom sink and wipe his hands on his khaki cargo shorts. He sat on the white-tiled floor, back to the tub, and frowned. "Stop brushing your hair over the sink, Al. You're clogging the drain."

Allison didn't bother to answer. How long had Jason been telling her that? The entire five years they were married? Before that even? Somehow divorce hadn't ended that part of the dance. Allison turned so he couldn't see her and unhooked her bra. She took it off and pulled a black slip on in its place. Then, tucked in her walk-in closet, she tried to decide which of her little black dresses to wear to tonight's charity dinner. Spaghetti straps and lace trim? Empire waist? She settled on a cute sleeveless sheath and pulled it carefully off the rack.

Allison felt Jason's presence behind her before she saw his reflection in the mirror. Same dark, curling brown hair, same broad shoulders that tapered down to form a perfect V. She'd always loved his body—its sinewy strength, its hardness—even when she'd disliked his attitude. Jason stood so close that Allison could almost feel his abs against her back and his breath against her skin. She knew it wasn't that long ago when this little scene would've played out differently. He would've reached around to cup her breasts, pulled the straps of her slip down, and let the material slide to her waist, maybe lifted the skirt up from behind. They would've made love on the bedroom floor until they were both breathless and sated.

"Sink's fixed, Al. What else do you need done?"

Ah, yes, she thought. In the here and now, we are friends, at best.

After searching his eyes for a hint of the regret that haunted her, Allison closed the closet door. She had been the one to end it, after all. A faint smiled played itself out on Jason's lips, but his eyes were guarded. Disappointed, she headed toward the bathroom.

Jason sat on her bed. He opened the drawer to her bedside table and rummaged around in the mess, pulling out a pair of nail clippers. He stuffed the tissues and magazines and stray notes back into the drawer and began clipping the already-short nail on his pinky finger.

She glanced at Jason over her shoulder while she struggled with the zipper on the back of her dress. "Zip me up, please." She backed to the bed.

"Sure." He pulled the zipper the remaining way up, placed the nail clipper back in the drawer and stood. "Is that all you needed? Because if so, I have a date of my own tonight."

That stopped her. "Really?" In the two years since the divorce, she'd never heard Jason so much as speak another woman's name. Allison slipped on her pumps, not liking the feeling of jealousy creeping along the edges of her mind. "So, do I know her?"

He smiled. Dimples creased the skin on each side of his mouth, under the stubble. "Fortunately, no. She's outside of your extensive social circle." He turned his head to the side and said, almost bashfully, "She's an underwear model."

Allison gave him a look that said *Yeah, right.*

"For department-store catalogs." He kissed the top of Allison's head. "Amber something or other."

"Must be serious. Make sure you learn her last name before the wedding." She reached out and stroked his cheek. "You'd better shave. You look like a slacker."

"I am a slacker."

This time, Allison smiled. Jason was a lot of things—difficult, argumentative, idealistic—but she knew that whatever he did, he did whole-heartedly. His sister Bridget's death had left a hole in his spirit wide enough for the Titanic to slip through. He'd taken his mom's side during his parents' divorce and, eventually, left his dad's company, where he'd run a small but busy legal department. Allison hadn't minded the career shift, exactly. But she had minded the new *laissez-fair* attitude that went with it. Just like with Mia, her mentor, it was as though Bridget's death zapped the will right out of him. Looking back, that accident signaled all of the changes yet to come in their lives. Mia's divorce. The birth of First Impressions. The rift in her own marriage.

Just when Allison's career picked up, Jason's took a U-turn, going from a high-profile corporate lawyer to an attorney in the DA's office. Despite what he thought, she hadn't given a damn about the reduced salary or the diminished prestige. But she did mind that, in her view, he'd given up on his dream of owning his own business. Her Jason had not been a quitter. The Jason who emerged from his family's troubles had lost sight of his goals.

"Come on," Jason said. "I gotta go. Walk me downstairs."

He grabbed her hand. She tried to ignore the familiar warmth of his fingers and the reassuring weight of his arm next to hers. It was too easy to remember the good and forget the bad. The all-night bar tours he'd pulled at the end. The fights over money, this house, his career, and her business. They'd been fencers, always sparring and their fights left emotional wounds.

Neither of them spoke as they made their way downstairs. In the foyer, Jason slipped his sandals back on. Despite the chilly weather, he wore shorts and sandals.

"I got a call today, Jason. One you should know about." Allison took a deep breath. She knew this would cause Jason pain, and that was the last thing she wanted to do. "From Detective Mark Helms. He's investigating the death of Arnie Feldman."

"I read his name in the news. So why does he want to talk with you?"

"I worked with Arnie's widow a long time ago." Allison paused. "And he wants to discuss Mia."

"*Damn.*" Jason's hands clenched into fists. "My mother called me today. My father stopped by the farm and practically accused her of killing Arnie. Talk about an ass." Jason shook his head. "If my mother were to murder anyone, it'd be him."

"How do you know it was murder? The papers didn't say that."

"My contacts at the police department." Jason's expression darkened. He reached for Allison's hand, seemed to think better of it, and fiddled instead with his keys. He smiled, but it was a humorless smile, one that made Allison ache to reassure him. Despite his bravado, she knew his parents' hatred of one another tore at him. Rather than suffer from divided loyalties like many grown children of divorcees, Jason loathed his father and coddled his mother. Mia's escape to that farm was something Jason still had trouble accepting. It worried him.

Allison wrapped her arms around her chest and leaned against the door. Mia's behavior worried her, too. She missed Mia. Sometimes desperately. Their relationship had been beyond that of in-laws. Mia had first been her mentor and boss, then her friend and, finally, her surrogate mother. But Allison's divorce from Jason had been a rude reminder that Mia and Allison had no blood tie—and in the end, Bridget's tragedy had been the undoing of their relationship, too.

"Besides," Jason said, breaking Allison's train of thought. "Vaughn called me this morning to find out what I knew, which was nothing, so I made some calls. It's good to have friends in high places."

"Why would Vaughn call you about Arnie Feldman's murder? Because of Helms?"

Jason gave her a strange look. "You're a funny lady, Al. Maybe Vaughn was just being nosey. You place him up on a pedestal, but he *is* human."

"I do forget that sometimes." Allison shook her head. "This whole thing is bizarre. What else do you know about the murder?"

"I know that my mother had nothing to do with it."

"Of course she didn't, Jason. But aside from that."

"Just that you should keep your door locked and the alarm system on. You don't pay enough attention to security." He closed her front door, then opened it and jiggled the handle to check the lock. "I wish you'd get over that fear of yours and adopt a puppy. Then I wouldn't have to worry about you so much."

"Not on your life. Puppies grow up to be dogs."

Allison balked at even the thought of owning a dog. Although she liked dogs in theory, in reality, they scared her. As a child, her father had kept an ornery wolf-dog mix named Thor as a guard animal. The dog lived in their backyard within the confines of a twenty-by-twenty pen. Even though Allison had been warned a thousand times to stay away from him, she'd thought—wrongly—that he'd never bite *her*. So one day, feeling sorry that he was all alone outside, she'd snuck in the pen with him. Thirty seconds later, he had her pinned up against the fence, his snarl so loud it echoed in her nightmares for weeks.

Her dad dragged Thor away before the dog did any physical harm. But her disobedience brought about the bite of her father's belt. She still had the scars to prove it.

While logic told her not all dogs were like Thor, she'd decided not to take a chance. Handing Jason the keys that lay on the foyer table, she said, "Is there something in particular that has you worried?"

Jason stepped outside, seemingly impervious to the sharp breeze that whipped through her lawn. "Just be careful," he said again, making Allison wonder what he wasn't telling her.

Allison waved good-bye before closing the front door. She glanced at her clock. A half hour before she needed to leave. Enough time to make a call.

She dialed Vaughn's number. He answered on the first ring.

"What's up, Allison?"

"Jason said you called him. About Arnie Feldman."

"I did."

"Then you know it was a murder."

"I do."

Baffled by Vaughn's clipped answers, Allison said, "Is this a bad time?"

"I'm at the gym." Vaughn's voice softened. "But that's okay. What do you need?"

"Can you do a little more digging? Make a few calls? I told Jason about the call from Detective Helms, and while Jason told me it was a murder, I got the sense he was holding out on me. I want to know what happened."

She heard him inhale, then a mumbled sound as though he had his hand over the receiver. "I already made a few calls."

Silence.

"And?"

"The police are questioning the ex-wife. And the widow. But then, you know that."

"There's more." Allison could tell by his voice he was hiding something, too.

Finally, he said, "Look, Allison, they're not releasing any details. Everything I know is secondhand."

"Stop beating around the bush, Vaughn. Just tell me what you heard."

He sighed. "It looks like ritualistic murder."

"Meaning?"

"Devil worshipping. That's why I didn't want to tell you. The whole thing was, or was made to look like, some sort of satanic ritual."

On the Main Line? That happened to homeless men on the city streets or lonely teenage girls in the boonies. Successful divorce lawyers were not targets of Satanists. And angry, bitter ex-wives killed out of hatred, not to appease Lucifer.

But what if it was true?

She looked around the foyer, at the windows that lined every wall of her house. Would the alarm system be enough of a deterrent to keep out a killer? She felt a sudden chill. She was sure Feldman had an alarm system, too. Everyone in these parts did.

"That makes no sense."

"Maybe not, but the police are sitting on the details because they don't want all the Main Line moms to get their thongs in a bunch. But it was most definitely a murder."

"Where does Mia fit into all of this?"

"Not sure. But one thing is clear. The police are casting a wide net. They will push to solve this as soon as possible. Devil worshipping on the Main Line? Not something you want plastered in the newspapers."

"What makes the cops think it was Satanism?"

"Hold on, Allison. I can't discuss this here." For a moment, Allison heard noise in the background, what sounded like men shouting superimposed over the blare of loud rap music, and then silence. A second later, Vaughn said, "Sorry. I promised my source I would keep this on the down low. Needed to get outside."

"No problem. You were telling me why the murder seemed like a ritual."

"Right." Vaughn huffed out a sigh. "Pentagrams, smeared blood messages, animal feces. No sign of robbery."

"What'd the messages say?"

"No idea."

"Any witnesses?"

"Not that I'm aware of."

"Alarm system?"

"Off."

"Suspects?"

"The ex-wife, Brenda Feldman, is a person of interest. So are Mia and Sasha Feldman, the new wife. But the detective told you that."

"The satanic stuff doesn't sound like something a spouse would do."

"Could've been a ploy."

Allison agreed. "But if you're a wife—or an ex-wife—why not just hire a hit man? Why go to all that trouble?"

"I don't know? Crazy people do crazy things."

Allison wasn't buying it. "Any chance it was real? That actual devil-worshipping was involved?"

"Really, Allison?"

"Humor me."

"It's not pretty."

"Spare me the chivalry. I can take it."

Allison heard the wail of sirens through the phone. They seemed to go on forever.

When the din quieted, Vaughn said, "Fine. You asked for it." He waited through another round of sirens before saying, "They found Feldman shirtless, with an upside down cross burned into his chest."

Allison's eyes widened. She clutched the mobile tightly. "That's awful."

Vaughn said quietly, "You don't understand. He was alive when this happened. I didn't want to tell you because I didn't want to scare you. Arnie Feldman bled to death, Allison. But only after he was tortured."

SEVEN

Vaughn clicked off the phone, acknowledging the sick feeling that assaulted him whenever he thought of Feldman's murder. The proximity to Allison's house was bad enough. The mere suggestion of Mia's involvement pushed him into hyperdrive.

He tucked the phone into the pocket of his shorts, took a deep breath, and pushed open the door to the boxing gym in West Philly. He might not be able to make things better for Mia or Allison, but at least here he could do some good.

A thick Puerto Rican with an angel tattooed on his arm dropped a barbell and mumbled *sonofabitch* under his breath as Vaughn passed. The guy looked up and nodded. Vaughn tossed him a nod back, said *Juan*, and kept going. Today was a training day, and the ropes were in the back, past the free weights. The kids were waiting.

The gym, hidden away on the first floor of a converted factory, stunk of body odor and mildew. Originally some investor's hot idea for a redevelopment project, the idea flopped and the second floor stayed empty. During the rare times that the gym was quiet, Vaughn could hear rodents scurrying along the upper floor. Didn't bother him. Didn't bother most of the guys who came here.

Vaughn made his way past a dozen muscular youths lifting along the rear wall. Rap music blared from an iPod docking station set on an old milk crate. Rows of fluorescent lights lined thirty-foot ceilings. In the winter, the cold air that seeped around the bank of industrial windows and the high ceilings meant Vaughn could see his breath. In the summer, the lack of air conditioning meant the place was no escape from hot pavement and Philly humidity.

"Hey Vaughn," said a small, wiry black kid with a missing ear. "Thought you weren't coming back."

Vaughn gave the kid a pretend punch, and said, "What would make you think that, D'Quan?"

D'Quan shrugged.

"Sorry. Had to take a call."

"A girl?" The boy grinned.

Vaughn laughed. "Something like that. Now mind your business and get warmed up."

The boy moaned, but he took off into the back of the gym, by the makeshift ring, where two other kids were also waiting. Vaughn barked out a series of warm-up exercises and watched as D'Quan jabbed the speed bag hanging in the corner. The kid was small for his age, but what he lacked in height he made up for in drive. D'Quan's stepfather had taken that ear off in a drunken fit. Boxing gave D'Quan an outlet for his built-up fury. Without it, the kid was a bomb poised to explode.

Vaughn understood. He'd been the same, once upon a time. Drunk father, timid mother, dangerous streets, smallish kid. As a teen, every time, it had been the same scene. His father would get plastered, hit his mother, and Vaughn would step in, full of youthful pride and protectiveness. He'd get smacked down. *Stupid, worthless boy.* Punch. *Get outta here, Christopher.* Punch. *Come back when you learned some respect for me.*

The memory of his father's words tasted like gun metal in his mouth and Vaughn tried to focus instead on the kids in front of him. No use reliving the past. Jamie's condition was enough of a reminder of how stupid he'd once been.

His work with the kids at the boxing gym was a sort of penance. He knew that the rigid schedule he imposed on himself created the sense of order he needed to get through each day. Discipline equaled order equaled peace. And Lord knew, after three years of juvie, then Jamie and the horrors that had followed, he needed peace.

Jamie. Vaughn hoped the nurse would stay till he returned. He'd asked her to, he was sure of it. Yes, he remembered now, she agreed to sleep in the spare bedroom. Angela. Sweet, kind Angela. Vaughn shook his head. He was letting himself get soft. But the lonely longing in his gut told him he wouldn't go straight home. Not tonight. Tonight he'd go where he was welcome.

After two hours with D'Quan and the other kids, Vaughn wiped his forehead with the square white towel and headed for the small locker room. A quick shower later he was dressed and heading outside. It was a new moon, and streetlights pierced the unrelenting darkness, exposing garbage that had accumulated in little windswept piles on the sidewalks. Not wanting to draw attention to his car, Vaughn had purposefully parked the BMW as far from a light as possible. But the darkness pressed down on him and the wind screamed. Even inside the car, the other luxury he allowed himself, a tough chill seeped around the windows and doors.

He thought about Allison and the Feldman murder. What he'd learned about the murder had scared him, for Allison more than Mia. The murder had taken place right in her backyard. And the police had no concrete leads. He wondered if it was just a coincidence that Hank McBride contacted Allison so soon after a Main Line murder. There was no reason to think they were connected, but still. Man, he thought, you're getting paranoid.

But Vaughn had acquired a sense about people from his years in that juvenile facility. There, as a scrawny kid with a scarred face, he knew he couldn't compete with his fists. He'd had to use his brain. He had to know what people were going to do before even they knew and use that knowledge against them. And after a few painful rounds, things he didn't want to think about, he learned. And now Vaughn prided himself on telling the good from the bad, the honest from the dishonest, the genuine article from the carefully crafted fake.

And Hank McBride was a fake.

But if Allison wanted to take the McBrides on as clients, he would respect that. Grudgingly. Allison had her reasons. Just as Vaughn could root out evil intentions, so he could spot when someone's reality was stretched thin. And although Allison Campbell might think she was happy, he knew that under the thick layer of professional devotion lurked a restless spirit. Yeah, he could relate.

Headlights snaked their way toward him and he adjusted his position to avoid the glare. He watched the glow grow stronger and then turn into a parking lot, illuminating a crumbling row house wedged between two intact ones. The abandoned house had a caved-in roof and boarded-up doors. In the lot out front sat a child's Big Wheel. No fancy hedges or flower beds here. Instead, the people living on either side of the condemned house would spend their days swatting cockroaches and chasing rats and hoping some crack head didn't set up camp in the ruins. He would know. He'd grown up just six blocks away.

Vaughn turned on to Route 30 and headed back toward the burbs. It wasn't coincidence that he'd chosen a gym out here in the 'hood. He made a point to remind himself of where he came from. Every single day. It was too easy to forget what lay on the other side of the Main Line divide. He guessed that's what he and Allison had in common: neither were natives. But she tried to run from her past. In his own way, he embraced his.

Vaughn grabbed his cell phone and dialed. On the fifth ring, a soft, husky voice answered, a voice that came to life when he asked if he could visit. "Come," she said, and he felt himself hardening. "I'll leave the front door unlocked."

He wouldn't stay all night, he told himself. Just long enough to lose himself in her. Just long enough to get his father and Jamie and all the stuff from years ago out of his head. Just long enough to make her forget her own troubles. Just long enough.

Mia stared at the receiver, rolled over in bed and stuffed her book back on the bedside shelf. *Damn him.* She hated the aching need she felt whenever he called or visited. It was a need she could ignore most of the time, a need for human companionship, pure and simple. The very fact of their differences, differences that went well beyond the color of their skin and the twenty years that separated them, created safety in their relationship. Mia knew that. Just like she knew that Vaughn would never betray her. Not like her ex-husband Edward, not like Jason and his ex-wife Allison, and, she hated to admit it, not like her daughter Bridget.

Death was the greatest betrayal, after all.

Mia swung her feet over the side of the bed and switched on the bedside lamp. Her eyes scanned the small room for clutter. Not that Vaughn would care. She held no illusions as to why he came. Poor Vaughn, with his striking looks and his troubled past and his crippled brother. Had Vaughn been born with less smarts and less character he might have been happy, but instead the stupidities of his youth served to rein in his future. Mia gave him what she could: the mother's love he yearned for and the sexual release he craved. What strange bedfellows we are, she thought. What would Edward think of that?

Damn Edward, too. Mia had tried to escape the anxiety her ex-husband's visit wrought. The events of four years ago plagued her as it was, but Edward's appearance stood as a great reminder of why she'd purchased this farm, thirty miles from anywhere that counted and down a barely passable dirt road. She would never—could never—forgive him for killing their daughter, Bridget. How someone she gave her body and heart to could kill his own and then use the legal system to rationalize his actions was beyond Mia. Further proof that you never really knew someone.

That's why her relationship with Vaughn worked. There was no pretense of love, no expectations for a future, and no way to disappoint. As long as he kept his word and didn't tell Allison. Jason must never know.

Outside, a cruel wind rattled the window frames and howled through the woods that bordered her land. Night was so absolute here. Living alone, Mia had trained herself to listen for unfamiliar noises. Eventually she heard tires on gravel, Buddy's welcoming bark from his spot in the kitchen. She smiled. Good noises, indeed.

Mia opened a dresser drawer and pulled out a black silk negligee, one of her few nods to vanity. She slipped off her flannel pajamas and stood in front of the mirror, her naked body haloed by the watery lamp light. Her breasts still stood high and firm and her waist and hips were slender. The frustrating inability to store fat as a young girl had served her well in later years. Only the slight bagging skin at her throat and the etched lines on her hands gave away her age. That and her wild gray hair. The tight curls hung in long, thick, wiry ropes across her shoulders and down her back. She'd stopped coloring it when Bridget was killed. Everything had seemed so pointless then.

Mia heard the front door open and close. She heard Vaughn's hello to Buddy, then his steps across the kitchen floor, soft and sure. She felt his presence in the bedroom doorway even before she caught sight of his reflection in her mirror. She made no move to cover herself. Instead, she studied his reflection: the cropped black hair, the tiny Lennon glasses, the thin scar that ran from his nose to his lip, the broad shoulders and defined pecs that spoke of hours at the gym. She watched him unbutton his shirt, take off his watch, then unbuckle his belt and pull his khakis down, all the while his gaze on her reflection. Her nipples grew hard. She turned to face him and saw that his excitement matched her own.

"I'm glad you came," she said.

He didn't say anything, just closed the space between them and joined her by the mirror. He wrapped his arms around her, one hand on her stomach, the other on her breast. The contrast between their skin colors—hers full-moon white, his night black—stole her breath. She watched his hand move across her body like a shadow. Despite his strength, his touch was gentle.

She turned to face him, then kissed his eyes, his neck, his lips. She led him to the bed. "Will you stay the night?"

If he'd heard the pleading in her voice, he didn't let on—and for that she was grateful.

He said, "Jamie." She nodded her understanding.

She pulled him close to feel the weight of his chest against her own. Strength, substance. That was what Vaughn was to her. Strength, substance and...oblivion. Beautiful, merciful oblivion. Gently, he kissed her throat. Mia threw back her head and moaned.

Vaughn punched in his pass code, waited for the familiar buzz, and then pulled open the security door to his apartment building. He took the elevator to his tenth floor apartment, twisted the key in the lock, and opened the front door.

Like always, that step from the outside world to the inside of his home was a shock to his system. First the smells: Lysol and the faint scent of urine and wisps of the spice-scented candles the nurses lit to hide both. Then the overwhelming warmth. Jamie had trouble regulating his body temperature and Vaughn needed to keep the thermostat set at seventy-five-degrees all year round. Then the sounds, so familiar to him now that he had to stop and listen for them: the gentle, life-supporting whir of the monitors and machines that helped Jamie function; the hum of the computer that ran all day because it was the only way Jamie could communicate; and finally, the lights. Night lights, overhead lights, fluorescents. Jamie would still wake up in a panic in the middle of the night, wondering why he couldn't walk or talk or crap on his own, his eyes rolling around and bulging from his head till Vaughn was afraid they would hemorrhage. Light was the only way to reassure. *No, it's not a nightmare, my brother. At least not one you can simply wake up from.*

Vaughn took off his coat, hung it in the living room closet and tiptoed toward Jamie's room. He could still smell Mia's citrusy scent on his skin, feel her arms around his neck. It was hard to leave that bed for cold spring air and the long drive home. What he wouldn't have given to wake up there—arms tangled in her hair, early morning love-making followed by fresh eggs and bacon and the sound of her damn rooster crowing. He could only imagine, though, for he'd never stayed.

He heard a rustling and froze mid-step. A second later, a pretty face peeked around the corner of Jamie's bedroom. Long, straight black hair. Short, curvy body. Sleep creases on her forehead. He saw a flash of embarrassment cross Angela's pretty features, then she smiled.

"Good night for him," she said.

"Will you stay?"

"Who's coming in the morning?"

"Mrs. Tildman."

Angela smiled again. Mrs. T was everyone's favorite. She put the kitchen to use and made soups and biscuits, homemade things he could store in his freezer to ward off chilly nights. She straightened blankets and plumped pillows and cleaned the oven. All the things he liked to believe his mama would have done had she lived. But best of all, she read books. To Jamie. They both loved mystery novels, and around his bed stood stacks of Elizabeth George, P.D. James, and Agatha Christie. The warmth and energy in her voice brought those characters to life. Jamie adored her. Vaughn wanted to pay her a premium to keep her there, but the woman would hear nothing of it. *My hourly rate is all*, she'd tell him. *I need to eat. But beyond that, I just like that boy's company.*

Angela took a step toward the spare bedroom. "I'll stay till Mrs. T gets here. Don't worry. Leave early if you have to."

Vaughn gave her a grateful smile and watched her close the bedroom door. He finished his trek to his brother's room and stood in the doorway. Jamie's blankets were pulled taut over his thin form, and Vaughn could see the slight indentation where Angela's head had rested next to Jamie's arm. Jamie was asleep. His eyes fluttered, restless even now.

The computer mouth stick hung just inches from his mouth in case he woke up and needed to say something. His words would show up flat, black against white, on the screen that stood just a foot away. Jamie wanted it that way. After the incident, Jamie never regained full use of his voice. The computer could speak the words, too, but they came out tinny and robotic-sounding, and Jamie said it was a reminder that he was mute as a dead parrot.

Vaughn obliged. Vaughn always obliged. How could he not when he'd taken up the yoke of Jamie's life—college and a real job and putting his brains to something other than creative drug deals—after Jamie had been paralyzed by the near-fatal gunshot meant for him over a decade ago? Once their mama died and Vaughn could see straight, he traded his own life for Jamie's. Some form of restitution.

Still, it was hard. Hard to see his brother motionless year after year with little hope for recovery. Harder to accept that Jamie stayed confined to the world Vaughn had created for him. Vertebra C3. Who knew one little body part could ruin two lives?

He looked again at Jamie. It was like viewing himself in a mirror. A fun house mirror that twisted and contorted and thinned out the image. That was his real penance. To look in that mirror every single day. To see himself lying there and not be able to do a damn thing about it and know it was his fault. Because in the end, it wasn't him. Worse. It was his identical twin.

EIGHT

The following day, Allison met with her Recently Divorced group.

The group was discussing change and how hard it could be to build a life as a single person when your world was predicated on coupledom. Unfortunately, each woman had a very different idea of what single looked like. Allison watched the group before her. For a moment their mouths seem to move soundlessly and she caught just a slow-motion glimpse of this hodgepodge of clients: Midge, with her pillbox hats and buttoned-up anger; the morbidly obese and timid Tori; sweet-natured Diane; and Kit with her plastic features and edgy personality. Some days this mix of personalities seemed like an inflamed volcano—ready to blow.

Today was one of those days.

"You put an ad online?" Midge was saying. "How does the guy contact you?" In her excitement, she sat forward too quickly and her pink pillbox hat fell across her forehead. "I don't understand these new dating rituals. It's a shame you and Bob split. Do you ever think about what you could have done differently to save your marriage?"

Oh, sweet Mary. Allison shook her head at Midge, who was cluelessly looking at Tori.

"Men are visual creatures," Kit said. "In any case, personal ads are not the way to go. You look desperate."

"*Kit,*" Allison said sharply. Then she looked around at the other women. "Ladies, you're being unfair. First of all, what Bob did was about Bob and his issues. It was not about Tori."

Tori turned her head toward the group room's window and stared straight ahead, avoiding Allison's gaze. But Allison knew her well enough to read the signs: rigid shoulders, face muscles taut, hands clenched into claws, reddened eyes. In a few minutes, Tori would be reduced to a crying mess, all her Bob memories from the last two years rushing at her alongside the swell of emotion caused by the group's fervor over her online dating.

Allison thought carefully about what to say.

Few of these women had stories Allison hadn't heard before, but Tori's was a new twist on an old theme. Her ex-husband, Bob, a forty-year-old investment banker, had had a succession of affairs, culminating with a poke to a nineteen-year-old blonde in Tori's bed while Tori gave birth to their third child, nine miles away. Tori's father found them together, the girl naked and bound, Bob wearing his son's Superman cape and nothing else. Unable to hide from the truth any longer, Tori was divorced before the baby was weaned.

Allison felt for Tori. There was something about Tori's pain at living in the body she'd been given that nudged at Allison's depths, reminded her of her own childhood memories. Allison looked at Tori now and saw the effort she had put into dressing that morning: black pants with a drape that softened the girth of her thighs, a subtle black-print blouse with material thick enough to hide the rolls of belly fat without adding bulk, a red scarf to draw attention to beautiful green eyes and glossy black hair, silver bracelets to pull the eye toward well-manicured hands rather than her enormous upper arms. Tori was beautiful. And she was learning. This was the polish that could make a difference.

"Tori?" Allison's voice was gentle. "Do you want to address the group?"

Tori didn't speak, just seemed to pull herself inside and disappear, away from Kit's gloating smile and the curious gazes of everyone else. Allison could hardly blame her. She needed time.

The room was silent. Allison heard the woosh of traffic passing by outside: a door slammed in the front office. She looked at Tori and tried to telegraph understanding and acceptance. For she did understand. More than Tori knew.

"Excuse me, Allison?" Kit raised her hand. "Allison?"

"Yes?" Allison turned toward the platinum blonde in the corner.

Kit Carson-Lewis. Her long hair was blown straight, her cleavage blossomed from the front of a low-cut magenta blazer. Nails like pink daggers.

"I want to address Tori." When Allison nodded, she continued, "Tori, I think I owe you an apology." She licked her obscenely plush lips. "I'm sorry."

Tori turned away.

"No, really. I was out of line. We all were." Kit looked around at Midge and Diane, who were nodding their agreement. "There are men out there who will love and accept you for who you are, Tori darling. And you shouldn't be willing to accept any less. The dating world can be scary. Online dating, especially. We're all just worried about you."

Allison smiled at Kit. She knew even that apology was difficult. Kit's ex-husband, a Philadelphia plastic surgeon, had urged her to undergo surgery after surgery: breast implants, liposuction, Botox injections, a face-lift, an eye-lift, labia reduction, a nose job. As she told it, she went along with his suggestions year after year. Then he committed the ultimate sin. He had an affair and later married a woman a few years *older* than Kit. According to Kit, the new wife was fat, wrinkled, and had a nose like an upside down ice cream cone. And still does. No plastic surgery for Wife Number Two, while Kit looked like someone created by Mattel. And the ex-husband seemed happy. Kit wore the bitterness like an overcoat. And her first instinct, always, was to hurt before being hurt. It was a habit Allison was trying to help her break.

Allison clapped her hands together. Tori's color had returned and the rest of the group had done the right thing. It was a good place to end before Helms arrived. Allison stood, signaling the ladies. Everyone but Midge filed out of the room.

When they were alone, Midge said, "I'm sorry about that. I guess I was really thinking about my own ex-husband. That maybe if I had been different, he wouldn't have chosen a man over me."

"You know that has nothing to do with you, either, Midge. His homosexuality isn't something you caused—or could have prevented."

"I know." Midge blushed. "He's living in Vermont with his lover. I guess I should have known years ago."

"Some people go their whole lives without realizing their partner is gay."

"I suppose I did overreact," Midge said, and laughed.

Yep, shooting him in the foot while he's naked and on top of another man is probably an overreaction, Allison thought. But hey, who am I to judge?

Allison pulled the group's file together and said, "So, for next time, you'll think about one small change you can incorporate into your life?"

Midge looked mildly ashamed. "Yes, I'll behave."

"Oh, I didn't say to behave," Allison said with a wink. "Just try to have an open mind."

"Adventure will be my middle name." Midge stood to go. "I used to be a pin-up girl, you know. In my heyday, I was quite a hottie." Her eyes brightened and Allison got a fleeting glimpse of a younger, more daring Midge. "I still have a postcard to prove it."

Allison said she hadn't known. "Bring in the postcard for our next session."

"Really?"

"Absolutely. I'd love to see it." Allison wanted her clients to bring in bits of their past. She could help them best if she had a broader sense of who they were, who they'd been. She believed people were often defined by their pasts, intentionally or not, and Midge was no exception. Midge had lost that sense of self somewhere in the forty years of marriage to a closeted gay man, but the old Midge was still there. Watching Midge now, Allison couldn't help but feel a twinge of pride.

"You're doing great, Midge. Next week, same time?"

"I wouldn't miss it." On her way out, Midge said, "Did you hear about Arnie Feldman? It's all people are talking about."

"I heard he was murdered."

Midge nodded. "His neighbor told my neighbor that there was blood everywhere. Sasha Feldman, that's his wife, had to hire an outside contractor to remove the carpeting and repaint the walls." She shuddered. "I'd leave that house, if I were her. But Sasha is a gold-digger. She probably doesn't care."

Midge said all of this with relish. The only thing more popular than shopping amongst some of Allison's clients was gossip. Allison swallowed. Curious or not, she'd feel better when the killer was locked away.

Midge smoothed the front of her navy shirtwaist dress. Echoing Allison's thoughts, Midge said, "Let's hope the police solve this one, Allison. I know I have trouble sleeping at night. And I keep a gun by my bed."

Vaughn had asked Lieutenant Helms to wait in Allison's office. Walking in, she expected to find a disheveled man in rumpled clothing, sort of the typical underpaid television policeman. Instead, Lieutenant Mark Helms was a tall, muscular forty-something, with striking blue eyes, an aquiline nose, and a thick head of salt-and-pepper hair. He rose when Allison entered the room and held out his hand. They shook. Out of habit, Allison glanced at his left hand. No wedding ring.

"Ms. Campbell," he said. "Your reputation precedes you."

"Well, I hope it's a good reputation," Allison said with a smile.

With one long glance, Allison watched him take in her three-inch Jimmy Choos, her tight beige pencil skirt, the fitted cream jacket and baby blue floral scarf that she'd knotted carefully around her neck. She tried to decide whether the look on his face was dismissive or one of practiced nonchalance. She decided to give him the benefit of the doubt.

She motioned for him to sit back down, and then she walked around her desk and took the seat across from him. "What can I do for you? I'm afraid I don't have much time. I have another appointment in thirty minutes."

"This won't take long, Ms. Campbell."

"Allison."

"Allison, as you know, we're investigating the death of Arnie Feldman. As we discussed on the phone, you worked with Feldman's widow, the former Sally Ann Reilly."

"Not for long."

"But you knew her before she married Feldman."

"I suppose. I didn't know she'd married Arnie, though."

"You didn't see them at social functions?"

Allison smiled. "Rarely. I'd met Arnie a few times at neighborhood events, but never his wife. They'd just moved in two years ago."

Helms nodded. "Rumor has it that Sasha—Sally Ann—wanted a bigger place."

"Rumor will have a lot of things, Lieutenant. The trick is parceling rumor from truth."

The lieutenant nodded. "I couldn't agree more."

"Then perhaps our two lines of business are not so different."

Helms laughed. "Perhaps not."

Allison had to admit, the guy had a nice laugh. She wondered why the police department sent the Lieutenant over instead of one of his directs. And while she wanted to help Helms, she honestly couldn't think of any information that would be of any help.

"Look, Lieutenant," Allison said, "What I remember of Sally Ann is probably not valuable. She was sent to me by her employer to work on some issues that were interfering with her job. We met a few times, she quit her job, and I never saw her again."

"Was she cooperative?"

"Moderately, although not particularly engaged."

"What does that mean?"

"She didn't really seem to want to be there. Lacked self-awareness about what was holding her back."

"What was holding her back?"

Allison thought back to the woman she'd seen. It had been in their old offices, when Mia still owned the business. "There was a naked sort of ambition about her. She knew what she wanted and you knew she would do whatever was necessary to get it."

Helms raised his eyebrows. "Did she strike you as a social climber?"

"I never gave it any thought."

"Think about it now. I'm sure I don't need to spell out the angle we're looking into."

"Was she capable of marrying for money and then disposing of her husband?" Allison replied.

Helms stayed silent, but Allison knew that was it. And there was probably a large insurance policy and maybe even a prenup with a death clause.

"I don't know. There was that naked ambition, but the woman I knew was socially awkward."

"In what way?"

Allison considered how best to answer. "Sally Ann was in her early thirties back then. Brash, a bit of a complainer, impatient. Not very likable, and I would think a successful social climber would be likable. She seemed smart, though."

"Smart intelligent or smart cunning?"

Allison smiled. "Smart cunning, I suppose."

Helms leaned back. He jotted something in his notebook.

"I'm intrigued by your comment about the neighborhood. How is it that you lived there two years and never ran into Sasha Feldman?"

"We don't travel in the same circles."

"But you're the area go-to lady."

"That doesn't mean I'm invited to every event. Or that I attend when I am invited."

"You said you met Arnie at a few affairs. Do you recall which ones?"

Allison didn't have to think hard to remember. Arnie Feldman was not a forgettable fellow. "A fund raising event for a charity for homeless teens. A neighbor held a dinner at a local restaurant. We were both there."

"But not Sasha?"

"Not that I recall."

"And the other events?"

"A graduation party for a neighbor's kid. Last summer. That was it." Allison gave Helms the name of the neighbor.

"Again, no Sasha?"

"Not that I recall."

Helms fished a manila envelope out of his briefcase. He opened it and pulled out a photo, which he handed to Allison. "Recognize her?"

Allison stared at the picture. Taken during an outdoor barbeque, the woman in the photo was sitting at a picnic table, arms crossed, an untouched hot dog on a paper plate in front of her. A frown creased an otherwise creaseless face. She had long, glossy black hair and her eyes were hidden behind oversize sunglasses. But Allison recognized the hard set of her mouth and thin, narrow shoulders. Sally Ann—Sasha—had had some major orthodontia and a boob job at some point. Double Ds strained the buttons on an expensive-looking silk blouse.

She handed the picture back to Helms. "Only because I know who she is. Truthfully, if I ran into her at a party, I wouldn't have known it was Sally Ann. She looks completely different."

"But if she'd come up to you and re-introduced herself?"

Allison nodded. "Yes, after a moment. But she didn't." Allison held up a hand. "But before you make too much of that, Lieutenant, remember what I do for people. Not everyone wants it known that they've worked with an image consultant."

"Understood. Her former employer told us she'd worked with you. That's how we made the connection."

Lieutenant Helms unfurled his long body and walked to the window. He spoke with his back to Allison. "And now a little closer to home. Mia Campbell?"

Allison tensed. "What do you want to know?"

"Her name has come up. Witnesses say they overheard Ms. Campbell making threats toward Arnie. She said, I quote, 'I'll get you one day.'"

"And who are these witnesses?"

Helms turned. "I get to ask the questions, Allison. Did you ever hear Mia Campbell threaten Arnie Feldman?"

"I heard a bereaved mother express anger toward a system that denied her daughter justice."

Helms walked across the room until he was standing over Allison. He placed both hands on her desk and leaned in so that she could smell his spicy aftershave. "Please answer the question."

Allison refused to be cowed. "Mia disliked the way Arnie treated her. He twisted words, tried to make her look unstable."

"Disliked him enough to hurt him?"

"Three years later? Hardly. She reacted in the heat of the moment. Was anything she said a true threat? Absolutely not."

"You said Feldman tried to make her look unstable. Is she? Unstable, I mean?"

Allison hesitated. "Not that I am aware."

But it was too late.

Like a hawk on a free range chicken farm, Helms swooped in. "A legalistic answer. Mia moved to the country, sold all her possessions and disconnected from almost everyone in her life—including you, her protégé and daughter-in-law."

"*Former* daughter-in-law."

Helms stood. His height was unsettling, but Allison matched his challenging stare with a hard look of her own.

After a moment, Helms said, "Admit it, Ms. Campbell, Mia is not who she was."

"Are any of us?"

Helms gave her a sharp look. "Stop playing games."

Allison stood. In heels, she could almost look him in the eye. "I'm not playing games, Lieutenant. Mia's daughter was killed at the hands of her drunk husband. She lost two people in one horrible split second. If that doesn't buy a person a temporary pass at sanity, I don't know what does. But that doesn't mean that years later Mia Campbell had the wherewithal or desire to murder her husband's lawyer. Frankly, you're grasping at straws."

Helms shook his head slowly, back and forth. In a split second, his expression went from angry to unreadable. The professional mask was back on. "That's all I need, Allison." He handed her a card. "Call me if you think of anything else."

As he was leaving, Allison stopped him. She'd meant to say something earlier, but the Lieutenant's question about Mia had thrown her off. "If Sally Ann Reilly married Arnie Feldman, Lieutenant, what happened to Arnie's first wife?"

"He divorced her. As I understood it, the circumstances were not amicable."

Allison considered this. She knew Feldman's first wife. The woman had been Mia's client a long time ago.

She said, "Hmm. I don't imagine they would be. Amicable, that is."

"Why is that?"

"Sally Ann's sister, Brenda Reilly, was Arnie Feldman's first wife. If Sally Ann is Sasha Feldman, that means that Arnie went from one sister to another." Allison opened the door to her office. The Lieutenant stood still, his eyes locked on Allison. "That, Lieutenant, could be one ugly love triangle."

After Helms left, and later between sessions, Allison read the headlines in the local newspapers and clicked through the online news, looking for anything related to Feldman's murder. The story was everywhere, including international syndicates. But each source only repeated the same tired information. A rare murder on the prestigious Main Line. Feldman died in his home under suspicious circumstances. No suspects in custody.

No mention of Mia; she was grateful for that.

Allison searched Google for anything on Sasha Feldman, the late Arnie, even Brenda, his ex-wife. Again, nothing new that would shed light on a motive to murder the attorney. Could it have been a sacrificial killing? A chill ran through her. She hoped not. That seemed too random. If that were true, then anyone could be the next target.

Allison put her head back, against her chair. Satansim. Torture. A disabled security alarm.

An inside job? A devil worshipper?

Or a very savvy killer?

NINE

Sunny arrived at four o'clock, without Hank. She walked into First Impressions behind her daughter Catherine while Maggie trailed a few feet behind them both. Allison greeted them at the door, taking in at a glance the distance between Catherine and her mother and Maggie. The weather had flip-flopped. It was a warm March day, but despite the tenacious sunshine, all three McBride women were dressed for winter.

In the light of her office, Allison could see Maggie's features more clearly. She had full, bow-shaped lips and black irises that spilled into the chestnut brown of her eyes, making little pools of ebony where there should have been none. A pretty girl, really. Or she could be.

Allison didn't have long to ponder this fact before Catherine said, "Mother and I were wondering how long you need with Maggie?"

"Three hours." Allison glanced at her watch. "You can pick her up at seven."

That got Maggie's attention. "No way. No effing way. Mom, you promised I could go out tonight with—"

Catherine shot a warning look at her sister. "Really, Ms. Campbell," Catherine said, "Don't you think that's overdoing it for the first session? We'd like her home earlier."

Allison looked at Catherine before glancing down at her schedule. She'd already decided to spend the better part of the afternoon with Maggie. Not only did she want a chunk of time to break through the barriers, but, if this relationship was doomed—if it was clear Maggie wouldn't work with her—Allison wanted to know up front. Before she wasted her time and the McBride's money.

Allison let the silence continue for another moment. She walked to a bookshelf and rifled through brochures, finally choosing one she normally gave to family members of clients, about supporting change in their loved-one. She handed the brochure to Sunny.

"I need three hours. After this, sessions will be one to two hours, max. But this is intake."

Maggie moaned. "Mom..."

"Really, Mother, think. We have my engagement party tonight. Seven won't work." Catherine took the brochure from her mother's hand. She leafed through it quickly and then tucked it under her arm in a dismissive gesture. "We'll be back at six," she said to Allison.

Allison matched icy smile for icy smile. When she spoke, it was to Sunny. "Seven o'clock. I can take her home, if need be. You agreed up-front to my rules, Mrs. McBride. If you're having second thoughts, please let me know now." Then Allison turned to Catherine and held out her hand. "The brochure."

Catherine gave it to her with reluctance, a scowl marring the glacial prettiness of her features.

"May I remind you, Catherine, that your parents and Maggie are my clients. While I'm thrilled for your engagement, and do wish you the best, I'd kindly like you to remember that I answer only to my clients."

Catherine looked like someone had punched her. Sunny, lips tightly knit into a barely discernible smile, seemed happily surprised. And Maggie grinned from ear to ear, the blow to Catherine's ego clearly more enjoyable than the pain of having to stay with Allison all afternoon.

"Okay, then. This way." Allison walked across the reception area to the front door. "Shall I bring her home?"

Catherine walked out in a huff, doing her best to slam the door behind her. Sunny turned before leaving and ran a finger across

Maggie's cheek. Maggie flinched. Sunny tilted her head to the side, sadness creasing the skin around her eyes, and gave Allison an empty smile. "If you don't mind. Thank you."

Allison watched them get into the Mercedes. Then she walked toward a small room off the back of the reception area, motioning to Maggie to follow. "This way, Maggie. Let's get started."

Allison led Maggie to the client room, a small room decorated in warm tones of beige, peach and chocolate. The room had been designed for intimacy. Allison wanted her clients to develop confidence in the relationship, to feel safe and secure enough to share goals and ideas. But glancing now at Maggie's angry scowl, Allison was pretty sure the studied coziness of the client room wasn't going to make a bit of difference.

Four armchairs faced each other around a mahogany table. In the corner, mostly hidden behind a small Asian-inspired screen, stood a scale. Next to the scale, a few feet from the table, was an old fashioned roll-top desk, the inside of which contained standing file folders, each labeled with the names of clothing manufacturers and filled with catalogues. Allison watched Maggie scan the room, still scowling.

Allison motioned toward one of the arm chairs. "Please. Sit." Then she walked over to the desk and pulled several catalogues from one of the file folders and a tape measure from a drawer. Before returning to the table, she pulled aside the screen that hid the scale.

When Allison turned back around, she saw that Maggie had pushed her chair back as far as it would go, until the back of it was lodged against a wall. She lounged with her head against the chair, her arms slung over the sides, feet propped on the table.

Allison ignored the scuff mark on the wall where the chair had hit too hard and the black line on the table top where the rubber from Maggie's boots maligned the wood.

"Here you go, Maggie." She placed a stack of clothing catalogues in front of her. Guess, DKNY, J. Crew, Abercrombie and Fitch. She took the seat opposite Maggie and spread the catalogues out on the table.

"This is what you do?" Maggie said, straining her neck to see, her feet still on the table. She snickered. "Catalogue shopping? That's your big secret to success?"

Allison chose to ignore her tone. "These catalogues help me get a sense of the style that appeals to you. Usually we start with a discussion of personal goals. I do a physical intake: weight, height, measurements. And then we prepare a personal plan. Together."

Maggie sat up and swung her feet down onto the floor. "No offense, Allison, but this is so stupid." She pointed to her skirt. "My style. What you see is what you get." Then she picked up the Guess catalogue, flipped through it much the same way Catherine had flipped through the First Impressions brochure, and tossed it back on the table.

Maggie sneered. "Oh, Allison, please give me perfect nails and a boob job and liposuction! Make me look like Catherine. Please, oh please. Or better yet, make me look like you, Ms. Perfect." She pushed the catalogues to the edge of the table and smiled. "But you were born perfect, weren't you? You were probably a cheerleader with loads of skinny, cheerleader friends. Well, that's not me. I don't need to look perfect to be happy, and I wish you and my stupid parents would just leave me the hell alone." With one finger, she pushed the catalogues over the edge of the table, onto the floor. She stared at Allison, her eyes challenging. "You make me sick."

Allison picked up the catalogues and took a moment to restack them, as much to buy time as to regain her own composure. How far from the truth Maggie was. Cheerleader? Perfect body? How about gorging alone in her bedroom in order to avoid the fact that she had no friends? The few she'd had had been terrified of her father, the criminal. Never mind that he was acquitted. Didn't matter. He and his family had been pariahs in a town of small thoughts and small dreams. And that made for a lonely existence.

No, she had been more like Violet than Maggie. Alone. Grateful for anyone's attention. Not like this spoiled child who sat before her now. But if she was going to make this relationship work, if she was going to give the McBrides some bang for their buck, she needed to think fast and not let her feelings interfere with work.

She looked at Maggie. The girl stared callously ahead, eyes hidden by gobs of eyeliner and mascara. Allison considered Sunny's description of her daughter. Could this all be chalked up to poor self-esteem? Oh, it made sense that the clothes, the hair, the piercings, were all designed to hide an insecure teenage girl from scrutiny. A mask of sorts, hiding the real Maggie. But Allison couldn't get a sense of what, exactly, Maggie was most afraid of—changing or not changing. Success or failure. She realized she couldn't really relate to Maggie's plight and the thought made her angry. How could someone who *could* have it all, especially the freedom and acceptance that go hand-in-hand with power and money, so blatantly throw it all away?

Don't be silly, Al, she thought. You've seen enough to know that money cannot buy happiness. The saying was cliché for a reason.

Allison stood up, walked to the small window over the desk, and looked outside. The sun shone. The oak trees that lined the street remained bare, but Allison could make out tiny nubs of green. Harbingers of spring. Hope and rebirth. She took a deep breath and turned to face Maggie.

"Get your coat," Allison said. "We're leaving."

"Where are we going?" Maggie asked. They were outside by Allison's car, and Maggie's ungloved fingers twirled a pentagram necklace around at the hollow of her throat.

"Get in and I'll explain."

Maggie climbed in, sat back, and said, "Tell me where you're taking me."

"The mall."

"I don't want to go to the mall."

"Please put your seatbelt on."

"I don't want to wear my seatbelt."

Lord. Allison rubbed her temple and wondered, yet again, about the wisdom of agreeing to this task. Maggie was a nightmare of Oppositional Defiant Disorder. Allison felt more like a babysitter than an image consultant. And she had no idea what she was going to do once she got Maggie to the mall. But nearly three long hours stretched before her and she needed to think of something.

She waited for Maggie to buckle her seatbelt. And while she waited, she thought of Violet.

A sense of futility weighed down on Allison.

As it had at the Meadows.

To a younger Allison, the name the Meadows had initially conjured up pictures of peaceful plains, resort-like rooms with clean corners and cheerful staff. Somewhere mildly neurotic children went to find comfort and understanding and the emotional space to heal.

She couldn't have been further from reality.

The building that housed the Meadows treatment facility was tall and imposing, a plain brick box with barred windows and a steel-door entryway. Instead of the rolling meadows the name suggested, a depressing mixture of scrubby lawn and low-trimmed hedges, plain and browning and uninspired, surrounded the building within the confines of a six-foot chain-link fence. A single-lane driveway led through the hedges to and around the front of the building and then disappeared around back, ending at the facility's parking lot.

The reception area had been carefully planned to give off an air of homey welcome. Plants surrounded a large oak reception desk. An oriental rug sat beneath chairs and a low round table, on which a carefully selected array of magazines—*Cricket, Good Housekeeping, Parent, Car and Driver*—had been arranged in a semi-circle. The walls were beige; the light fixtures illuminated the room in a soft glow and kept the corners dark.

But if you looked closely, and Allison had, you'd see that beyond the reception desk, on the other end of a beige hallway, stood another metal door. Beyond that door, the homey atmosphere ended. Beyond that door were gray corridors and metal bars and stained furniture bolted to the floors. Beyond that door you could hear the shrieks and moans of girls who missed their mothers or their boyfriends or their crack. You could see the care-worn faces of staff burned out from too little pay and too much responsibility. You could smell the hopelessness.

Allison came to learn that, for many, the Meadows was the last stop, a residential treatment program where Pennsylvania counties sent their worst female offenders—and their most horribly offended—before incarceration or, for the sickest kids, a psychiatric hospital. This meant rules. Lots of them: no smoking, no cursing, no physical contact. No hairspray (flammable), no nail-cutters (weaponry), no boys (temptation). Lights out at nine; wake up at six. Mail was read, beds were inspected, delousing was mandatory. And the list went on.

The rules went for staff also: no fraternizing, no friendships, no fun. The Meadows was a serious place where serious counselors performed the wizardry of therapy on seriously disturbed adolescents. The Meadows was the place Allison worked during graduate school. The Meadows was where she met Violet.

Allison recalled her first glimpse of the girl. During intake, Violet had sat hunched over on the nurse's stool, a thermometer dangling from her mouth, her legs drowning in baggy brown corduroy. A beat-up blue duffle bag, barely large enough to fit gym clothes much less the worldly possessions of a teenage girl, had been propped next to her.

"New kid," the nurse said, her heavy chest heaving with the exertion of filling out forms and sorting through paperwork. "She'll be ready to go to the dorms soon enough."

The girl didn't move, didn't look up from beneath her bangs. Allison saw purple bruises on her jaw line and aged, white scars on the backs of her hands.

"She has her period. We'll send her up with pads." The nurse pulled the thermometer from the girl's mouth, glanced at it, and stuck it back in a jar of alcohol. "Wait a minute, Allison, and you can take her with you. She doesn't talk much, this one. But she's no dummy. Don't let her fool you." She handed Allison a stack of paperwork and a white bag full of pads and tampons. "Good luck."

Allison motioned for the girl to follow her. "What's your name?" she said.

The girl stared stonily ahead.

"Violet Swann," the nurse called from down the corridor. "With two n's. Not like the bird."

Violet Swann. A stoner fourteen-year-old with stringy brown hair and a waist that spanned the length of one of Allison's outstretched hands. A self-mutilator. Defiant. Allison had read her case file with a mixture of grief and rage. The fourth time Violet ran away she was raped by a teenaged neighbor looking for a way to prove his manhood. Six days after the rape, Violet set fire to his parents' garage, earning her the hard-to-place label "fire-setter." After nine placement rejections, her caseworker finally sent her to the Meadows.

Allison knew Violet didn't have a chance, really. The details of her history had read like any clinical file in any residential treatment program in any state in America. Abuse, neglect, drugs, sex. Probably in that order. Two therapists at the Meadows fought to have Violet taken off their caseload. She wouldn't talk, wouldn't listen, wouldn't even shower unless a staff member dragged her kicking and screaming, her hand clutched around an ancient, eyeless, smelly stuffed hippo. She needs a psychiatric placement, they said. She's psychotic, they said. But no one listened. Poor Violet was too sick for foster care and too well for a psych hospital. The truth was, she had nowhere else to go.

So eventually Allison asked her boss, Dr. Nutzbaum, to transfer Violet to her caseload. Doc shook his head and said, "Allison, don't bet on a sore loser. She has a 145 I.Q. and spent the last ten years of her life wasting it, one I.Q. point at a time. She's oppositional, probably has Borderline Personality Disorder, and is incapable of bonding. Find a better use for your graduate education. Use it on someone who has a chance at making it."

As she pulled into the mall parking lot now, a sullen Maggie beside her, Allison tried to picture Violet's face, but all she saw were sunken gray eyes and the dark hole where her right eye-tooth had been. She knew that wasn't really fair; there were moments when Violet had looked beautiful. Specks of gold had glittered in her eyes in the sunlight, making them appear translucent. Those eyes, together with her dark hair and fair skin, gave her an ethereal countenance. In those moments, Allison saw the author, the artist, the scholar that Violet could have been.

And it made her want to weep.

TEN

Allison switched off the ignition and glanced at her watch. 4:58. Another two hours before Maggie was expected home. With a twinge of guilt, Allison wished she hadn't insisted on the full three-hour intake session. But she wasn't about to change that now.

Maggie said, "Why are we here?"

"To browse."

"I don't want to be seen here with you."

Allison grabbed her purse off the floor behind her seat. "Look, Maggie, you agreed to this, remember? 'Daddy said my last chance is coming over today.' Those were your words, not mine. So cut the attitude and let's try to make this work."

Maggie sat, arms crossed, and stared straight ahead.

"Let's go, Maggie."

"No."

"You only have two more hours. Let's put them to good use."

"I said no."

Allison took a deep breath. "Think, Maggie. Your parents expect you to fail. At least, that's how they'll see it. Why don't you throw them a curve ball? Cooperate. Consider what you might get out of this relationship before you do something that causes more trouble."

Maggie twisted in the seat to face Allison. "I don't like you. You're here because they're paying you to be here."

Allison weighed a response and decided to be candid. "That's true."

Maggie shook her head. "I want to hate you."

"So hate me." Allison got out of the car and shut the door. This time, Maggie followed.

"Look, Maggie, I'm not trying to dictate how you feel about me. I have a job to do. You have a desire to stay out of boarding school, and I'm the ticket to freedom. Despise me, if that's what it takes. Just cooperate and everybody wins."

Maggie looked for a brief second like she would capitulate. Then suddenly, from a few rows over in the parking lot, Allison heard car doors slam and the competing voices of teenage girls talking and laughing over nothing much. Maggie's features hardened.

"The hell with that," she said and stormed toward the mall.

Allison jogged in three-inch wedges to keep up with her. After catching her breath and thanking the good Lord for thick, strong ankles, Allison said, "I'm sure we can find some common ground."

Stormy silence.

Allison tried to think of things teens liked to talk about. Of course, they liked to talk to *each other*, not thirty-three-year-old women. She gave it a go anyway. "Do you have a boyfriend, Maggie?"

"None of your business."

"I heard you mention going out tonight and I thought maybe a guy was involved."

A glimmer of interest flashed in Maggie's eyes. Allison hoped she'd cave. Boy-talk would at least be common ground.

"I *said* it's none of your business."

Allison counted to ten silently to keep from telling Maggie what she could do with *her business* and led the way into Neiman Marcus.

Maggie marched through the women's dress section as though unfazed by the sequined materials and lithe mannequins that lined the aisles. Allison steered her toward the escalator and a trendier department. Maybe being around girls her own age, and around fashions most teens would kill for, would motivate her.

"What do you like to do in your spare time, Maggie?"

"No comment."

"This isn't an interrogation. I'm just trying to get to know you."

Maggie flashed her an evil grin. "Okay then. I'm a witch."

"Really?" Allison had been eyeing a Kate Spade bag she thought would be perfect for one of her clients. When Maggie spoke, she turned to give her full attention. "A witch? As in rides a broomstick and has a thing for black cats?"

"Make fun of me if you want, but it's true. I go by Lanomia. My parents told me not to tell you."

"Should that matter to me? That you're a witch?"

"Aren't you afraid of witchcraft?"

Allison shrugged. "Should I be?"

Maggie let out a huff of exasperation. Then, all of a sudden, her attention shifted to something or someone behind Allison. She moaned. Allison turned. Two girls and a woman were snaking their way through the thin crowd in the center aisle, heading right toward them. Maggie was doing her best to disappear behind Allison's back, but her skirt billowed on all sides behind Allison.

"Maggie McBride?" The older of the two girls smirked. "Never thought we'd see you here."

"Yeah," the smaller girl said. "We thought you did all your shopping at the Salvation Army."

Both girls laughed. Allison stood in front of Maggie, feeling protective of her client and debating what to say. She sized up the people in front of her. The woman looked vaguely familiar. She was tall, lean, and brunette. Not so much beautiful as sensuous in a lazy, sleepy sort of way. Heavy eyelids, full mouth. High, heavy breasts that strained against a black wool turtleneck sweater. She carried an assortment of over-stuffed shopping bags from The Limited, Neiman Marcus, Bloomingdales, and Gap. She shifted impatiently from side to side.

The two girls, presumably her daughters, looked nothing alike. One was about Maggie's age, but taller and much thinner. She had her mother's dark hair, but her face was elfin, more cute than pretty. The younger girl's strawberry blond hair had been pulled back in a ponytail. She flashed sultry green eyes and wore a tight sweater that outlined a body ripening too quickly for her age.

"Desiree Moore." The woman held out her hand to Allison. "And these are my daughters, Sarah and Megan. You're the image consultant and writer, Allison Campbell. *From the Outside In.* Loved the book. I went to one of your workshops on leading with the right side of your brain. Fabulous." She waved her hand casually toward the girls. "I'm sorry about my daughters. Silly teenagers. They're harmless." She shot the older one a warning look.

Allison became aware of Maggie's hand on her back, pushing her forward. Allison took a step to leave, a fast but polite exit on the tip of her tongue, when one of Desiree's daughters spoke up.

"Is she your girlfriend, Maggie?" A mean giggle.

"*Sarah.*" Desiree smiled apologetically, and Allison saw tiny, perfectly white teeth, all lined up in a carnivorous row.

Allison felt another sudden—and surprising—need to protect Maggie.

"We have to get going. I promised Maggie's mother I'd drop her off."

"Is she getting an image makeover?" The younger girl said. "That's what you do, right?"

"She certainly needs one."

"Sarah!" Desiree pulled the girl close to her, although whether it was an act of protection or reprimand, Allison wasn't sure. Maggie looked horror-stricken. All Allison knew was that she needed to leave before she said something she'd regret.

Allison fixed the older girl with her most condescending smile and said, "Actually, Sarah, Maggie's a friend of the family. I'm just picking her up at the mall. She was hanging out with friends."

Allison could see a little of the tension drain from Maggie's face. It was worth the lie. Maggie cocked her head up a notch and stared back at the sisters. *That a girl! Don't let them push you around!*

Sarah shrugged. "Whatever." She and her sister shared a knowing smirk.

Still annoyed, Allison pulled a card from her purse. She held it out to Desiree and said, "I give lessons on manners and etiquette, too. Just in case you're interested."

Without waiting for a response from Desiree, she grabbed Maggie's arm and led her to the exit. When they were safely out of earshot, she said, "What was that all about?"

"Nothing."

"Do you know them from school?"

Maggie squirmed. Her eyes shifted to the right. She nodded.

They were passing through the makeup department, on their way back out to the parking lot. Allison had decided to call it a day. She wouldn't charge the McBrides for anything other than the first hour. The mall trip had been a waste of time, and after the run-in with Desiree and her girls, Allison didn't think she could salvage it.

A skinny woman with a bad dye job and fire engine red lipstick sprayed perfume on a card and held it out to them. Allison declined, but Maggie reached for it. Allison saw the woman take in Maggie's clothes with a long swallow of a glance.

Maggie put her nose to the scented card.

"Marc Jacobs," Allison said. "Nice, huh?"

Maggie scrunched up her features. "It's alright."

"You don't have to like it, you know." They had arrived at the double doors that led outside and Allison paused before opening them. "Everyone is different. What smells good to you might not smell nice to me. Perfume works with your body's chemistry, so to really get it right you have to try the scent on."

Allison watched a flicker of interest light up Maggie's eyes. Her white face powder had begun to wear off, and the sallowness of the skin underneath came through. She had shadows around her eyes too pronounced for a fifteen-year-old. There was something moving about the way Maggie stood there, looking at that perfume card and fighting the urge to know more.

"Want to try out some scents?"

For a moment, Maggie looked as though she was going to say yes. But then she caught herself, tossed the card to the floor, and scowled.

"Your world, not mine," she said.

Allison reached for the door, disappointed. "Then let's head back to your world, Maggie," she said. "After we grab a bite to eat."

* * *

Mia counted. Ninety-six egg cups, six different types of seeds, six-teen plants of each. She looked at the mess spread out on the make-shift porch table and warmed her hands under her wool sweater. It was still chilly for March, especially out here when the wind was blowing, like now. She picked up a spoon and opened the bag of potting soil. Three spoonfuls for each seed, a few drops of water, and then into the greenhouse and under the grow lamps. By some miracle, in a few months she'd have food to last through the sum-mer: tomatoes and eggplant, green beans and spinach, lettuce and squash. She'd done something wrong last year, and only a third of her seeds had grown into seedlings, and then only half of them pro-duced a vegetable, which is why she'd spent the year trudging back and forth to the Whole Foods twenty miles away. Not this year. She'd get it right.

Buddy nosed his way under her armpit and gave her love nips with his front teeth. "Not now, boy," she said and pushed him gen-tly away. She glanced at her watch. Jason was supposed to stop by and fill her in on the Feldman murder. She'd baked him a loaf of honey wheat bread and some chocolate chip cookies. Next she'd make coffee, start the fire in the living room, and hope he'd stay awhile. Anything to keep her mind occupied. And Jason, she was sure, could use the company as much as she could. Maybe he'd even stay for dinner.

The phone rang. She wiped her hands on her jeans and pulled out her mobile.

"Mom, I got held up with work. I'll have to make it another day." Mia heard the regret in Jason's voice and swallowed her own disappointment. She thought of the bread cooling by the stove, of the tin of cookies on the counter. She'd freeze them.

"That's fine."

"You sound upset. Are you okay? Dad didn't call to harass you again, did he?"

"I'm okay, Jason. Just in the middle of spring planting, that's all. What's the news on the Feldman case?"

"Some sort of satanic ritual. At least that's what it looks like." She heard him breathe deeply. "If the police haven't contacted you already, they will."

"Someone came by today. Lieutenant Helms. Like I told him, Jason, I didn't do anything."

"Of course you didn't. How did the conversation go?"

"Fine." She sighed. "I told him what I know, which is that Feldman was a bastard, but I didn't wish him dead. At least not recently." She laughed, and it sounded a little crazy, even to her. "Look, I haven't seen Arnie Feldman in almost three years. I cooperated with Helms. There's nothing more to say."

"You should have called me. I would have come by for the discussion."

"He surprised me."

Jason paused. "Did he seem satisfied with your answers?"

Mia thought about the conversation. Helms had been hard to read. He'd wanted an alibi for the night of Feldman's murder. That was the one thing Mia couldn't give him. She said truthfully, "I don't know."

After a few seconds, Jason said, "Let's see how things go. I'm worried because of the pressure Helms is under. The fact that he's doing legwork himself underscores his anxiety over this murder. We might find you a lawyer, just in case. You did threaten to kill Feldman *during* court proceedings. Not the smartest thing to do on record."

"I get it. It was dumb. That's the past." And that's where she wanted it—in the past. The police visit was forcing her to live through it all over again. Just thinking about Helms caused her heart to pound away in her ribcage. She gripped a container of seeds too hard. The bag split and the tiny gray dots scattered under the potting table as though happy to get away from her.

Jason said, "Mom, still there?"

Wearily, she said, "Sorry, just thinking. What were you saying?"

"Kids. They're also looking at the possibility that kids were involved."

"How could kids do something so horrible?"

"They're looking at every possibility. There's a lot of money in this town. People want answers."

"But a kid, Jason?"

Jason sighed. "Kids. Plural. They're even questioning Feldman's own son, Ethan."

ELEVEN

The McBride house was dark when Allison and Maggie arrived at 7:05. Allison pulled into the circular driveway and idled in front of the double-doored entryway. Where were Maggie's parents? She and Maggie had finished a silent dinner nearly an hour ago—Mexican, Maggie's choice—but Maggie was insistent that they not return to her house until the designated time. "They'll think I didn't cooperate," she said. "And I'm *not* cooperating, just for the record. But they don't need to know that."

Too tired to argue, Allison took Maggie back to First Impressions where the girl had been drawn to the very catalogues that had prompted the mall trip in the first place.

"I'm just bored," Maggie said while flipping through DKNY. Her flat black hair, end-of-the-day limp, fell across her eyes. "So don't get any ideas. This is all so very *lame.*"

And Allison had to agree. It was by far the lamest session she'd had since she'd bought the business from Mia. Three torturous hours of lame. Maggie had used every spare second to remind Allison of how uncool/corporate/phony she was, and even the image-consultant armor Allison usually donned to ward off client projection was starting to wear thin. Time for Maggie to go home.

But her house was dark. So now what?

Maggie opened the passenger door.

"Uh-uh," Allison said. "I'm not leaving you here alone."

"*Ohmyfreakingoddess.*" Maggie shook her head. "You *cannot* be serious." She swung her feet out of the car.

"I am serious." Allison turned off the ignition. "Unless your housekeeper is here, you stay with me. Or I come inside with you."

"Udele is always here. She's a fixture. An old, cranky fart from Daddy's prep-school childhood." When Allison didn't budge, she shrugged. "Fine, suit yourself."

Maggie turned the knob on the door on the right side. Locked. She pounded on the door and screamed, "Udele! Open up!" When there was no response, she finally pulled a key from her skirt pocket and unlocked the door. Allison followed her inside.

"Weird. Udele's always here." Maggie walked through the center hall toward the back of the house, flicking on lights as she went. "Maybe someone died."

Bite your tongue, came to mind. Instead, Allison said, "Let's call your parents' cell."

"I'm home by myself all the time. Just go."

"You just said Udele's always here, so you're *not* home by yourself all the time."

"Same thing. She never talks to me."

"Do you try talking to her?"

Maggie uttered a "Yeah, right" under her breath. "She hates me and the feeling is mutual."

Maggie led Allison through a large dining room to a professionally equipped kitchen. Stainless steel appliances, two islands, double ovens, a forty-eight-inch Viking stovetop. Very chic, and with all the generic charm of a showroom. Allison wondered who did the cooking. Maggie must have seen her eyeing the space, because she said, "No one uses it. Except Udele. And mostly she just reheats stuff she gets from restaurants."

Maggie handed Allison the phone and repeated her mother's cell phone number. No answer. Allison tried Hank's number and Catherine's as well and was plopped into voice-mail each time. She glanced at her watch: 7:12.

"Where can I wait?"

"Wherever."

Maggie opened the Subzero doors and pulled out a plate of cheese. She took it over to the counter, grabbed a knife from a butcher block, and sliced a large wedge of cheddar for herself. She looked up while chewing and said, "What? Want some?"

Allison shook her head no. She was wondering how Maggie could possibly still be hungry after wolfing down three cheese enchiladas, a basket of chips with salsa, and an entire dish of fried ice cream, but she knew better than to say anything. Their working relationship had moved from loathing to some sort of ice-cold truce, but the wrong words would have it sliding backward again.

Allison took a seat at the table in the adjoining sun room. Maggie opened her mouth, as though to speak, then seemed to think better of it. She sliced another piece of cheddar, pulled the plastic wrap back over the cheese, and left the plate and the dirty knife on the counter.

"You know," she said while punching the ice dispenser, "you really don't have to stay. I'm not a baby. My parents won't appreciate it. They'll just be annoyed."

It seemed to Allison there was a tiny pinpoint of kindness in Maggie's tone, a slight loosening of the defensiveness she wrapped around her like a winter cloak. In the vastness of this house, Maggie looked like a little girl playing dress-up. Even her attempts to look tough—the black clothes, garish makeup and Gothic accessories—only accented her youth. It occurred to Allison that Maggie was an outcast here in her own home, the child perpetually left out of playground games. But the old chicken-and-egg adage held true: was Maggie reacting to a dynamic present since toddler-hood or had she created her status with her behavior?

She decided to take a gamble. "Your parents seem like tough people to please."

Maggie took a sip of water from the full glass and then dumped the rest in the sink. "Not my mother. Just Daddy. And Catherine."

"So you get along with your mother?"

"I didn't say that."

"There must be someone in the house you're close to."

She shook her head. "They're all wacked. Daddy's a jerk, Catherine's mean." Maggie's cocky stare challenged Allison to respond. "And my mother does what she's told."

Ah. The scorn Maggie had for conformists when they first met. She had been reacting to her mother's willingness to obey her father.

Allison said, "My father wasn't a nice man."

"Join the club. What he'd do?"

"He could be abusive."

Allison could tell Maggie was trying to look nonchalant, but the sudden interest in her voice gave her away. "Happens all the time. My boyfriend, his father used to hit him when he was smaller. He hates his father because of it."

"Parents shouldn't hit kids, I don't think." Allison shifted in her chair so she was facing Maggie. "So you *do* have a boyfriend?"

Maggie nodded. She smiled in a girlish way that warmed Allison to the possibility that there was something soft and gentle in this difficult child. But the warmth died quickly when Maggie said, "Ethan Feldman. We've been dating for a year."

As Allison drove home from the McBride residence, Maggie's words echoed in her mind. She knew the fact of Maggie's relationship with Ethan Feldman meant nothing. But it made things messy and Allison's natural response, especially when it came to kids, was to avoid mess.

But she'd made headway with Maggie tonight. She'd gotten a glimmer of someone vulnerable, someone light-hearted and kind. Okay, a faint glimmer. Like the voltage from a lightening bug. But she'd take it. Sometimes it was the peek underneath the mask that could lead to a breakthrough.

Allison twisted the pearl necklace around her neck. She couldn't help it. After spending the evening with the congressman's daughter, she began to understand why Maggie reminded her of Violet. The pervasive sense of loneliness. Despite Maggie's privileged upbringing, the oppositional behavior covered up isolation and insecurity. As it had with Violet.

Allison supposed her breakthrough session with Violet had come four weeks after Doc finally transferred Violet to her caseload.

By that time, Violet had already been at the Meadows three months. Rather than improve her disposition, life at the Meadows seemed to drive Violet deeper into her shell. Her skin was pasty white. Fresh scars, as thin and superficial as nail scratches, criss-crossed her hands and the fleshy spots on her arms. Dark circles shadowed her eyes. She avoided looking or speaking to anyone. During sessions, Violet sat across the desk in Allison's claustrophobic cubicle that masqueraded as an office. She'd crossed her arms over her chest and refused to speak. Allison would ask a question and Violet would stare blankly at the wall or look down at her slippered feet or, if the question was pointed enough, glare briefly at Allison. Day after day.

But as these sessions wore on, Allison started to notice something about Violet: although she never spoke, she didn't space out like the other girls, whose eyes would roll and faces slacken so Allison knew their silence meant they were with their boyfriends or dreaming about escape or Grandma's pumpkin pie or a big, fat joint. With Violet, Allison had her attention. So Allison began to wonder if Violet's silence wasn't a form of control, the only control Violet had.

Violet was a hopeless insomniac. In the beginning she'd wander around the dorm late at night, restless and agitated, until Doc prescribed a sleep aid. Violet was way too smart to keep up her nocturnal wandering for it would have been a dead giveaway that she was palming those pills. Still, Allison suspected that Violet was twisting in her covers, unable to sleep, still plagued by her nighttime terrors.

So late one night, Allison snuck in her dorm with a package. Sure enough, when Violet sensed her enter, she rolled over and closed her eyes. If Allison hadn't been watching her so closely, she might not have noticed the ruse. But she was, so she did.

After making sure the other girls were asleep, Allison tip-toed to Violet's bed and laid the package next to her elbow. "Don't rat me out or I'll deny it," she whispered, and left. She didn't stay to see whether Violet opened the bag and, if she did, whether she used it. But somehow she knew she would.

Allison's shift was over at midnight. When she came in at four the next day, she met with Violet in the little cubicle. Again, Violet didn't speak for the full forty minutes, but it seemed her glare was a little less unfriendly. And when Violet stood to go, Allison swore she heard her say "thank you" as she walked out the door.

Later that same night, Allison peeked at Violet when she made her evening rounds. Rather than roll over and close her eyes, Violet looked up at her through the dim reddish light of the emergency bulbs the Meadows kept on 24/7. Then, in one fluid motion, she held up the tiny flashlight Allison had given her and shined it on Allison's old, tattered copy of Ayn Rand's *We the Living*, a particularly apt book for a young woman in search of control. Violet must have agreed because though she was just beginning her second night with the book, she was already to the end. When Allison looked back at Violet's face, she saw a smile cross those lips.

A real honest-to-goodness smile.

After that, Violet kept Allison poor with her demand for books. Her appetite for reading was, unlike her appetite for food, voracious. She went through four or five books a week, sometimes more. *The Awakening*; *Girl, Interrupted*; even *Les Miserables* and *Gone with the Wind*. She was like a paraplegic who suddenly discovered she could walk and who decided then and there never to sit again. She carried books to the dining table, on outings, to the bathroom. Together she and Allison even tackled Shakespeare; *Romeo and Juliet* was her favorite. Violet was, underneath it all, a romantic. Of course, the Meadows staff was quite careful about the reading material provided to patients, so, by tacit agreement, Violet kept the more controversial books for night-time consumption.

Sessions progressed. It seemed in order for her mouth to work without being censored by that big brain of hers, Violet's hands had to be kept busy. Allison noticed she'd fidget with her paper clips, making little people and animals out of the wire, or she'd pick up her pens and doodle on her hands or scrap paper Allison had given her. Allison nabbed drawing paper and charcoal pencils from the art instructor and put them on the desk one day when Violet showed up for her appointment. Violet's hands inched toward the paper. Allison nodded. Tentatively at first, then with more vigor, Violet began to sketch: flowers and houses, birds and crosses.

Over the course of weeks she progressed to people. Allison's favorite was a drawing Violet had done of her. In it, Allison's head was cocked to the side. Her hair, long and straight at the time, was tucked behind her ears. Her neck looked exceptionally slender, her eyes particularly kind, and her smile almost beatific. Allison thought it looked nothing like her, or perhaps it was her angelic twin. In any case, Allison kept that portrait. It was now tucked under her bed in a box along with three months of letters from another Violet, one burdened less by the expectations of an idealistic counselor and more by the realities of the urban underground.

After leaving the Meadows, Allison couldn't bear to look at that portrait any more than she could bear to read Violet's letters. She'd tell herself it was because the portrait reminded her of the Violet that could have been. Sometimes Allison wondered if it wasn't more personal than that. Perhaps the picture reminded her of the *Allison* she might have become.

TWELVE

When Allison finally pulled into her driveway, it was after nine-thirty. Jason's truck was parked off to the far side of the garage, in the shadows. What's he doing here, she wondered? She made her way to the door, an unwelcome mixture of apprehension and happiness creeping along the edges of her mind.

She turned the knob to her front door. "Jason?"

He didn't respond. Allison could hear the faint murmur of a television coming from upstairs. She followed the sound up the steps, through the hallway, and to the second guestroom. The door was closed. Allison thought of Jason's underwear model, Amber-something-or-other. The image of him with some waif-like model was almost too much to bear. She pushed open the door, curious about what brought him here.

After a second, her eyes adjusted to the dim light, the only source of which was the glow of a twenty-inch television. Jason *was* on the bed, dressed in a pair of dirty cargo shorts and no shirt. His feet were bare.

"Hey, sleepy head," she said. She sat on the bed next to him and shook his shoulder gently.

Jason blinked, sat up, and looked around. When his eyes focused on Allison, he smiled. She jumped up and turned off the television.

"What are you doing?"

He yawned. "You mean besides sleeping?"

"In dirty pants on my handmade quilt. Yes."

"Worked late, and then I swung by my mother's house. I gave her a hand with some greenhouse planting. I had originally canceled on her, but she sounded so...sad." He smiled warmly. "You think the pants are dirty, you should have seen the shirt. At least I took that off first."

"So what brings you here?"

"Just checking on you." He reached down and picked his t-shirt up off the floor. Dirt was splashed across the "Penn" logo.

She held out her hand. "Give it to me. I'll wash it."

"I know how to work the washing machine."

"I know you do. But I'm offering to do it for you. If you can wait for it, that is."

He looked at her, and Allison wasn't immune to the longing in his eyes. "I can wait."

Allison's pulse quickened. Her eyes locked onto Jason's and she could feel herself softening. The moment stretched. Finally, the tension in the room suddenly too much, Allison said, "Come on."

Jason held her stare for a second before standing. "Allison-" His voice was thick with emotion.

She shook her head. "We both know where it will lead. We've been down that path, remember?"

"It wasn't so bad."

Allison smiled, but the sadness in her eyes belied the gesture. "Let's go downstairs and get your stuff cleaned up." Before he could say anything else, she led the way to the laundry room. He followed.

They didn't speak while Allison threw his shirt in the washing machine. He stood with his back to the wall, watching her. She liked having him here and she was touched he had stopped by.

When she was finished with the laundry and trusted herself to speak, she said, "I had an interesting evening." She filled him in on her conversation with Helms, the deal with the McBrides, and her outing with Maggie. "Can you believe the McBrides didn't show up until after nine? I think even Maggie was worried. They turned their cell phones off, out of respect for the groom's family, they said. An engagement party. I felt bad for Maggie. I think it's not unusual for them to leave her out of things." She shook her head.

"Not that I can totally blame them. The kid's not easy to deal with."

They were in the kitchen. Jason rummaged around in the freezer and found the remnants of Faye's pierogis. He took out the container and popped it into the microwave. "Did they at least apologize?"

"Sunny did, sort of. Well, she said, 'Udele should have been here. It was not your responsibility to stay.' If you can call that an apology."

"Who's Udele?"

"The housekeeper." The microwave beeper went off. Jason removed the container and set it down on the stone countertop. He fished a fork from the drawer and stabbed a pierogi. Allison watched him. How many times had they sat here like this, each of them filling the other in on their workday while they munched leftovers or Chinese or pizza? She knew midway through a pierogi, Jason would remember the butter.

Sure enough, after one bite, he put down the fork, pierogi still attached, and said, "Butter?"

She shook her head. "Olive oil."

He made a face. "Not the same." He picked the fork back up and continued eating. The container was empty ten seconds later.

"So where was Udele?"

Allison shrugged. "They still didn't know when I left. I'd be worried, if I were them."

"The Feldman murder?"

Allison nodded. "It's all I'm hearing about." She paused. "Speaking of the Feldman murder, I also found out that Maggie dates Ethan Feldman, son of the late Arnie Feldman. How's that for a strange coincidence? And stranger yet, Maggie didn't seem to know Arnie was dead."

Jason's eyes widened. "I didn't tell you," he said.

"Tell me what?"

"I told my mother. I thought I told you, too."

"*Tell me what?*"

"Because there was no breaking and entering, and because of certain pieces of evidence found at the scene, the authorities think it was someone Arnie knew well. Maybe even someone in the family. Ethan has no alibi for that night. They're questioning him, Allison. But if he's involved, they don't think he acted alone."

Allison woke up in a sweat. She turned over and patted the empty space next to her. *Damn.* Her head throbbed, her tongue felt like sandpaper. Friday night came back in a rush: casual conversation had led to a bottle and a half of Pinot Noir and a home viewing of *Shawshank Redemption.* Too drunk to drive home, Jason camped out in the guest room. Only at two in the morning, when she couldn't sleep, she'd wandered in and asked him to join her in her room. So much for resolve.

Sleep. That was all she wanted. Strong arms holding her, the feel of muscles against her back, someone to ward off the loneliness of the night and the recurring thoughts that came with it. Had it led to more? She peeked under the blankets. Her pajamas were still on. After two years, it would have been weird or wonderful or awful but certainly memorable. She'd have remembered.

Relieved, she swung her legs to the floor and stretched. Last night had been stupid, plain and simple. She and Jason were dangerous together. Obviously he thought so too or he wouldn't have taken off so early, scrambling out of her house like a sorority sister doing the walk of shame. They made great friends, true, but as lovers and especially as partners, it was Chernobyl on a bad day.

Allison peeled off her top and her pajama bottoms. A hot shower would feel good. Then she'd treat herself to coffee and a croissant at Starbucks and check in at First Impressions to catch up on paperwork and set up the book signings her publicist had been nagging her about.

She stood naked at the window and lifted the shade just enough to see bright sunlight, a clear sky. What a perfect spring day.

The home phone rang. She considered running for the handheld but decided against it. Whoever it was could wait until after her shower. The ringing stopped. She was three steps from the bathroom when her bedroom door swung open and Jason walked in. He smiled when he saw her there, arms wrapped reflexively around her chest, naked as the day she was born.

"*Jason.*"

He stood there, her phone in his outstretched hand. He turned his head, but not before Allison caught that look of longing again. He said, "It's Vaughn. He says it's important."

Allison backed up and grabbed a bathrobe from the closet. "Can you just find out what he wants?" When the robe was safely cinched around her waist, she focused on the brief conversation occurring between her ex-husband and her colleague.

Jason clicked off the phone and handed it to her. "Hank McBride is looking for you. He wants to see if you can spend some time with Maggie today. Vaughn said it sounds like yesterday went well and he wants to *build on that foundation.*" Jason used two fingers to put air quotes around the last four words.

She nodded, still too rattled to speak. With the bedroom door open, she could smell the dueling aromas of coffee and bacon coming from downstairs. This was all too much.

Jason said, "I made you breakfast. Thought you might like something hardy after last night."

She found her voice. "Did we..."

Jason smiled tenderly. "You drank too much wine and came on to me. I saved you from yourself."

"Very funny."

He leaned in to kiss her cheek. She pushed him away playfully. "Funny, Al. But true."

When Allison arrived at First Impressions, the door was already unlocked and Vaughn was sitting in his office. He looked worn. Allison tapped twice on the doorframe and then took the seat opposite him, propping her elbows on the desk.

"Busy morning?" she asked.

"You could say that."

"It's Saturday, my friend. You shouldn't even be here."

Instead of answering, his eyes seemed to size her up. Suddenly, she was conscious of her unwashed hair, thrown up in a pathetic excuse for a ponytail, and her lack of make-up, without which she still looked like she was twenty and not in a good way. She'd needed to get out of her house, away from Jason. She would shower later, at the gym, once she'd had a chance to work out her feelings with honest sweat and physical discomfort.

"I'm sorry you had to deal with Hank this morning."

"My job." He picked up a pen, scribbled something on a piece of paper, and handed it to her. She looked at him questioningly.

"McBride's office number. He wants you to collect Maggie from his house at two o'clock. He wouldn't get off the phone until I promised you'd be there."

Allison made a face. "So soon?" She filled Vaughn in on the happenings of the night before, including Maggie's revelation that Ethan Feldman was her boyfriend.

"I spoke to my buddy at the police department. Ethan was brought in for questioning yesterday, Allison. That's not good."

"No, I don't imagine it is." Allison was thoughtful for a moment. "I can't figure the McBrides out. Hank's a bully. Sunny seems to kowtow to him, yet there is something distant about her. But I believe she cares about Maggie, she just doesn't know how to reach her. And Catherine is clearly her father's daughter. That leaves Maggie to play the family scapegoat."

"You sound like you like the kid."

"Like?" Allison smiled. "She has such a tough shell, but I think there just may be a decent kid underneath it all." She shrugged. "Anyway, I don't need to like all of my clients. I just need to understand them."

"Ah, yes."

Allison sat back. "You're awfully icy this morning."

Vaughn took a deep breath and let it out. His eyes looked tired and red, as though he hadn't slept—not unlike her own before she'd put drops in them in the car. What drove him? She'd never met anyone so willing to work, so utterly committed to his job and his paycheck. Not even the executives she coached displayed Vaughn's single-mindedness. It wasn't ambition exactly, or a need to prove himself. To Allison, it seemed more like a desire to lose himself in work.

Allison wondered about this man with whom she trusted her business, both professional and personal. And she did trust him. That was one of the few things she knew about Christopher Vaughn. She trusted him with her life.

Allison raised her eyebrows. Vaughn smiled. This time when he spoke, his voice was softer, without the accusing edge. "Sorry. Rough night."

"Girlfriend troubles?"

"Not exactly." He picked up a pen and twirled it around his fingers. He seemed suddenly sad and wise, like a man burdened with knowledge beyond his years. Allison regretted the flippant question. Clearly something was troubling him, but she knew he wouldn't share it. Vaughn generally kept mum when it came to his own personal life and it looked like today would be no exception.

"Aren't you wondering why Hank McBride contacted you, Allison?" he said after a moment. "At the same time that there's a murder of a prominent person in the community? And now we learn that his daughter is dating the victim's son. Coincidence?"

Allison felt her face heat up. "You think Hank had something to do with Arnie's murder?"

"I didn't say that."

"The man is a bastard, I'll give you that. But why would he risk his career to kill Feldman?"

Vaughn held up a hand. "I'm simply wondering why McBride is so insistent that you work with his daughter, that's all. I don't trust the man. You are brilliant at what you do, Allison, but it sounds like that girl needs a lot more help than you can give her."

Vaughn was right. She probably couldn't help Maggie any more than she had helped Violet. And Hank's timing *was* odd. But Allison thought she understood.

She remembered the first time she met Sunny and Hank, the way Sunny looked at her, desperate for some kind of help, some form of hope. She remembered her own father, his desperation to end his pain all those years ago, desperation that led him to drive over that embankment, a stupid, insane act.

Allison didn't know if Hank's dogmatic pursuit of her was out of love for Sunny or just a desire to appease his wife, but whatever his motivation, Sunny was the reason, not Maggie. But how could she explain that to Vaughn without explaining her own family life? She couldn't.

"Look, we have a business here," she said. "Hank McBride is willing to pay us a ridiculous sum of money to work with his daughter. She's difficult, it's true, but I don't see how this can hurt." A headache hovered behind her temples. She stood to leave. "Would you mind calling Hank for me? I'm going to go to the gym. Tell him I'll pick Maggie up at two. Lord knows what I'm going to do with her today. I need to find some way to connect."

Vaughn nodded, still looking glum. Allison placed a hand on his shoulder. "Go home," she said. "Get some rest. There is nothing here that can't wait." When he didn't respond, she leaned down and whispered in his ear, "No one dies over image consulting, Vaughn. Go home."

Allison bristled. The nerve. After making her wait for hours on Friday with no apology, no thanks, just that half-hearted excuse about their housekeeper, McBride was late today too? Allison said she'd pick up Maggie, but now that she'd worked out, showered, and had some time to clear her head, she was having second thoughts. Maybe Vaughn was right. Hank's disrespect for her time indicated a lack of cooperation. Image consulting couldn't work without some level of mutual ownership. Here, not only was the kid defiant, but so was the parent.

She rang the McBride's bell one more time. When no one answered, she walked back to the Volvo and climbed in. It was a sunny day, and with the windows down, the musky scent of spring was strong. She could be doing some yard work. She could be working on her next book. She could be doing a lot of things that didn't involve the McBrides.

Allison had her hand on the cell phone. She was ready to dial Hank's number, to tell him no in a way he could understand, to explain politely, but firmly, that she called the shots. The sound of the phone ringing jolted her into awareness.

The caller I.D. said it was her sister, Faye. Still smarting from the last situation, she picked up.

"Mom fell." Faye said without introduction.

The tension Allison had shed at the gym returned.

"She's all right," Faye continued. "We met with a social worker after the fall. The social worker is concerned that next time it will be more serious. She's recommending we start looking at nursing homes. Just in case. And Dad, well." Another deep breath. Faye's voice sounded unusually calm and even and that fact alone troubled Allison. "While the social worker was here, Dad called 9-1-1. He told the operator he was being held hostage by a group of drag queens."

Allison laughed, despite herself.

"It's not funny."

"I'm sorry, but you have to admit, it is *kind of* funny."

"It's not funny when you're living it. I shouldn't have called. You're obviously not willing to help. You can't even take it seriously."

Allison rubbed her face. It *wasn't* funny, but it was all so absurd, so pathetically, unreasonably absurd. And unfair. What could she do *but* laugh? It beat crying.

"So then what happened?"

"The operator called back, thinking it was a prank, so no cops showed up, thank God. Daddy said later he thought the social worker was a man in drag, she was so ugly. Luckily, he waited until she left to make *that* proclamation. But he was such an itch during the entire interview, vying for my attention, spouting off about the liberal left and the good old days when a woman was a woman and a man was a man. He's more of a problem than Mom, I think."

"What do we need to do?"

"The social worker laid out our options. We can put Mom in an institution that accepts Medicaid."

"Or...?"

"A private nursing home. We'll have to sell the house either way, but then what do we do with—"

"—Daddy."

"Exactly."

Or you, Allison thought. What will you do, Faye?

Allison chose her next words carefully. She knew she had to make the offer with the right mixture of nonchalance and sincerity or Faye would be offended.

"When the time comes, you and Daddy can live with me. We'll sell the house to pay for private care for Mom."

Silence.

"Realistically," Faye said, "even selling the house won't pay for more than a month or two at a reputable place. The neighborhood is rundown, and Daddy has almost as much debt as the house is worth."

"Then you could all live with me. We'll hire a private nurse."

"Listen to yourself, Allison," Faye said. "You don't really mean it."

Allison was quiet for a second. She *did* mean it. It's what she should do, what was expected of her. Then why the trouble breathing at the mere thought of such an arrangement? So she wasn't thrilled at the prospect. She had, after all, spent the last twenty years trying to escape her childhood. She didn't have to like the arrangement to offer it willingly.

"I have extra bedrooms, Faye. We could sell Mom and Dad's house and invest the money. Then, when we can no longer care for Mom, we use the money to pay for a private nursing home. A state institution is out of the question."

"You couldn't handle Daddy, Allison. You've never been able to handle him. Do you think I didn't see that growing up? No. We'll find another way."

Allison twisted in her seat. She thought about Maggie. Maybe she wouldn't be saying no to the McBrides today after all. Together with her savings, the sum the McBrides were offering would help pay for private nursing care right there in her parents' home—for a while, anyway. Her mom *and* dad could stay put and Faye would have help. And, most importantly, no depressing institution.

"Let's find a private nurse, then."

"How in the world will we pay for that, Allison? Use your head."

Allison refused to bite. "You find the right person, Faye, and let me worry about the finances. Okay? If need be, I'll sell *my* house."

Faye didn't speak, but Allison could hear her breathing, more pronounced now, on the other end.

"Faye?"

"Okay," Faye said finally. "I'll let you know what I find."

Allison hung up and put her head back against the car seat. She would think of her mother when dealing with McBride. That would temper her pride.

THIRTEEN

"Daddy wants to be president, you know," Maggie said.

"Stay still for just a minute, Maggie. I need one more measurement." Allison wrapped the tape around Maggie's upper arm and made a notation in her notebook. "There, you can get down now."

Maggie stepped off the dressmaker's platform, turned a chair backward and straddled it. She wore a pleated black peasant skirt and the stiff material bunched around her thighs, exposing thick, black-stockinged legs. A jagged runner ran the length of one calf, ending at the edge of a polished Doc Marten.

"That's the real reason for this bullshit," Maggie said. "He doesn't care about the Senate race. The selfish jerk doesn't want any skeletons in the closet in six years when he tries to become the big cheese."

"He's still your father, Maggie, so maybe you could *try* talking about him without the derogatory terms." Allison stretched backwards, taking care not to snag her own stockings. "He may have trouble showing it, but I suspect there's at least a little concern in there for you somewhere." Allison winked. "He did hire me, after all."

Maggie snorted. "Please. He thinks your corporate brainwashing will fix his only skeleton. Me." Maggie shook her head. Allison had to wonder. While she certainly didn't believe everything that came out of Maggie's mouth, she'd heard rumors that McBride viewed the Senate as merely a stop along his political train ride.

The air in the office of First Impressions felt stuffy, and the scent of patchouli drifting in waves off Maggie's body made Allison faintly nauseous. She opened two windows. Fresh air. From outside, she heard the sounds of traffic and a wailing police siren, reminding Allison there was a world out there, a world that included the Main Line Murderer. One glance at the morning's papers had told Allison that the rest of the Main Line was as worried about catching the killer as she was.

She toyed with asking Maggie what she knew but thought better of it. She doubted Ethan was involved and, anyway, she didn't want today's session to get off to a bad start.

"He's not my real father, you know."

Startled, Allison turned from the window. "Who?"

"Hank. I mean, I'm pretty sure he's not my real father. We're nothing alike. He has blond hair and blue eyes and is left-handed. My mother must have gotten so tired of him and his crap that she went out to a bar one night and slept with a musician or an actor. Or maybe a famous scientist. That would explain my interest in the occult."

Allison had no idea how a scientist-father would explain Maggie's interest in the occult, but she decided to stay quiet on the lack of obvious connection. Instead she said, "Maybe you just wish he wasn't your father, Maggie. That's not such an odd thing for a teenage girl to want."

Maggie shot her a *you-don't-know-anything* look. "Trust me. He's not my father." She scooted backward off the chair, stood up, and picked up her sack of a purse. "Now what? More catalogues? Another fun trip to the mall? What's the next chapter in Maggie Makeover 101?"

Allison ignored the sarcasm and thought for a moment. With a normal client there would be at least two or three sessions of interviews, during which Allison would get a sense of the client's taste and an idea of what he or she wanted to focus on. These interviews would dictate both the sessions that followed and the experts Allison would partner with. Makeup artists. Nutritionists. Personal shoppers. Voice coaches. Allison and her team could help with any number of goals: public speaking, dressing for success, overcoming shyness, returning to the workforce, weight loss. But what she could *not* do was work magic. She was hoping something would click soon. In the meantime, she'd march onward and hope for the best.

"You pick it," Allison said.

Maggie just stared at her, head cocked, as though Allison had suggested a flight to Mars.

"You're joking."

"I never joke with my clients," Allison said.

"*Ohmyfreakinggoddess.* Don't you get it, Allison? I don't want to go anywhere with you. That's the point. I don't want to be seen with you."

Allison smiled. "Fine, then I'll pick."

Maggie plopped back down on the chair and crossed her arms over her chest. "This should be good."

"Don't say I didn't give you the opportunity to choose."

"Where are we going, Allison?"

Allison stood, pointed toward the door and said, "The zoo."

"You took her *where?*" Vaughn put down the file he was updating and stared at Allison. He'd never known her to go off script. Ever. When it came to her clients, the woman towed the line like a rookie in his first World Series. "No offense Allison, but are you *nuts?* Her father's a House Representative. He's paying you to fix his disaster of a daughter and you take her to the *zoo?*"

Allison flashed him a smile that said *I have this under control,* but he wasn't so sure. He watched her smooth her hair back from her face and stretch her long legs out in front of her. She did seem pretty confident. He wished he shared the feeling.

Vaughn glanced at the clock. 7:16. Mrs. T. had to be out of there at 8:00 and he had no one lined up for the night, so he and Jamie were on their own. He'd rented *American Pie*—Jamie never seemed to tire of its teenage humor—and Vaughn would watch clothes dry if it made his brother smile. But he promised himself he'd get through these files, finish up the billing and check up on the Feldman case today. He had to hurry.

"Fine," he said. "Then don't tell me what you were thinking. I'm not sure I want to know anyway. Going to the zoo with that kid?" He shook his head, picked the file back up and stood to return it to the cabinet. Vaughn wished the whole damn family would just go away. He couldn't shake the feeling that Allison was playing with fire. And taking McBride's kid to the zoo was, in his opinion, a risky move. "McBride is paying for serious image consulting. He's going to see a zoo trip as high-priced babysitting."

Allison shrugged. "Not sure it helped, but how could it have hurt? I was looking for a way to get through to her. Thought maybe a change of scenery would do some good." Allison stood up and reached for her coat, which lay draped across the extra chair in Vaughn's office. "Maggie was not happy, but once we arrived it wasn't too bad."

"But why the zoo?

"The professional spin or the truth?"

Vaughn closed the file cabinet and turned to face Allison. She looked tired. He wondered about that morning, when Jason had answered the phone. Since their divorce, Jason had never answered Allison's phone. Did this mean they were together again? He didn't want to think about Allison sleeping with Mia's son, but he had to admit, he'd rather see her back with Jason than making the rounds with some other guy who didn't appreciate her. Jason was good people. Still, it was all a little *too* cozy.

He said, "Both. Start with the spin."

Allison held her coat in her hands and sat back down. "I wanted to make the point that one of the things that separates us from the animals is choice. A lion is a lion, a monkey is a monkey. Animals don't have the wherewithal to change colors. A monkey can't reinvent itself as a lion. A giraffe can never be an elephant."

"And? Did she get it?" He glanced at the clock again: 7:22. He put the last of the files away and sat facing Allison across his desk.

"Eventually. At first she took the analogy literally and thought I was saying she was an ugly duckling who could never become a swan. But I think I convinced her that I didn't mean that at all. Humans have a wondrous ability, unlike those animals, to choose our thoughts and, eventually, change our behavior. All I was saying was that Maggie has the choice, like the rest of us, to set her sights on what she wants to be and make it happen." Allison shrugged. "So that's the spin. A bit of hands-on learning."

"And the truth?"

"I had absolutely no idea what to do with her."

Vaughn laughed, relieved that Allison had a reason for the zoo trip, bullshit or not. "How'd she handle it?"

"Like any other kid, I suppose. She grumbled and complained. Threatened about a thousand times to tell Daddy. And finally shut up when I bought her a stuffed gorilla and French fries."

"Ah, bribery."

She nodded. "She mentioned Ethan Feldman again." Allison frowned, stood up, and reached for her purse.

"What did Maggie say?"

"They're dating behind their parents' backs. The McBrides have forbidden her to see him, and Arnie Feldman had done the same. Arnie caught Maggie and Ethan having sex in the Jacuzzi one afternoon last fall."

Vaughn said, "Was Maggie upset? About Ethan's involvement with the police over this murder?"

"Very. In usual teenage fashion, she was overly dramatic about the whole thing: they're going to run away together, it's the world against them, she can't live without him." Allison looked thoughtful. "I know the police are questioning the Feldman boy about his father's murder. It's just odd though—"

"Yeah?"

"Jason said Ethan has no alibi for that night."

"So?"

"So Maggie let it slip that she and Ethan were together. Why wouldn't Ethan admit to that?"

The clock read 7:29. Vaughn needed to have left ten minutes ago to get home in time. "Maybe she snuck out later to be with Ethan."

"Maybe." Allison opened the door. Vaughn could feel tendrils of cool air reaching across the foyer to where he stood. He shivered, but whether it was from the cool air or Allison's next words, he wasn't sure. "Or maybe the kids are lying."

Vaughn said, "Have you heard anything more about Mia?"

"No, and that worries me. I'm going to call Jason when I get home. I'm not sure whether the shift in police focus to the kids has taken the heat off of her. Do you know?"

Vaughn shook his head, feeling like an ass. Although he didn't know where the police thinking was currently headed, he did know more than he was letting on. And he hated keeping things from Allison.

Allison looked worried. "I wish Mia's name was off the list."

"Me, too."

Allison made a what-can-you-do gesture with her hands. She said, "Dinner?"

Vaughn shook his head. As much as he would've liked to join her, he had to get going.

The corners of Allison's mouth turned down in disappointment. "A date?"

He looked away from her, toward the door. He hated lying again. But Jamie was his best kept secret. He couldn't explain Jamie without explaining his own past. And he wasn't ready to come clean yet, not even to Allison. Especially not to Allison. So Vaughn said, "You could say that."

On his way home, Vaughn called Mia. Her voice sounded hoarse, as though she'd been crying. "You okay, babe?" he said.

"Sure."

His heart ached for her. He knew the police, the questions, were dredging all of the pain again, it was like a goddamn soul excavation. He wished there was something he could do to make it better.

"Want some company? I have Jamie tonight, but you can join us. We'd love it."

"No, but thanks, Vaughn." A pause. "I got another visit from the police. One of Helms' henchmen."

"What's the latest?" he asked gently. He shifted into fourth gear and eased up on the clutch. The night was warmer, and he rolled the window down for some fresh air.

"Same questions, over and over again. And they won't let up on my whereabouts the night Arnie was killed."

"Then tell them, Mia. I'm tired of the lies, anyway. It's time."

"No."

"Allison won't care. And Jason—Jason's a big boy. He wants you to be happy."

Mia took a moment to respond. "It's not just them, Vaughn."

"Then what the hell is it? We were together the night Feldman was killed. There is no way you coulda been there and been with me. Why can't you tell the police that?"

"You, Vaughn."

"*Me?*"

"Your past. What if they don't believe we were at my house? If they start digging, they'll find out about your record. The arrests. Then Allison will find out. Do you really want to risk that?"

Vaughn turned into his apartment complex and killed the ignition. No, he thought, I don't want to risk it. It's the reason I haven't told Allison about Jamie. It's the reason I live in a goddamn house of cards. But it wasn't worth Mia's pain.

Vaughn sighed. "I don't want to hide anymore, Mia. I paid my dues. We both have. Maybe it's time to come clean."

But Mia had other thoughts. "I can't risk it, Vaughn. Not now. We all have too much at stake. I didn't kill Feldman. The real killer will come to light eventually."

Jason sounded frustrated when Allison spoke to him over the phone a little later. "They brought my mother in for questioning. She said Helms treated her with kid gloves, but I don't like it."

"What was their angle?"

"She says they just asked a few questions. She was vague."

Allison had just made herself dinner: celery and peanut butter, cranberry juice and two Fig Newtons. The supper of champions. She sank into a kitchen chair and put her phone on speaker.

"Can't you ask around at work? Find out what's going on with the investigation?"

"I've tried that," Jason said. "All I know is that my mother is still a person of interest."

"That sounds ominous."

"Helms and his staff have a few leads, but right now it's a process of elimination. And for whatever reason, they haven't been able to eliminate her. Or the Feldman kid, for that matter."

Allison smoothed the peanut butter on the top of a long celery stalk. "Then maybe we need to help the police a little."

"What are you suggesting?"

"I'm suggesting that we know people. I can call Sally Ann— Sasha Feldman. She was my client once upon a time. I'll get Vaughn on the case. Between the three of us, we know half this damn town."

Jason didn't answer. Allison heard his breath over the phone, pictured his kind eyes as he mulled it over. "Think the widow will talk to you?"

"Eventually," Allison said.

"It's worth a shot." But Allison heard apprehension in his voice. "Just be careful. Mia didn't do it, but someone did. And that someone is still out there."

Allison found Sasha's home number in the White Pages. She glanced at her watch and dialed, feeling slightly guilty for invading the woman's privacy. Her husband *had* just been killed. On the fourth ring, a husky male voice answered. The guy sounded too old to be Arnie's son, Ethan, and too rough to be local.

"Yeah?" said the voice.

"May I speak with Sasha? This is Allison Campbell."

He hesitated. "Nah, she's sleepin'."

"Could you ask her to call me?" Allison left her home and mobile numbers.

"Yeah, sure. I'll tell her," said the voice.

Allison hung up, feeling pretty certain that the message wasn't making its way to Sasha.

She logged into her computer and did another search on Arnie Feldman. Who were his contacts, what were his interests, how did he spend his free time? There were volumes about Feldman online, but from what she could tell, the man had few interests outside of work. On impulse, Allison checked the state's website for properties held in Feldman's name. Nothing other than the $1.2 million dollar home he lived in now. So what could be the motive?

Allison was getting sleepy. She did one more search in a referral site for lawyers. She skimmed through a staggering number of reviews. The Custody King was an attorney people sure felt strongly about, and they either loved him or hated him. Allison made note of a few of the comments, largely about child custody, and logged off. She couldn't shake the feeling that his death was somehow linked to his work. The man courted controversy. And eventually, controversy could lead to trouble.

FOURTEEN

A week later, Allison woke up with a horrible headache. It was Monday morning. She'd spent the past week tunneling her way around the Feldman murder, getting nowhere. Sasha Feldman hadn't returned a single call and even Vaughn's network of Main Line connections wasn't panning out. On top of that, she'd spent the rest of her week working with Maggie in the hopes that they would forge a connection. She wanted to show Maggie—and the McBrides—what a lovely girl was underneath the Goth snarl. But Maggie resisted—and it was time for Allison to get her own schedule back on track.

She rolled over in bed, carefully to avoid sudden movements, and tried to remember what appointments she had for the day: Judge Lint at noon, his wife at one-thirty, a Dressing for the Seasons presentation at three. Could she get away with another hour in bed? She cradled her aching head in her hands. Yes, she would have to. She was fumbling around the bedside table for her meds when the phone rang.

"Allison Campbell," she said without looking at the caller I.D.

"It's me, Allison," rang Vaughn's voice. "You sound like a sailor the morning after a bender."

"I feel terrible." She glanced at the clock. "I'll be late today. Wish I could cancel altogether. All I want is a double dose of Imitrex and a hot mug of tea. Anyway, what's going on?"

"I'll keep it short. McBride called. He says he needs to speak to you about the direction you're taking his daughter."

Allison twisted the sheet around one hand. "Oh, for Lord's sake."

"He sounded...curt."

"Did he say anything specific?"

Vaughn hesitated, which made her think Hank had said a lot more than whatever Vaughn was about to say. "Not really, just that you were not making the kind of progress he had hoped for. Tangible progress, that is."

Ah, yes. Maggie wasn't suddenly dressing like Catherine after two whole weeks. Allison could see why he was upset. The sessions of the past week had mostly gone like the first two, which meant Maggie had been as cooperative as a rodeo bronco. Nevertheless, to Hank, Maggie should be hosting her own talk show by now.

Allison said, "Well, he can kiss my you-know-what."

Vaughn laughed. The sound, usually welcome and comforting, raked through her skull like the tines of a fork down a ceramic plate.

"Anything else, Vaughn? 'Cause if not, I'm going to knock myself unconscious for a while."

Again, he hesitated before saying no. He was sitting on something. But right now, Allison was in too much pain to even care what—or why. She wanted to feel the fog receding, even if just a little bit. If she took the medicine before a full-blown migraine set in, she could get the pain to ebb, like an outgoing tide. If she waited too long, it grew into a tidal wave. It felt like tsunami time.

She said, "Just don't book anything else for today. I'm going to take a power nap. I'll see you by noon."

"McBride?"

"I'll deal with him when I get in."

Five minutes later, the phone rang again. Allison was set to ignore it until she saw it was Faye.

"Hello?" she said tentatively, the smallest noise amplifying the screaming in her head.

"Your birthday is coming up. I'd like to take you out."

Surprised, Allison said, "That would be nice."

"There's a restaurant in the city. Trattoria Bianca. I've been wanting to try it."

"Isn't Philadelphia a little far for you? We can meet closer to home."

Faye hesitated. "I'll be in the city. A routine test. Nothing to worry about. I can meet you there at six-thirty. Will that work?"

Allison thought her sister's invitation was odd. She never ventured into Philadelphia, much less alone. Why now? But Allison's head hurt too badly to question. And sleep was calling.

"Sounds nice, Faye. I'll see you then."

Allison dreamed of Violet.

Even in sleep, Allison told herself it wasn't real. The old woman in her dream, for the magic of slumber changed fifteen-year-old Violet into a toothless, graying senior, was pulling at her breast, needing to nurse. Violet's face morphed into her mother's face and then into Faye's, with the features of each sliding and melting into the features of the next. Repulsed, she struggled to wake.

Buzz, buzz, buzz.

Allison rolled over. The buzzing seemed to come from her head, from the same depths that produced the perverse women-babies. Allison clutched at her chest. Dry. Clothed. She murmured "Thank God" under her breath.

Buzz, buzz, buzz.

The doorbell. *Oh, man.* Allison swung her feet over the side of the bed and glanced at the clock: 9:45. Still in a dream-fog, she walked to the window and peeked outside. No car. *Buzz, buzz. Buzz, buzz. Buzz, buzz...*

"What the heck?" Allison grabbed her robe and threw it on as she ran down the steps. "Coming!"

She heard a dog bark, and then the sound of pounding joined the buzzing. She knew she should've been cautious, there was, after all, a killer loose on the Main Line, but she never heard of a killer announcing himself with such a racket. She threw the door open.

She was about to yell at whoever was pounding when all at once she took in the scene before her.

Maggie, a gash on her left arm and a bleeding wound on her hand, stood on the step with a monster of a dog next to her. Maggie was leaning over, grasping the dog's frayed collar in her good hand. She wore a school uniform—pleated green skirt, white polo shirt, knee socks—and her school backpack was flung over one shoulder. Tears stained her face.

"Help me."

Allison couldn't take her eyes off the dog. Her pulse racing, she pushed the door open wider and motioned for Maggie to come inside.

"Just you, Maggie. The dog stays outside."

"He's the reason I'm here. Please?"

The dog looked up at Allison, its lip curled in what looked like a sneer. It was truly the ugliest creature she had ever seen. It looked like a Boxer but had an oversized head and a severe under bite. Its teeth, yellowed and sharp, stuck out from its bottom jaw like an uneven picket fence. Drool dribbled from its mouth down to the front step. What looked like gum and tar matted the dog's fur. A large bald spot in the shape of Florida was splayed across the beast's back. Allison shook her head back and forth and backed away. Cujo looked ready to pounce and she doubted Maggie's ability to hold onto him.

"I don't do dogs, Maggie. I'll get you some rope and you can tie him—"

"Please? Pleeeeease?"

"No."

"Come on, Allison. Please?"

Just then the dog broke free of Maggie's grasp and ran into the house.

"Get him!" Allison slammed the door shut, leaving Maggie outside. Then she remembered Maggie and opened it again. "Come in here and get him! Hurry!"

Maggie called, "Here Brutus! Brutus, come!"

"Brutus?"

Maggie shrugged. "That's what the collar says!"

Allison could hear the dog in the kitchen. "Get him!" Allison ran for the powder room and locked herself in. Her hands shook. She had to get hold of herself and then call Animal Control. What the hell were Maggie and some dog doing here anyway? Her heart pounded itself right into her throat. She couldn't breathe.

Allison pressed her ear to the door. Silence. What was she going to tell Hank McBride if Brutus ate Maggie? *I'm sorry, but I hid in the bathroom while a wild dog mauled your daughter?* She had to get out of there. She willed her hand to the doorknob and turned just as she heard a tap on the door.

"You can come out now," Maggie said.

Allison opened the door a crack and peeked out. She saw Maggie but no sign of the dog.

"Is he outside?"

"Sure."

Allison tucked her robe around her waist and pulled the belt tight. She took a deep breath, forcing herself to be calm, and opened the door. Still no Brutus, a good sign. But then she saw a granola bar wrapper on the floor near the kitchen. She was bending to pick it up when she saw a yogurt container. A few feet from that was an empty meat wrapper—she recognized the brown paper that once covered the hamburger she'd pulled out for dinner. Her head started to pound again.

"The truth, Maggie. Where is he?"

Maggie's lips turned up in an apologetic smile. Then Allison heard it: the slurp-chewing of a wild boar. She followed the sound to the kitchen. The dog was eating out of her newest All-Clad pan— raw beef, cinnamon granola, All-Bran and yogurt.

"He was hungry, is all." Maggie went into the kitchen and pulled out a chair. "He must've been half-starved."

Allison grabbed the doorframe. She wanted the dog out of her house. "Hand me the phone."

"Why?"

"I'm calling Animal Control."

"You can't! They'll put him to sleep."

"He's obviously unhappy, Maggie. Look at his teeth. He can barely breathe. He needs to be taken care of. "

As though he understood her, Brutus put his head up and looked at her. A black paste of ground food stuck to his jutting lower teeth. Breathing and eating seemed to be competing needs and he choked and snorted his way through the food in his mouth as he stared at Allison. She looked away, half-convinced he was pleading with her, too.

Maggie stood in front of the phone, blocking it with her body. "No way, Allison. Just listen to me. Please?"

Maggie took the receiver off the wall and, phone in hand, crawled over to the dog. She put her arms around his neck and nuzzled his head against her own.

"Maggie, be careful! Not while he's eating!"

Maggie ignored her. Brutus licked her cheek and then returned to the bowl. Allison had to admit, despite his disgusting table manners, he didn't *seem* vicious.

"Now will you listen to me?"

"Fine, talk."

Allison pulled out two kitchen chairs, placing one between herself and the dog. She sat on the other while keeping a watchful eye on Brutus. "But keep that mutt over there." She sniffed. "He smells like the local dump."

"He's homeless. What would you expect?"

Allison glanced at Maggie's arm, alarmed. "Did he bite you?"

Maggie shook her head. "He was standing in the middle of traffic when my friend and I were driving to school. We stopped. I chased him through the woods and cut myself on a branch or something." Maggie's eyes started to water again. "He was shaking when I found him."

Allison steeled herself against Maggie's tears. She had a dog in her house. No dogs were allowed in her house, especially not huge, teeth-baring dogs in need of doggie deodorant and an orthodontist. No way. This was simply another of Maggie's attempts to manipulate.

"You should have brought him to *your* house."

Maggie snorted.

"Why bother? Daddy hates animals. He would never let me keep him. He would have had my mom take him to the pound or he would have shot the dog himself."

Allison cringed at her last statement. She could certainly picture Hank being less than accommodating. But then, she didn't want to deal with the dog, either.

She remembered Vaughn's phone call, the fact that Hank had contacted her earlier that day. She hadn't called him back. And now Maggie was here, not in school and injured by her run-in with Brutus.

She doubted this was the direction Hank McBride wanted to go in either. She saw her fee for this deal slipping away and along with it, her reputation and the money for her parents' care.

Maggie said, "He's so sweet."

Allison looked again at Brutus. "He's not that sweet."

"You don't know him yet."

"Yet? Oh no, Maggie. I draw the line here. No dogs."

"Wasn't it you who told me people have the ability to shape their future? If you want to get over your fear of dogs, you can. You have that power. Please? Look at that face! Please, please, please?"

"I *am* looking at that face. Even if I wasn't scared of him, I'd be worried about disease and fleas. There's something wrong with his fur."

The dog stopped licking the pot and sat next to Maggie, his flank against Maggie's side. Making what sounded like a contented grunt, he sprawled on the floor, his head in Maggie's lap. Maggie stroked his ears.

"Please? Just for a few days? It will give me time to find him another home."

"Doesn't he have a tag? Just call his owners."

Maggie fingered the metal circle that hung from the dog's collar. "I can only make out his name. The metal's worn away."

It did look as though he'd been panhandling for quite some time. Still, Allison said, "We should call the AASPCA to see if anyone's lost him."

Maggie just stared at Allison, a soulful pleading in her eyes.

"Oh, for goodness sake, Maggie. I have a life here. I work round the clock. There's a reason I don't have kids or pets...or plants, for that matter. You don't even like me. Why would you want to trust me with a dog?"

"I like you a little bit."

Allison looked at her, trying to decide if this was manipulation on Maggie's part or the expression of real feeling. What she saw surprised her. While Allison had no doubt that Maggie wanted something—namely, help with the dog—there was also genuine warmth and trust in her eyes. Allison felt her resolve melting.

"Come here, let's clean you up." She walked over to the sink, careful not to turn her back to the dog, and pulled Neosporin and Band-Aids from a cabinet. These she laid on the counter. "Roll up your sleeves."

She washed Maggie's hand first. The scratches seemed superficial: a few long trails of dried blood covering thin lacerations. The arm was worse. A chunk of skin was missing, and the area around the wound looked red and puffy.

"You need to keep an eye on this. When was your last tetanus shot?"

"Like I know."

"This could get infected. Tell your parents you need a trip to the doctor."

"Um, no." Maggie cocked her head to the side and rolled her eyes. Her dyed-black hair had blue highlights in the morning light.

"Then I'll tell them." Allison covered the wound with triple-antibiotic cream and a bandage, the whole time keeping one eye on the dog in case he decided a pot of raw meat wasn't enough sustenance for one morning.

"You can't tell Daddy. I will be *so* dead for skipping school."

"I'm sure the school called your mother. She probably already knows—"

"Even if they did, she won't tell. She's afraid of upsetting my father. Everyone's afraid of upsetting Daddy."

"You saved that dog. They'll be proud of you."

"Yeah, right. If you haven't noticed, Allison, Mr. Conservative Values is less about helping others and more about appearances. He doesn't want that ugly dog saved any more than he wants to turn me loose to the media. Anyway, I told you. He hates animals."

"There's still your arm to take care of."

"Will you keep Brutus for me? I know it's a lot to ask, but I don't have anyone else to turn to." Maggie's eyes were teary. "Please?"

Allison looked from Maggie to the dog. He did seem harmless enough, certainly nothing like her father's wolf-dog, Thor. Maybe Jason would take him. She could put him in the basement until Jason arrived. What would an hour or two hurt? And it would make Maggie happy. She seemed so worried about the animal, and it was nice to see a human side of her.

"I'll make you a deal. If you tell your parents you hurt your arm and get them to take you to a doctor—use whatever story you want—I'll try to find a temporary home for Brutus until we find his owners."

Maggie smiled. "Deal."

As though on cue, Brutus let out a low, long fart. He looked quite pleased with himself afterwards, rolled over onto his side, gave a wheezy sigh, and closed his eyes again. Maggie laughed.

"Nice. All that All-Bran," Allison said. "Anyway, so how did you know where to find me?"

"The Internet. You can find all sorts of stuff if you know what you're looking for."

True, Allison thought. No one had privacy anymore. "Who drove you here?"

"A friend."

"And where is said friend?"

"At school."

"So I guess you need a ride back?"

Maggie nodded. Allison eyed Maggie's clothes to see whether a spin in the washer was required first. Despite the uniform, Maggie had managed to accessorize à la London underground: that pentagram necklace, black Doc Martens, anarchy-symbol earrings and her signature bed-head hairdo. Mud streaked the white Polo and pleated skirt. Nothing a little warm water and soap couldn't handle.

"Let's get you upstairs and cleaned up. You can't go to school like that. And you certainly can't go home like that. Your mother will know something's up. You smell like a barnyard and there's dog hair all over your skirt."

Maggie looked down at her uniform. "So what do you suggest?"

"I'll give you some sweats. We'll throw your uniform through the rinse cycle, and then I'll drop you off at school."

"In the meantime?"

Brutus farted again. The sound startled him, and he jumped up in surprise. Maggie giggled.

Oh Lord. "You can bathe that dog. If he's bunking with me for a few hours, he needs to smell less like Eau de Waste-Treatment Plant and more like Johnson's Baby Shampoo."

FIFTEEN

"I can't take him, Al," Jason said. "My apartment doesn't allow dogs."

"Since when does Jason Campbell follow the rules?"

"Since I like having a roof over my head," he said over the phone. "Would you prefer I live there again?"

"No." She answered quickly—too quickly—but the fact was, the question gave her pause. Allison tried to decipher the tone in Jason's voice. Was there even a hint of wanting, or was it just Jason being playful? Not that it mattered. She'd made her choice. They both had.

"Well, what am I supposed to do with him? If I send him to the AASPCA, Maggie will have a stroke."

"Maybe he has an owner out there."

"Maggie and I called every shelter in a fifty-mile radius. No one has reported him missing."

"Then it looks like you're a dog owner."

Allison watched Brutus. She'd made Maggie barricade him in the kitchen before she'd dropped her off at school, but he wasn't looking too thrilled about being corralled. The dog paced back and forth restlessly, head down, tail between his legs. Even Allison knew a non-wagging tail meant an unhappy dog.

"That's not an option, Jason. I'm far too busy to care for a dog." At the sound of her voice, Brutus walked over to the where she stood and sat, looking at her expectantly. "Besides, he wants to eat me."

"You're being ridiculous."

She glanced at the clock: 11:14. "No, I'm not. I'm standing here staring at this dog. Soon he'll have to go to the bathroom. Then what will I do? If I try to put him on a leash, not that I own one, he might bite me."

She didn't like the panic in her voice, but she couldn't hide it. She wanted to add that she was still in jeans, hadn't showered, had a headache-medicine hangover and needed to meet with a Third Circuit judge in forty-five minutes. But Jason already viewed her as an anal-retentive freak of nature, and she wasn't about to give him more ammunition.

"Mia," he said.

"Huh?"

"I'll call my mother. She has the space, and she loves animals. Maybe she'll take him for a few days."

"There's one little problem with that plan. She won't talk to me, remember?"

"Don't take it personally, Al. She's just a little sensitive after everything with Bridget and then the divorce."

"I think not returning a single phone call in two years is a pretty good indication of her feelings toward me, Jason. We both know she thinks I abandoned you."

Jason didn't respond. Rather than entertain the thought that he, too, felt Allison had abandoned him, she said, "If your mother will take him, I'd appreciate that. I'm desperate."

"I'll give her a call. For now, don't show your fear, Al. Dogs can smell it. It'll only get you into trouble."

Judge Norman Lint sweated. Public speaking terrified him, and by the end of any speech he would be drenched: armpit stains, collar ring, a damp nest of white hair against his reddened forehead. The man had made it through two years on the bench of the prestigious Third Circuit only by using a mix of Paxil, behavioral therapy, and weekly sessions with Allison. She had no idea how he'd gotten through law school or managed a successful twenty-year stint as a litigator. Even with the meds and an audience of only one, Allison had a tough time keeping him calm and focused.

"Norman, remember to breathe. Find one person in the room and focus on his or her face...Good, now speak like you're only talking to me... And breathe. That's it. If you feel yourself starting to panic, take a deep breath and focus on your point person...Deep breaths. Good!"

Allison placed a hand on her diaphragm. "Here, Norman. Deep belly breaths."

Norman stood six inches shorter than Allison, and his small-featured, mustachioed face tilted up toward hers. She tried to ignore the starry-eyed wanting in his eyes. For a shy man, he certainly wore his heart where you could see it. At least he wasn't staring at her feet today. She'd dressed casually in charcoal capris, a white sweater set and ballet flats to remove any temptation. She hoped she'd remembered to put away her extra pumps. Last time they disappeared after his session.

After a moment, Norman said, "Labor law has changed over the years. There was a time when the Third Circuit heard cases..." In his typical monotone, the judge gave the short speech he had prepared for today's session.

Allison usually suggested fun, easy topics like a hobby or sport, but Norman insisted on providing her with in-depth educational spiels about the legal system. She smiled. "Good, Norman. Very interesting."

From the other side of the closed door, Vaughn's voice rose above Norman's. "You can't go in there, Congressman. She's with a client... no, Congressman. I'm afraid she's busy. Hey—"

The door flung open with a bang and the doorway was suddenly filled by Hank McBride's unwelcome presence.

"Ms. Campbell, what in damnation were you thinking?" He stopped when he saw the judge.

Vaughn's angry face hovered behind Hank. He mouthed, "Sorry."

Allison was livid. Behind her, she heard Judge Lint's breathing go from slow and steady to quick and labored. She had to get Hank out and Norman calm. They'd recognize each other, of course, both being powerful men traveling in a very tight Philadelphia political circle.

Confirming her thoughts, Hank said, "Norman."

The judge nodded, but his cheeks were bloated and his face beet red. That telltale sweat was already beading across his forehead.

"Out, Congressman. Now."

Hank looked from Allison to the judge and back again, considering, it seemed, whether to back down. Allison pointed toward the door. She made no attempt to hide her anger. "I'll see you when we're finished here."

Vaughn placed his hand on Hank's shoulder, but the man shrugged it off. After a final glance at Norman, Hank left the room with Vaughn at his heels.

Allison turned her attention back to the judge, who stood, back against the wall, arms clutching his chest. "I'm so sorry, Norman. Remember to breathe. Good, good, straighten up. That's it." She helped the judge to the couch and handed him tissues to blot his face. "Part of public speaking is learning to roll with the unexpected, so consider that a good lesson."

Allison took her time with Norman. When they were finished, she apologized again and walked the judge out. She'd finally calmed down enough to give Hank McBride—the blooming bastard—a piece of her mind.

She found him in her office with Vaughn, who glowered over Hank like an angry prison guard. Allison thanked Vaughn. "You can go," she said, "we'll be fine." Then to Hank, she said, "What were you thinking? I had a client in there, Congressman. You can't barge in that way."

Hank walked over to the window, one hand clutching his mobile, the other arrogantly planted on his hip. His face was a mask of infuriating calm, though the red creeping from underneath his collar told Allison that he was feeling less than serene.

"Are you finished yelling at me, Ms. Campbell?"

"I wasn't yelling. To the contrary. I would love to yell at you, but I'm a professional."

He looked away. "I apologize for the misunderstanding. I thought you were alone."

Bullshit. "What do you want, Congressman? My time is limited."

Head still turned away from her, he said, "Maggie."

"What about Maggie?"

"I received a phone call from one Mark Helms this morning. Ring a bell?"

"*Lieutenant* Mark Helms?" With sudden understanding, she said, "He's investigating the Feldman murder. But what does he have to do with Maggie? Or me, for that matter?"

Hank took two menacing steps toward her. "Why don't *you* tell *me* what Helms has to do with my daughter, Ms. Campbell?"

"I have no idea what you're talking about."

He took another step, closing the distance between them. Allison stood her ground.

His eyes squinted menacingly. She said, "I think you should leave, Hank. Before you do something you'll regret."

"The police are investigating my daughter for the murder of Arnie Feldman." He spoke through clenched teeth. "Do you have any idea what that means?"

Allison's mind sorted through the implications. Maggie must not know at this point, or she would have mentioned it this morning. But once she found out, once Hank got a hold of Maggie...This was the end of the line for Maggie, regardless of the legal outcome. Boarding school would look like Disney World.

Allison said, "I'm sorry to hear that. Maggie must be terrified."

"You knew Maggie was dating Ethan. It's awfully coincidental that the Lieutenant comes knocking on our door just weeks after we hire you."

"I have no idea why the police are questioning Maggie, and I certainly haven't talked to anyone about Maggie in relation to this case."

He tossed the cell phone on the floor and came at her in one swift move. He rammed her hard against the door with both hands, digging his thumbs into her shoulders. His breath smelled like onions and cigarette smoke.

"You bitch," he hissed. "You told Helms that Maggie was with Ethan the night of the murder."

His fingers pressed deeper into her collarbone, twisting the light cotton of her sweater. She tried to push him away. He didn't budge.

"Get off me! You will be very sorry, Congressman. I had nothing to do with Helms." Another push. McBride was dead weight against her. She tried to knee him in the groin, but the best she could manage was a stomp on his foot. She wished she'd worn stilettos.

Hank winced. He lightened his grip. "Maggie told Sunny that you knew. I'm not stupid—"

"Listen to yourself." Allison gave him another shove and this time he backed off. There was a loud knock at the door.

"Allison, everything alright in there?" Vaughn said.

"Fine, Vaughn." Allison shot Hank a warning stare.

"I'm right here if you need me."

"Everything's under control," she said to Vaughn. She turned her attention to Hank. Her heart was racing. Sweat beaded across her brow. She wiped it away angrily and said, "What the *hell* were you thinking? I could have you arrested for battery. I don't give a rat's ass if you are a congressman!"

"I just assumed." Hank looked down at his hands as though surprised at what they'd just done. He walked slowly back toward the window, still facing Allison. Allison rubbed her collarbone where his fingers had squeezed.

"Maggie seems even less compliant since she met you, not more. You come along, then Lieutenant Helms. It was a logical deduction. I'm sorry. You must understand. She's my youngest, after all."

Allison detected a hint of real concern in Hank's tone and mannerisms. She *wanted* to believe the fear was for Maggie—and not his political career—but instinct told her otherwise. She said, "We're through, Congressman. This engagement is predicated on trust. I'm afraid I can't work with you anymore."

He stood straight, a look of surprise replaced by the glare of righteous indignation. "We had a deal. You signed a contract."

"Didn't Sunny tell you? I refused to sign the contract. Our deal is off." She opened the door and motioned toward the waiting room. She wanted Hank out of here, out of her building and her life. I should have trusted my gut, she thought. She felt awful for Maggie and, if she was being honest with herself, she would actually miss the kid. But the truth was, without the support of her family and a willingness to roll up her own adolescent sleeves, change was nearly impossible.

"Payment is dependent upon completion—"

"Then don't pay me. I don't want your money." She pointed at the front door. "Please leave, Congressman."

He picked up his phone and walked through the open door. In the waiting room, he paused and turned toward Allison. "You'll be sorry, Ms. Campbell. Few people cross me and survive with their careers intact."

"Don't threaten me, Congressman." Allison walked him to the front door of the office. She opened it, waiting for him to leave.

He flashed a crooked smile. "Oh, it's not a threat Ms. Campbell. Merely a fact." He held his wrist up to the light and made a show of checking the time. "I'm late for a press conference. Fancy that. I never know what will come out when I speak with the media. You know how rumors start."

Allison tried to keep her voice even. "I also understand how fragile a politician's reputation can be. And I'm sure the press would like to know about the stunt you pulled today." Allison put her hand on her throat. Then, before he could respond, she slammed the door in his face.

Damn him. Media. Threats. Let him try. She rubbed her collarbone again, the unpleasant sensation of his fingertips still chafing against her skin. She wondered how often McBride resorted to violence to get what he wanted.

Sunny's unhappiness was suddenly understandable. And Maggie's. Tonight would not be a pleasant one in the McBride household. Allison would keep her promise about that dog, but otherwise, she was afraid there was nothing more she could do.

SIXTEEN

Mia switched off the ignition and stared at Allison's house. Until Jason had called earlier in the day, Mia had been under the mistaken impression that he was as bitter as Mia over his and Allison's divorce. Perhaps I'm too sheltered up there, she thought. I'm projecting my own feelings onto my son.

Too many memories lingered here. Allison had been like a second daughter to her. She remembered the wounded creature who showed up at her doorstep a decade ago, looking for work. When Allison told her she was a semester shy of a doctorate, Mia had turned her away. She'd needed an assistant—someone to do intake, file, answer the phone. Allison had been overqualified. And hopelessly plain. But something about her dejected air had tugged at Mia, and when Allison showed up a second time, assuring Mia the job was exactly what she was looking for, Mia gave her a chance.

The assistant position had grown as Allison blossomed. She soaked up all Mia had to teach her. The clients loved her. She was warm and no-nonsense at the same time, a wonderful contrast to the Main Line exclusiveness that surrounded them. After Bridget's death, Mia had clung to Allison. Sold her—no, practically gave her—the business and watched it grow in ways Mia never imagined, all the while feeling a mother's pride in Allison's accomplishments.

And then Allison left Jason. Her only son. Indeed, her only surviving child.

Mia forced herself out of the car. She opened the trunk and grabbed a leash and a dog blanket, which she spread over the backseat. When was the last time she had come here, to this house? Three months before Allison and Jason had announced their divorce. Allison had come home late that night. She'd just heard that her book, *From the Outside In*, was to be published. She'd seemed overjoyed...whereas Jason had not.

One more thing separating Allison and Jason: success.

Was divorce inevitable? Mia liked to think they could have salvaged their marriage. They were good for one another. Jason had had a succession of girlfriends during college and afterwards. Mia found most of them vapid and boring and wondered whether her son wasn't too fixated on the physical, for all of them were beautiful. Tall, short, thin, voluptuous but always beautiful.

But then he met Allison through her and something changed. He stopped going out so much. He listened to people. He wanted a family. Allison broke her son's heart. This Mia knew deep in her soul, and it was this knowledge that had caused her to turn Allison away two years ago. Losing a child to her own husband's drunk driving was bad enough. She couldn't bear to watch her other child suffering.

Perhaps she had been unfair.

Mia knocked on the door. She heard shuffling and then a dog barking. Something crashed. Allison screamed. Mia knocked again, more loudly this time.

Another scream. *Hurry.*

Mia tried the doorknob. Unlocked. She dropped her purse and the leash and ran inside. Another scream, followed by a giggle and a moan, came from the dining room.

Mia sprinted through the foyer and kitchen and into the dining room... and there they were, dog and woman. Allison lay on the floor with the largest boxer Mia had ever seen sitting on her chest. The dog had a face only a mother could love—jutting jaw, protruding bottom teeth. Allison's face was scrunched up, eyes squeezed shut. The dog was watching her face. Every so often, he'd reach his head down and lick her, stubby tail wagging.

Mia said, "I wish I had a camera."

Allison opened her eyes. "Help!"

"It looks like you're doing just fine."

"Ha, ha." Allison lifted her head. "Can you get him off? Please?"

Mia grabbed the dog's collar and pulled. "What's his name?"

"Brutus."

"Come on, Brutus." Mia tugged again. The dog seemed determined to remain on top of Allison, as though claiming his prize. "How about a treat?"

Allison said, "In the kitchen. He loves Meaty Bones."

Mia jiggled the Meaty Bone box. That was all it took. Brutus came running into the kitchen and sat before her, tongue hanging out. She gave him a bone, and he devoured it as splinters of Meaty Bone flew from his lower jaw and clustered in his jowls. Mia shook her head. This dog was a mess.

"His table manners are lacking," Allison said. She came into the kitchen. She wore faded jeans and a cotton blouse, which she was tucking back in. She looked at Mia warmly and said, "Thanks for coming." She nodded toward Brutus, who was waiting for another treat. "He escaped from the kitchen and tackled me. Jumped right over the barricade."

Mia laughed. She knew Allison had a bad experience with a dog when she was younger, so she was surprised to see her so calm now. Mia took a long look at her former daughter-in-law. She'd aged little since Mia had last seen her—a few faint crows-feet around her eyes and light lines on her neck and around her mouth. Allison's hair seemed shorter and blonder than before, cut shoulder length and angled around her face, giving her a more mature air. All-in-all, she still had a pleasant, easy smile and features that leaned toward cute rather than beautiful, although there seemed to be a calmness about her now that hadn't been there before.

Mia took stock of her feelings and was surprised to find only a vague sense of regretful longing. She'd expected to feel anger and bitterness.

"Tea?" Allison said with a wistful smile. "You didn't use to be a coffee drinker, unless that's changed."

"Tea would be lovely."

While Allison filled the teapot, Mia watched her tall, slim frame, still so familiar, at the sink. When they'd parted ways, Allison had been just on the cusp of career success. But despite her promise, she had always seemed a little bit of an outsider. Maybe that had been her appeal for Mia. She'd been a refreshing change from the Main Line sameness. But this Allison was a published author, a respected professional, a sought-after speaker. Had she finally managed to fit in?

Mia looked around. The house was a study in contradiction. Some rooms, like the kitchen, were professionally decorated and spotlessly clean. Others, like the dining room, were nearly devoid of furniture or anything personal that hinted at the woman who lived here.

"Chamomile, Mia?"

"Perfect."

Allison poured water into the teacups. As she carried them to the kitchen table, Brutus hit her elbow with his massive head, causing one cup, then the other, to spill. Some of it splashed on the dog's back.

Allison yelled, "Brutus!"

Brutus yelped and dove under the table. Mia climbed after him. His skin, though wet, seemed fine. When Mia looked up, she saw Allison standing there, looking at the dog, her shoulders shaking with big, chunky sobs that caused rivulets of black mascara to snake down her face.

"Hey," Mia soothed. "It's okay, Allison. He's not hurt."

"I didn't mean to... the poor dog." She backed up and wiped at her eyes. Mia stood up and handed her a paper towel.

"He's fine."

"It's not just the dog. It's everything." Allison blew her nose into the paper towel. "I'm sorry, for whatever I did. To make you so angry."

"Stop. You have nothing to apologize for. *Nothing*."

"I let you down."

"You didn't let me down. I was crushed when you divorced Jason, yes. But only because I love you, and I was afraid. Afraid I'd never see you again." Even as she said the words, she understood the irony. It was she who'd initiated the freeze between them, not Allison. The divorce hadn't taken Allison away; Mia had pushed her out of her life. Before Allison could hurt her, too.

"Oh my, Allison." Mia took Allison's hand. "It's I who am sorry."

Their eyes met.

"You'd been through a lot. With Bridget." Allison gently pulled her hand free. She dampened the paper towel at the faucet and wiped it over her swollen face. Then she pulled out a kitchen chair for Mia and took the seat opposite. "I know her death broke your heart, Mia. Jason and I, we weren't sensitive to that. We should have waited to tell you."

"Her death did break my heart. It was the most crushing pain I've ever felt. But I survived." Brutus pushed his head up under Mia's hand. She stroked it absentmindedly. "Maybe that's the funny part of it. That any of us can go on, can continue to do and think and be, in spite of what happens. And before that, that we keep making music, or painting, or cleaning, or punching numbers on a cash register, all the while not realizing what horrible things wait for us around the corner."

Mia rubbed under Brutus's chin. The dog seemed to like it and raised his head up further to lean against Mia's arm. Allison's house was quiet except for the hiss of the tea kettle releasing the last sprays of steam. Mia thought about Bridget, about all the times she and Bridget had sat, waiting for water to heat, talking about things that meant nothing at the time but, looking back, meant everything, really.

"Maybe those of us who've never experienced the worst life has to offer get along with a peculiarly human kind of denial," Mia said into the silence. "And maybe those of us who've touched the void and lived—and losing a child *immerses* you in the void, Allison, believe me—maybe we survivors just need to protect ourselves from ever visiting its depths again."

Mia looked up to see Allison staring at her. Her eyes showed only kindness.

"I've spent the last few years being so angry at Edward. For killing. And at Bridget. For dying." Mia swallowed, biting back her own tears. "I judged her, Allison. I judged her in my heart and condemned her for being the one to go. And I am just now realizing that the anger I directed at you was my anger toward her. For leaving me."

Mia felt her own tears come in a rush, long overdue. Then she felt a warm hand on her shoulder and a wet nose under her arm. She was grateful for the comfort, for the knowledge she was not alone.

It was as though Bridget was there, smiling and, finally, offering her forgiveness.

Mia shook her head. "I'm not taking him, Allison. He might have something my other dog could catch, like mange."

Mia knelt on the kitchen floor and stroked the dog's back. She and Allison had spent the last two hours catching up, but now it was time for her to leave. Allison wanted her to take Brutus with her. The dog didn't have mange—Mia was pretty sure the patch on his back was just a skin allergy—but Mia needed some reason to leave Brutus here. It was obvious that Allison and that dog needed each other.

Allison put her head down. "Now what? I can't have a dog, Mia. Especially not one like him. He's so big and needy."

"Take him to the vet. I'll give you the name of a good one. A few decent meals, some medication, and he'll be in great shape."

"Look at him."

Mia smiled. He *was* about the ugliest dog she'd ever seen. "So what? Underneath that face is a sweet dog, Allison. You could always take him to the pound, though they may...."

Allison's jaw clenched. "No. Never mind." She sounded resigned. "I promised Maggie, no ASPCA. I'll keep him for now if I have to."

"Maggie?"

"A client. A former client, actually."

Mia stood up. "Since when do you take clients' dogs?"

"Since I was trying to bond with an oppositional teenager." She gave Mia the gory details, ending with her confrontation with McBride earlier in the day. "We're through now. But I can't go back on my word on this dog. I promised Maggie."

Mia felt her pulse quicken at the mention of McBride. There were rumors: job losses, broken deals, country club cancellations, all following fallings-out with the congressman. She knew of him from her image consulting work and through Edward. The Main Line was a large suburb but, at its core, a small town. The big players knew each other. And so McBride had played golf with Edward on occasion, and even Edward, arrogant ass that he was, didn't trust him.

She handed Allison the leash she'd brought from her car earlier, and then jotted a veterinarian's name on a piece of blank paper.

Mia said, "Stay away from Hank McBride, Allison. He's a powerful man, more powerful than his political title warrants. He comes from money, and he's not afraid to throw it around."

"You know him?"

"I've met him. He and Edward used to play golf together."

Mia considered the other part of Allison's story: that Maggie McBride was being questioned by police. She imagined that the threat to McBride's family status, to the image of the McBrides as an all-American unit, would make him even more dangerous. And the congressman's visit to Allison, an indication that he somehow blamed Allison, silly as it was, made the whole situation that much more worrisome.

She said, "Stay away from Maggie, too, Allison. Any connection to the McBrides can only cause you trouble. Remember my first rule of imaging consulting?"

Allison smiled. "How could I forget? 'Know your limits.'"

"Exactly. If you can't fix it, the problem belongs to someone else."

Allison nodded toward Brutus. "What about him?"

Mia laughed. "I'm afraid Brutus needs more help than any of us can give him. From an image consultant's standpoint, he's beyond redemption. But I think there's a carve-out in the consultant handbook for hopeless canines."

When Hank came in, Sunny was lying down, a cool towel over her eyes. He slammed the door shut and then plopped down on her bed. She felt his hand on her shoulder, rough fingers digging into her flesh. She could hear his breathing, rough-edged and excited. Oh god, no, she thought. Not now.

"You're so beautiful," he said. "Even like that."

His fingers pinched her breast through the thin material of her blouse. She peeked from beneath the towel, expecting to find him looking at her with that lascivious stare that meant he had other things on his mind. He didn't disappoint.

"Hank—"

"Come on. It's been weeks since we've done it. You know how I get when you deny me."

Today she didn't have the stomach for it. Not on top of Catherine's constant complaining and Maggie's...well, the Maggie situation, as she'd come to think of it. Worry about her daughter loomed over every waking moment and haunted her restless dreams. She'd never understood Maggie. Unlike her own childhood, Maggie had everything. Money. A beautiful house. A private education.

Growing up in Georgia, an olive-skinned girl in a peaches-and-cream world, Sunny knew only isolation and poverty. But not Maggie. Yet Maggie had thrown it all away, scorned everything her parents' offered with a contempt that stabbed and insulted. Sunny both loved and hated her daughter, and that fact alone was difficult to bear. She had had such high hopes for the Campbell woman. Another failure. Another waste of time.

"What do you want?" she said to Hank, careful to keep her tone neutral.

"I want you to want it, too."

"Well, that's not going to happen, Hank."

"Then I'll settle for your submission."

She toyed with whether to refuse. He'd let her, but she'd pay for it in other ways. He was a vindictive little boy at heart. She knew she could pretend to want it—to want him—but she was so scared and exhausted that she just didn't have it in her. Better just to let him have his way and get it over with.

She said, "Fine."

He pulled the towel from her head. "Sit up."

She pushed her way into a sitting position, temples throbbing.

His eyes followed the curves of her body. "Get undressed," he said. He watched as she unbuttoned her blouse and slid it off her shoulders. "Yes," he said, and smiled.

When Sunny was bare, he turned her over, so her head was facing the head board. She could hear the unzipping of his pants, the brush of material against skin as he pulled his trousers down. She let her mind drift, so she didn't quite feel Hank's rough entry, his hands pulling her head back, his teeth on her shoulder. It only took a minute. It always took a minute.

When he was done, he pushed her down on the bed and collapsed on top of her. She could feel his wetness running down her thigh. She forced her mind elsewhere.

"I made a few calls," Hank said into her ear. "You distracted me and I forgot to tell you."

Sunny was having trouble breathing. She lay still, hoping he'd shut up and go away.

"I called Allison Campbell's graduate program. She was telling the truth. She left before she finished her dissertation."

"So?" Sunny said into the pillow, because she knew he expected her to respond.

"Don't you find that curious? Why would someone go through years of school and give up before finishing? Allison hardly seems a quitter." He rolled off her, onto his back. Sunny rolled over, too, and tried not to look at him lying there, that arrogant look on his face.

"So I tracked down a former colleague, a nurse," he said. "Allison used to work at a residential treatment home for messed up kids. Place is closed down now, but I had my assistant do a little digging."

Sunny was tired. She wanted sleep. She didn't care about Allison Campbell, revenge for perceived wrongs, posturing for the sake of the media, or any of Hank's obsessions. She wanted to close her eyes and drift away. But she said, "What did the person say?"

Hank rolled onto his side. "Seems our Allison was involved with another girl. Years ago. A girl who ran away to be a prostitute. There was a scandal. Allison was blamed."

"How could that be Allison's fault?" Sunny said.

"The woman didn't say, exactly. Hinted that Allison's relationship with the girl was inappropriate." He grabbed Sunny's arm and shook it. "Don't you see? Our girl has a past. A person with a past is vulnerable. We can use this, Sunny. If we need to." He stood and pulled his pants up over his thighs.

"If Maggie is arrested, why would we bother?"

"I don't like that woman."

"That's your ego talking."

"Bullshit. We hired her and Maggie became more defiant, not less. And now this mess. Campbell never signed the nondisclosure. We have no way to get at her." He paused. "That woman's involved somehow. For all we know she put Maggie up to it."

"You don't really believe that, Hank. Let it go. For Maggie."

"For Maggie? Maggie started this."

"Maggie's a child." Sunny, her eyes heavy, shook her head. "You never used to be this—"

"Mean?" Hank sighed and tilted his head. Sunny got a glimpse of the confident, thoughtful man she'd fallen in love with. Long ago, they had been in love.

"Yes, Hank. Mean."

Hank sat next to her. "I prefer to think of myself as practical, darling. When you're a politician, you need to mind your reputation. Let one person walk on you, and the whole world follows suit."

Sunny heard him, but just barely. Her last image before drifting off to sleep was of Arnie Feldman, lifeless and bloody, as he must have been the day he was killed. God help Maggie and Allison Campbell, she thought. She clutched the blanket to her chest. God help us all.

SEVENTEEN

Late that night, Allison could hear the dog scratching at the kitchen barricades. Brutus didn't like being confined, and she couldn't say she blamed him. Maybe he could come up. It wasn't like he had mange, after all. What had the vet called it? Allergic dermatitis. From living in the woods. He'd been bathed and inoculated and dewormed. Okay, so he was ugly. As Mia had said, so what?

She heard him whimper and then bark. She threw back the covers and crept down the hall. In the first guest room, she rummaged through the mess in the walk-in closet until she found an old comforter. She made a bed in the hallway and then went downstairs and let him up.

He jumped ecstatically, wagging his tail and nipping at her hands. "Okay, okay." She stifled a laugh. "Now don't get any ideas. This is all just temporary."

Brutus followed her into her bedroom. "Oh, no! In the hallway. Right there." She walked back out into the hall and patted the comforter. "Here you go."

Brutus stood in her bedroom doorway, an expectant look in his eyes.

"Fine." Allison sighed wearily. She dragged the blanket to her room and placed it next to her bed. "That's as good as it's gonna get."

She lay back down and turned off her light. Brutus's breathing was labored and loud. It had a wheezy rhythm to it that made her sleepy. White noise.

Br-r-ring. Br-r-ring.

Who now? Allison reached for the telephone, expecting Vaughn or Jason. "Hello?"

"It's Maggie."

Brushing off Mia's warnings, Allison said, cautiously, "Are you okay?"

"How's Brutus?"

"Fine. He's here next to me."

"Can I see him?"

Oh boy. "I don't think that's a good idea, Maggie. You and I, well, we're not working together anymore."

"I know. I'm going to boarding school next term."

"I'm sorry, Maggie."

"I don't care about that. I just want to see Brutus."

Allison took a deep breath. She wasn't deaf to the pleading in Maggie's voice. But she thought of Hank McBride, of his desperate behavior in her office. He was a man on the edge and pushing him over that precipice wasn't going to do his daughter any good. "No, Maggie. Not now."

"Please, Allison? I won't bother you, I promise. I just want to see him...because ...everything else is not so good right now..." Her voice broke and she stopped talking. Allison could hear her quiet sobs through the line.

For Lord's sake, how could she say no to that? Judgment out the window, she said, "When?"

"Tomorrow afternoon? After school? A friend will bring me by."

"Okay. Just this once."

"Thank you, Allison! I mean that. You're not so bad." She paused. "Give Brutus a kiss for me, okay? I'll see you tomorrow."

Allison turned the phone off. She was so tired. First Hank, then Mia, now Maggie. And her mother. She couldn't forget her family, always in the background, like a toxic cloud threatening to rain down misery. Ugh. Allison, get a grip, she thought. You're being a little dramatic. Still, what happened to her neat little life with its clear rules and hospital corners?

Allison slid off the bed and onto the floor. She rubbed Brutus's head for a minute, gathering strength, then reached under the bed for the box that she'd stored there years ago and had felt, for some reason, compelled to keep. She opened the box...and out poured a Pandora's mix of emotions.

Every emotion, it seemed, except hope.

"Tell me more about home, Violet," Allison had said years ago. It was late, maybe two A.M., and the other girls at the Meadows were sleeping. The dorm was dark. From her vantage spot on the couch, Allison could see shards of the living room illuminated by the glow of moonlight: navy blue furniture, a brown carpet, both juice-stained and littered with cigarette burns. Violet lay sprawled on the floor, her head propped up on a couch pillow, her legs buried under the regulation scratchy brown blanket pulled from her bed. The two insomniacs. Allison imagined a fly on the wall would've had to strain to hear them talk, so trained they were at keeping their voices low.

"You've read my file."

"Okay, so I know what your caseworker knows. Now tell me something new. Something positive."

Violet rolled over so she was facing Allison. She pulled her little book flashlight from under her and positioned the head under her chin. She flicked the light on. In the glow, her skin took on a ghostly pallor. With one slim finger, Violet pulled back her lip and showed Allison the blank space where her eyetooth had been.

"Aunt Kay," she said. "Cousin Jimmy knocked it loose, but Aunt Kay punished *me* by pulling it out with pliers."

Allison flinched. She reached down and stroked Violet's hair. "How was that positive, Violet?"

Violet grinned, but there was a hollowness to the smile that left Allison chilled. "When my father found out, he tried to strangle Kay."

Allison remembered that from her file. It was the incident that had landed John "Junior" Swann back in prison.

* * *

"Who's Sparky?"

Three months after John Junior went back to jail, Violet was due to return home. It was late September, and Allison had been looking forward to celebrating the holidays with Violet, but her county decided Violet's residential money had run out and Violet needed to leave the Meadows. Her father had been let out of prison only to land back in for grand theft auto, but her grandmother was willing to take her back.

Doc pushed for foster care, but Violet wanted none of that. Allison hated the idea of Violet going back to her family, especially without the misguided protection of her father, but, even more so, she didn't want Violet moved to another family where she wasn't really wanted and where she might fail. And so Allison had campaigned on Violet's behalf, negotiating with Doc and Violet's caseworker so that Violet could go home.

"Sparky's a friend of a friend." Violet stared at her shoes while stealing glances at Allison out of the corner of her eye, a gesture that always meant she was hiding something. "How'd you hear about him?"

"I listen to dorm gossip." In truth, all Allison heard was a name, one whispered in awe down the dorm when the residents thought the staff were too stupid or inattentive to notice. Allison thought he was a teenage boy, someone from a neighboring town whom all the girls had a crush on. She assumed he was harmless.

Allison watched the way Violet's fingers drummed the chair. Nerves. She'd noticed that Violet had grown her hair out in the last few weeks and had started wearing makeup. She seemed thinner than ever, but her skin glowed from plenty of milk and fresh fruit. Allison had wondered, not for the first time, how Violet would survive back home. As always, she pushed the thought away. *You have to let her go,* Doc had said just that morning. *You're too attached to her. You're not seeing clearly.*

"Your final home visit is tomorrow, Violet. Are you sure you're ready?"

Violet looked up and met Allison's gaze, head on. "Trust me, Allison. Please." When Allison simply held the stare, Violet said, "Did my file tell you I found my mom after she'd killed herself?"

Allison shook her head. All she knew was that Millicent Swann had committed suicide. Alcohol and pills. She braced herself for more. She wasn't sure why Violet was telling her this—maybe to change the subject—but experience had taught her that the girls were most open right before they left. And it seemed Violet would be no exception. So she waited through the silence.

"I was nine and in third grade at Our Lady of Guadalupe," Violet said, her voice a low murmur. "It'd been the best year of my life. Dad was home and working at a gas station. I set my alarm clock to wake the two of them up before school and we all had cereal together in the morning. Cookie Crisp and Cap'n Crunch. Sometimes we'd fight over the prize, but it was a play fight, and, in the end, they'd give it to me. Sometimes Mom didn't want to wake up and I'd have to shake her and yell till she'd roll over and pull me in the bed with her to shut me up. I loved that, when she'd hold me, and I'd pretend all was right and we'd live in our little apartment forever."

Violet's eyes possessed a faraway glaze. She was no longer talking to Allison, but was lost in the land of memories. The office was cold, and Allison could smell the stinging disinfectant housekeeping used to keep the dorm germs at bay. Allison thought of her own mother, the mornings she'd spent wrapped in her mother's frail arms when a migraine was finally subsiding, and she understood Violet's ability to pretend the world was sane and just.

"It was a Friday, Al. Mrs. Colliver gave me an A on my social studies project. I wrote about Martin Luther King, and she said it was the best paper she'd ever seen a third-grader write, and I believed her because Mrs. Colliver never, ever smiled, but that day she did. So I thought maybe my parents would celebrate and order a pizza or we could go to Burger King and I could have a Whopper. I used to love those, before I knew what they really were."

She took a breath and let it out in one long sigh. "But my mom was dead. Her arm was across her face, and her body was so still I knew something was wrong. When I couldn't wake her, I crawled in bed next to her and prayed. I prayed and prayed just like the nuns said to do and hoped when I opened my eyes she would be awake and smiling and proud of my A, but she wouldn't wake up, no matter how many Hail Mary's I said."

Tears ran down Violet's face, making her mascara smear in ghostly circles around her eyes. Allison could picture that little girl trying to glue her world back together with the recitation of some magical words. Allison had wiped her own eyes and waited till Violet said her good-byes to her mother, good-byes that were long overdue.

"I'm afraid," Violet said.

Allison had moved around her desk so that she sat next to her and took her hand. "You're allowed to be scared, Violet."

"But I have to go." She said, as though convincing herself.

"You can do this, Violet. I believe in you."

And those were the last words Allison ever said to Violet Marie Swann. After six months of building a tunnel to let light into that murky head of hers, it was really Allison who had been kept in the dark.

EIGHTEEN

From its plastic hideaway, Allison pulled out the portrait, now yellowed with age. The young, angelic Allison that Violet had captured over a decade ago stared back at her. She thought of Mia's words earlier that day: "*Before we know what horrors lie around the corner.*" How true. The Allison in that picture would soon learn just how cruel life could be. For it was one thing to suffer. It was another thing to know a child whose short life was *only* pain and suffering. And then to be a party to that suffering? Unforgivable.

Allison dug deeper in the box until she found the letters. Crinkled from tears and handling, marked by the police, there they still hid, held together with a fat black clip. She wanted to put them back in the box, close the lid, and forget. But she couldn't. As though with a will of their own, her hands undid the clip, her eyes began to read.

October 2
Dear Allison,
Please, please don't be angry. Please. It's beautiful here. You should see it. I have my OWN room with a pink comforter and pink curtains and I only share a bathroom with one other girl. Her name's Suze and she's so pretty. And nice. Long, red hair and green eyes. Huge boobs, like a 34DD. And they're real. She's gonna teach me to pole dance. Says I can make $50 a night at the club (after Sparky's cut). Sparky got me a fake ID so I can dance. Nothing bad, Alli-

son, so stop thinking the worse. Sparky's not like that. He's a gentleman. You should see my room if you don't believe me. A framed poster of babies in flower costumes. Anne Geddes, it says. And a Monet poster. Maybe someday I'll paint like Monet. What do you think?

Anyway, Sparky says I don't need to gain weight. I thought for sure I'd be too skinny to work for him—you should see the bodies on some of these girls—but he says no, that some guys like their girls to look young. Gross. But whatever. As long as they pay. Imagine, $50 a night just to dance. After a few months I'll have enough for Mexico or Colorado or at least Ohio. Anywhere but Philly. Sparky keeps our fake IDs locked up in a safe—for our own protection, he says, so we don't get busted. But maybe he'll give me mine when I have enough money to go. He's nice like that.

So don't be angry (see, I said angry, not mad, like you taught me). I know you wanted me to make the best of living with Gram and Aunt Kay and maybe my father if he ever gets himself straightened out, but I can't go back. They'll never change and I'm so tired of telling people that because no one listens. Foster care would've been even worse. Sparky's offering me a future. And he doesn't mind that I don't talk much, says guys don't want to listen to a lot of chatter anyway, or that I always have a sketchbook in my hand. Draw, he says. Whatever makes you happy.

I like it here, Allison. So stop worrying and don't be angry. Please. I like Sparky and I like Suze and I love my room and my unlocked door and my freedom. See why I left, Allison? Home wouldn't have worked. I had to go.

Love,

V.

Ps. Don't try to find me. You can't anyway. I'll be okay. Promise.

* * *

November 1
Dear Allison,

It's cold here. And damp. Late at night, I try to use my charcoals but my fingers are too stiff. I don't think Sparky has heat or if he does he won't use it. It's too dark to see. Once we finally turn in—around 4, sometimes later—Sparky puts towels in the windows and won't let us turn on the lights. Sometimes I watch the shadows dance around my room, they follow the waves of light that still flow in around the windows and under the door when morning comes, and I imagine what things will be like when I have the money to free myself. I'll sell my sketches and learn to paint. I should get started now. Maybe I'll try to use that flashlight you gave me, prop it up next to my pillow with a book so I can see better. Think Sparky would notice that? As it is, I go to bed thinking I drew a masterpiece and wake up to a muddle of lines and blurred edges.

Sparky says I need to dumb it down, that the joes don't like too many syllables coming out of a girl's mouth. Sparky calls them johns but that name makes me think of my father, John Junior, and then I want to cry. No good crying when you have some 200 pound man panting in your face. It only seems to egg them on. I remember the day you read Romeo and Juliet with me, Al. It was late and the other staff slept. Remember that? The two insomniacs, you called us. I think I understood love then. Line by line you translated that funny English till I finally understood why they stuck together. There's no Romeo here, that's for sure. Yesterday a guy came into Sparky's club, all smooth skin and after-shave. A suit. Suze wanted him bad (more money, she said), but he chose me. Me, Allison. It was just a lap dance but I still can't get used to the little rooms, to shaking my boobs in some guy's face till his pants rise up under me. Sparky says to keep going, grind down on his lap till the boner goes *away so I'll get a bigger tip but I can't seem to do that. I concentrate on his eyes and wait for the second he hands me control. It always happens. Eventually. But the control never lasts, does it? I want it to last.*

A few days ago I sketched a skyscraper. Sparky took us to Love Park to meet a joe—me, Suze and Nicki. He let me take my charcoals so we looked legit. My lines were long and lean. Perfect. Think the buildings are so tall so they reach up to God, Allison? I like to think so, that there's someone up there watching over us and he likes the straight lines and sharp angles as much as I do. Sparky says there is no god, that it's up to us to make our way in a cruel world and sometimes you have to be cruel to do it. He says that when he slips into my bed at night. Not often, Al, so don't worry, okay? I just squeeze my eyes shut when it happens and pretend he's Romeo and I'm Juliet. Even when it hurts. Sometimes love hurts, right?

Tomorrow I have to take Suze to the doctor. For a you-know-what. She cries all the time now. It pisses Sparky off and I can tell he wants to punch her but she's money to him so he doesn't. But he finds other ways of punishing her for all the tears, like giving her scraps to eat and taking her share of the tips. I watch and listen, so I know to keep my money hidden. I won't even write the location here in case he gets hold of this letter before I send it. I must have close to $300 already. But then I don't tell Sparky about all the money. Some I slip into my body before he gets to me—or I hide it in the club. I also know not to trust Nicki. I see her watching Suze. I think she's told Sparky that Suze wants out, that she has a boyfriend now—a joe—and doesn't want to dance. Nicki is beautiful, all sleek black hair and wild eyes, like a cat. And she's sneaky like a cat. I don't trust her and neither should Suze.

I'm tired, Allison, and in a few hours I have to get ready for work, so I'm signing off. Don't try to find me. I know people are looking for me. Suze has a friend who's connected and this friend said the cops are on the watch for a "Sparky" and his underage girls. It's no use, Al. They'll never find me. Sparky has a million aliases and he moves us around a lot. I always have a friend of a friend deliver these letters, so the postmarks mean nothing. I don't want to go home, Allison. Ever. Cockroaches are better than rats. Know what I mean?

Love,

V.

* * *

December 17

I have to write fast. Sparky's in a rage. Suze ran. She slid a driver's license against the edge of her bedroom door till she pushed up the latch. I saw her go. She shushed me and I signaled that the coast was clear. I want her to make it, Allison. She was always nice to me and I know how much she wanted that baby. It was his. The guy who treats her nice and bought her those sneakers and that crystal necklace, the one with the two amethyst birthstones. Suze said she never had anything with her birthstones in it. Sparky made her get rid of the baby. Held her head upside down in the toilet till her skin turned blue and her eyes bulged and told her no one would miss her if he killed her. So she went to that doctor. I have a sketch of Suze under my bed. She was pregnant and sober and happy and her eyes look so exotic in the sketch. She's an eighth Cherokee, you know.

Tonight I watched her slink past Sparky's door. She had a fist-sized bruise on her cheek. Sparky must've been pissed to leave a mark. He never leaves a mark. Says joes don't like damaged goods.

Shit. I hear him coming. He can't know I helped her, he'll kill me Al. I wish you were here to help me. But I'll be okay. Just hope that bitch Nicki doesn't tell.

V.

* * *

December 18

Oh Allison, I did something stupid. Real stupid. I'm afraid. And cold, so fuckkkkking cold. I wish I could call you, come to your house, something. I bet you're still mad at me for leaving the way I did Allison and now I know it was a Bad Choice, but then I felt trapped and scared and so sure Sparky was the real deal. He was real alright, a real Killer, a real Ass, a real Pimp.

When I left I felt old, like twenty-one, and ready to tackle the world. Now I feel old, like Gram, and afraid I'll never get out of this. I have to think.

Once you told me all problems seem bigger at night, that if I close my eyes and sleep, in the morning things won't seem so bad. Remember that? It was the day after you snuck me the book and the flashlight. We the Living. *About the girl who ran away. I still have that book, it's all beat up now and the pages are folded cause I've read it a million times. Thing is, I ran but maybe it wasn't such a great idea. Stupid. The girl in the book—what was her name? I can't remember anything right now! Left looking for freedom. Maybe I had freedom all along, a different kind of freedom. Now I'm in it BIG, Al. My life is cursed. I always do things backward and that's why I end up in so much trouble.*

Trouble. I'm in a crap load of it. It's late. Like 3 in the morning. And I'm tucked in between a WaWa and a Dunkin Donuts, writing with a pen and your flashlight. Everything seems hopeless. Maybe in the morning it won't all seem so bad.

V.

* * *

December 24
Dear Allison,
Suze is dead. I think Sparky's dead. I'm gonna tell you what happened but only because by the time you read this I'll be long gone. Maybe even in Mexico.
The answer came to me in the morning, like you said. I can't believe I didn't think of it before. Find a new joe. Someone kind who will take me west or south or anywhere far, far from Philly. One last date. I can do this. I'll have to pretty myself up cause right now I must look like a crack whore, all dirty and torn and hungry. I haven't eaten since, jeez, days ago. Some lady with a red hat and Jesus Saves pin gave me a bag of donuts and a flier for a Christian Bible study. I ate the donuts and am writing to you on the back of the flier. Oh, and a man with a little Hitler mustache and real bad acne offered me $20 to give him a blow job behind the Asian convenience store on 11th and Race. There's a spot behind the Dumpster there where the cops can't see. It smells bad but if you press your nose against the guy's stomach a little you can't smell the trash so much. You'll be happy to know I refused, though. No more joes. Other than the one who will take me far away from here.
So back to what happened. I'm running out of space and will have to write inside the church outline soon. Who-ever made this flier had no idea how to draw. The church is all wrong—the perspective is off and the steeple is out of proportion. Look at it, you'll see. I could have done it better.
Anyway, Suze ran but Sparky had one of his boys go after her and bring her back. I'll never forget the look on her face when he dragged her through that door. She knew what was coming. Once Gram took me to see my great Un-cle Ray where he worked at a slaughterhouse. I saw pigs being herded off a truck. I could hear the squeals and screams of the pigs already in there and it was clear those animals leaving that truck knew what was about to happen cause, I swear, their eyes looked human. That was how it

was with Suze. She stood in the doorway of the tiny kitchen and even though two of Sparky's thugs were pulling her toward Sparky, she dug her heels in and refused to move. I wanted to scream, Allison, anything to distract those men but I was too scared to move. And Nicki was laughing, all quiet and sneaky in the corner but I saw her eyes light up and the edges of a smile behind the hand she held to her mouth. Bitch.

I won't give you all the details Allison not because I think you'll be grossed out but because I can't remember them, it all happened so fast. The thugs pulled Suze inside and Sparky told them to leave. Then he made me and Nicki watch "for a lesson" while he kicked and punched Suze until she lay on the floor like an old shirt. Blood oozed from her mouth and ears and her legs were splayed at a weird angle. She managed to pick her head up though and look at Sparky and he went for her again. That's when I did the stupid thing. He raised his big boot to kick Suze in the head and I grabbed the closest thing, a screwdriver, and stabbed him in the back over and over and over just wanting him to stop hurting Suze. He turned on me and grabbed me around the neck and started to choke me. I couldn't breathe, and the room started to spin then everything looked dark and far away. Then all of a sudden he let go. I looked down and saw Suze on the floor with her teeth sunk in Sparky's leg. There was blood everywhere. Sparky yelled something and Nicki ran out the back door, I figure to get the thugs. Sparky started to kick Suze again and I knew I had to do something fast. I didn't think, Al, I dove for the drawer where Sparky kept his cigarettes and pot and grabbed a can of lighter fluid and a lighter and some matches. I splashed fluid on him and held a lighter to his back. His shirt caught in flames, then his hair and he was screaming with anger and hate and coming for me. I pushed him as hard as I could against the counter and the flames caught the curtain and the room started to burn. I glanced down at Suze and she was lying there bleeding her eyes open staring at nothing like my mom did ages ago. I knew he'd killed her. So I ran. I ran until I heard sirens and then I ran some more. It wasn't until I'd run so far my feet were bleeding in my high heels that I realized I'd left my money stash at the house. Too late.

So that's it, Allison. I think I killed Sparky and I burned down the house. Me, the fire setter. You know what the system does with murderers and fire setters. No more nice residential treatment program. Jail. I can't go to jail, Allison, it'd be worse than the cockroaches AND the rats.

I'm sure you're worried now. I can almost see you—hand running through your long blond hair, that frown on your face. You'd tell me that I should trust the system to do the right thing. And you'd mean it, Allison, because you of all people would never tell me something you didn't believe. But I can't risk it. I'm only 15. That's a lot of years left to live with regret.

So you won't hear from me again. You should know if I could have had another mother, I'd have wanted her to be like you. I'd have wanted her to be you. So remember me, okay? You said Romeo and Juliet was a tragedy and I thought that was kind of beautiful in a strange sort of way. No happy ending. That's life, right? Maybe that Shakespeare is wrong. Maybe I'll make my own happy ending. I think we all get a second chance, Allison. Or at least we should.

Love,
Violet M. Swann

It was 2:12 when Allison finally crawled into bed, her face still wet and her heart tangled in her ribcage. She felt numb. So numb, that she didn't object when Brutus jumped in bed beside her and laid his great, ugly head on the pillow next to hers.

NINETEEN

"Being a witch is not easy," Maggie said.

"I don't imagine it is."

Maggie plopped down on the living room couch and stretched her legs out on the cream silk, Brutus's head in her lap. The dog closed his eyes, clearly enjoying the thorough ear-rubbing Maggie was bestowing upon him. Allison smiled. Dog and teenager both looked content.

"I had to learn the herbs. There are so many of them. And the incantations."

"How did you get into Wicca?"

"I read about it. Then I made some calls. There's a coven in Devon. I can't attend meetings—Daddy won't let me—but I talk to the other witches online. When I can."

Allison sat on the floor and stretched. She had piles of work to finish and then she was due to meet with her personal trainer. Maggie had arrived late and in a cab. Her parents thought she was at the mall. Allison tried to ignore the rational little voice that said she should get Maggie out of here now. Maggie seemed relaxed and happy. And it *was* kind of nice to have some company. What harm could an hour here do?

"That must drive your father crazy."

"He doesn't know."

Allison considered this. Maggie seemed to do a lot Hank didn't know about. Ethan. Wiccan. And now Allison and Brutus. She wondered what other secrets Maggie managed to hide.

She decided to ask the question she'd been avoiding. "I heard you were questioned by the police, Maggie. How did that go?"

Maggie seemed intent on rubbing a patch of hair above Brutus left eye. "Fine."

"Were you scared?"

She shrugged.

"I imagine you're scared for Ethan."

"He didn't do it. And neither did I. We were together that night." She looked up at Allison. "Daddy and I had had another fight. I left without asking. My mother knew, she saw me go. But I made her swear not to tell."

"Would your mother cover for you?"

"She's scared of Daddy. I told her I'd tell *her* secrets if she opened her mouth. She told anyway, of course. She's such a mouse." Maggie frowned. "But I won't tell on *her*. My Wiccan oath and all. It was just a bluff."

Allison was dying to ask what secrets Sunny McBride was hiding, but she figured some things were best left unknown..

"Udele never came home."

This was news. "Where did she go?"

Maggie said, "We don't know. She hasn't been home all week."

"Really? Aren't your folks worried? Given the circumstances surrounding Mr. Feldman's murder, I'd think they'd be very concerned."

Maggie shrugged. "Daddy filed a missing person report. He's convinced Udele stole something and ran. Only nothing's missing."

That did seem odd. Udele hardly seemed like the fly-by-night type or a thief, for that matter. What would make her suddenly leave the family she'd been with for decades? And with no warning? And why would McBride say something like that about a woman he'd known so long?

Maggie looked around the room. "Where's all your furniture?"

"You're sitting on a couch."

"Yes, but there are no chairs. Or tables."

"My ex-husband took some stuff. I haven't had time to buy new things."

"When did you get divorced?"

"Two years ago."

"Aren't you an image consultant? Wouldn't you want the house to look all fancy and put together?"

"I don't entertain much."

"Two years is a long time. Aren't you lonely here by yourself?"

"No."

"It feels so empty. Like no one lives here."

Allison stood up. Enough questions. "Why don't you take Brutus for a walk?" She walked to the window and looked outside. "The drizzle stopped."

Maggie tilted Brutus's face up and looked in his eyes. "Would you like that, boy?" His tail stump thumped against the floor.

"The leash is over there." Allison pointed to a hook on the wall by the front door. "He pulls. And he isn't good with other dogs, so be very careful. If you see another dog, go a different way."

"Aren't you coming?"

"I have work to do."

"Come on, just for a little while? You're already dressed for it." She pointed to Allison's yoga pants and t-shirt. "Besides, I don't know my way around here."

She was right. It probably *was* better if Maggie didn't go alone. Brutus could be a handful, and there was no telling what trouble Maggie could find on her own. The presentation she was working on for an upcoming workshop could wait. Only so much one could say about interview etiquette, anyway.

"Fine. Let's go." She grabbed an anorak from the closet while Maggie clipped the leash to Brutus's collar.

Outside, the air felt damp and cool. She watched Maggie and Brutus canter down the driveway, toward the sidewalk. Maggie's hair, flat and loose today, curled around her face, making her look younger than her fifteen years. She still wore her school uniform, knee socks slouchy around her ankles, and no coat.

"Do you want a jacket?" Allison yelled after her.

"No way! Come on!" Maggie yelled, and stuck out her tongue. "You can't be that slow!"

"Oh yeah? Race me to the corner!"

Allison took off, running as fast as she could go, which wasn't particularly fast. Maggie, pulled along by a very excited Brutus, beat her by a few inches.

"Ha!" Maggie bent over, breathing hard. "I win."

"Want to go another round?"

Between breaths Maggie said, "No way. I always fail gym. Can't you tell?"

Allison laughed. Brutus was straining on the leash, and the three walked slowly so Maggie could catch her breath. The lenses of Allison's glasses were covered with a fine mist, and she wiped them on her t-shirt. She had forgotten to take them off earlier. Habit.

"So, are you like blind without them?" Maggie said.

"These?" Allison held up her glasses and smiled. "Want to know a secret?"

"Sure."

"I have almost twenty-twenty vision."

Maggie stopped walking. "Then why wear glasses?"

"They make me look older and smarter." Allison slipped them off, looked at Maggie, and then slipped them back on again. "See?"

"Sneaky." Maggie laughed. "But you're right, they do."

They walked past a few more houses: large, newish homes with neatly landscaped lots. Allison knew the neighborhood couldn't compete with Maggie's, but still, she always felt a stab of pride when she considered how far she'd come.

"So why do you care what people think?" Maggie said.

The question caught Allison off guard. "It's my job to care, Maggie. Image is important. Without the glasses, the people I work with might not take me as seriously."

Maggie threw her a sideways glance. "No offense, but that's really sad. You're basically saying you're a fake."

Allison stepped over a small muddle puddle in the center of the sidewalk. "I'm not saying that at all."

"You have a big house with nothing in it. You wear glasses you don't need. You run a business teaching losers like me how to look and act like winners. Doesn't it get to you?"

"You're not a loser."

"You know what I mean. Don't you sometimes wonder what's real?"

Allison looked up at Maggie, surprised by the question. Of course she knew what was real. Rules of etiquette were *real*, posture and syntax were *real*, color and fabric were *real*. What were not *real* were relationships and hopes and dreams. Just look at her mother, boxed in by the walls of a twelve-hundred-square foot house, any happy memories erased by Alzheimer's. Or Violet, dreaming of being an artist, only to have it all end because her therapist was too stupid to see the signs that she was about to do something dangerous. No, *real* meant tangible, tenable, and safe. Allison lived for *real*.

But that was something some people would never understand.

"Um, Allison—"

Allison looked up slowly. Too slowly. Across the street was old Mrs. Briar and her miniature poodle, Peaches. Before Allison could react, Brutus lunged. He pulled Maggie off the curb and onto her knees. Maggie howled, then let go of the leash.

Brutus sprinted across the street, right for Peaches and Mrs. Briar's cashmere-cloaked form.

"Brutus! No!" Allison helped Maggie up, and they both dashed across the street.

"Get that monster away from Peaches this instant!"

Brutus, fifteen inches taller and seventy pounds heavier than poor Peaches, was trying to mount her. Thankfully, Peaches would have none of it. Allison tugged at the leash. Brutus, obstinate as ever, held his ground, despite his lack of success. "Brutus! No!"

Maggie grabbed his collar and pulled. On the third pull, Brutus stopped humping the air over an anxious Peaches and sat on the pavement, an innocent expression on his face. Mrs. Briar swooned. Allison grabbed her arm.

Mrs. Briar looked at Maggie and Brutus in turn, then at Allison. She scowled, bent down, and picked up Peaches. Mud and saliva dotted the fur on Peaches's backside where Brutus had tried to have his way with her.

"I would have expected better from you, Ms. Campbell," Mrs. Briar said. She pushed a lock of stiff, white hair off her forehead, and nodded toward Maggie. "Peaches and I came to this neighborhood to escape the hooligans."

"I didn't introduce you. Mrs. Briar, meet Maggie McBride. Congressman McBride's daughter."

This time, Mrs. Briar's eyes widened in surprise. She backed up, stumbled and smiled apologetically before turning to leave. "Forgive me, dear," she said over her shoulder. "I didn't recognize you. I left my glasses inside."

Back inside Allison's house, Maggie fell on the foyer floor and let out a howl of laughter. "Did you see Brutus trying to do it with that silly little dog?"

Allison laughed. She had to admit, the whole scene had been pretty funny. And she'd never really liked Mrs. Briar anyway. Allison's clothes were dripping. No use getting the rugs dirty. She peeled off her anorak and t-shirt, both now splashed with water and mud, and stood in the hallway in her black yoga pants and a teal sports bra. "I'll be down in a minute, Maggie. I'm going to change. Stay there and I'll throw some towels down for you and Brutus."

Maggie stopped laughing. "What's that?"

Allison turned around. Maggie was pointing to her back. It took a moment to realize what Maggie was talking about. Her scars.

"My father. I told you, Maggie. He used to beat us." She shrugged. "He was particularly fond of the buckle side of a belt."

"Jeez, you weren't kidding before."

"I would never kid about a thing like that."

Maggie looked thoughtful. She twirled her pentagram necklace around between her fingers. Allison stood on the bottom step and waited for Maggie to make some sarcastic remark. By now she should have built up immunity to Maggie's comments.

Instead, Maggie surprised her by saying, "I'm sorry."

"For what?"

"For assuming you were one of *them*. I didn't realize you were a misfit, too."

TWENTY

"Gabrielle, move your left arm about an inch. That's good. Stay like that."

Sunny adjusted the lamps in her attic studio so that soft light fell across her model's bare breasts, leaving her face in shadows. Gabrielle was not a beautiful woman, but she had a lush, womanly figure and flawless skin. Sunny's paintbrush made her high cheekbones and almond eyes sing on the canvas.

Sunny had two regular models, Gabrielle and Elise, a younger woman with white-blond hair and pale skin. Sunny liked to paint them together. Next to each other, naked, they were the yin and yang of womanhood: one dark and voluptuous and knowing, the other the lithe embodiment of female innocence.

Each of them was sworn to secrecy, given a cell phone that was to be kept on at all times so that Sunny could reach them when the need to paint was strong and Hank was away. She paid them in cash, an hourly rate that would have made her husband weep, and told Hank the money went for social lunches and charity events. She knew Gabrielle and Elise would keep their promises, for they loved to be adored as much as she loved to capture them on canvas.

She mixed ochre with white and blotted her brush on the palette. "Almost finished. Open your legs, just a little bit. I want to tease."

Sunny watched Gabrielle shift slightly on the cushions, her breasts heavy against red silk brocade. A curl of black pubic hair hid her lips, and it was this promise Sunny wanted to capture.

Sunny's more recent paintings, the ones she was known for, were nothing like the abstracts hanging in the foyer and hallway. Those paintings were sanitized, fit for Hank's conservative bedfellows. These were magnificent: brazen and sensual, paintings meant to stir up the beast inside. Hank would kill her if he knew.

Sunny painted the last bit of shadow and hair, stepped back to take in the finished piece, then placed her signature "Tournier" in the corner. Tournier was her grandmother's maiden name. But Hank didn't know that, either.

"Tomorrow?"

Sunny shook her head. "Hank will be back."

"How do you put up with that *trou de cul?*"

"That asshole, as you say, pays for these sessions." Sunny handed Gabrielle her jeans and sweater, which had been thrown across a bench in the corner. Gabrielle slipped them on over bare skin. "Besides, he has his secrets, and I have mine." She kissed Gabrielle on the lips. "I'll call you next week."

"Will you sell this one?"

"Perhaps."

"He will find out eventually."

"Perhaps."

"He could find this studio. It's in his house, after all."

Sunny smiled. "You worry too much." She stroked Gabrielle's cheek—let her fingers follow the curve of her jaw, trail down her neck and under the swell of her breast. "He never comes up here."

Gabrielle arched her back against Sunny's touch. "Udele could say something."

Ah, Udele. Where was that blasted woman, anyway? Sunny had too much to do, with the wedding coming up and Catherine's demands. She needed the housekeeper now more than ever. She pulled her hand from Gabrielle's breast and said, "Udele isn't here right now. Anyway, she knows better than to say a word."

Not that it mattered. Hank had three mistresses and two illegal offshore accounts. And those were the things Sunny knew about. But Hank could be rough. Her wrists still smarted where he'd grabbed her for not making Allison sign the contract. She rubbed her wrist now, absently. But if he should decide to snoop...well, he'd better think twice before giving her an ultimatum. She had her own insurance. People would pay to know his secrets.

Gabrielle shrugged. Her nipples stood erect under her cotton sweater, and Sunny longed to reach under the thin material and stroke them. But Maggie would be home soon, and it was no good starting something she couldn't finish.

"I'll see you out."

Sunny opened the attic door and Gabrielle followed her down the steep, narrow steps, then through the upper hall. The evening was turning gray and the cold, damp spring air seeped under the windowsills. She reminded herself to call a contractor to have the windows replaced. The chill seemed ever-present in this old house. She did wish Udele was around, to start a fire in the study and heat some soup. Instead, she and Maggie would be on their own tonight.

Downstairs, she picked up her purse from the foyer table and opened her wallet. She handed Gabrielle three hundred dollar bills, then opened the front door.

"You're forgetting I'm parked around back. You need to open the gate."

Damn. She'd have to go out into the cold. Sunny grabbed a shawl from the hall closet and wrapped it around her shoulders. She stuck her feet in a pair of Catherine's slippers. Then she picked up the key ring they kept in a small bowl on the table. The two women walked around the side of the house.

A sharp wind rattled the tree branches. The gloom depressed Sunny, almost as much as the thought of an evening alone with Maggie. At least Hank would be away for another night. That was some consolation.

Sunny unlocked the carriage house. Gabrielle's Honda sat next to the carriage house, which contained the Mercedes and Hank's Porsche. He only drove the two-seater in the summer, on winding back roads away from the city grime and traffic. And even then the weather needed to be perfect. In truth, Sunny resented that car. Hank treated it special, the way he treated her when they'd first met.

"You promised you'd show me the Porsche one day," Gabrielle said. There was a petulant tone to her voice Sunny didn't like. "I want to go for a ride."

"Not now. Maggie will be home soon."

"Just a quick trip around the block." She put her arms around Sunny and nibbled at the skin on her neck. Sunny shivered.

"Not here." She pushed Gabrielle away gently. "I'll just show you the car, okay? We'll go for a ride another day."

Hank allowed no one but him in the Porsche, but she certainly wasn't going to pour salt in Gabrielle's wounds by saying that now. Sunny opened the carriage house door and flipped on the lights. She noticed a smell, faintly sour and rotten—dead mice, no doubt— and reminded herself to call their handyman, too.

Sunny watched as Gabrielle, grinning mischievously, peeled the cover back from the Porsche, exposing red paint and sleek lines. Gabrielle gasped.

Then she screamed.

It took Sunny a moment to understand the reason for Gabrielle's hysteria. Udele's body sat slumped against the steering wheel. Her unseeing eyes bulged from her bloated, purplish face. Dried blood was smeared across the driver's side window in the shape of a pentagram. Sunny's breath came in short, tight gasps before she, too, started to scream.

"You've really done it now, you little delinquent." Catherine hissed in Maggie's face.

She grabbed Maggie's arm and pulled her toward the door. Allison moved between the sisters. "Stop. You're going to hurt her."

"Not your problem," Catherine said. But she let her go.

Police cars lined the congressman's street, red lights slashing into a tin-colored sky. Yellow tape cordoned off part of the McBride's driveway, its cheery shade a sharp contrast to the horror it symbolized.

Allison watched a boy on a blue Colnago park his bike next to the curb and stare, eyes wide, at Maggie. She turned and caught a glimpse of a neighbor's curtain moving to the side. A set of eyes looked out at the street, taking in some rare excitement in this corner of town.

Sunny came outside. She looked gaunt, her beautiful face haggard and gray. Next to her, a dark-haired, dark-eyed woman hovered possessively. Allison wondered about her relationship to the family.

"Ms. Campbell." Sunny nodded curtly before turning her attention to her daughter. "Maggie, you're wanted inside." Her tone was brusque, and Allison was quite sure being *wanted* was not a good thing.

Catherine said, "I tried to tell you, Mother. What did you do, Maggie? You couldn't wait till after the wedding to cause more trouble?"

Catherine again grabbed Maggie and pulled her toward the open front door. Maggie's eyes searched Allison's for a few seconds before she gave in and followed her sister. Allison looked on helplessly.

Sunny had called just a half hour before, while Allison and Maggie had been playing with Brutus. She'd spoken first to Maggie, but her speech was so slurred from crying that Maggie had trouble understanding her. Maggie had handed her mobile phone to Allison, who agreed to drive Maggie right home.

On the phone, Sunny had been clear about one thing: Udele had been murdered. And it looked like another ritualistic death. With Udele dead, it seemed even Maggie's family suspected Maggie's involvement. So much for rallying around your own.

"Allison," Sunny said, "please don't try to see my daughter again. She's fragile. When Hank finds out she was with you, he'll wonder what's been going on. And now Udele. You have to see. It all looks bad."

Sunny sniffled. Catherine came back outside and took her mother's arm. Allison watched the three women go inside, Catherine and the stranger supporting Sunny on either side. Sunny was weak, that was evident. She would be little help to Maggie. And Catherine obviously didn't give a hoot about her sister. Sunny's words rang through Allison's head: *When Hank finds out she was with you, he'll wonder...*

Yes, he will. And he will blame. What was the old saying? *Fool me once, shame on you. Fool me twice, shame on me.* Hank didn't scare her. But, against her better judgment, she'd gotten herself mixed up in a murder investigation. And worse, Allison recognized that niggling feeling, that creeping, crawling gut sense, as fear. Fear for another teenager about to be caught up in the vagaries of youth and fate.

Allison headed back to her car. She knew she should run far from the McBride family. Let Maggie go...*que sera sera.* Focus on work and writing and presenting and all the things she was good at, and leave the caring for people who were better equipped to deal with the fallout. She told herself: Get in, drive, don't look back.

And she did. She pulled out of that driveway like she was escaping Satan himself, ran the first stop sign, and plowed through a yellow light. But Maggie's face, her eyes searching and pleading, stayed with her, replaced after a moment with Violet's. *Damn.* There was nothing she could do for Violet. But for Maggie there was hope. Allison thought about Maggie with Brutus, the way she risked her own neck to save a stray animal. Maggie wasn't a murderer. But Allison didn't trust a single person in Maggie's family to care more about that kid than they did about themselves, and that terrified her.

But what could she do?

The phone rang, breaking her train of thought. Caller I.D. told her it was Vaughn.

"You'd better head over to the office," he said. "I have something to show you."

Allison was about to tell him about Maggie, but something in his tone stopped her. "Is it bad?"

"Just come in. We'll talk when you get here."

TWENTY-ONE

It wasn't the worst thing. But it was bad enough.

"Sit," Vaughn said when Allison arrived at First Impressions. His manner was curt, his rage barely contained. She took the chair opposite his desk. He tossed her a copy of *Philadelphia Living*. An article was circled and a few sentences were highlighted in neon green.

Vaughn said, "Just read the highlighted portion."

Allison looked down at the paper in her hand, head pounding, and read:

> In her book, Allison Campbell says there are no nightmare clients. While that may be the case, this reporter spoke to one client who said it's Allison who is a nightmare. Catherine McBride's family hired First Impressions to work with her sister. "What we thought we were getting and what we received were two very different things," Ms. McBride said. "Allison Campbell took on a role she couldn't handle. My sister got worse, not better. In my book, she's nothing but a neatly packaged fraud." Indeed, this reporter discovered that Allison has skeletons in her own closet, including a patient who ran away and disappeared almost a decade ago. Perhaps image consulting boils down to some simple concepts, as Ms. Campbell says in her book, but it seems some jobs are too difficult for even this local wizard.

Allison read it twice, and then skimmed the rest of the article. Details about the Meadows, her humble rise to success. Violet's name was never specifically mentioned, but Allison felt no less violated for that fact.

"I knew McBride was trouble from the start," Vaughn said. "Bastard."

Allison threw the article onto Vaughn's desk and took a deep breath. She needed to think. She felt a fist-sized knot in her stomach. Udele's murder, the implication that Maggie did it, even Mia's involvement. It was all too much. And now this. If McBride continued on his campaign, he could ruin her. She could fight back with the truth, but even the mere insinuation that she was incompetent from the right people could mean *adios* in this business.

"I'm afraid that's not all." She gave Vaughn an abbreviated version of what had happened at the McBride's. "If Maggie gets charged with the murders, the McBrides have paved the way for linking this all to me. Just mention of my name next to a scandal could be disastrous for the business."

Vaughn looked skeptical. "The timing is off, Allison. You didn't even know Maggie or the McBrides when Feldman was killed."

"Won't matter. Most people won't take the time to understand the details. They'll connect my name with Maggie and the murders. This line of business is not that different from restaurants. True or not, just a rumor of rodents or bugs and a restaurant fails. We can't risk that."

Vaughn nodded his agreement. His hands were clenched by his side. He stared at Allison with concern in his eyes and said softly, "Are you going to be okay?"

Allison shrugged. "Do I get a choice?" She forced a smile. "There's just one thing I don't get."

"What's that?"

"Why does McBride hate me so much? He and Catherine seemed to take an instant dislike to me."

Vaughn reached across the desk and squeezed Allison's hand. "It's what the Allisons of the world do to the McBrides of the world. You make them feel small. And they're not used to feeling small."

Allison stared at him, unsure of his meaning.

Vaughn used his hands for emphasis. "Look, you're attractive and successful. People like McBride expect you to be superficial and vapid, too. When he found out you had a heart *and* an I.Q., it wasn't so easy to dismiss you. And you didn't kiss his ass. Then there's Maggie. She hates McBride, but likes you. And instead of becoming obedient like Hank wanted, she's started to assert herself in healthy ways. That's threatening. For folks like the McBrides, people who can't be controlled upset their whole world view."

Allison thought back to her first outing with Maggie, to the day this all started, really. Maggie had referred to her own mother as someone who does what she's told. Disdain for herself on some level? Maybe Vaughn had a point.

"I don't mean to make anyone feel small."

"Doesn't matter." Vaughn shrugged. "The harder you try to make some people feel good, the more they'll resent you for it. With certain individuals, you can never *really* win."

"I guess."

Vaughn sized her up from across the desk. "Something else is eating at you, Allison. Out with it."

"I'm that transparent?"

"Kinda."

Allison looked at her hands. Her nails were short, bitten almost to the quick, a habit she'd thought she'd broken long ago. Her head still hurt and her aching jaw told her that she was grinding her teeth again. It didn't take a PhD in psychology to know that these were all signs of stress.

"Mia and Maggie," Allison said finally. "If it's not bad enough that there's a murderer out there, two people I care about are involved."

"There's nothing you can do about that, Allison. Let it go. Focus on work. Mia's innocent."

Allison glanced at him sharply. "And Maggie?"

Quietly, he said, "I don't know."

Allison stared at him. She closed her eyes, counted to ten and focused on her breathing. Even Vaughn was questioning Maggie's innocence. Was she crazy? Was she missing something? It had happened before.

Allison stood. Her watch said it was 4:35. She could be in Mt. Joy, Pennsylvania in an hour and a half, two hours with traffic.

"Do me a favor? See if you can find out the time of Udele's death from your police contacts."

"Mia's alibi?"

Allison nodded. "The sticking point for Mia has been her whereabouts at the time of Arnie's murder. The day Udele disappeared, Jason was at Mia's. If she can prove an alibi, her name could be cleared—for that murder, at least. "

"Of course, Allison, but where are you going?"

"I have some thinking to do."

"That doesn't answer my question."

Allison grabbed her purse. "I'm going back to my professional roots, Vaughn. It's a trip I should have made a long time ago."

Night fell fast in the country. Allison pulled the Volvo through an old chain link gate, now hanging by one hinge, and onto blistered, buckled blacktop. The sun was already sinking low in the sky. Mature pines and maples danced shadows across the parking lot that once belonged to the Meadows.

Long abandoned, the Meadows had become a graveyard. The imposing building sat empty, its windows shattered behind iron bars, proof that nothing could be kept safe. Allison parked at the far side of the lot, behind the building. She climbed out of the car, traded Jimmy Choos for her running shoes, and walked toward the institution that had been such a part of her past.

Surrounded by a tall chain link fence, then acres of woods, and then farm land, the Meadows was a prison within concentric circles of green. Nature had reclaimed what she could. The roof had caved in places, and the thick branch of an oak tree speared through asphalt shingles like a knife through a body. The neat hedges had turned into wild sentries, their bristling green tentacles reaching into broken windows. Gnarled vines, bits of paper and cardboard and discarded cans had accumulated in corners. The steel-door entryway remained intact, but next to them, someone had spray painted "Love Shack" in red bubble letters. Allison shook her head. So far from the truth.

She stepped over a broken iced tea bottle and through a thicket of tall grass that had sprouted between sidewalk cracks. She stared into a broken window at the former lobby. It was empty, except for one lone chair that sat propped on three legs next to the built-in receptionist desk. On the chair was a towel soiled with black stains. Cobwebs hung from the corners of the room.

Allison closed her eyes.

The silence was overwhelming. The Meadows had been built miles from town. It took four back roads to get there, and she couldn't even hear highway noise. She opened her eyes. Over the horizon, the setting sun glimmered in vibrant shades of red and purple, but the kaleidoscope of color did nothing to soften the memories.

Somewhere overhead, a crow called. Allison heard a rustling in the overgrown shrubs that lined the building's façade. She froze, listened. A squirrel dashed out in front of her and Allison let out a long, hard breath. She pictured Violet, leaving the Meadows for the last time. Allison had watched her from a window as the teen made her way out the door and into her caseworker's car. Violet had looked back, her expression unreadable through the blur of Allison's tears.

Allison trudged alongside the old building and made her way toward the recreation center in the rear. A separate chain link gate led into a field encircled by what once had been a paved track. Like the parking lot, the gate was broken and the track was cracked and overgrown with weeds. On the other side of the track, propped up against a razor-topped fence, stood two sets of bleachers. Vines and saplings were growing between and around the metal benches, as though holding the bleachers captive. Allison made her way to that side of the rec field. She stared for a long while at those bleachers, remembering the young girl who would sit by herself on the end, refusing to play whatever sport was going on.

And Allison would join her. So she wouldn't be alone.

Allison wiped a spot on the edge of one bleacher. Night was near now. The ghost of what was once the Meadows spread out before her, she took stock of the place that robbed her of her confidence and, through Violet, had broken her heart. Allison watched a hawk swoop from a nearby tree. The odd rustling in the foliage no longer scared her. Nor did whatever memories lingered in the shadows of this forsaken place.

She thought of Violet. There was nothing she could do for her now. She thought of Maggie McBride. Maggie still had a future.

Eventually, Allison stood and made her way back toward her car. Once upon a time, she came to a crossroads and made the wrong decision. This time, she would make the right one.

TWENTY-TWO

The next afternoon, Allison was just leaving her sixth message for Sasha Feldman when Vaughn knocked on her office door. He came in and closed the door behind him.

"Still won't answer?" he said when he saw her frustration.

Allison shook her head. "Doesn't pick up, won't return my calls. I know she has a lot going on, so I feel bad disturbing her, but I expected some response."

"What are you going to do?"

"I'm going to head over there myself," Allison said. "Today if I can."

"Well, it won't be now." He pointed toward the front door. "Visitor."

Allison knew exactly who it was—and this time she wasn't surprised to hear from him. "Lieutenant Helms."

"Shall I tell him you're unavailable?"

"No." Allison sighed. "Might as well get it over with."

Vaughn escorted Helms to Allison's office a few minutes later. Today the detective wore a navy blazer and tan pants. No tie. Although his eyes shone with a certain dogged intensity, his manner was friendly. He shook Allison's hand and sat in the chair across from her.

"Thanks for seeing me without notice, Allison. This will only take a few minutes." He pulled a notebook and pen out of his coat pocket. "I'd like to talk about Maggie McBride." He looked up. "How long have you known her?"

Allison thought. It felt like forever. "Almost a month."

"How would you categorize your relationship?"

"Professional."

"She seems to consider you a friend."

Despite herself, Allison smiled. "Did Maggie say that?"

Helms nodded.

Allison shrugged. "We share a dog." He gave her a quizzical look, and Allison gave him an abbreviated version of how Brutus came to be in both of their lives. She watched his face for a reaction, but he remained impassive. He wrote something in his notebook.

Helms said, "Any signs of violence from Maggie?"

"Absolutely not."

"A temper? Fits of rage?"

Allison shook her head.

"Has Maggie told you she practices witchcraft?"

"Yes. Wicca."

"And that she believes in black magic?"

"She didn't say that specifically."

"What *did* she say?"

Allison took a moment to think. Mostly, Allison had dismissed whatever she said as the babblings of a teenager searching for identity. Allison said, "Not much. We didn't really get into it."

The Lieutenant frowned. "Are you aware that Maggie kept a knife in her room?"

That came as a surprise to Allison. "No."

"Udele Daldier was killed with a knife."

For some reason, it was odd hearing Udele's last name. She had always been simply Udele to Maggie and her family. It struck Allison that Udele Daldier had a past and a life and, probably, dreams and hopes bigger than running the McBride household. Udele had not been particularly friendly to Allison, but nevertheless, Allison felt a pang of sorrow for the fact that whatever Udele Daldier wanted out of life, it was not to be.

"The same knife?"

The Lieutenant simply stared at her. "Ms. Campbell, do you understand what a troubled girl Maggie McBride is?"

"Maybe having everyone refer to her as troubled is part of the problem."

Helms stood and walked over to Allison's book shelf. He took his time perusing the books on the shelf before saying, "Did Maggie ever mention spells, curses, that sort of thing?"

"Do you think Udele died because of a curse, Lieutenant?"

He turned abruptly. "Please. Just answer the question."

Allison took in his demeanor: all business. Lieutenant Helms had reason to be worried. It didn't look good to have had a second murder go down on the Main Line under his watch, especially with the first one still unsolved. But worry could turn to desperation—and desperation into a witch hunt. Allison decided for Maggie's sake to play along.

"No, no curses, Lieutenant. I think Maggie was mostly playing at the witchcraft. For a reaction. But she certainly wasn't out to harm anyone."

The Lieutenant stuck the end of his pen in his mouth, bit down on it, and gave her a condescending smirk. "You believe that?"

"Yes." Allison bristled. "Besides, Wiccan is a peaceful religion. It's not the same as devil worshipping."

"But it's a slippery slope. What begins as interest in the occult can broaden, deepen, especially if fueled by anger or illness." Helms shrugged. "We've seen it before. It's not that big a leap."

Allison studied him. His eyes had softened until they had the look of sad resignation. She was sure he'd seen the worst of what humanity had to offer. Of course, to him, the leap from Wiccan to more sinister occult interests wouldn't seem so huge. But Allison didn't agree. "Look, Lieutenant," she said, "I really have nothing to add to this conversation. I've known Maggie for a few weeks. She has an attitude, perhaps—"

"Perhaps? She's the most recalcitrant kid I've ever had the misfortune to work with. She has a record, you know. Shoplifting. Loitering."

"That doesn't make her a killer."

"Has she told you anything about school? About her relationships with other kids?"

"I know she's been in trouble a few times."

"It's a little more serious than that. She was suspended for threatening to kill another student."

Allison paused. "Kids make threats all the time. That doesn't mean anything."

"With references to the devil, Ms. Campbell? She threatened this other student with a letter written in what she claimed was blood." His eyes widened. "Now I ask you, is *that* normal kid stuff?"

After the Lieutenant left, Allison walked back to find Vaughn. There was so much she didn't know about Maggie. Why hadn't the McBrides mentioned more about Maggie's school problems? Were they afraid telling her everything would scare her away? Probably. But even so, she'd been owed the truth. Suspension—and near expulsion—from school, psychiatric counseling, anger management classes.

What had Lieutenant Helms said? The fight between her and the other student had started over a boy. And not just any boy: Ethan Feldman. Was there a connection between the letter and Arnie's death? The police thought so. Feldman had forbidden Ethan to see Maggie after that. He'd called the school and demanded that the teens be kept separated during school hours. He'd threatened a restraining order if she continued to call their home.

Any kid would be upset. Arnie Feldman's actions, though perhaps understandable, would have been humiliating, especially to an emotionally unstable teen. But would they have been enough to cause Maggie to kill him?

She'd read between the lines Lieutenant Helms had drawn for her. From his perspective, Maggie killed Feldman as vindication for trying to keep her and Ethan apart. It was a logical step given the threats she'd made in the past.

Allison considered what she knew of Maggie. Difficult? Yes. Antisocial? Perhaps. On the surface anyway. Capable of murder? No. Allison had experienced Maggie's moodiness, her unwillingness to please, her desire to get in those little painful jabs. But she'd also seen her smile, had watched her protect her mother and save a dog no one else bothered to help. The kid had a caring side. Not the profile of someone incapable of empathy.

Unless it was all an act.

Allison had been fooled before. She thought of Violet, at the shock of finding out that Violet had run away to be with Sparky. At the shock of realizing how very, very wrong she could be about people.

Was she wrong here? Was Maggie simply playing her? This was bigger than running away. Murder took a brutality of character she didn't think she could miss. But Maggie was fifteen. Teenagers' brains were still developing. They often made decisions without considering consequences, focusing only on their immediate desires.

But these murders, for Allison had no doubt that the murders of Udele and Arnie were connected, didn't seem like impulse kills. Rather, they seemed calculated. And anyone who knew Maggie would know of her interest in the occult. Between that and her personality, Maggie was an easy target.

Further support for Allison's burgeoning theory: someone was framing Maggie.

But if Maggie was innocent, *who* had killed Arnie Feldman? And, even more baffling, who would want to kill Udele too?

Vaughn didn't agree. "All roads lead to Maggie, Allison. That's the sad truth." They were in the client room, straightening-up after the long day. Allison was pooped. She sank into a chair and focused her attention on Vaughn.

"Then all the roads are leading in the wrong direction."

"Okay, then, let's play whodunit. We know Mia is off the hook, at least for Udele's murder. Coroner puts time of death sometime in the morning between nine and noon and Mia was volunteering at the local soup kitchen. Has three witnesses who will swear to it. So how about Hank McBride?"

"Why would he frame his own daughter?"

"Maybe he wants her out of the picture. What better way to make that happen?"

Vaughn stacked catalogues and put away files as they spoke. He was art in motion. She watched him, not even trying to hide her skepticism. "How so?"

He put down the file he was holding and took the seat across from her. "McBride wants a seat in the Senate. What if Arnie Feldman had something on him? He had to get rid of him. Both Feldman and Maggie stood in his way. There was one way of getting both of them out of the picture and grabbing some public sympathy."

Allison said, "Go on."

"He paints himself as the poor father with a psychiatrically ill daughter. He does everything to help her. Hires professionals. Even hires a popular image consultant to work with her. Nothing works. In fact, things get worse. It isn't his fault."

Allison said, "It's too risky. There are easier ways to get rid of someone. Why would you purposefully bring the police into your own house? And that's assuming Feldman had something on McBride. We don't know that, although it's worth exploring." She put her head in her hands, squeezing her skull as though the pressure would keep the looming headache at bay. "The fact is, we don't know much of anything."

"True enough. From what you've said, all this conjecture might be moot," Vaughn said. "They haven't arrested Maggie, but it sounds like it's just a matter of time."

"We need to know more about Feldman. What he was working on, who his clients were. Something tells me if we understand why he was murdered, our questions about Udele may be answered as well."

"Sasha Feldman's a must. And Arnie's ex-wife, Brenda."

Allison nodded. "Makes sense. I'll visit Sasha, you take Brenda. Between you and Jason, we should be able to pull together basic info."

Something the lieutenant said was niggling at the corners of Allison's mind. The knife. The crime scenes. The pentagram. Maggie's necklace. She needed to understand the significance of Wicca and how it fit into this.

"I think we should also explore Wicca. I'll do some Internet research on witchcraft and local covens to see what I can find out."

Vaughn looked at her. "Are you thinking that the real killer is part of that world?"

"Maybe. Or maybe the real killer knew enough about it to frame Maggie and Ethan. Either way, it's worth researching."

He seemed to consider this. "Why don't you let me handle the Internet stuff? I have a friend who's a computer genius. He's kind of bored right now. He may be able to track down the local covens."

Allison felt hopeful. It *would* save her hours in front of a computer. And she was no computer genius. "You trust this friend?"

Vaughn nodded.

If Vaughn trusted him, Allison would trust him, too. She thought of another detail that Maggie had told her, one she'd forgotten to share with Lieutenant Helms. "Maggie said her witch name was Lanomia. I have no idea if that will help, but it might."

"I'll be sure to pass that along."

"Thank you. And thank your friend."

Vaughn looked away, but not before she saw the shadow that fell across his face. "I will."

"You don't really think Maggie was involved, do you, Vaughn?"

"I don't know. It is still a little *too* neat," he said after a moment, the shadow gone as quickly as it had appeared. "The more I consider it, the more I think the biggest defect in the police's logic is the most basic reason of all."

"Which is?"

"Premeditated murder takes planning and foresight. When was the last time you met a teenager who could organize her closet, much less orchestrate two cold-blooded killings?"

TWENTY-THREE

The Feldman home was a newly-built architectural stew of modern American, French Colonial and English Tudor, culminating with a three-car garage. The neighborhood abutted two streets of older Main Line estates without so much as a nod to their formal grace. Like the Feldman residence, the other houses on their street marked an identity crisis of style. But all the houses had one thing in common: size. Allison didn't think any were under 5,000 square feet, and that was probably a conservative estimate. Things were bigger on this side of the neighborhood.

Clearly, Arnie had been good at his job.

Allison rang the doorbell. She heard a yippy dog barking, but no one answered. She rang again. Her watch read 8:08. Rudely early for an image consultant; perfect timing for an investigator hoping to catch someone at home.

After a few minutes, the door opened slightly. Allison saw a pair of squinting eyes looking at her from the other side of the chain-locked door. A Chihuahua's pink face poked its way through the crevice, cradled in the woman's hands.

"Mrs. Feldman?" Allison wedged the front of one red pump in the door, cringing at the thought of marred leather. "May I speak to you? Please? It will only take a few minutes."

Sasha stared at her through the opening.

"I know it's early," Allison said, "but I was hoping to catch you before you left for the day. I'm Allison Campbell. Do you remember me?"

The woman squinted, nodded, her eyes slowly widening in recognition. "Of course. What do you need, Allison?"

"Just to talk. About your husband." Allison flashed an apologetic smile. "I can explain if you let me in. I tried calling first, but—"

"I've been busy." Sasha hesitated for a moment before unlatching the chain lock. Allison followed her into a spacious foyer. A round table sat in the entryway, on it a multi-colored Chinese vase too big for the circumference of the small table, and a set of brightly-patterned Russian nesting dolls. The foyer had been painted a deep red; the carpeted floor was white. Small stains dotted the rug. The house smelled of cloying floral perfume and cinnamon room spray.

Allison took a sideways look at the woman in front of her. Sasha Feldman was short, maybe five feet tall, and wore Lycra shorts and a sports bra that accentuated a slender, sculpted figure—including a good dose of surgical enhancement. Her long hair was pulled away from her face with a teal headband. Despite the cosmetic transformation, everything about her was harsh: overly-square fingernails, sharp chin, long, chiseled nose, even the stony look in her eyes. She certainly didn't *look* like the grieving widow.

Allison remembered Arnie Feldman. Significantly older than Sasha, balding, with small tortoiseshell glasses and a lipless smile. Had Sasha been the trophy wife, or had there been love between them? She was having difficulty picturing them together based on appearances. But then, appearances could be deceiving.

The Chihuahua snuggled against Sasha's chest, managing to look simultaneously indignant and frightened. Sasha stroked the dog's head.

"My personal trainer is on his way here," Sasha said. "I don't have much time."

Sasha sashayed through a narrow archway and into the living room. Allison tried to take in the layout of the house, picturing in her mind how an intruder would get in. The house was a maze of interconnected rooms, each one contained and claustrophobic. She had to admit that she had no idea what ingresses and egresses lurked behind these walls.

"You can sit over there." Sasha pointed to a leather couch the color of sand. The whole room was sand-colored, except for an abstract oil painted in viscous strokes of crimson and orange..

Sasha cleared her throat.

Allison said, "You're probably wondering why I'm here—"

Sasha simply stared at her. The dog stared at her, too. Allison shifted in her seat, feeling suffocated by Sasha's overwhelming perfume and the awkward stillness. She waited it out, though, understanding all too well the power of silence.

Finally, Sasha said, "How can I help you?"

"I'm so sorry for your loss. This must be an extremely difficult time for you."

"I don't think you came here to tell me that, Allison." Sasha said the words without a hint of malice or emotion—just a flat matter-of-factness that Allison found even more unsettling.

"I'm here because of what happened to Arnie, Sasha. My mother-in-law was a client of Arnie's. She's understandably concerned that certain, well, uncomfortable information about her divorce could make it into the public forum."

The dog growled, a pathetic sound from deep within its skinny throat. Sasha's perfume assaulted Allison in waves, sickly sweet and nauseating. She held back a sneeze.

Sasha picked at a loose thread on her shorts. "I don't understand."

"Because of the police investigation. Records will be reviewed. Information could leak out."

Sasha said, "The police aren't focused on Arnie's clients, so she doesn't have to worry. They know who did it."

It was Allison's turn to play dumb. "Really?"

Sasha huffed impatiently. "Ethan's little whore of a girlfriend. With Ethan's help."

Allison feigned surprise. "His own son?"

Sasha shrugged. "I know it's hard to believe. I didn't want to accept it, either." Sasha ran her long, manicured fingernails down the dog's back, leaving little trails of fur like garden furrows. "He's almost a son to me. But the evidence was huge. Gi-normous."

Allison cringed. Vaughn's voice rang out in her head: once you establish your reason for being there, just keep her talking until you get what you need. Proud of her new-found ability with one-word sentences, Allison said, "Really? How?"

"The crime scene: a silver cup, a parallelogram like Maggie wears around her neck. Knives. An upside down crucifix. And there was no breaking and entering," she said. "So the police think it was someone who lived here. And I didn't do it, so that leaves Ethan."

Allison fought back the desire to say "pentagram, not parallelogram." And she wondered what Sasha meant by "silver cup." A chalice? She asked, "Did Arnie try to get away?"

"He couldn't. His hands and mouth were bound with duct tape."

"How could two kids overpower a grown man?"

"Surprise. Have you met Ethan? He's a bull." Sasha looked down at the dog. "And Maggie's a witch. Literally. All along we thought maybe she was just a devil bunny. You know, one of those teens who thinks it's cool to be into Goth and worship Satan? Stuff she'd grow out of. Boy were we wrong."

Allison thought for a moment. "Does anyone else have the security code, Sasha?"

"Now that would be plain stupid, wouldn't it? Of course not."

"Maybe someone arrived and Arnie let him in?"

Allison knew she was grasping at nothing, but Sasha was so blasé about all of this. For a woman who was recently widowed, she certainly didn't appear bereft. And if Ethan was like a son to her, wouldn't she be defending him, maybe even trying to prove he hadn't murdered his father? But Sasha Feldman seemed to take it all in stride, like she would a broken shoe strap or a missed Bloomingdale's sale.

"No. Impossible. Look, Arnie was a busy man. He had few friends outside of work. I was his life. No one came to the house. As I said, I didn't do it, and my Arnie did not kill himself. That leaves Ethan. And that little slut he hangs out with."

Allison remembered Vaughn's words: *All roads lead to Maggie.*

"Did anyone hold a grudge against Arnie that you knew of? A client?"

Sasha snorted. "He was a divorce attorney. Everybody he went up against held a grudge against him."

"Anyone threaten him?"

"What are you, the police? I don't know. Like I told that lieutenant someone-or-other, Arnie didn't talk about work. When he came home, he liked to have a drink, relax."

"What can you tell me about Ethan's relationship with the McBride girl?"

Sasha laughed, but it was a bitter, mean sound. "I'd hardly call it a relationship. Maggie McBride is a witch. Literally. Ethan is no angel, certainly, but together...they had no regard for authority."

"When did they start dating?"

Sasha rolled her eyes. "Like a year ago, maybe? Two? I don't know, exactly. I'm not the family secretary. Does it really matter?"

"When was the last time Maggie was here?"

"With Arnie's permission? About four months ago. Without Arnie's permission? Who knows. The night he was killed, probably."

"Why did you forbid Ethan to see Maggie?"

"The Jacuzzi incident was the last straw. Arnie found them together." Sasha's lips twisted into a look of disgust that gave no doubt as to what *together* meant.

"You said 'the last straw.' Were there prior incidents?"

Sasha twisted on the ottoman and glanced at her watch. She didn't answer.

Allison decided to help things along. "Letters, Sasha? Did you know anything about Maggie getting suspended at school for sending threatening letters?"

Sasha nodded. "Sure. Ethan was in the middle of that, too. Troublemaker. I wish to God Arnie had left the brat with Brenda."

"The letters?"

"Yes, those." She sighed and then picked at the dog's rhinestone-studded collar. The Chihuahua sat shivering on her lap. Allison thought it looked like a hairless rat. It made Brutus look cute.

"Maggie thought another girl was after Ethan. She sent her a series of letters threatening some sort of mumbo-jumbo curse if the girl didn't lay off."

"Anything else about the letters?"

Sasha nodded. "Little witch. She deserves to rot in prison. What do the Scriptures say? 'Thou shalt not suffer a witch to live.' She's a bad kid, like I said."

"How about her father, Hank McBride? Did Hank and Arnie get along?"

"Hardly." Sasha scowled. "Although frankly, they agreed on one thing. Their kids should stay away from each other. Far away."

"Did Hank and Arnie have any other contact? Maybe business dealings?"

"My Arnie was a divorce attorney," Sasha said in a tone that suggested that Allison was stupid for even asking. "The McBrides are married."

"Golf? Country club?"

"You mean did they hang out socially?" Sasha shook her head. "They traveled along different paths, if you know what I mean. McBride thought he was too good for my Arnie."

Allison heard a car pull into the driveway and said quickly, "Who was the other girl, Mrs. Feldman? The one Maggie sent the letter to. Do you remember?"

Sasha stood up and placed the shaking dog on the ground. It ran up to Allison, just out of her reach, and growled. In a high-pitched, baby-talk voice, Sasha said, "Now, now, Muffin, behave."

"The other girl, Sasha? Do you know who she was?"

She looked up from the dog. "Of course. She and Ethan hung out for a while. She was here all the time."

Patience, Al. "Can you tell me her name?"

With the same bored tone, Sasha said, "Sarah Moore."

Why did that name sound familiar? With a sudden flash, Allison remembered being at the mall with Maggie during their first session together. Two girls and a mother. Rude teenagers, a mortified Maggie. Her reaction made sense now.

She said, "As in the daughter of Desiree Moore?"

"One and the same." Sasha looked out the window. "If you'll excuse me, my trainer is here. I have some serious work to do on my abs."

Allison said, "Thanks for your time."

Sasha twisted her lips into a smile. "Remember me when you write your next book." She turned, gracing Allison with a side view, and flexed her bicep, which was toned and defined. "Maybe you could write about Main Line moms who stay in shape."

Back in the car, Allison called Vaughn. She wanted to hear the results of his conversation with Brenda and wondered whether the ex-wife could shed some light on Ethan and Maggie's involvement. But when she opened her phone, to her surprise, there was a text message from Maggie.

Things bad here. Luv 2 Brutus. U2. – Mags

Touched, all judgment out the window, Allison texted her back: *Hang in there, kid. Brutus misses U2.* She hoped it was good for a smile. Then she called Vaughn.

"The ex-wife refused to see me," Vaughn said, frustrated.

"Did she say why?"

"No."

"Did she say anything?"

"Slammed the door in my face. That count?"

Allison watched the young, built, and very male personal trainer as he talked with Sasha on the front step. The two disappeared inside the Feldman house. "Well, Ethan is her son. I imagine she's not going to be too sympathetic to our problems. She's got bigger fish flopping around in her pan."

Vaughn muttered something that sounded like agreement. Then he said, "Mia!"

"Mia?"

"Let's send Mia. We should have thought of that before."

Catching on to his reasoning, Allison said, "Of course. Brenda was her client. And Mia can sympathize on a level that neither of us can. But do you think Brenda will talk to her? And will Mia agree to go?"

"Worth a shot."

Allison started her car. Mia's house was almost an hour away at this time of day, but Allison could use the time alone to clear her head. "I'll drive out there. Can you shuffle my schedule?"

"Consider it done." Vaughn cleared his throat. "Aren't you forgetting to tell me something?"

"You want to know about Sasha Feldman?"

"Be nice, seeing as how I just got a door slammed in my face and all. I hope you had more luck than I did."

"I did, actually." As she wove her way through the morning traffic, Allison relayed her conversation with Sasha. "Either she's still in shock, or she's one cold-hearted lady. My gut says the latter."

"Drugs? Maybe tranquilizers?"

Allison thought about Sasha's demeanor. "Not that I could tell."

"Had she ever met the Moore parents?"

"I didn't have a chance to ask."

"So now that we know who Maggie wrote the letter to, one of us should pay a visit to the Moore household."

Allison agreed. "I'll do it."

"Then let me do some research on the Moores so you have some background. And while you're chatting with Mia, I'll check in with my computer expert to see what he's discovered about local covens."

TWENTY-FOUR

An hour later, Vaughn pushed open the door to his apartment and was met with a sobering, still darkness. For a moment, he felt a catch in his breath, the anxiety over the recent Main Line murders mingling with his ever-present fears for his brother. He forced himself to breathe. You're losing it, man, he told himself.

Walking through the darkened living room, he became aware of the scents of cornbread and spices, the faint but comforting sounds of Mrs. T. in the kitchen. Here, at least, all was as it should be.

"Hello," he called.

"In here, Christopher!" Unlike everyone else in his life, she refused to call him Vaughn. *That's no Christian name,* she'd said, *and you are a good Christian gentleman.*

Yeah, right. He walked through the hall and into the small galley kitchen.

"No orange juice, no milk. How is a young man like yourself supposed to survive on coffee and peanut butter?"

Mrs. T didn't even give him a chance to respond. He watched as she picked up a carton of Ensure and poured it into a glass for Jamie. Then she popped a flexible straw in the glass.

"You take care of your brother better than you care for yourself. Well, I won't be a party to it, Christopher Darnell Vaughn. Uh-uh. I made you some chili, cornbread, and a nice, fresh salad. None of that store-bought stuff." She poked Vaughn in the ribs with a thick finger. "You need to find a lady to fatten you up."

"I don't think any lady will want a part of my crazy world." He smiled. "Anyway, I have you."

Mrs. T made a face. "You just need to find the right lady. That brother of yours is special, workin' legs or not, and don't you ever go feelin' sorry for yourself. God don't make no waste. Jamie's mind's as sharp as my Granny's sewing needle, and let me tell you, that's sharp." She rubbed her ample backside. "I've had Granny's needle jabbed down where the sun don't shine once or twice, so I would know." She chuckled. "Sit down."

"I'm only here for a minute, Mrs. T. I have to talk to Jamie."

She frowned and jerked her head toward Jamie's bedroom. "Go on, then. He'll be happy for the company. Been working on that darn computer like a madman all afternoon."

Vaughn turned to go but turned back to give Mrs. T a kiss on the cheek.

She grinned and waved him away. "Now, now, what was that for?"

Vaughn said, "Just 'cause."

Vaughn found Jamie intently focused on the computer. The lights in his room were dim, but the small overhead lamp that Jamie could turn on via a thin cord that dangled by his head shined down on the keyboard.

"How did you make out, Jamie?"

Jamie took his mouth off the piece that allowed him to work the computer and smiled.

"That good, huh?"

Jamie manipulated the mouthpiece and Vaughn walked over to the large computer monitor. He read: YOU WOULD BE SURPRISED BY THE NUMBER OF WITCHES IN THE AREA. OKAY, MAYBE YOU WOULDN'T BE SURPRISED.

Vaughn smiled at Jamie's attempt at humor. Vaughn wished he could treat this man on the bed the way he knew his brother wanted to be treated: like a man. But guilt always got in the way.

Jamie said: LANOMIA BELONGS TO A COVEN IN WAYNE. THE OTHER MEMBERS LIKED HER IN THE BEGINNING, BUT NO ONE REALLY SEEMS TO KNOW HER WELL.

Vaughn sat on the edge of the bed. "Why?"

Jamie's response read: SHE NEVER ATTENDS CEREMO-NIES. MOST OF HER INVOLVEMENT IS OVER THE WEB. SHE LEARNED RITUALS, RECEIVED INFORMATION ABOUT THEIR CALENDAR, INCENSE. FOUND SUPPORT. THEY ONLY MET HER A FEW TIMES WHEN SHE FIRST JOINED.

"That makes sense. Her father had forbidden her to attend. She was doing this on the sly." Vaughn considered what Jamie was saying. "How'd you learn all this?"

I PRETENDED TO BE A WITCH. ASKED AROUND ABOUT LANOMIA. AT FIRST, NO ONE WOULD TELL ME MUCH. BUT EVENTUALLY THEY OPENED UP. IT TOOK ME AN ENTIRE MORNING JUST TO LOCATE THE COVEN. YOU KNOW WOM-EN. He caught Vaughn's eye. THEY LIKE TO GOSSIP, WITCH OR NOT.

Vaughn laughed. "True enough, my brother." He walked closer to the bed. "What else did you learn?"

SOUNDS LIKE HER PERSONALITY CHANGED. HER EMAILS SEEMED ANGRY SOME OF THE TIME. SHE'D WAFFLE BETWEEN BEING A MODEL WICCAN AND TALKING ABOUT BLACK MAGIC. THEN, ABOUT A MONTH AGO, THERE WAS DISCUSSION ABOUT KICKING HER OUT OF THE COVEN. FOR ASKING ABOUT THINGS THAT ARE FORBIDDEN BY THE WIC-CAN RELIGION.

"Like what?"

EVIL SPELLS. BLACK MAGIC. SATAN-WORSHIPPING.

This was going from bad to horrible real quick. Poor Allison. She really believed in this kid. "So what the police are saying makes sense that Maggie's interest in the occult led to something darker?"

Jamie leaned his head back on the pillow and took a deep breath.

"If it's too much right now, Jamie, we can talk about this later."

Jamie opened his mouth, and then closed it again, as though stretching his jaw muscles. He took the controller back in his mouth and said: SOMETHING DOESN'T ADD UP. THE TIME-LINE. IMPORTANT.

Vaughn stood up. This was tiring Jamie out, and he should make his brother stop. But Jamie's eyes glowed with an enthusiasm he hadn't seen in years.

"What is it, Jamie?"

Jamie closed his eyes. Vaughn could hear the clatter of Mrs. T cooking in the kitchen. She was humming something to herself, loudly. A cinnamon candle burned on the bedside table, blending with the earthy scent of cumin and the faint, stale aroma of sickbed.

Jamie opened his eyes again and grabbed hold of the mouthpiece with his teeth.

MAGGIE DID MOST OF HER INTERACTING ON THE WEB. THE OTHER MEMBERS SAID HER PERSONALITY WAS INCONSISTENT. THIS COULD MEAN MAGGIE CHANGED.

"That's not good. It could fit with the police's theory."

TRUE. Jamie paused. OR IT COULD MEAN THERE WAS MORE THAN ONE MAGGIE.

"An impersonator?"

THERE IS NO REAL PRIVACY ON THE WEB. ALL YOU NEED IS THE RIGHT ADDRESSES, HER WICCAN NAME. THESE WITCHES TALKED TO ME, A FREAKING CRIPPLE. WHO KNOWS WHO ELSE INFILTRATED THEIR COVEN.

Vaughn flinched at the word cripple. But Jamie was right. In a matter of a few hours and the right code name, he had been able to get this much info on Maggie.

Jamie cleared his throat so Vaughn would look at the screen. It read:

DO YOU SEE? IT'S POSSIBLE SOMEONE PRETENDED TO BE LANOMIA. SOMEONE WHO WANTED TO FRAME MAGGIE MCBRIDE.

TWENTY-FIVE

It felt like a scene from *Little House on the Prairie*. Allison drove up the long driveway, along nearly a mile of fenced-in fields, past terraced gardens, a small flock of sheep, and a few wandering goats. *Goats*. She tried to picture the old Mia raising livestock, but couldn't do it. Not even a dog.

Closer to the house, Allison made out what looked like a chicken coop next to the old barn, which had been given a fresh coat of red paint. The small house had also been painted. It was now a pleasant white, with dark green trim. Stone steps wound their way from the driveway to the house, leading up to a porch door. Mia had planted flower beds everywhere: around the barn, near the house, along the drive. The whole thing was quaint. Lovely, really.

But not what she expected.

When Mia had first purchased the place, it seemed remote, removed from the events that had transpired in Mia's life. Allison understood that. But she guessed she'd expected Mia to wave her magic wand over the property and make the old house, the crumbling old barn, disappear—to recreate her old life out here in the country. Instead, Mia had simply restored everything to some semblance of yesteryear.

Allison pulled alongside a stone wall and clicked the car into park. A brown and white dog ran up to the Volvo to greet her, his rear end swaying back and forth from the frantic movement of his tail.

From the house, Mia called, "Buddy!" The front door opened, and Mia emerged. She wore jeans and a gray fisherman's sweater and was waving a blue checkered dishtowel at the dog. "Buddy! Enough!"

When she saw it was Allison, Mia smiled. Then, suddenly, her smile disappeared. "Everything okay?" she said as she neared the car.

Allison had rolled down her window, reluctant to get out of the car. She recognized the dog's rapid tail movements as a sign of canine-happiness, but she wasn't sure if the dog was happy to have her company or happy to have the chance to eat her, and she wasn't taking any chances. Finally, thinking again of Brutus, she climbed out of the vehicle but kept a wary eye on the mutt.

"Everything is fine, Mia." She clutched her purse to her chest, back against the Volvo, and tried not to look Buddy in the eye. It was no use. The more she avoided him, the more excited he was to see her. He pressed his side against her legs and gave a sharp bark.

"He's friendly," Mia said.

"I'll take your word for it." Allison patted his head, which Buddy reacted to with increased pressure on her hand and even stronger gyrations. Allison laughed. "Some watchdog."

Mia grabbed the dog by the collar and pulled him toward the house. "He just sort of showed up here about a year ago. What could I do?" she shrugged. "Come on inside."

Allison followed Mia, curious, despite her sense of urgency, to see the inside.

"I'd give you a tour, but it would last about ten seconds."

They walked through a small, utilitarian kitchen and into a hallway lined with pictures of Bridget and Jason. From there, they entered a spacious living room with a wall-length mantel and a deep stone fireplace at one end and a bank of windows on the other. Mia had placed simple brown plaid couches, facing each other, and an oversized cocoa-colored chair in the center, atop a patterned wool rug. Books, gardening magazines, and newspapers littered the wooden chest that doubled as a table in the center of everything. Allison sank into the couch, which was as comfortable as it looked.

"A little different from my old house, aye?"

"Just a bit."

Mia laughed. She wore her hair loose today, and curls framed her face. Even without make-up, her skin looked fresh and well-scrubbed. Next to her, Allison felt fussy and overdressed in a black pants suit, silk blouse and red sling backs.

"This place. It's beautiful," Allison said.

"I think you mean that." Mia tilted her head and jutted her chin out in a gesture that made her look almost girlish. "I'm not as crazy as Edward made me out to be?"

"I never thought you were crazy."

Mia stretched, her posture as impeccable as ever, and smiled warmly. "I figure you have an agenda, Allison. So out with it."

Allison swallowed, unsure where to start.

Mia gave her an encouraging nod. "You didn't come all the way out here to talk about me. I'm guessing it has to do with the McBride girl and the Feldman murder? Based on our previous conversation, it sounds like you've traded in your tape measure and three-by-five cards for a magnifying glass and a pipe."

Allison laughed. "Something like that." She brought Mia up to speed on Sasha Feldman, on Maggie's text message, on Brenda's refusal to speak with Vaughn.

"So you want me to talk to Brenda?"

Relieved that Mia had beat her to the punch, Allison nodded. "Will you?"

Mia was silent for a moment. She seemed far away, as though she was thinking about something else altogether. The wind outside rattled the bank of windows, a cacophony of sound in the quiet of Mia's home. Mia didn't seem to notice.

"I'll do it, Allison," she said. "Under one condition."

Allison nodded for her to continue.

"You're playing with fire, but I don't see that you have much choice, frankly. If the police nail Maggie for this, her father will make sure you suffer, too. He's a spiteful bastard. I saw that newspaper article. It was a warning."

"Agreed."

"If I speak with Brenda, I want you to be careful. Keep Vaughn involved. And you," she said, pointing at Allison, "you should never have texted Maggie. You've let yourself get attached to that girl. No more contact, understand? You need me, Allison. If for no other reason than to be the voice of reason."

Allison recognized the truth in Mia's words. But Maggie needed her. She would be damned if another young woman was going to have her life ruined on her watch. If this was the only way to get Mia's help, so be it. Reluctantly, she said, "Deal."

Mia stood. "I'll go see Brenda. I'll try to get out there today."

Allison followed back toward the kitchen. Mia stopped short in front of a room off the small hall, near the living room.

"Your office?" Allison asked.

"My bedroom. Want to see it?"

"Sure."

Mia led her into a small room. Bed neatly made and covered with a handmade patchwork quilt and coordinating pillows. Full-length, wrought-iron mirror. Two Shaker-style dressers. A matching bedside table. The room was painted celadon. Cheerful green, blue, and butter-colored curtains hung from the windows. Like the rest of the house, the room looked understated, warm, and immaculately clean.

"Beautiful," Allison said, and meant it.

"Thanks," Mia said, already back in the hallway.

Allison started to follow, but something on the bedside table caught her eye. It was a man's watch, tucked up against a box of tissues and a worn copy of *The Red Tent*. So Mia's not *completely* alone, Allison thought, and smiled. *You go, girl.*

TWENTY-SIX

Although it was Mia's intention to visit Brenda Feldman later that same day, it was a full two days before she could bring herself to drive there. She opted not to call first, afraid she'd be refused. She wouldn't have blamed her. Mia may have acted nonchalant about Allison's request, but in actuality, she felt uneasy. Brenda Feldman was part of her past. Mia doubted Brenda wanted to be reminded of her own failures any more than Mia did.

Mia stood in front of Brenda's door and waited. She'd knock, eventually. For now, she was taking in the property, all Brenda got out of twelve years of marriage to the late Arnie Feldman. It was a small ranch house on the outskirts of Paoli, in a neighborhood of split levels, ranches, and bi-levels. A short, steep driveway ran alongside the house and ended next to a small patio adorned with cheap plastic furniture. An overflowing ashtray lay atop the table.

A dog barked somewhere nearby. Mia could smell mesquite—an early spring barbeque. Neighborhood sounds, neighborhood smells. This reminded her of her old house, her old neighborhood, and for a second she felt a pang of longing she thought she'd quashed long ago. She knocked, suddenly impatient to be done with this. No answer. She knocked again.

A car sat in the driveway, an older model Honda Accord, and Mia assumed it belonged to Brenda. She raised her hand to knock again when the door swung open and Mia found herself face-to-face with a young man, maybe fifteen or sixteen. He was tall and husky, with wiry brown curls, vibrant blue eyes, and lips that seemed too full for his face. When he opened his mouth to speak, metal glistened. Not the invisible braces most kids wore these days. Ethan had some serious orthodontia.

"My mom's not here."

"Her car is here."

"She went for a walk." He started to close the door, an insolent expression on his face.

Mia put her hand against the door. "Please tell your mother that Mia Campbell is here to see her."

"She's not here—"

"Save it." Mia smiled. "Look, I know she's here. I know who you are, and she'll know who I am, so let's cut the bull, Ethan. Get your mother."

The boy's eyebrows arched in surprise. He nodded and backed into a carpeted living room. "Hold on," he said.

Mia waited. It wasn't long before Ethan was back. This time, he let her in. "She's in a mood. Don't say I didn't warn you."

"Thanks for the heads-up."

Mia followed Ethan through the living room and into a small kitchen beyond. He opened a door, and together they descended steps into a finished basement. On one end stood a small, wooden bar and two worn barstools; on the other, a sectional sofa and a huge flat-screen television. Brenda Feldman sat on the sofa wearing a pink velour pantsuit. Her dyed-platinum hair was pulled back into a ponytail. Gobs of makeup did little to soften sharp features or enlarge tiny, beady eyes. She dangled one cigarette from her fingertips. Another sat unlit next to an ashtray by her side. Smoke wafted across the dim interior in a haze of gray.

"Well, well," Brenda said, her tone vitriolic. "If it isn't Mia Campbell, the queen of etiquette. What brings you here without notice? Isn't that a breach of the Miss Manners by-laws?"

Mia tensed. She could see Brenda taking her in. Mia had purposefully dressed down for the occasion: jeans, a black t-shirt, sneakers. Her own hair was pulled into a loose bun, her face was bare. She wanted to stand before Brenda humbled and honest, a change from their last meeting, nearly twelve years ago, six months after Arnie admitted to his first affair. Brenda would be nearly fifty now. And from the look of her, the years in between had not been kind.

"I'm sorry to barge in like this," she said. "But we should talk. We have some mutual interests to attend to, Brenda. And I'm coming here one mother to another. I hope you'll hear me out."

Brenda was silent for a moment. The television was blaring the Home Shopping Network and an enormous woman in a red jumpsuit was going on about the versatility of the gold chain in her hand. Ethan was still there, standing next to Mia, his eyes on his mother. Finally, Brenda said, "Sit."

Mia looked at Ethan. Brenda, understanding, pointed at the steps. "Go on, honey," she said.

Ethan lingered for a moment, then left. Mia heard the upstairs door slam shut.

Mia sat on the couch and twisted to face Brenda. Brenda was pulling another cigarette from her pack. She laid it next to the ashtray. The cigarette version of a lady-in-waiting.

"Is this about Ethan?"

"In a way," Mia said.

"What else would it be about? That's all the talk right now. Arnie's murder. How my son has been questioned in the death of his own father. A sin, all of it."

"It must be hard."

"Hard? Damn right. It's been hell. Absolute hell." Brenda stubbed out the cigarette, though she'd taken only one puff, and picked up the next one. "I hated that bastard. God, how I hated him. I'd like to say I'm sorry to see him dead, dying the way he did and all. But I'm not." She inhaled, coughed and put the lighter down on her lap. "But as in all things where Arnie was concerned, he had to make a helluva mess with his death, too. He lived to make me miserable. Why stop now?"

Mia stayed silent. What could she possibly say? When Brenda had come to her, she'd just found out that the father of her three-year-old was cheating. All Mia could offer her was a fresh color palette and a new hairstyle. Brenda had put up with two sessions and then quit, telling Mia she catered to the rich and clueless. She hadn't been wrong. That was the thing.

"So what can we do for each other, Mia?" Brenda pointed with a new, unlit cigarette. "You look different, I gotta say. Not so polished anymore. You let your hair go gray. I never figured you for a blue-hair."

Mia smiled. *Fair enough.* "I think we have a mutual interest in finding out who Arnie's real killer is, Brenda."

"It wasn't Ethan."

"I know that."

"Ain't no way a teenager did that. No damn way."

"Agreed."

"I told the cop that. He questioned me, too, you know." Brenda laughed, and the sound rang out across the low-ceilinged room, mean and bitter. "Seriously. I'd have killed that bastard years ago if I was gonna do it."

"I hated him, too."

Brenda met Mia's gaze. "Because of your divorce? I read about your daughter, you know. About the accident." She took a puff and blew it out slowly in gray concentric circles. "I was sorry."

Mia recoiled inwardly. "Thank you. I hated Arnie because of how he handled my divorce. Because he couldn't see me as a person, dying inside, and instead he used my pain to his advantage."

Brenda nodded. "Sounds like Arnie." She rose, walked to the bar, and, over her shoulder, said, "Want a drink? Scotch. Vodka. Merlot?"

"Merlot. Just a bit."

Brenda raised the bottle to the room's murky light and looked inside. "A bit's all I got." She poured Merlot into a tumbler, then a few fingers of Scotch for herself, straight up. The former she handed to Mia. She carried herself as though in pain, her slender form hunched and twisted.

Brenda must have caught her looking because she said, "Car accident. About three years ago. The old back is cranky as an Atkins dieter at a vegan buffet." She sat back down with a thud, pulled out another cigarette, and lit it. Then she pointed to the flat-screen television. "Paid for that, though." She smirked. "So what do you want to know?"

"Who else might have had it in for Arnie?"

Brenda threw her head back and let out a howl of laughter. "Who? Who *didn't* want to kill Arnie? His clients worshipped him. The rest of the world hated him. Name me a Main-Liner and I'll say if they were for or against Arnie. Seriously, Mia. That's what I keep telling the police. But they don't listen."

Mia thought about that. Motive, she knew, was prime when it came to murder investigations. Establish a motive. "Why would Ethan want Arnie dead?"

"He didn't do it, I told you," Brenda said sharply.

"I know. But why do the police seem to think he'd even *want* his dad dead?"

Brenda waved her cigarette. "They fought all the time. Over grades, school, that girl he was seeing. They're looking at her, too. Maggie McBride. The congressman's daughter. I heard they've questioned her."

Mia choked down a mouthful of the cheap Merlot. "I know who the McBride girl is."

"Well, she's another one. Doesn't follow the rules, mixed up in some satanic crap. I tell Ethan, dump her. You don't need that in your life. But he doesn't listen. Men never do."

Mia said, "Tension over grades and girls hardly sounds like motive."

"That's what I say. But the police, they say something different. They say they have evidence that links Maggie and Ethan to the crime scene. Satanic stuff. And they have no alibi. Ethan is no Satanist. A Jew, yes. He speaks Hebrew. A Satanist, no."

"How about Maggie?"

Brenda took a quick sip of Scotch and a drag on the cigarette. She blew out smoke, sat back and shrugged. "Ethan says she's a Wiccan. He says witches aren't Satan worshippers. I don't know. I'm a fallen Catholic from Northeast Philly turned Jew. I converted for Arnie." She laughed again. "What the hell do I know about religion? Squat, that's what."

Mia figured the Ethan-Maggie angle was a dead end in this conversation. The police would only disclose so much to the family and, anyway, she was looking for other leads, something beyond the obvious.

"Did Ethan have friends besides Maggie who may have had a grudge against Arnie?"

"Not that I know of."

"How about Sally Ann?"

Squinted eyes, deep frown. "My sister's dead to me."

"Think, Brenda. Were there any other clients who may have had enough of a beef to do him in? Someone close enough to the family to know about Ethan and Maggie, to know about the witch-craft?"

Brenda stared at her drink for a long time. "I only know from Ethan, mind you. Arnie and I didn't speak. But Ethan, he said his father was always on the phone with this Kenburg guy. And they talked about child abuse. A lot. In a heated sort of way. It creeped Ethan out." She put her drink down and sat forward. "You think this guy could have offed Arnie?"

Mia stood. This was something at least. "I don't know, Brenda. But I'm going to try and find out. Did this man know about Ethan...and Maggie?"

"I don't know."

"Do you know his full name?"

Brenda shook her head. "I'm lucky I remember his last." She yelled for Ethan. When he didn't answer, she screamed for him again. After a minute, Mia heard the door open and Ethan's pound-ing footsteps on the stairs.

"What?"

"You know how your dad used to talk to that child molester?"

Ethan said, "Yeah, so?"

"So what was his first name?"

"Jack."

Brenda turned toward Mia. "Hear that? Jack Kenburg."

Ethan said impatiently, "Not Kenburg. Bremburg, Ma. Jack Bremburg. He's the head of Star Oil. Dad was always complaining about him. Drove Sasha crazy." He turned his attention to Mia. "Why do you want to know, anyway?"

Before Mia could respond, Brenda said, "We know you didn't do it."

Ethan rolled his eyes. "Doesn't matter what you think, Ma. It's the police that matter."

Brenda stood and pointed her cigarette at her son. "Yeah, well, if they had enough evidence to get you, your ass would be in jail right now. So thank your lucky stars they don't, and stop being such a smart ass."

Mia walked toward the steps. She had a name. It wasn't much, but it was something. "It was good seeing you, Brenda," she said, hoping to avoid witnessing an all-out brawl between mother and son.

Brenda stopped arguing with Ethan long enough to say, "No it wasn't, Mia. But then, you always did like to pretty the truth."

TWENTY-SEVEN

Desiree Moore, the mother of the girl who received Maggie's threatening letters, agreed to meet Allison at the Ardmore Art Center, right after her one o'clock pottery class but before she had to trek across town for yoga. For Allison's part, that meant canceling a session with a wealthy, albeit neurotic, philanthropist and rescheduling her Reentering the Workforce group, but that was okay. She could feel Vaughn's edginess at taking time away from the clients, but she saw these as special circumstances. She'd do what she needed to do.

She pulled into the art center's parking lot at 12:45 and leafed through the Internet articles Vaughn had printed out for her. There wasn't much, and what there was focused mainly on Kyle, Desiree's estranged husband. Allison was grasping at straws, she knew, looking for something that would help her build a connection to this woman in the hopes she could explain what had happened with Maggie. She needed to know whether Maggie was capable of something more sinister than a few threatening letters and she couldn't shake the feeling that Desiree Moore could help her reach that understanding.

The first print-off was a short article from *Entrepreneur Magazine*, about businessmen with innovative ideas. Kyle Moore was the first featured interviewee, for his work at TECHNO, Inc. His picture was at the top, next to the byline. A tall, skinny man, he had a thick mop of flaming red hair. A large mole marked his left cheek. He wore oversized horn-rimmed glasses, which gave him an absent-minded, professorial air. There was nothing extraordinary in the substance of the article except for the date and a sentence Vaughn had highlighted for her. When asked about his success, Kyle credited his wife as both his support and inspiration. The article was dated November of the previous year. According to another piece dated two months later, Moore had separated from his wife. Next to these two highlighted facts, Vaughn had written "what's up with this" in his slanted print.

What *was* up with that? But of course, giving kudos to his wife two months before separation could mean a lot of things: a happy façade for the benefit of the business; a sudden marital issue, like an affair, that occurred in the interim; a one-sided relationship; an attempt to fix a broken marriage.

The real reason didn't matter. Allison wanted to know what happened between Maggie and Sarah. Knowing that Desiree was going through her own marital pain could only serve to give context to the events between the girls. When you're already under stress at home, additional stress seems amplified. So perhaps Desiree had overreacted to the letters. At least that was Allison's hope.

And Allison would only know if she asked.

She unbuckled her seatbelt, tucked the articles back in their envelope, which she placed under the passenger seat, and got out. It was a warm day and the sun laced through the budding maples and oaks that bordered the art center's parking lot, throwing webbed patterns on asphalt. Allison took a deep breath and made her way toward the blocky building. Desiree had wanted to meet in the vestibule, next to the iron tree sculpture. *You can't miss it*, she'd said on the phone. On her way inside, Allison's cell phone beeped. She ignored it. She wanted to be mentally prepared for this discussion, afraid, on some level, that it would prove her wrong about a child yet again.

"Allison Campbell?"

Allison had been waiting by the iron tree sculpture—and, indeed, she couldn't have missed its vast, ebony, waving branches—

for almost ten minutes when the sound of a male voice startled her. She looked up. Standing before her was a twenty-something man wearing paint-stained jeans, an NYU t-shirt, and a broad smile. He laughed. "You look startled. Sorry. I'm Jeremy." He held out his hand. Allison saw brownish material, which she assumed was clay, under his fingernails. His hands were slender, his fingers long and shapely. She returned the handshake.

"Desiree asked if you wouldn't mind talking to her in the studio. She's finishing a breakthrough piece."

Breakthrough piece? Allison searched for a hint of sarcasm in his tone, but there was none. His eyes shone green and sincere. "Desiree's a good student. I'm her instructor. She really *gets* the medium."

Allison nodded, amused.

Jeremy looked her over. "You may get splattered. I'll get you a smock."

Allison followed him through the vestibule, her heels clicking on the tile floor and echoing in the room's high walls. Paintings and ceramic sculptures lined the path. Off to the right was an entryway into a small art store. Three well-heeled women, talking and laughing, each carrying a different brightly colored Vera Bradley bag, followed three toddlers out of the shop. Somewhere behind them a baby wailed.

"Are these private lessons?" Allison asked.

"For Desiree? Yes. But I also offer group lessons."

Curious, Allison said, "Are the private lessons expensive?"

Jeremy smiled. "Depends. If you want to know the truth, I think they're outrageous. But around here," he gestured toward the three women they'd just passed, "it seems they're not. I'll get you a price sheet if you're interested."

Allison smiled. "That's okay."

Jeremy turned down a narrow hallway and then opened a heavy wooden door into a small studio. The first thing Allison noticed was the smell: pungent and earthy. The room was cold, and Allison wrapped her arms around herself to ward off the chill. Inside the room, to the left of the doorway, were shelves. Stacked on these shelves were a hodgepodge of plain clay dishes, vases, bowls, and other ceramics in various states of completion. In front of the shelves sat a square, wooden table, its surface gouged and scarred. An assortment of pottery tools, strange-looking flat knives and other items, were laid out neatly on the table next to an enormous block of clay wrapped in heavy plastic.

Across the room stood a utility sink and a potter's wheel. On a bench in front of the wheel, one foot on a pedal, sat Desiree. Her long straight hair had been pulled into a loose bun, and she wore clay-smudged jeans and a fitted white t-shirt. She was focused on a willowy vase perched on the wheel. Desiree ran a wire through its top, using two wood handles to guide the wire so that about an inch of clay was removed in one neat band. Then she used her thumbs to smooth and flatten the edge. Allison watched, fascinated, as the clay moved and writhed against the pressure of her fingers.

"Cool, huh?" Jeremy said.

Allison nodded. After a few minutes, Desiree stopped the wheel and took her hands off the piece. She looked at Jeremy, grinned, and then glanced at Allison. "So sorry," she said.

Allison said, "Not a problem. I appreciate your time."

Jeremy said, "Looks good, Desiree. Want me to take it from here?"

Desiree shook her head. "I'll clean up. Would you mind giving us a few minutes alone?"

"Sure. Let me take care of the lady here, first." Jeremy dug around in a bin next to the utility sink and pulled out a large yellow men's dress shirt, its sleeves torn, the body stained. "Here you go."

Allison put it over her suit, feeling slightly ridiculous. It was huge. "Thanks."

Desiree and Jeremy exchanged a look, one Allison couldn't quite read, and then he was gone.

"Do you want to sit while I scrub up?" Desiree nodded toward the benches that surrounded the room's lone table.

"I'll stand."

Desiree walked to the big sink and filled it with water. Allison followed, wanting to see Desiree's face as they talked. When the tub was three-quarters full, Desiree dumped tools in and began to scrub with a slimy wedge of sponge. The water looked muddy. Allison wasn't sure anything was actually getting *clean*, but maybe that didn't matter.

"I won't beat around the bush, Desiree. I'm here because of Maggie McBride."

If Allison was expecting a reaction from the other woman, she was disappointed. Desiree's face remained blank, and her impossibly long lashed eyes stayed fixed on the sponge and tools.

"What about Maggie?" Desiree said.

"I want to know about Maggie and Sarah. What happened at school. The letters."

Desiree stopped scrubbing. "You know about the letters?"

Allison nodded.

"Do you mind if I ask why you're interested, Allison? What's Maggie to you?"

Allison thought for a moment. What was Maggie to her? Finally, she said, "A friend."

Desiree began scrubbing again. "It started about a year ago. As you saw that day at the mall, my daughter, Sarah, can be high-strung, I'm afraid. Maggie was—is—different. Eccentric. The two clashed. They haven't gotten along since grade school, really."

"They've known each other that long?"

Desiree nodded. "They were friends once. Third, maybe fourth grade. But then Maggie, well, she started to change. She withdrew. She stopped playing with Sarah. They didn't have much contact until last year, when circumstance had them in the same classes and after the same boy."

"Ethan Feldman."

Desiree sighed. "Yes, Ethan. I didn't understand what either girl saw in the boy, but who knows what goes through the adolescent mind."

Allison smiled. "True."

"At first it was harmless stuff. They'd call each other and hang up. Send nasty texts." Desiree took a handful of tools and wrapped them in a big off-white towel, which she placed on the floor next to her. Then she pulled the drain plug. While the tub emptied, she said, "The letters began coming late last spring. At first it was just hands-off stuff. Stay away from my boyfriend, that sort of thing. But eventually," she paused to run cold water over the sponge, "eventually they turned darker."

Allison's shoulders tensed. "How so?"

"Witchcraft references. The letters took on a threatening tone. My husband at the time, Kyle, he called the police when the last letter came." Desiree turned so she and Allison stood eye-to-eye. "It was written in blood."

"How do you know it was real?"

"I had it tested. I wanted proof, in case...in case we had more problems with Maggie down the line."

Desiree had taken the sponge to the wheel and was wiping down its surface. Streaks of clay followed the sponge and dried that way, leaving tracks.

"How many letters were there?"

"Three."

Allison said, "Were you afraid for Sarah, Desiree?"

"Yes and no." Desiree stopped wiping and stood straight. "I was afraid because of the effect it had on my daughter. Sarah was scared. Nightmares, anxiety. Did I think Maggie would actually do anything?" She shook her head. "Not really. But Kyle, well, he was in Papa Bear mode. He wanted Maggie expelled."

"In the end, she wasn't?"

"No. Hank McBride fought us. We threatened a restraining order. The issues spilled over into school and Maggie was suspended. Arnie Feldman forbid Ethan to see her. To be honest, I felt bad for Maggie."

"Why was that?"

"Because she's a lonely kid."

Allison nodded. "She is. I guess that's why I'm here."

Desiree pulled a duffle out from underneath the table and unzipped it. "Do you mind if I change? I have to be at yoga in twenty minutes."

"I'll leave—"

Desiree laughed. "No, stay. We're both girls, right?"

Allison looked away while Desiree pulled off the t-shirt and jeans, replacing them with a fitted tank and yoga pants. Desiree made no attempt to cover up, even when Jeremy came back into the room to retrieve Desiree's *breakthrough* piece. In fact, Desiree seemed to flaunt her figure, smiling mischievously at her instructor.

Allison said, "Art, yoga...how do you find the time?"

"I have lots of interests. It was one of the sore points between me and Kyle, actually. He was jealous of the time I spent away from him." She shrugged. "Couldn't get past it."

"That's a shame for the girls."

"He stays in contact with them, so that's good, I guess."

"He lives close enough to see them regularly?"

"Oh no," Desiree said. "He lives in Virginia where his main office is. He never sees them. But they talk on the phone. We have an amicable separation."

Allison knew there had to be more to that story, but as curious as she was about the Moores' arrangement, their marriage was not the reason for her visit. Still, she had to wonder how Desiree could afford to keep up her non-working lifestyle now that she was separated. She assumed Kyle was still footing the bill.

"I have one more question, Desiree, if you don't mind."

Desiree was sliding pedicured toes into lavender flip-flops. "Go ahead."

"In all of the letters and interactions between Sarah and Maggie, did Maggie ever specifically mention Satanism?"

Desiree paused. Allison noticed a sudden clenching of Desiree's jaw. She felt herself tense, unsure she even wanted to hear the answer to her question.

"Kind of," Desiree said finally. "She talked about the devil." She pulled a light jacket out from her bag and tugged it over her arms. Her gaze met Allison's. "But more than that, it was the tone of the letters, her verbal threats to Sarah." Desiree shook her head. "I understood Sarah's terror. Maggie was a child in over her head. It was just a matter of time before she crossed that line. And I was damn sure it wouldn't be with my child."

* * *

Back in her car, Allison's hand shook as she dialed Vaughn's number. He didn't answer. She checked her voice mail. Three work-related calls and one from Mia, asking her to call as soon as possible. She dialed Mia's number. No answer.

"Dammit," she said under her breath.

She put her head back on the seat and took a deep breath. *Think, Allison.* Desiree had left her feeling unsettled. The woman's confidence, her calm manner. Allison realized she had been ready to dismiss the raving lunacy of an overinvolved mother, but Desiree seemed neither crazy nor overprotective. To the contrary, she came across as rational and legitimately concerned. Maybe I'm the one who's crazy, Allison thought. She hit the speed dial for Vaughn again.

Did she want to believe Maggie to the point of not seeing clearly? Just like all those years ago when she, the one person charged with caring for Violet, had failed to see the signs?

On the third try, Vaughn picked up.

"Finally," Allison said.

"Mia may have a lead."

"Were you talking with Mia? I've been trying to reach you."

Silence met her on the other end. She thought she heard coughing in the background. "Vaughn, are you alone?"

"No. Look, I can't really talk now. Why don't we meet at the office? I'll be there in an hour."

Feeling even more unsettled, Allison said, "Fine." She hung up, wondering about that cough and Mia's lead. She pulled out of the parking lot, feeling a sudden sense of loss at the previous simplicity of her life. What had she written in her book? Life is only complicated if you let it be. Well, somewhere along the line she had lost control.

And she wanted it back.

* * *

Vaughn hung up, feeling guilty. He rolled over and pulled Mia to him. "This is so wrong. You know that, don't you?"

She smiled up at him, the beautiful angles of her face haloed in the ripe afternoon sunlight. She pulled his face to hers. He kissed her gently.

"Yes," she said finally.

He wanted her again, but there was no time. It was bad enough they'd stolen the last hour when he should have been at home, with Jamie, or at First Impressions. Anywhere but Mia's bed.

"I need to meet Allison."

"What are you going to tell her?" Mia suddenly looked concerned. He reminded himself that she had as much at stake here as he did. A newly-healed relationship with Allison, for starters.

"The truth. That I met with you to talk about your meeting with Brenda. And that I followed up with Jason about that lead on Jack Bremburg."

Mia looked thoughtful for a moment. He felt her legs, long and muscular, snake through his own. He forced himself to disentangle and slide out of bed.

"Don't forget your watch," Mia said. She reached over and pulled his gym watch off the bedside table. He rose, pulled on his pants and tucked it into his pocket.

"What do you think?" Mia said. "Bremburg have any relevance to this case?"

Vaughn considered the few facts they had while he pulled his polo shirt over his head. "Who the hell knows. Child abuse sounds like an excellent motive. I guess we'll see."

TWENTY-EIGHT

Allison arrived at First Impressions ahead of Vaughn. She decided to put her anxiety aside and concentrate on work until he arrived. She did still have a business to run. For now, anyway.

She turned on her computer and then walked into the small kitchenette sandwiched between her office and the client room to make some tea. When she returned to her desk, she opened her email and scanned her mail. Her eyes fell on a name: Catherine McBride. She opened it. It was short and sweet.

> *Dear Ms. Campbell:*
> *We know you have been texting Maggie. Given your influence over her and in light of recent circumstances, we would like you to desist all contact. If not, in Maggie's best interest, we will have to request a restraining order against you.*
> *Regards,*
> *Catherine McBride.*

Allison wasn't stupid. She knew Hank was setting her up, planting the seeds of suggestion so that, eventually, he could point the finger at her. Building a case through his daughter to keep his own hands clean. Allison also knew that if Maggie went down, he fully intended to bring her along, too.

Allison's vision blurred with anger. If their intent was to see her cower, they had misjudged their target.

"Allison?"

Allison jumped. "Vaughn, I didn't hear you come in."

He smiled. "Working too hard, as usual?"

"No, unfortunately. Not working at all." She motioned toward the email and he read it over her shoulder.

"McBride's getting antsy."

"I know. And it's only going to get worse."

"Well, remember, no one has arrested Maggie at this point. The police are probably afraid to act too hastily. They don't want the congressman after them, either." He paused. "You going to reply?"

She'd considered that. "No, I don't think so. Anything I say will be used against me—or worse, Maggie."

"I think it's time you talk to a lawyer."

"For what? I haven't done anything wrong."

"Still. This makes *me* antsy. McBride has it out for you."

"McBride has nothing *on* me." Allison shook her head. "I refuse to react." She pointed to the email. "This is all nonsense, distracting me from the real issue. If only McBride would cool it, maybe we could work together. He may dislike me, but you'd think he'd want to clear Maggie at least as much as I do."

"I guess. Unless he suspects she's guilty." Vaughn pulled out the second chair in Allison's office and sat across from her. He filled her in on his friend's online research and the fact that Maggie changed over time.

"Supports the theory that Maggie was framed," Allison said.

"I guess." Vaughn paused. "Now, for Mia's news. Name Jack Bremburg ring a bell?"

Allison thought. "Vaguely. Why? Should it?"

"Head of a major local energy company?"

Why did she know that name? "I think I worked with an ex, years ago. So?"

"So his most current wife accused him of molesting their daughter. A six-year-old. Feldman was representing him on both the divorce and seeking sole custody for Mr. Bremburg."

"Are you thinking that maybe Bremburg's wife did it?"

"That was Mia's first thought. She called Jason. The wife did go to the police with this, but no evidence of abuse was found—"

"Of course, what's a little girl going to say? She'd be scared to death."

Vaughn held up his hand. "Exactly. So no charges were filed and Feldman somehow managed to keep it out of the local papers. Anyway, I'm going to visit the wife later this week. But I would think if she'd go after anyone, it'd be the husband, not his attorney."

Allison nodded. "If I knew my husband was molesting my child, I think *I'd* kill him." She picked up a pen and started doodling circles on a piece of notepaper, thinking. "Besides, unless this woman knows enough about Maggie to frame her, she wouldn't fit the bill."

"True. But there's another possibility."

Allison put the pen down. "Out with it."

"Jason told me lawyers can report client conduct if they believe it will result in bodily harm to someone. What if Feldman knew Bremburg intended to continue molesting his daughter? What if, afraid he would look complicit in his client's crimes, he told Bremburg he could no longer represent him? Or he threatened to go to the police? Maybe Bremburg killed Arnie."

"But that doesn't explain the Maggie connection."

"I thought of that too." Vaughn stood and paced the room, his hands in his pockets. "Mia said Ethan knew about Bremburg because Arnie was always moaning about him at home. What if the reverse was true? What if he was always complaining about home—Ethan and Maggie—to his clients? Or at least certain clients?"

Allison said, "Well, it's something. And something is a heck of a lot better than nothing." She glanced at her watch, and reached to turn off her computer. "I have to get going. Jason's coming for dinner."

"For your birthday tomorrow?"

Allison nodded. "Faye and I are going out tomorrow night. She's in Philly for a med appointment and asked to meet me." Allison had a sudden thought. She said excitedly, "Join us tonight. It's nothing fancy, but I'd love you to be there. We can talk shop. Or not. It's been a while since we've seen each other outside of the office."

"Are you sure? Three's a crowd and all."

Allison smiled. "Absolutely, please come."

"What time?"

"Seven."

"Maybe I'll take you up on that, if you're sure it won't be a romantic dinner for two."

Allison laughed. "That, I can guarantee."

"Balsamic vinaigrette or bleu cheese?" Allison reached down and absentmindedly patted Brutus's head.

"Blue cheese for me." Mia pulled something out of Allison's oven. It was wrapped in tin foil and smelled heavenly.

Allison had been surprised when Jason called earlier in the week and suggested he come over and help her celebrate her birthday. She was even more surprised when he showed up with Mia. But Allison had to admit, tonight felt cozy and comfortable. Mia had brought pork loin and garlic mashed potatoes, Jason brought wine, and Allison made a salad.

"Vinaigrette," Jason said. He walked behind Allison and gave her rear a surreptitious pat. She turned, ready to say "hands off," but something in his eyes stopped her. She saw wanting. And it stirred her own feelings.

"Brutus has certainly taken to you," Mia said. "He doesn't leave your side, does he?"

"Yeah, you look kind of cute together. Beauty and the beast." Jason put a bowl of garlic mashed potatoes on the table, then reached for a bottle of Pinot Noir. He poured three glasses.

"You'll need a fourth glass," Allison said. "Vaughn may stop by. I hope you don't mind. I invited him, too."

Mia dropped a serving fork on the table.

"What is it, Mom?" Jason put the bottle down. "Did you burn yourself?"

Mia shook her head. "I'm okay. Really, I'm fine. Just clumsy."

Allison went back to tossing the salad but kept her eye on Mia. She didn't look well all of a sudden. "How about Vaughn?" Allison said. "Neither of you answered me before."

"Sure," Jason said. "It's your birthday celebration."

"Mia?"

"Of course." But her voice, Allison noticed, seemed strained.

Dinner was incredibly tense and Allison had no idea why. The tension started the second Vaughn arrived. He was unusually distant; Mia was uncharacteristically quiet.

"So you think someone is out there impersonating Maggie?" Jason said. "Why would someone go to the trouble of impersonating a fifteen-year-old?"

"To frame her for murder," Allison said. "Either to get to her or her father."

"Maybe a political opponent?" Jason said.

Allison looked at Vaughn. "Did your computer whiz get a sense of timing? When did the personality shifts and strange questions start?"

Vaughn said, "You're wondering whether this coincides with the letters to Sarah Moore?"

"Exactly. If it does, then it seems more likely that it was Maggie. If it was later, then someone who knew about the letters could have gotten the idea."

"I don't know. I'll ask my source."

Allison saw Mia give Vaughn a hard look. She wondered what that was about.

"How about you, Mia? What do you make of this?"

Mia shrugged, not taking her eyes off Vaughn. "I have no idea. Though it seems to me it would take someone an awful lot of work to frame Maggie. Going on the Internet? Building up a history of pretending to be someone you're not?" She shook her head. "It's too complicated. I think there must be a simpler answer." She shot Vaughn another look.

Vaughn picked at his pork roast, twirling his fork around and around on his plate. Allison stared at him. He'd barely touched his food, which was nearly unheard of for Vaughn. Usually he could be counted on for thirds or fourths.

"Are you okay, Vaughn?" Allison said. "You're not eating."

Vaughn glanced at Mia and said, "I'm fine."

"Maybe it was Sarah Moore who is trying to frame Maggie." Jason speared some more pork from the serving dish and then reached under the table and fed a handful to a very grateful Brutus. He stared at his mother as he did so, obviously challenging her to say something. Or testing her, which meant even Jason had picked up on the tension. "Maybe Sarah and a band of forest fairies got together and killed Arnie Feldman."

Allison made a face. "Very funny. Don't forget about this Bremburg fellow." She turned to Vaughn. "Maybe you could ask your researcher to do some digging on Jack Bremburg?"

Vaughn nodded. "Already have."

"Who is your computer friend, anyway?" Allison said in an attempt to steer the conversation in a more benign direction. But as soon as she asked, both Vaughn and Mia looked up, startled.

"She really doesn't know?" Mia said.

"Not now, Mia," Vaughn said.

"Know what?" Jason said.

Allison glanced at Vaughn, then Mia. There was obviously some unspoken communication going on between them, and it wasn't friendly. They'd known each other for years, through the business. But to Allison's knowledge, they hadn't seen each other since Mia sold it, so what they could be communicating about now was a mystery to her.

"Would one of you care to tell me what's going on?" Allison said.

Mia cleared her throat. Her eyes shot daggers at Vaughn. He looked down at his plate.

"Vaughn? You owe it to Jamie. We both know he's your computer whiz." Mia put down her fork and raised her voice. "He's not something to be ashamed of. For goodness sake, he's your *twin*."

Allison's head swam with questions. Twin? Since when did Vaughn have a twin? And why did Mia know this and she didn't?

"More wine?" Jason said. He poured before anyone could answer and refilled his own glass to the top. "Mom, maybe you shouldn't be the one to out people's secrets. Glass houses and all."

"What do you know about my life, Jason Campbell?" Mia shook her head. "You stop by when it's convenient or when you feel guilty. Don't talk about my secrets. You have no idea what you're talking about."

"I've been there for you all these years, Mom. When you shut everyone else out, I was there. And I know you deserve to be happy. If he makes you happy, it shouldn't have to be a secret."

Allison said, "What am I missing here?"

"How do you know, Jason?" Mia said. "I didn't want you to know."

"I came by one night when you weren't answering your phone. I was worried about you. His car was in your driveway. I could see you through the window."

"Holy Hell, Jason." Mia seemed to age ten years in an instant.

Vaughn put his head in his hands. "Oh, man. Damn," he said.

"It's okay. Really. That was months ago. I didn't say anything because it doesn't bother me. I just want you to be happy."

Allison slammed her hands on the table. "Would someone please tell me what you're all talking about?"

"My mother is seeing Vaughn," Jason said.

Allison stared, open-mouthed. "What?"

Mia looked pointedly at Vaughn, her face a collage of shame, anger, and defiance. "There's more, Allison. While we're sharing secrets, Vaughn has something to tell you."

Vaughn nodded. Slowly, he said, "I do have a twin. Identical. He's...paralyzed." Vaughn looked over at Mia, who, still looking as though someone had walloped her, reached out and grabbed Vaughn's hand. "He took a gunshot meant for me. Drug dealers. Mistaken identity. We were nineteen."

Jason said, "I had no idea."

"He lives with me. He's my life."

Allison rubbed her temples, her head spinning. How could they have hidden these things from her? *Why* would they hide these things from her?

Vaughn said, "I'm sorry, Allison—"

"All these years? Seriously?"

"Look, I'm sorry—"

"I wish you had trusted me," she whispered. "Who you see is your own business, but a twin? I could have helped you."

Vaughn didn't say anything, just stared down at his hands.

Allison looked around the room at these people she'd thought she knew. To think just fifteen minutes ago she'd felt surrounded by people she loved. Now they seemed like strangers.

She heard Jason say, "Why don't you two go? I'll talk to her."

Vaughn said, "I wanted to tell you, Allison. I just couldn't ever find the right time. I'd have had to explain my past. It would have changed everything."

Vaughn stood up to leave. He folded his napkin into a neat little square and placed it on his still-full plate. He looked so hurt. Allison wanted to hug him, tell him it was alright. She, if anyone, understood the need to hide from your past. But she felt shocked, couldn't move.

To Mia, Jason said, "Was that why you were so vague about your alibi the night Arnie was murdered."

Mia nodded.

"Seriously, Mom. You would go to those lengths to hide your relationship? You're divorced. Why would I care if you're seeing someone?"

"You're my son. He's younger—and not your father." Mia pushed her seat back. She looked up at Jason. "Vaughn has more character than twenty Edwards."

"You don't have to convince me," Jason said. He walked over to Allison and put his arm around her shoulder. "I don't understand why you feel this need to punish yourself. Hiding Vaughn? It's as though you think you're undeserving of happiness."

"It's not that."

"Then what is it?"

Mia put her hand on Vaughn's arm. It was such a natural, gentle gesture that Allison wondered how she hadn't seen their connection earlier.

"I had my chance. God gives you one opportunity to get it right, that's it. I don't want to use up Vaughn's one shot at happiness. He deserves someone younger, someone who can give him a family."

When Vaughn opened his mouth to speak, Mia smiled gently at him and reached out a slender hand to stroke his face. "I think he's seen enough pain in his life. He's also learned the hard way—sometimes one chance is all you get."

"Stay with me," Allison said. She couldn't meet Jason's eyes. He stood next to her in the now-darkened kitchen, cleaned earlier by the two of them working in a heavy silence.

Allison felt Jason's arms slide around her waist. He pulled her close, gently pushed the hair away from her neck, and kissed her exposed ear.

He whispered, "Are you sure?"

No, she wasn't sure. She was feeling the foundation of her life crumble under her. Nothing was as it had seemed. But Jason, present, strong, and dependable, was here, and she suddenly wanted him very badly. In her bed, maybe even back in her life.

He pushed against her tenderly so that she could feel his excitement. Her body responded. He kissed her again.

"I'm sure," she whispered back.

TWENTY-NINE

"Kids?" Allison rolled over so she was facing Jason. Early morning sun poured through the blinds in waves, bathing the ivory bed in ripples of white. Jason's hair hung limp across his face. Allison pushed it back with tentative strokes.

He said, "Kids. One, maybe two."

Allison stared at him, unsure what to say. They'd discussed having kids years ago, before the divorce. But she was having a hard enough time with the fact that she was lying naked in a bed with him again. Kids?

"What is it, Al? Why are you so dead set against it?"

"Have you met my family?"

"Once or twice."

"Doesn't that say it all?"

Jason moved closer to her so she could feel his breath on her face. His left hand idly strummed the skin on her belly.

"Allison, my mother is having an affair with a man nearly half her age. My father is a cruel son of a bitch who killed my sister in a car crash yet has never taken an ounce of responsibility for it. Do you really think your family is any worse than mine...or worse than any other family out there?" He kicked back the covers and sat up. "So your family's a little weird."

"Understatement. You of all people should know better."

He paused. "Don't you think you've used them as an excuse long enough?"

Allison sat, pulling the sheet over her chest.

She said, "An excuse? For what? For trying to make something of my life? What's your excuse? You wanted nothing but to run your own business someday. And you gave that up."

"Is that how you see it?" His tone was iron.

Allison hesitated.

"It is."

He stared at her, disappointment in his eyes.

"I never gave up. Bridget's death changed me, made me reconsider what I wanted out of life." He shook his head. "Wake up, Al. People don't come all neatly packaged. You've spent your whole adult life trying to force people into these tidy little boxes. Things don't work that way. People mess up. They get scared. They change their minds. What's under the surface comes out, and you know what? It's not always pretty. That's okay. It's called life."

Jason stood up. She was afraid he would storm out of the room and leave, further proof that coupledom was not in their future. One night, and it had come to this. Instead, Jason bent down and stuck his hand under the bed. He pulled out the flat container that held her memories of Violet's life.

"What about this, Al? You accuse me of running away, but what about this?"

Allison was stunned. "That's different."

He placed the box containing Violet's letters on the bed and started to open it.

Allison grabbed the box and pulled. "Don't."

Reluctantly, he let her take it.

"I know, Allison. Don't you see? I've known all along." His tone was tender. "I know what happened. Or at least I know the parts I could put together from the letters."

Allison couldn't look at him. She felt the bed move and the box slide away. His fingers traced lines up and down her arm in soft, comforting strokes.

"That was a long time ago." With a gentle finger on her chin, he turned her face to his. "And it wasn't your fault."

Allison felt tears sting her eyes. "How do you know...that it's not my fault?"

"Because I know you. And I could see the love that girl had for you in those letters. If something did happen to her, Al—and you don't know that for sure—then, despite whatever went wrong, at least she knew what it felt like to have someone care."

Allison picked up a pillow and held it to her face, hoping to stifle what felt like a torrent. He was right. Violet lay behind her refusal to have kids. Violet— not her own family—lay behind her need for a neat life. Restitution, safety, predictability. Maybe she wasn't so different from Vaughn after all.

Jason took the pillow away from her face. "I still love you, Al."

"I still love you, too. I never stopped loving you—"

"But?"

"But my life is a mess right now. My parents. Maggie." She looked up at Jason. "And there will always be Violet."

Jason kissed her forehead. "We can work through all of that. And as for Violet, you've shouldered this guilt all these years, yet you don't even know what really happened to her. Why don't we try to find out?"

She shook her head.

"I'll help you. Vaughn can help you."

"I know where her father lives. I've known for years."

"Then go see him. Nothing's stopping you."

"I can't."

"Why?"

Allison looked toward the window. She felt the warming sun on her face, but it wasn't enough to dull the chill that ran through her. "Because," she said, "because I know in my heart that she's dead."

Later that evening, Allison made her way to Trattoria Bianca, on the corner of Ninth and Chestnut, in what had once been an old apartment building. She found Faye standing outside, nervously fidgeting on the sidewalk. Faye looked out of place in the urban setting, her arms crossed over her chest in a feeble act of self-protection. She was wearing a plain black skirt, too loose and three inches too long, a cream silk blouse tied with a bow at the throat and one-inch black heels. Allison recognized the pearls around her neck—they had been their grandmother's. Faye's hair was tamed into a neat twist, and rouge lent a warm glow to pale skin.

"Happy birthday, Allison." Faye didn't smile.

Allison gave her sister a hug. Faye's body went rigid. Allison told herself to have patience. Peace would not be won in a day.

While Faye went inside to see if their table was ready, Allison watched the swirl of activity outside the restaurant. Dim light spilled from the street lamps. Three young women and a man with a shaved head climbed out of a cab and ran, arms linked, to the front entrance. Between the front door and a side alley, an old woman squatted, wrapped in blankets, a beat-up shopping bag stuffed with random objects next to her. She huddled close to a heater grate. A passerby handed her a dollar and she shouted "God Bless" in slurred syllables.

Faye was back a few seconds later. "Come on, Allison. The table is ready." She motioned impatiently for her sister to follow. "Are you okay?"

"I'm fine. Let's just go."

Faye stared at her for a moment, searching, Allison thought, for the truth in her eyes. But then she smiled. "Good then."

Allison and Faye sat at a table for two, wedged between a window and a couple. The owner had divided the restaurant into small dining rooms, each with a fireplace and an ornate crystal chandelier that took center stage in otherwise plain space. The tiny rectangular tables, large enough to sit two comfortably, four in a pinch, were covered in ivory linen. A small spray of red roses in a crystal vase and a tiny brass hurricane lamp had been placed in the center of each table. The effect should have been calming and romantic. Allison found it all a bit too forced: the lights too dim, the waiters too solicitous, the tables too close together, and the coloring too carefully neutral.

Allison glanced at their neighbors. The man looked to be a well-dressed sixty-five. Wrinkles lined his mouth; his forehead had the plastic-y stillness Allison knew from her client, Kit Carson. Facelift or Botox, or both. The woman couldn't have been more than thirty. Tiny, with thin, straight blond hair and round blue eyes. Allison wanted to believe they were father and daughter enjoying a special night out together. But the hand he had on her leg under the table and the silly way she giggled at his jokes said otherwise. He wore a wedding ring. She did not.

Faye said, "Allison."

Allison watched the man pick up the woman's wine glass and hand it to her. "Bottoms up." The woman laughed before lifting the glass to her lips. "Good girl," he said.

Good girl.

"Allison?"

Allison looked up to see Faye and the waiter staring at her. "Are you ready to order?" the waiter said.

Allison's menu sat closed. She shook her head.

After the waiter walked away, Faye gave Allison an apprising stare. "Is something bothering you?"

"Sorry. I have a lot on my mind." She gave Faye a brief summary of the local murders and her involvement with Maggie. "Rough few weeks."

"This was bad timing. I'm sure you had better things to do than meet me for dinner. On your birthday, of all days."

Allison looked stricken. "That's not true at all. I'm glad you called. I'm glad we met."

Faye studied her. "Mom remembered your birthday."

"Really?"

She held up a hand. "Don't get too excited. She does that sometimes. Memories from long-ago are within easier reach. Still," Faye said with a shrug, "it's something."

"It is something." Allison smiled. "How did your test go?"

Faye frowned. In a determined burst, she said, "I lied before. I came into the city to meet with someone else. An Alzheimer's specialist."

Confused, Allison said, "Why didn't you tell me?"

Faye looked away. "This is my decision to make, Allison."

"What's your decision? How to help Mom? You're not making sense. Start from the beginning."

Just then, the waiter returned. Allison opened the menu, and quickly ordered the Chilean sea bass with a side of broccoli rabe. Faye mumbled *lasagna* and twisted the cloth napkin on her lap.

When the waiter was gone, Allison said, "Are you trying to tell me that you've made some decisions on your own about Mom's care?" She fought to keep accusation out of her voice. It was a struggle.

"If Dr. Hom says that in the normal course of the disease, Mom has six months to live, she can get hospice care. In the house." Faye looked up, her eyes beseeching. "*Everything* would be paid for by Medicare."

"But hospice means no more treatment. It means she's terminally ill, Faye. Think about that."

Faye sat, silent.

"Does Mom's GP agree?"

Again, Faye twisted her napkin. She squirmed in her seat, avoiding eye contact. Allison took a deep breath. She needed to think this through. Maybe there were facts she didn't know. But Faye was digging in her heels the way she used to when they were kids. Her way or no way.

Allison turned and caught a glimpse of a kiss between the older man and his younger mistress. Elsewhere in the restaurant, someone dropped a tray and the piercing clang of metal against ceramic startled her. She searched for somewhere to rest her gaze, somewhere that was not Faye's face or the couple next to them. Her eyes settled on a red-headed man across the narrow aisle. There was something eerily familiar about his long neck, the arrogant cock of his head. She strained to see his date, who sat across from him, partially blocked from view by Faye.

"I'm with them all the time, Allison. It's really my decision to make. You should see that."

Redhead's date stood up. She looked young, maybe sixteen or seventeen, though it was hard to tell through the six inches of makeup caked on her features. She started to wobble by Allison's

table, a little unsteady on cheap silver stilettos. Allison saw Redhead's hand jut out to balance her. He whispered something, and
then put a groping hand on the curve of her buttock, sliding it down
the length of her thigh.

Allison felt sick.

"Are you listening, Allison?"

Allison looked down and saw Faye holding out a pamphlet
about hospice. She had no idea her mother was that far gone. Questions swam through her head, demanding answers, but she needed
to ask them when she could be calm or Faye would become defen-
sive. Right now, she didn't think she could manage calm.

She glanced up in time to see Redhead's date make her way
toward the bathroom. The girl wore a lavender satin dress that
looked two sizes too big on her thin form. A floral scarf draped
around her neck. It was knotted at the base of her throat, one end
hanging in the shadows of her cleavage. Her clothes were bor-
rowed. Allison could tell the same way she could tell that there was
something fishy going on between her and Redhead.

"I've made an appointment with Dr. Hom, Allison. This is happening."

Allison was about to respond when the waiter returned to
Redhead's table with the check in his hand. Redhead turned to take
his credit card and Allison got a clearer view of his face in the can-
dlelight. A large mole marred pasty-white skin. She knew that face.
Her mind edged sideways, searching for a connection. She flashed
to a picture she'd seen recently, a photo printed off a website just as
the waiter said, "Thank you, Mr. Moore."

"Allison, say something."

But Allison couldn't move. She could barely breathe.

Kyle Moore. Desiree's husband.

What the hell was he doing here, in Philly, when he was supposed to be living in Virginia?

"Allison, I'm speaking to you. I've made up my mind."

And who was that girl?

* * *

Allison said, "We agreed to wait until we can both meet with Dr. Hom."

Jason remained silent. Allison could hear the murmur of canned television laughter through the phone. "I didn't know your mother was that ill, physically."

"I didn't either. And I'm not sure she is. I think Faye is completely overwhelmed and grasping at what she sees as solutions."

"Well, that's a big step. Hospice means no more treatment. If Dr. Hom is willing to attest to that—"

Allison sighed. Her head and neck were sounding the warning bell. Stress meant a migraine, and she couldn't afford a migraine today. "He hasn't seen anything other than her medical records. He needs to examine my mother, and even then we would want to consult with her general practitioner."

"It wasn't fair of Faye to spring it on you that way."

"She's scared. For my parents, for her own future. I get that." Allison sat on her bed. She cradled the phone against her shoulder. "I need to be there for them."

"You're one person. You can't do it all alone."

Very true, she thought. What did she tell her clients? Sometimes it made the most sense to tackle one problem at a time. Right now, she had to think straight, had to process what she'd learned yesterday about Kyle Moore and figure out if it meant anything.

Jason continued, "I'd forgotten how great we are together, Allison."

"Whoa." She stood up from her bed and walked toward the bathroom for a glass of water, little headache miracle pill in hand. Brutus lifted his head from her pillow and yawned. "Lord, I've missed you—true. But just because we slept together doesn't mean we're a couple. We need to think this through."

"What's to think about? Please don't overanalyze it."

"There are reasons we divorced. And none of that has changed. I'm still me and you're still you and once upon a time that wasn't such a great combination. Remember?"

"You *have* changed."

"No, Jason. I haven't."

"Something's different, Al. Maggie, the dog. You're softer somehow."

"Even if that's the case, have *you* changed?"

He was quiet for a moment. "Don't I deserve a second chance?"

Allison swallowed the pill and turned off the faucet. Her mind wandered to Violet, to Mia's words the night before. "Maybe there are no second chances. We all have to live with the consequences of our actions. And sometimes *wanting* things to be different just isn't enough."

"That's a load of horseshit, Al. *You* have the ability to give us a second chance. *You.*"

He paused, and Allison pictured him as he was last night: strong and caring and gentle. The man she'd fallen in love with years ago. But what if they couldn't have that back? What if they tried again and failed? How many marriages did she see end in divorce? Too many to count. Allison wasn't so sure she could share Jason's hope for a second chance.

When she didn't respond, Jason said, "Love is a leap of faith. There are no guarantees. Whether it's a lover or a child or a dog, you love because you have no choice. So figure out what you want, Al. In the meantime, you know where to find me."

THIRTY

Allison called Vaughn while climbing into her car. She was left with a vague sense of sadness over Jason and her mother and a maddening desire to get to the bottom of Maggie's situation. She wanted to get on with her life, to help Faye and her parents deal with theirs. She wanted Maggie to be able to get on with hers.

"I know you're visiting Jack Bremburg's ex today," she said to Vaughn, "but I wanted to let you know that I'll be late."

"You're still upset with me."

"I've thought about your brother, Vaughn, and I'm trying to understand why you felt you needed to hide the very fact of his existence."

"Can you honestly say it wouldn't have mattered, Allison?"

She turned on the ignition and thought about all the times she'd asked Vaughn to take on a late assignment, do weekend overtime, deal with an irate husband, attempt some detective work. Would she have still asked him? No, probably not. Not without advance warning and plenty of time to make whatever arrangements were needed for his brother.

She grunted into the phone. "Okay, maybe a little."

"I want you to see me the way I am now, not the little punk from years ago. If I'd told you about Jamie, you'd have known about everything."

"That's not what I meant, Vaughn. I don't care about that. Jeez, if anything I admire you even more for pulling yourself together, looking after Jamie, going to school. I just meant, well...I thought you were this ladies' man, with no commitments. I might have been less likely to ask you to do things had I known you were taking care of your brother."

This time, Vaughn laughed. "Touché, then. Maybe we underestimated each other."

"I think that's true."

"Where are you heading anyway?"

"To drop in on Desiree Moore." Allison backed out of her driveway and headed in the direction of the address she had for Desiree. As she drove, she told Vaughn about her unexpected sighting of Kyle Moore. "Something's not adding up."

Vaughn said, "TECHNO has an office in Philly. The fact that he was dining there doesn't necessarily mean anything."

"True. But with a young woman? A *very* young woman?"

"She was probably older than you think. And anyway, even if there's something illicit going on, what does that have to do with the McBrides?"

Vaughn didn't need to say it. Allison could tell by his tone that he thought she'd lost it on this one. She accelerated to get around a car double parked on Route 30.

"Maybe. But I think it's time to pay her another visit. I can't shake this feeling that Desiree isn't telling me the whole story—about Maggie, at least. She's my connection to another side of Maggie. The truth may all add up to nothing, but then it will be one more thing I can cross off my list."

"And one more Main-Liner who will read what the McBrides have to say about you and believe it." Vaughn paused, and Allison resisted the urge to protest. He was right. "But do what you need to do, Allison. At the end of the day, you have to be able to live with yourself and your choices. That's what really matters."

"Allison. What a pleasant surprise." Desiree's flat tone told another story.

Allison knew she was overstepping her bounds by showing up this way. She didn't need Vaughn to tell her that. She'd found Desiree's home address in her client database, unsure whether she'd even use it. And yet here she stood, nervous about what she might learn.

"I'd like to chat for a few minutes, if you don't mind."

"Oh?" Desiree motioned for Allison to come inside. "About?"

Allison knew the connection between Maggie and the Moores was solid, but what about a connection between Kyle Moore and Arnie Feldman? Tenuous, at best. Still, it had bothered her to see Kyle at the restaurant, with that girl, after Desiree told her Kyle lived in Virginia and never saw his daughters. She'd meant what she'd told Vaughn. If this was a dead end, she'd let it go and move on.

Allison said, "Maggie McBride."

Desiree nodded. "I heard the police had questioned her. Poor kid. Doesn't look too good." She clucked sympathetically.

Allison took off her coat and, at Desiree's urging, handed it to her. Allison glanced around the house. A genteel Yankee quality permeated the décor. The ceilings were high, the floors polished oak, the oriental rugs clearly authentic imports. But something about the house struck her as odd, and it took her a moment to figure out what: there was a distinct male presence.

Kyle had left months ago, yet Allison could smell the faint, lingering scent of aftershave. A decidedly masculine umbrella sat perched against one hallway wall. A brown fleece with leather trim hung from a white peg by the door. Maybe Desiree had a new boyfriend. Or maybe she wasn't being completely honest about Kyle.

Vaughn had an image of Marta Bremburg as older, angry, and bitter. When she opened the door of her apartment to greet him, he realized that he'd let his years at First Impressions color his thinking about divorcees. Allison's divorced clients fit a stereotypical pattern: middle-aged women who'd given up careers to raise a family only to be left by unfaithful husbands for much younger women.

But clearly, Marta Bremburg was not the typical First Impressions divorcee.

Her apartment was on the third floor of a complex in Bryn Mawr, which, from the look of the parking lot, was home to mostly graduate students from one of the nearby colleges. Vaughn knew she'd be there. He'd called from the car first and then feigned a wrong number when she answered. He felt slightly guilty about the trick.

Vaughn had wedged the Beemer between an ancient Datsun and a two-door Nissan and made his way to the front entrance, which had a security door. He adjusted his tie and then fumbled in his suit pockets, pretending to look for his key, until a twenty-something guy in a backward baseball cap came out and held the door for him to go inside. Vaughn smiled his thanks and gave a silent prayer for the trusting collegial population.

He hadn't been expecting the blonde beauty who opened the door.

"Yes?" She peeked out from behind a door chain. Vaughn saw striking blue eyes, nearly level with his own, and impossibly full lips. "Do I know you?" She had a thick Eastern European accent.

Vaughn said, "Christopher Vaughn. I'm investigating the Arnie Feldman murder, Mrs. Bremburg. I'd like to talk to you for a few moments about your ex-husband, Jack."

She stood there and, for a second, Vaughn didn't think she would let him in. But then he heard the chain slide off and she opened the door. "I thought I was finished with this," she said.

The slice of her face he'd seen through the crack in the door hadn't done her justice. She was tall and curvy, almost plump, with long, thick, wavy blond hair and full round breasts, probably fake, that pressed against the thin material of a nurse's aid uniform. Vaughn guessed her age at twenty-five, tops.

"I will be leaving for my work in a few minutes," she said. "So I hope this will not take long."

He entered the cramped apartment, and she motioned toward a worn couch in a tiny living room. "Sit, please." A child's toys lay scattered on the floor: Barbie dolls in various states of dress, a dollhouse, broken crayons, and a stack of well-used coloring books. Marta said, "My daughter's things. She is at school."

Vaughn sat on the couch. Marta pulled a chair from the dinette set perched against a wall, placed it across from Vaughn and sat down gracefully. A small television teetered nearby on a milk crate. A DVD player sat on the floor next to it, beside several battered-looking Disney movie cases. Clearly, Marta had not done well in the divorce.

"I'll get right to the point, Mrs. Bremburg. What can you tell me about Arnie Feldman?"

Marta's hand drummed nervously against the arm of the chair. "He is—was—my husband's lawyer."

"Had you met him?"

"Of course. Several times." She glanced at the children's toys. "Jack and I fought over our daughter, Kira. This Feldman was involved."

"In creating the custody agreement?"

"I told the police this already," she said impatiently.

"I'm sorry, Mrs. Bremburg, but I need to ask you to go through it once more. Please. It could be important."

She frowned, but continued. "Jack was a bad father. He had...desires. He could not have her in his custody. Mr. Feldman did not believe me or Kira. He thought we were lying."

Vaughn looked at a framed photo of Kira on the wall. Big, round blue eyes. Longish brown hair. Cute, dimpled smile. She couldn't have been more than four in that picture. Vaughn pictured a father violating someone that young and felt his own rage awakening. Unconsciously, his hand clenched into a fist.

As though sensing his anger at what had happened to her daughter, Marta said, "Yes, yes, I will cooperate some more."

Vaughn knew he was treading on fragile ground. Marta assumed he was with the police. Despite the risk, one more glance at that photo told him he didn't want to dispel that notion unless he had to, in case Arnie's murder *was* linked to child abuse. But he also didn't want to repeat questions she'd been asked already. That would only make her suspicious. He decided to hone in on what he really wanted to know: was she capable of having killed Feldman? Was her husband?

"Had you ever been to Feldman's house?"

"No."

"Did you despise Arnie Feldman, Mrs. Bremburg?"

The question seemed to catch her off-guard. "He was doing his job. It is my husband I hate."

"Because of what happened with your daughter?"

Her eyes flared. "Yes. Jack wanted Kira only to hurt *me*." She turned her head and made a spitting noise. "He is a bad man."

Softly, Vaughn said, "Why did you marry Jack, Marta?"

She looked at the floor. "Out of love."

Vaughn doubted that. Perhaps she was angry and bitter after all. Perhaps all divorcees were angry and bitter. But then, that was the nature of all relationships...to end, one way or another. In bitterness or heartbreak.

Though he thought he knew the answer, he said, "Why did you separate?"

"I told police this. He touched Kira...she told me, and I believed her." She looked up again, conviction in her blue eyes. "At Jack's house, we lived like princesses. Beautiful bedrooms, a pool, so many clothes." Marta shook her head wistfully. "Here it is dreary. He will not give us money. That was the agreement. I do not tell the news people what he did and I keep my daughter. I have a new job." She shrugged. "It is not so bad."

"If he says he's innocent, why would he care if you went to the media?"

"He is an important man. He does not want any hint of scandal."

"Aren't you worried he will do this to another little girl if you don't pursue it?"

She looked at him defiantly. "My daughter is my main concern, Mr. Vaughn. If I pursue it, as you say, he will take her away from me."

"Even with Feldman gone?"

"I did not kill Mr. Feldman, if that is what you are thinking. There will always be another Mr. Feldman. Men like my ex-husband have unlimited resources."

"How about Jack, Mrs. Bremburg? Do you think he could have killed Arnie Feldman?"

Marta shrugged. "Jack is old. Infirm." She glanced at the picture of her daughter. "Before we married, I was Jack's nurse."

Vaughn considered this. "Is Jack retired from his company?"

"He is still on the board of directors," Marta said. "Or at least he was. He uses...how do you say...computer from home?"

"Remote access?"

"Yes, that."

Jamie's voice was suddenly echoing in Vaughn's brain. Anyone could have impersonated Maggie online. Even an elderly invalid with a grudge.

"Is your ex-husband good with a computer, Marta?"

Marta smiled, and for the first time Vaughn saw something that looked like actual admiration for Jack Bremburg. "Oh yes, Lieutenant. As you Americans say, he is whiz. A real genius on the computer."

Desiree Moore led Allison to a small, rectangular room lined with books and bric-à-brac. Three overstuffed arm chairs surrounded a square coffee table stacked with photography books on Ireland, the Mediterranean and impressionist painters. Behind the chairs, white built-in shelving lined with books and pictures covered the wall from floor to ceiling. A lopsided vase, glazed milky red, had been placed on the top shelf. One of Desiree's pieces?

"Tea or coffee?"

Allison turned her attention back to Desiree. She wasn't in the mood for either but wanted a chance to look around for a minute or two, uninterrupted, so she said, "Coffee, if it's not too much trouble."

"No problem at all." Desiree disappeared into the hallway.

Allison's looked over the length of the bookshelf. She didn't know what she was searching for, just something that would give her a better sense of who this woman was and how Kyle fit into the scene—if he did. But it all seemed so innocuous.

Undated pictures of Desiree, Kyle and the girls had been placed at odd angles here and there in front of the books. Allison walked closer to get a better view. Many showcased special events: cheerleading tryouts, horse shows, gymnastics finals. In nearly every picture, one of the Moore girls was shown holding a ribbon or trophy, smiling mechanically, with Desiree hovering nearby.

A snapshot of the Moore family in front of an Ocean City Ferris wheel caught Allison's eye. In it, the family had carved a spot amidst the typical resort beach crowd—kids in strollers, fathers in Polo shirts, teens looking too cool to care. Although each of the Moores was smiling, they were those perfunctory smiles born of happiness on demand rather than genuine emotion. Neither the forced smiles nor the setting were odd in and of themselves, but when Allison looked at the other photos in the room, she noticed a consistency. No one ever *really* smiled and Kyle always seemed a little bit removed, with Desiree and the girls standing to one side, Kyle on the other. Why? Was that just the unconscious manifestation of a family already falling apart? Or was something more sinister lurking in the Moore household?

"That was taken after Sarah graduated from grade school." Desiree placed one cup of coffee on the table and then took the photo from Allison's hand and placed it back on the shelf. "We celebrated with a trip down the shore." She motioned toward the couch. "Please. Sit."

Allison sat, but not before she caught a glimpse of a series of titles about child rearing: *Raising Girls, Surviving the Teen Years*...and a few others she couldn't make out.

"Kyle is a reading fanatic. He stocked this library." She smiled. "I kept the books in the divorce, of course."

Why "of course"? What did Kyle do, Allison wondered, that caused Desiree to make out so well? Her mind flitted back to Kyle with that young woman—no, girl—at the restaurant. Could Desiree be blackmailing Kyle? She snuck another look at the photos dotting the bookshelves, at the way Desiree positioned herself between Kyle and the girls in almost every one. Was he a child molester? But even if that was the case, and Allison hoped for the sake of the girls it was not, how would that tie in to Arnie's murder? Or Udele's murder, for that matter.

"What can I help you with this time, Allison?"

Allison caught the thinly-veiled annoyance in Desiree's voice, but she chose to ignore it. She could hardly blame her. "Thanks for the coffee." She put down her cup. "I was hoping to read the letters Maggie sent your daughter."

"I'm not sure I have them any longer."

Allison doubted the veracity of that statement. Someone who went to the trouble of testing the ink would have kept copies, even if the originals stayed with the police.

"Would you mind checking?"

"Why do you care?"

Allison decided to be honest. "Because I need to understand Maggie. I need to know what she's capable of."

Desiree sat there for a moment, an odd expression on her face. Finally, she rose and glided over to a small writing desk in the corner. She pulled a monogrammed keychain from her pocket and unlocked the top drawer. After rummaging for a moment, she pulled a paper-clipped stack of papers out. From this, she separated three sheets of paper and handed them to Allison.

Feeling apprehensive, Allison began to read. The first one was written in black marker, in large, uneven script. It seemed innocuous: mostly ramblings about Ethan and love, with a few four-letter words thrown in here and there. The second letter felt more sinister. At the top was a hand-drawn pentagram in a circle, at the bottom, an anarchy symbol. The letter was short:

> *Get out of my life, get out of his life. You know what I mean. I can't take it anymore. By the powers of the mighty Horned One, I will see to it that you can't hear or speak. I have said my prayer to the god of death and dying. Leave us alone...or else! – Lanomia*

Chilled, Allison flipped to the last note. It was slightly longer and written in a dark ink that certainly *looked* like dried blood. The beginning was much the same, orders to leave Maggie alone, orders to leave Ethan alone. At the top, another pentagram. At the end was written:

This is your last warning. Don't underestimate me. By this blood oath I vow that you will torment me no more. Oh Mighty Horned One, Oh Mighty Hunter, I have cast my wishes, I have made my sacrifices. God of death and dying, hear me.

Again, it was signed Lanomia. Finished, Allison stood and handed the letters back to Desiree. She understood now why the police were focused on Maggie. For a second, her vision fogged and her temples throbbed. *Sacrifices. Blood oath.* Oh, Maggie.

Desiree stood up and walked toward the window. She spoke with her back to Allison. "So now you understand."

Allison found her voice. "I do. This must have been hard on the family, especially your daughter."

"Oh, you have no idea. Hank McBride was a...well, a bastard to deal with, to put it nicely. He fought us every step of the way. Nothing was his fault. This ordeal caused my divorce. The tension, the stress. It's my girls who've lost out."

At the mention of divorce, Allison remembered the other part of the reason for her visit. She said gently, "Desiree, I could have sworn I saw Kyle at a restaurant downtown recently. I recognized him from the newspaper."

"You must have been mistaken."

"I don't think so. He was with a young lady, maybe your daughter's age. But it wasn't your daughter."

"I can assure you, it wasn't Kyle."

Despite Desiree's dismissal, Allison sensed she'd hit a nerve. When Desiree turned, Allison saw the other woman's facial muscles tighten and her eye twitch, ever so slightly. But for all Allison knew, Desiree's reaction was related to unresolved relationship problems, arguments over visitation schedules, or memories of transgressions.

Allison thought again about the letters. Clearly, Maggie's waters ran deeper than Allison had originally thought. But still, her gut said there was something she was missing, some piece to all of this that would make events clearer, the puzzle whole. But sadly, Allison had to admit that in her fervor to help another teen, she could have let her imagination run rampant. Perhaps that man had not been Kyle Moore. Perhaps she had been wrong.

"Thanks for your time," Allison said. She'd promised Vaughn, and herself, that she'd leave this avenue alone if it turned out to be a dead end. And for now, at least, she was staring at a brick wall.

While Desiree retrieved her coat, Allison looked at the parenting books again. Childhood bulimia, anger management, parenting in the computer age. One book caught her eye.

The book wasn't about child molestation. It wasn't about parenting at all. The book was called *Satan's Cohorts: Devil Worship in a New Millennium*.

Vaughn couldn't shake the feeling of foreboding. Like someone was walking on his grave. He'd known Allison for ages, but the woman sitting next to him was not the calm, rational ice queen he was used to. And that left him rattled.

They were in his car, on the way to meet Jamie. He finished describing his meeting with Marta Bremburg, leaving out the part about how gorgeous she was, and waited for Allison to say something.

Finally, she said, "Bremburg's still a possibility."

"Right, but he's old and sick."

"He could have hired someone."

"True. And he has the computer know-how," Vaughn said. "But what's his motivation, Allison?"

"Blackmail?" Allison was silent for a second. "Same with the Moores."

"Maggie and Ethan are still the most probable suspects. They had motive *and* opportunity. And don't forget the physical evidence linking Maggie to the murder scene. Her hair, for one thing"

"What about Sasha? Or Brenda, the ex-wife?"

"Jason said Sasha's cleared. She finally admitted that she was getting a little workout with the personal trainer when Arnie died. Brenda's still on the list as a possibility. Claims she was home alone. But the cops don't seem too interested in her."

"You can't dismiss the Moores out of hand, Vaughn. What about the Satan book? Your brother said someone could have been impersonating Maggie online. Yes, the letters were damning, but Maggie's witch name was on them. What if Kyle figured that out and began impersonating Maggie?"

"The book is just coincidence, Allison. I'm afraid you're looking for meaning where there is none." Vaughn pulled into his parking space next to Mrs. T's five-year-old Toyota and cut the ignition. He turned to watch Allison's face and saw that thinker's crease that told him she was still mulling over something.

"Then we have a series of strange coincidences."

Vaughn decided to try to see things her way, give Allison the benefit of the doubt. "Fine. Maggie and Sarah didn't get along. There was some adolescent love triangle between them and Ethan Feldman. So what? Maybe Desiree bought that Satan book to read up on the crap Maggie put in her threat letter."

"How do you explain Kyle at the restaurant?"

Vaughn took a deep breath. He knew he had to play it carefully here. "Maybe, just maybe, it wasn't Kyle Moore."

"I didn't imagine that. I recognized him. And then the waiter said his name."

"Restaurants are loud."

He saw that set of her jaw that meant she wasn't giving in on this one. "I know what I heard, Vaughn."

"Okay, fine. Maybe there was some innocent reason for that rendezvous. The daughter of a client? A woman who looked younger than she was? I don't know. What I do know is that you're letting your imagination run away with you. Ask yourself, Allison: Why would Kyle Moore want to murder Arnie Feldman? And why the hell would either of them want to murder Udele?"

"I don't know."

"Exactly. Motive. You need a motive. And right now you don't have a clear motive for the Moores. Or Bremburg. That leaves Maggie McBride."

"Just do me a favor?"

He tensed. "Of course."

"Watch Desiree's house for a few days? See if Kyle shows up?"

"Allison—"

"Please? Just humor me."

Vaughn wondered who was going to humor him when he needed to have Allison committed. "Okay," he said. "On one condition."

Allison waited.

"Tell me why you're so hell-bent on proving Maggie didn't do this."

Allison looked out the car window, letting the charged silence hang between them. When she spoke, Vaughn heard resignation, not anger.

"My gut says Maggie's innocent. My gut may be wrong. I just need to know the truth." She met his stare, and he glimpsed that iron will of hers again. "We all have devils from the past, Vaughn. It's time I face up to mine."

Vaughn nodded. It was a reason he could understand. "Well then," he said. "You ready to face my past demons? Jamie's waiting to meet you."

THIRTY-ONE

Vaughn opened his front door. He said nothing as they entered, his handsome face taut, as though he was trudging toward the inevitable. They walked through a long living room. Two black leather loveseats faced each other on one end, a bold, patterned red carpet between them. Atop the carpet sat a glass and chrome coffee table, its surface bare and spotlessly clean. A large entertainment center stood next to the couches, a flat-screen television and complex stereo system visible behind glass. The room was painted white. No art on the walls.

"This way."

Allison followed Vaughn through a narrow hallway toward a small kitchen and dining area. Like the living room, the kitchen was tidy—modern but austere. Jamie's nurse was standing by the stove.

"Mrs. T, meet Allison Campbell. My boss."

Vaughn put an arm around a large black woman. Her hair had been smoothed back into a neat bun and she wore a faded red apron, the dowdiness of which contrasted strongly with her long, shapely fingernails and ankle-length aqua skirt. Everything about Mrs. T was full and round: her face, her lips, her body. She exuded a motherly aura that was not lost on Allison's maternally-deprived soul. But Mrs. T's maternal feelings were clearly for Vaughn, and she was summing Allison up with the intensity of a mama lion protecting her cub.

After a moment, Mrs. T said, "Please, sit." She pointed to a small wooden table, already set with one place setting. While she gathered another plate and utensils from the cabinets and drawers, she said to no one in particular, "Flapjacks and sausage. My Ray makes the sausage himself."

She put a plate of pancakes and the beautifully browned meat in front of Allison and Vaughn.

"Jamie's working anyway. He had a rough night. Bad dreams again. I'm heading out soon, Christopher, so eat up an' I'll clean up this kitchen before I go."

Allison picked up her fork, still feeling dazed. Despite the nervous tugging in her belly, the food smelled good and she found her plate empty before she knew it.

"His boss, huh?" Mrs. T mumbled to herself while she bustled around the kitchen, picking up dishes, washing surfaces that already looked clean to Allison. "Work and sleep, work and sleep, that's all Christopher does, you know. That's not good. You're his boss, then you should know how hard he works. That's all I'm saying."

Vaughn started to say something, but Mrs. T cut him off.

"I'm not being disrespectful, Christopher. Miss Campbell looks like a nice lady. She should know you're working yourself to the bone."

Allison stood up. "I agree." She brought her dish to the sink and stuck it into a tub of soapy water.

"I'll get that—"

Allison waved her away. "Thank you for breakfast, best sausage I've ever had. The least I can do is the dishes." She said to Vaughn over her shoulder, "Mrs. T is right, you know. All work and no play makes Christopher Vaughn a very dull boy."

He laughed. "Is that so?"

"It is. Maybe we've both been too focused on work."

"You think?"

"Maybe you need to go out more, take a vacation."

Mrs. T said, "Now that's what I'm talkin' about."

Allison dried her dish and turned around. Vaughn was staring at her with wariness and surprise.

"And how am I supposed to take a vacation?"

Allison smiled. "Now that I'm finally meeting your brother, I'm sure I could help you out."

Mrs. T nodded. "That's right, Christopher. And you give me some notice, I'll be here every day." She smiled approvingly at Allison. "You got people, Christopher. It's time for a vacation. And a nice lady friend."

Vaughn shook his head, but he looked amused. "Remind me never to get you two together again. You're a dangerous combination."

Allison was unprepared for everything about meeting Jamie: the change in atmosphere from the rest of the apartment, the stifling warmth in the room, the faint, mingling odors of disinfectant and scented candles, and, most especially, the man himself.

Vaughn went in alone. She could hear what sounded like a one-sided conversation during which she heard Vaughn explaining to him who she was.

Vaughn's words were punctuated by silences, which Allison could only believe were filled with Jamie's side of the exchange, though she heard no other voice. Every so often she heard Vaughn say, "I'm sorry."

Allison felt jittery. She glanced at her watch. It was still morning, yet it seemed like a whole day had elapsed.

"Allison, ready?"

Vaughn had opened the door to Jamie's room. He moved back to let Allison through.

"Allison Campbell, meet my brother Jamie. James Emerson Vaughn, former first-string basketball player and class valedictorian. Allison Campbell, image consultant extraordinaire."

Jamie Vaughn was strapped into a motorized wheelchair at his desk. His painfully thin frame looked too weak to hold up his head. His graying hair was cropped short. He wore silver spectacles that only magnified the bright intelligence in his eyes. His face was attractive, his smile generous. This was Vaughn's twin alright, but a twisted version of his brother, at once smaller and larger than life.

They stared at each other for a long while, Allison conscious of the tube that ran from Jamie's body into what looked like an air compressor that hung on the back of the wheelchair. A thousand questions ran through her mind, from the concrete to the meta-physical: How can someone live like this? What are the machines, the technologies, helping Jamie survive? How can Vaughn deal with the guilt, the reminder, the stress, day after day? And how the hell had he managed to hide such a huge piece of his life?

In answer to a question she had not asked, Vaughn said, "Mrs. T is a registered nurse. They all are, the folks who attend to Jamie. He's as self-sufficient as he can be, but...there are limits."

Indeed, his limits were evident by this room, which was as high-tech as it was clean. Allison looked around, trying to compre-hend how Jamie managed without any mobility. Next to a specially equipped bed was a computer monitor connected to a mouthpiece that extended out, a funny-shaped nozzle on the end. A lift sat in the rear left corner of the room. In the other corner stood a U-shaped desk housing a series of turntables that held files and books and another computer. Like the computer by the bedside, a mouth-piece was connected to this computer's keyboard.

Vaughn had clearly made an effort to soften the tech-lab feel of the room with satin comforters, a graceful loveseat and chair near the bed, rich chocolate-colored drapes and ice-blue accent pillows. But still, the room contained more high-tech toys and wires than a Best Buy.

Jamie took the mouthpiece between his teeth and words began to glow on the monitor in front of him.

MRS. T IS MY FAVORITE. THOUGH I THINK ANGELA MIGHT BE VAUGHN'S.

Vaughn laughed. "Hey now—"

ALL YOUR PARTS WORK, MY BROTHER. AT LEAST ONE OF US SHOULD BE HAVING SOME FUN.

Vaughn smiled. "There's a lady present."

SORRY. MY MANNERS SEEM TO HAVE DISAPPEARED ALONG WITH MY MOBILITY. ALLISON, IT IS A PLEASURE TO MEET YOU.

"Likewise, Jamie."

VAUGHN SAYS YOU ARE A GREAT BOSS AND A GOOD FRIEND. MY BROTHER HAS SPENT MORE THAN A DECADE PUNISHING HIMSELF FOR SOMETHING THAT WAS NOT HIS FAULT. MAYBE NOW THAT YOU KNOW HIS SECRETS, YOU CAN HELP HIM FIND FORGIVENESS.

Jamie was looking at Vaughn as he spoke, but Vaughn didn't seem ready to hear his brother's absolution. He'd turned away and stood near the window, where he busied himself adjusting the shade. Allison was certain he could not see the screen from that angle.

VAUGHN TELLS ME YOU'RE SOMETHING OF A SLEUTH. A MODERN-DAY NANCY DREW, STICKING YOUR NOSE WHERE IT DOESN'T BELONG.

Allison smiled. "Is that so?"

I LOVE IT. TELL ME WHAT'S HAPPENING.

Allison glanced at Vaughn, who still seemed engrossed in the shades, so she said, "Are you sure you want to hear all the gory details?"

I HAVE AN AEROBICS CLASS TO ATTEND IN AN HOUR, SO YOU'LL HAVE TO MAKE IT QUICK.

The smile on his face made light of his words, and Allison found herself getting comfortable. Jamie would humor her, listen to the pieces, and tell her if she was crazy to pursue this. She explained how Hank McBride had come to her, her involvement with Maggie, the little she knew about the Bremburgs, the Moore family.

NOTHING YOU'VE TOLD ME SO FAR WEIGHS IN ON THE ISSUE OF MURDER. WALK ME THROUGH YOUR FACTS ABOUT EACH PERSON AND TELL ME HOW THEY FIT IN THE PUZZLE. START WITH MAGGIE.

"Okay, Maggie. We know she probably disliked Feldman for keeping her from Ethan. We also know she is into Wicca and has had some exposure to the occult. To me, she's still a kid and how could a kid—"

Allison watched Jamie take the mouthpiece. His features scrunched into an impatient frown.

FACTS. TELL ME FACTS, NOT CONJECTURE.

"Okay, sorry."

She tried to hide her ruffled feathers. He was right, of course. Facts. They needed to focus on the facts. She started over. "Maggie. Fifteen, infatuated with the first victim's son. Feldman had forbidden Ethan from seeing her. She has a history of antisocial behavior in the form of shoplifting, opposition to authority, making threats to a fellow student. Has dabbled in Wicca and has at least some knowledge of the occult. No decent alibi for either murder. Symbols at the scenes of both crimes, as well as the presence of Maggie's hair and handwriting, have led the police to link Maggie to the murders."

DOESN'T SOUND GOOD SO FAR. YOU HAVE MOTIVE AND OPPORTUNITY. PLUS DIRECT EVIDENCE LINKING HER TO THE SCENE.

He stopped for a second and appeared to be thinking. It amazed Allison how the vitality in his eyes contrasted with the deadness of his body. Vaughn came over and sat next to her on the loveseat. Jamie cleared his throat, and Allison turned back to the screen:

GO ON.

Allison reviewed what little they knew about Ethan Feldman, Brenda Feldman, Sasha Feldman, and the Bremburgs. "Jack's ex-wife had motive—to keep custody of her daughter—but it doesn't look like she'd have opportunity, and she would not likely have known about Maggie and the witchcraft. And as for Jack, a possibility, but he'd have to have hired someone."

ANYONE ELSE?

"They, along with Ethan Feldman, were the more obvious ones. Of course, the police may have leads of which we're not aware." She paused, but Jamie was looking at her expectantly. "Kyle Moore. I know this will sound absurd," she spoke quickly, letting the words spill out, one on top of the other, "as he seems so unconnected to the case. But listen. I have to pull the few facts together with conjecture." When Jamie didn't object, Allison filled him in on her encounters with Desiree Moore.

She stopped, suddenly aware as she spoke of how tenuous and absurd the Moores' connection sounded. Where was her head? Out of the likely cast of characters, Maggie was the only one who knew both victims, had motive and opportunity. Why was Allison so desperate to prove Maggie innocent when the writing was written in blood on the wall, just like those letters?

Allison stood. "I'm sorry I wasted your time with this. Thanks for listening to me, really."

She turned toward the door when she felt Vaughn grab her arm gently. He pointed toward the screen.

TELL ME ABOUT THE LETTERS.

Allison sat back down and told him what she could remember.

WRITE THAT DOWN.

Vaughn disappeared for a moment and then returned with a legal pad and a pen. Allison recreated what she could recall of the letters, including the symbols, and put the pad by Jamie. He glanced at them.

DID YOU KNOW THAT LANOMIA, MAGGIE'S WICCAN NAME, IS THE NAME FOR AN ASSASIN CATERPILLAR? ONE OF THE MOST DEADLY CREATURES IN BRAZIL.

Allison swallowed. Not what she wanted to hear.

BUT THAT DOESN'T NECESSARILY MEAN ANYTHING ALLISON. IF SOMEONE FRAMED HER, THEY WOULD KNOW THAT. IT WOULD MAKE THEIR ACTIONS MORE BELIEVABLE.

"And how does that help?" Allison asked.

FORGET ABOUT MAGGIE FOR A MOMENT. THINK ABOUT ONE OF THE COMMON DENOMINATORS IN ALL OF THIS.

"Besides Maggie?"

YES. SOMETHING ELSE. THE OTHER PLAYERS. WHAT DO THEY HAVE IN COMMON?

She shook her head. "What?"

THINK.

They were all well-off people on the Main Line. So what? They traveled in intersecting circles. So what? She thought about how they all knew Arnie Feldman.

"Divorce."

EXACTLY. DIVORCE. AND WHAT DO YOU NEED TO COM-
PLETE A DIVORCE?

"A divorce attorney."

YES. AND WHAT HAPPENS DURING A DIVORCE?

"Secrets can come out. People can get hurt."

Jamie smiled.

Vaughn said, "The Moores weren't clients."

DO YOU KNOW THAT FOR SURE? THE MOORES WERE
ALSO GETTING DIVORCED. ALLISON NEVER FOUND OUT
THE REASON FOR THEIR SPLIT. IF I UNDERSTAND HER
THINKING, SHE SUSPECTS THAT KYLE COULD BE A PEDO-
PHILE AND THE MURDER OF FELDMAN WAS SOMEHOW RE-
LATED. SHE MIGHT BE RIGHT. MAYBE BLACKMAIL WAS IN-
VOLVED AFTER ALL.

Allison sat back down, on the edge of the couch. She tried, un-
successfully, to hide the excitement in her voice. "If that's the case,
then Kyle Moore could have set up Maggie. He'd have known about
Maggie through the letter ordeal. He could have impersonated
Maggie—Lanomia—online to bolster the appearance of guilt. He
would have known Feldman and Feldman may have let him in the
house, which would explain why there was no breaking and entering.... as for Udele..." She realized she had no explanation for Udele.

Allison read Jamie's screen: NO DOUBT RELATED.

Allison could see the exhaustion in Jamie's face, but his in-
sights and confidence had lent her hope. Maybe there was a way to
solve this. Maybe she wasn't crazy. But one thing still bothered her.

"Even if we're right, why go to all that trouble to frame anyone?
Why not just hire someone?"

Vaughn said, "Two reasons. One, hit men talk. Two, Congressman McBride."

"Hank?"

Vaughn nodded. "For some reason, McBride seems untoucha-
ble in these parts. But he's *not* loved. Maybe whoever is using Maggie is also trying to get back at her father."

"I thought of that. And what better way than to destroy the one
thing he loves—not his daughter, his career. If Maggie is convicted,

his career is toast." Allison could feel her adrenaline soar. "Vaughn, you'll still watch Desiree's house, to see if Kyle visits?"

He nodded.

"We need to establish a connection between Feldman and Kyle Moore."

YES. WITHOUT THAT CONNECTION YOU HAVE NO MO-TIVE AND YOUR THEORY FALLS APART.

Vaughn said, "Sasha. She may be able to confirm whether Moore was a client. If she doesn't know, she may have access to his client records."

"Good idea. One of us should visit the grieving widow."

EVEN SO, SHE WON'T BE ABLE TO TELL YOU ABOUT FELDMAN'S INTEGRITY AS A LAWYER, AND THAT'S WHAT YOU HAVE TO FIND OUT, TOO. WAS HE HONEST? IF HE DID LEARN THAT MOORE OR BREMBURG WAS A PEDOPHILE, WHAT WOULD HE DO WITH THAT INFORMATION?

Vaughn said, "I can check to see if there have been any ethics complaints against Feldman. And we can check with Jason to see if either Moore or Bremburg has a record."

Allison thought of something. Mia. She leaned over and kissed Vaughn, then stood and kissed Jamie. "You're a genius. You both are." She looked at Vaughn again. "Mia! I've been trying to figure out who would know about Feldman's character. Who better to answer that question than a woman who sat in a courtroom with him? Mia battled Edward and Arnie after Bridget died. If anyone would have a sense of Arnie Feldman's ethics, she would."

THIRTY-TWO

Mia shrugged. "I'm afraid I can't tell you much."

That wasn't what Allison wanted to hear. She leaned against the broken fence post and felt her heels dig into the soft ground. While she waited for Mia to say more, she watched her kneel, pick up a piece of plywood, and nail it to the rickety fence frame. Mia's wild gray hair was pulled back in a loose ponytail, and wayward curls framed her face. A streak of dirt ran the length of one cheek.

"In my opinion, Allison, Arnie Feldman was a shyster. A real shark. Other than that, what can I say? My feelings for him are recorded for all posterity in that court transcript."

Allison handed Mia another piece of plywood. She scanned the property. Here, not even that far from the city, the air smelled of damp leaves and burning wood, not car exhaust. There were still working farms and Sunday church dinners, and people didn't lock their doors. Mia had taken it upon herself to fix the fence alongside her driveway, and it was this task that Allison had offered to help with.

"Grab the nails," Mia said. "And hold this hammer." She handed Allison the tool, straightened-up and then stretched backward, arching her back as she did so. She was still slim. A sinewy length of arm peeked from beneath her gray flannel shirt. Flannel. When Allison had first met Mia, back when First Impressions was a no-name operation run out of the first floor of a Route 30 storefront, Mia would have worn silk. Or cashmere. But not flannel.

But, Allison had to admit, flannel looked good on her.

Mia positioned a nail against the wood. She spoke with another nail between her lips. "Allison, I had just lost my daughter. My husband had a blood-alcohol level more than twice the legal limit. Witnesses told police that Bridget didn't want to get in that car. Arnie went into our divorce hell-bent on making me look like a deranged woman for wanting Edward to take some damn responsibility. Does that sound like an ethical man to you?"

"I don't know, Mia. Maybe there's a difference between spinning the facts to advocate for your client and breaking the law."

Mia slammed the hammer against the head of a nail, pushing it beyond the surface of the wood. She eyed the circular impression and said, "Arnie filled Edward's head with nonsense. I have no doubt it was Feldman's idea to make me look mentally unstable. And so he allowed Edward to get away with what basically amounted to murder."

"Arnie was a lawyer. Lawyer ethics don't always comport with normal ideas about ethics. What I need to understand is whether Arnie was willing to go beyond lawyer ethics. Whether Arnie was capable of blackmail."

Mia was quiet for a moment. She nailed another piece of plywood to the fence and then stood back to examine her handiwork. She took a long, flat-headed nail and pounded it into the bottom of the board.

"Do you know why I maintain this fence?" Mia said.

"To keep people off your property."

"No." Mia picked up a stick, looked it over, and then tossed it into a nearby bush. "I maintain it so that my neighbors know where their property ends and mine begins. I don't like the lines to be fuzzy."

"And Arnie—"

"Some people are too comfortable with ambiguity, Allison. Some people see everything—property lines, the accumulation of wealth, life and death—as negotiable. No hard rules, no absolutes. For them, ambiguity means opportunity. That was Arnie."

"So you do think he was capable of blackmail?"

Mia pocketed the rest of the nails and tucked the hammer under her arm. "Honestly, I don't know. But I do suspect," she said, and turned to look straight into Allison's eyes, "that his comfort with ambiguity finally caught up with him. I suspect he knew too much about the wrong person. And for that he was killed."

Disappointed, Midge clicked off the phone. It was unlike Allison to cancel appointments and this was the second one in two weeks. Something was going on. Midge held the postcard up to the light. She'd been excited to share it with Allison and to tell her she got the job. Midge turned the postcard over in her hand. Marjory Louise Minion, pin-up girl, 1960. There she was in her glory days. Jet black hair formed in thick curls around her face. She'd worn a red bathing suit, modest by today's standards, but back then its strapless neckline and bare midriff seemed so risqué. Midge could still remember the excitement.

It had all lasted about ten seconds. And then she met Randolph.

When he came upon Midge stranded with a flat tire at the side of the road in coal mining country, Pennsylvania, he thought he was rescuing a damsel in distress. And that's how he treated her the entire forty years of marriage, like a fragile flower he had saved from ruin. Midge returned the postcard to its hiding place in the manila envelope tucked underneath the china dessert plates.

Randolph. Midge closed the door to the China cabinet and turned the tiny pewter key in the lock. Looking back, there were so many clues, if only she'd had her eyes open. The long stares at men—not women—when they went to restaurants. She'd thought he was warning them away. And the sex. The sex should have been her first clue. She'd been no virgin when they met, true, but she'd been innocent enough to think maybe his behavior in the boudoir was normal.

For the first ten years of marriage, they'd done it once every two weeks, like clockwork. Always on a Friday night. Always with the lights out.

And she spent years trying to ignore her disappointment over their sex life because any boredom in the bedroom must have been *her* fault. She was too demanding or unattractive or scatterbrained or uncreative for him. She had to accept her lot and move ahead with life.

So she did. She gave birth to two babies. She volunteered at the local women's shelter. She made casseroles for shut-ins and taught piano lessons to runny-nosed grade-schoolers. She sang in the choir, lunched with the neighbors, and planted a magnificent rose garden. Like her mother before her, she made something out of nothing. And she kept the bits of what could have been under lock and key in the china closet.

Of course, when she found him with the neighbor's married son, well, the poor dear didn't have a chance. She could still picture Randolph running down the stairs, his pants around his ankles. The neighbor was nude. And the lights had been on. That was what had thrown her over the edge. The blazing lights.

And after everything, it was Allison who helped her find the will to live again. She owed that woman a great debt. And, by golly, she would find a way to repay her.

Midge turned off the dining room chandelier and headed toward the kitchen. Something was going on, Midge just knew it. Allison was sick or depressed or someone in her family had died. Allison never let them down...and now, two sessions in a row? She clicked on the phone and dialed Tori's number. This time, Allison needed *them*. They'd march over there and show her how much they cared.

Vaughn sat in the BMW and waited. He disliked Desiree's neighborhood. Big chandeliers with hanging crystals shining through oversized foyer windows. Three-car garages. Engraved nameplates over double-wide entries. What was all that about? Too many white folks trying to look richer than they were.

Outside, the wind was starting to pick up. He thought he'd make it to the gym, maybe visit with Mia later, catch a movie, have some dinner. Surveillance was his least favorite activity. And Desiree sure was boring.

The lights were on in Desiree's home. He watched her daughters walk home from the bus stop and go inside. At one point, he could make out Desiree's profile in a window.

His phone rang. Allison. "Yo," he said.

"Anything?"

"*Nada.* And I called Jason, but haven't heard back from him."

"Can you try Sasha?"

"You already met her. Wouldn't it make more sense for you to go?"

"I have something I have to do," she said.

He enjoyed a moment of relief thinking she was back at her old game and had some work, real work, to handle. A politician with a speech to deliver or a book club to address. But when she said, "Maggie," the relief turned to dread.

"Fine. I'll talk to Sasha, Allison," he said. "Of course I will. But it's a bad idea to go see that kid. McBride warned you off, and that should be enough reason to keep your distance."

Allison laughed. It wasn't quite a sane laugh. In fact, it was a downright crazy laugh.

"Hank can go to hell," Allison said. "Sunny called me while I was at Mia's. Maggie was arrested. And now Hank is trying to have his daughter declared insane."

THIRTY-THREE

"Out with it Maggie. All of it. I want the truth this time," Allison said.

If Allison was expecting Maggie to look depressed or repentant, she was wrong. Without the Goth makeup and layers of black garb, she appeared scrubbed and healthy and very, very full of spit and fire. Maggie was being held at a juvenile lock-up, so their conversation had to take place under police observation. They sat on two tape-covered vinyl chairs across a battered table, its feet stuffed into sliced tennis balls to protect a scarred wooden floor. The smells of body odor and stale cigarette smoke overwhelmed the senses.

Maggie said, "How's Brutus?"

"You tell me the truth, Maggie, and we talk about Brutus."

Maggie scowled. For a moment, Allison thought she would refuse to cooperate but a second later, she said, "Fine. What do you want to know?"

Allison leaned in, keeping her voice a whisper. She said gently but urgently, "Were you involved with Arnie Feldman's murder, Maggie?"

"No."

"Udele's?"

"Of course not!"

Allison tried to read her expression. Was she being honest? She thought of Violet, of the session with Violet right before she'd run away. Allison had had no real clue that Violet was up to something, just a vague sense of anxiety and "Sparky," that unfamiliar name. And now with Maggie, how could she really know what the truth was? Wasn't that what teens did: bend the truth to suit their needs, consequences be damned? Back then, she had ignored her instincts. Now, she decided, she would trust them.

And her instincts said Maggie was innocent. Troubled. Unruly. Oppositional and dramatic. But innocent.

Maggie said, "You believe me?"

"Yes."

They regarded one another for a moment. Maggie smiled. "Is that it?"

"No." Allison reviewed what she'd found out about her and Sarah.

"All true," Maggie said. "I hate Sarah Moore."

"But you knew she'd get you in trouble, Maggie."

"I didn't care. She was trying to steal Ethan. She made fun of me constantly at school. She pretended to be nice, got good grades. Teachers would never believe she'd do the things she did. I had to do something."

"You could have told your parents. Maybe not your dad, but your mom?"

Maggie snorted.

"Your mom's the one who gave me permission to speak with you today, you know."

Maggie looked surprised. "That's a first. Daddy will kill her." Her eyes darkened. "Watch out, Allison. I wouldn't trust her. Daddy may be up to something."

Allison had thought of that. She wouldn't have put it past McBride to use Sunny to try to ensnare her somehow, especially now that Maggie had been officially charged. But Sunny had sounded desperate, and upset. Very upset. Allison's gut told her the grief was genuine. But Maggie's concern still touched her.

"I read the letters, Maggie. The ones you sent to Sarah Moore."

Maggie shrugged. "That was stupid. I paid the price for it."

"You're paying the price now. Don't you get that? Those letters tie you to the Feldman crime scene."

"I didn't kill anybody."

"But you admitted to Satan worship in those letters."

Maggie laughed. "Hardly."

"'God of death and dying,' 'Horned One'?"

"*Ohmyfreakinggoddess!*"

The guard stood up and looked menacingly at Maggie and Allison. "Shhhh," Allison said. "They'll make me leave."

She glanced at the large clock on the wall, its face secured by a network of crisscrossed bars. "I only have another ten minutes as it is."

Maggie lowered her voice. "The Horned One is Cernunnos, not Satan. A Celtic god. I told you, Wiccans don't believe in doing evil."

"But the letters mention sacrifices."

"Personal sacrifices. Giving up chocolate, not swearing. I wanted Sarah to go away."

"Then why make references to this Cernunnos? You had to have known he sounded like the devil."

Maggie looked abashed. "Maybe I wanted to scare her. But only a little bit! I wouldn't have hurt her. And I would never hurt an animal!"

"Then whose blood was on the letter, Maggie?"

"Mine."

She thought about the Feldman crime scene. The chicken blood and dog feces. The handwriting that matched Maggie's. "You never used animal blood?"

"Ohmygoddess, Allison! I don't even eat meat—you think I would kill an animal to write a stupid letter? Anyway, I only used the blood in the last two letters. The first two were written in ink."

Allison looked at her. "How many letters did you send?"

"Four."

But Desiree said there were three.

"Are you certain?"

"Of course I'm sure! I wrote them."

So Desiree was lying. Or she didn't know about the fourth letter. Allison thought about the crime scene, about the bits of Maggie's handwriting found near Feldman's body. How easy it would have been to use that fourth letter to plant Maggie at the scene of the murder. Too easy.

"Do you have a lawyer, Maggie?"

Maggie rolled her eyes. "Daddy hired some old guy with disgusting nostril hair. He wants to argue that I'm not responsible for my actions because I'm crazy. But I didn't do it, Allison." She stood up. "How can I be held responsible for a murder I didn't do?"

The guard shot them another warning look.

"Sit down, Maggie," Allison hissed. "They're watching."

"I don't care," Maggie said. But she sat down. "God, Allison. Don't you get it? Daddy doesn't care whether I'm innocent. All he cares about is trying to keep me out of the news."

Allison had to agree.

Maggie chewed the end of a worn and jagged thumbnail. "So he hired some Dr. Loser to dissect my brain so Attorney Nose-Hair can get me locked up in a nut house. They can all kiss my—"

Allison stopped her with a raised finger.

"Focus, Maggie. There has to be something you can tell me that will help your case."

"Nothing."

"Think."

"I have been thinking, Allison. I was with Ethan the night his father died. They don't believe either one of us, so how do we prove that? And the day Udele disappeared, I was with you."

"Not till the afternoon, Maggie. Where were you earlier?"

She sat silently for a minute. Behind her, a girl with dyed-orange hair and a nose stud let out a smoker's cough. She swore in Spanish at another resident. "I was shopping," Maggie said finally. But she avoided Allison's gaze. Allison knew there must be more.

"Why didn't you tell the police that?"

"Because. They wouldn't have believed me anyway."

"But there would be purchase records, surveillance cameras."

"Not where I went."

"Where did you go, Maggie?"

Maggie sat forward, pulled her legs up on the chair, and wrapped her arms around her legs. "New Hope."

It certainly wasn't immediately obvious to Allison why Maggie would want to go there. The small Bucks County town had a lot to offer in terms of restaurants and culture...but for a fifteen-year-old? And it was over an hour from Villanova. "Why in the world would you go to New Hope? And *how* did you get there?"

"I took the train as far as I could. Then I called a cab." She chewed her thumbnail again. "I went to The Witches Brew. It's a Wicca store. I knew they would use that against me, Allison, which is why I didn't say anything."

"But there would still be a trail. A train ticket, a receipt. Cell phone records. All proof that you weren't home when Udele was killed."

"I've got nothing. No receipts, no tickets. I didn't buy anything."

"But the phone company will have a record of your cell-phone call to the cab company."

"I used a pay phone at the train station."

Allison's mind spun. This was still something. The cabbie might remember her. There should be records. "Why did you go, Maggie?"

"To look at the spell books. I jotted some notes. But they're not dated. They don't mean anything."

"Spells for what?"

Maggie hesitated. "For home. To make things better. So I...so I didn't have to work with you." She looked ashamed. "I'm sorry. But seriously, Allison, you came into my house acting all stuck up and important. What else could I do?"

Allison smiled, despite everything. "It's okay. I think the feeling was mutual. But you turned out to not be so bad, you know."

Maggie rolled her eyes again, dramatically. "You either, Allison." Maggie held Allison's gaze for a minute and then said, more seriously, "But what about New Hope?"

Allison nodded. There had to be an alibi in there somewhere. If not the cabbie, the staff at the Witches Brew would remember Maggie. Hopefully.

"Was Udele home when you left?"

"Yes. She made me breakfast, as usual. Sugarless, tasteless, low-fat food. Daddy's orders for his chubby daughter. The first thing I did when I got to New Hope was have a chocolate croissant and a café mocha."

"How long were you gone?"

"Four hours. Maybe less."

"You left when you would have normally gone to school?"

Maggie nodded.

"That means you got home well before you came to see me. So, who saw you come home?"

"No one."

"No one? Not even your mom? I thought she was usually home during the day."

Maggie's mouth twisted into a grin, but it was a smile that left Allison cold. "My mother was home, but she was busy. I saw her. And I'm pretty sure she didn't see me."

Allison tried to hide her impatience. It was Maggie's butt on the line, yet she was playing games. "What was she doing that she wouldn't see you?"

"Not what, Allison. Who."

Startled, Allison could only say, "What?"

Sunny was having an affair? She would expect that from her husband. But Sunny? The woman didn't seem the type. But then again, she'd seen enough nasty divorces to know there really wasn't a type.

"Who was she with, Maggie? Did you know him?"

"Not him. *Her.* My mom's a rug-muncher, Allison. I've seen her with women before. Just one of the things she doesn't want Daddy to know."

Allison looked at Maggie, trying to discern if this admission was true—and, if so, whether it upset her. If it did, she wasn't letting on. To be fifteen and have seen so much, know so many sordid secrets. Poor Maggie. No wonder the kid was so mixed up.

Allison remembered the dark woman who was with Sunny and Catherine the day Udele's body was found. Maybe that was her lover. They certainly seemed familiar with each other. And the woman did seem protective of Sunny, territorial even. Allison realized the news didn't completely surprise her.

"Did you recognize the woman your mom was with?"

"Oh, I recognized her alright. Which is why I stayed out of sight."

"And?"

"I'll give you a hint," Maggie said. "You asked me why I didn't tell my folks about Sarah instead of going after her myself."

"Yes, so?"

"I knew it was pointless."

"I'm not following you, Maggie," Allison said, before sudden comprehension forced a shiver down the length of her spine.

"My mom was with Sarah's mom," Maggie whispered, confirming Allison's fears. "Mrs. Moore."

Allison tried to call Vaughn. Six rings, then his voice mail. She texted him. No response. *Where is he?*

She put the car into drive and pulled out of the juvie parking lot. Too many coincidences. Sarah and Maggie, Kyle Moore at the restaurant...now Desiree Moore and Sunny McBride? Desiree had been in Udele's presence on the day she disappeared. That might mean Kyle had access, too. She needed to find out whether Arnie Feldman had ever represented Kyle Moore. And if Moore had been Arnie's client and there had been a disagreement between them, that could constitute a motive...Tenuous, at best, Allison had to admit. But something.

At least "Horned One" was not a reference to the devil. Hallelujah!

But even if Vaughn could prove that Arnie Feldman had something on Moore, how could she convince the police? They had their girl. Why look further? It would only make them look incompetent. Hank McBride, too afraid of bad publicity, wasn't fighting Maggie's arrest. So it would be up to them to glue the pieces together. She believed the Moores were somehow involved. But she needed to find the proverbial smoking gun.

But how?

She tried Vaughn again. No answer. Maybe she'd head back to the office. Catch up on some paperwork, take time to think. There was a pattern here. If she could just connect the dots, the real killer would be revealed. But before she went to First Impressions, she'd call Sunny. Maybe Sunny could shed some light on this mess. And if Sunny was involved? Allison didn't even want to consider how a mother could do that to her own child. She hoped to hell that wasn't the case.

THIRTY-FOUR

Vaughn didn't go right to Sasha's. Instead, he stopped at home first to visit his brother. Jamie had been keeping up with his online research, and Vaughn wanted to see what news he had today.

"Chicken soup," Mrs. T yelled from Jamie's room. "And biscuits. Fix yourself a big bowl. There's plenty to go around."

Vaughn dumped his phone on the entry table and then followed his nose to the kitchen. There, he dipped a spoon in the soup, blew on it and sipped at the broth. Perfect.

Vaughn grabbed a few biscuits and walked into Jamie's room. Mrs. T was sitting on the loveseat, reading from a novel.

"Want me to stop there, Jamie?" Mrs. T was saying. Vaughn couldn't see Jamie's response on the monitor, but Mrs. T closed a book and stood up. "He's all yours, Christopher."

When Mrs. T was out of earshot, Vaughn filled Jamie in on the recent events between bites.

"Allison is with Maggie now," he said. "And for the last few hours, I've been watching the Moore house. Nothing."

HOW ABOUT MIA? ANY SUCCESS THERE?

"Nothing new. Mia thinks Feldman may have known too much. She hated him. So I take Mia's opinion with a few grains of salt."

BREMBURG?

"Other than the wife's allegations, nothing. Absolutely clean."

DOESN'T NECESSARILY MEAN ANYTHING.

"True." Vaughn sat on the edge of the bed and absentmindedly straightened Jamie's blankets with his free hand. "But anyway, Mia doesn't think Arnie was the blackmailing type. So I guess that says something, if even Mia wouldn't accuse him of blackmail. She's accused him of everything else."

I NEED MORE INFORMATION ABOUT THE CRIME SCENE.

"I can ask Jason, but why?"

BECAUSE I DID SOME RESEARCH ON THE DIFFERENCES BETWEEN WICCA AND SATANISM. IT'S POSSIBLE MAGGIE WASN'T REFERRING TO SATAN IN THAT LETTER. THERE'S A CELTIC GOD NAMED CERNUNNOS. HE IS SOMETIMES REFERRED TO AS THE GOD OF DEATH. IN SOME WICCAN TRADITIONS, HE IS THE MASCULINE COUNTERPOINT TO THE GODDESS. HE IS ALSO CALLED THE HORNED ONE.

"Hence the mix-up."

THAT'S WHY I NEED MORE INFORMATION ABOUT THE CRIME SCENES. ALLISON SAID PENTAGRAMS HAD BEEN DRAWN. SATANISTS USE AN UPSIDE-DOWN PENTAGRAM WITHIN A CIRCLE. IN HER LETTERS, MAGGIE DREW AN UPRIGHT PENTAGRAM—A WICCAN SYMBOL. WHICH ONE WAS USED AT THE CRIME SCENES? IT FEELS MORE AND MORE LIKE SOMEONE IS TWISTING MAGGIE'S IDENTITY TO SUIT THE SITUATION.

Vaughn's stomach twisted into a knot. "If that's the case, and it's someone we've touched, Allison could be in danger."

Vaughn picked up the phone in Jamie's room and dialed Jason's cell. This time, Jason answered.

"I looked into Kyle Moore, Vaughn," Jason said. "He's clean."

Bremburg, now Moore. Vaughn thought about what that meant. Had Allison been off-base about Moore? Or had he just been lucky so far? Vaughn explained Jamie's question about the crime scene and the pentagram.

"I didn't think there was a difference," Jason said.

Vaughn said, "Me either. But Jamie said the Wiccans use an upright pentagram. The Satanists, an inverted one."

"I just recall the word 'pentagram' in the reports I read. But I'll go back and ask to see the photos. Can I call you back?"

"The sooner the better."

Vaughn was looking down at his hand, thinking about the players in this situation, and didn't immediately see Jamie's next words. When he looked up, he said, "Are you sure?"

I'M SURE. THE CHANGES IN MAGGIE'S PERSONALITY BEGAN WEEKS AFTER THE LETTERS WERE SENT TO SARAH. PLUS, I WAS ABLE TO CONFIRM THAT LANOMIA HAS BEEN LOGGING IN USING TWO DIFFERENT EMAIL ADDRESSES. ONE IS REGISTERED TO JANE DOE. Jamie paused, took a deep breath, and continued. I THINK ALLISON IS RIGHT. MAGGIE IS BEING FRAMED.

Vaughn was just pulling into Sasha Feldman's driveway when he realized he'd forgotten his phone. But his need for expediency outweighed his desire for his mobile. He'd get it later, before he took another swing past Desiree's house.

He knocked six times before Sasha answered. He knew she was there: he had seen her car in the driveway and that little Chihuahua kept running up to the living room window and away again, as though alerting someone that a stranger was outside. So he waited. When Sasha finally opened the door, she said nothing, just ogled him with an intense once-over that made him feel exposed.

"Yes?" she said, with a look that could have been boredom or vapidity. He couldn't tell.

Vaughn decided not to sugar-coat his reason for the visit. "I work with Allison Campbell," he said. "You spoke with her a few days ago."

Her eyes lit up.

"I have a few more questions for you."

"Oh." She looked less eager, but stepped outside in her bare feet, closing the front door behind her. "What do you want? I already told Allison what I know."

"Mrs. Feldman, was Kyle Moore Arnie's client?"

"No."

"Red haired man, freckles—"

"I know who he is. I said no."

A helicopter flew overhead. Sasha looked up and, in that instance, Vaughn saw someone pull aside a living room drape and peek outside. A bare-chested male someone. Hmmm, Vaughn thought. No wonder it took her a few minutes to answer the door. Allison's description of Sasha came back to him. No grieving widow is right.

"Kyle Moore," Sasha said. "Sarah Moore's father."

"Right. You're sure he wasn't a client?"

"I'm sure. Ethan and Sarah knew each other from school. Kyle wasn't Arnie's client."

Vaughn's impatience was growing. He felt a sense of urgency, and Sasha's obstinacy wasn't helping to hurry things along. "Yes, I understand that—"

"But Desiree was."

Vaughn froze. This was news. He'd been focused on Kyle, but there was no reason Desiree wouldn't have hired Arnie. He tried to consider the implications. "Had she ever been to the house, Mrs. Feldman?"

Sasha thought for a moment. "Yes. At least once. To pick up papers and talk to Arnie." Sasha shrugged. "Maybe more, but I wouldn't really know."

Vaughn thought about this. It meant Desiree would have known the lay-out of the house. She could have even seen Arnie punch the code for the alarm.

"Was Desiree Moore Arnie's client until the divorce went through?"

Sasha laughed. "Are you joking? As far as I know, their divorce was never finalized."

More news. He was pretty sure Allison thought they *were* divorced. Vaughn was starting to see the full picture here—and he didn't like the shape it was taking.

The dog barked, and Sasha turned to go back inside. Vaughn put his hand on her arm gently to stop her. He still had one more pressing question and couldn't lose her now. "Can you remember whether Desiree and Arnie had a falling out? Did they argue? Did she threaten to fire him?"

Sasha took his hand and moved it off her arm. "I doubt it. *No one* fired Arnie Feldman. It was like a marriage. Till death do you part. Once Arnie was your attorney, you stuck with him until the end."

THIRTY-FIVE

Sunny agreed to meet Allison at a Starbucks along the Route 30 corridor. Allison arrived first. She parked the Volvo and sprinted inside, her hands shaking. Feeling dazed and slightly feverish—she hoped it wasn't a cold coming on—she ordered hot tea and then grabbed a table next to the window. She tried on scenarios while she waited for Sunny.

Maybe Kyle Moore, angry at the two women's affair, killed Arnie Feldman and framed Maggie, hoping to get revenge on the McBride family. Maybe Arnie had been blackmailing the Moores because of the affair. But how would he have known? Allison wished she knew the Arnie-Kyle connection. She pulled out her cell and checked to see if Vaughn had called. Nothing. She was dying to hear whether Arnie had represented Kyle.

"Allison?"

Allison looked up to see Sunny standing over her. Sunny's hair was twisted into a chignon, and she wore a pink trench coat and sunglasses. A cream-colored scarf had been tied in a neat knot around her slender throat. She looked thin, drawn, and pale—very much the tragic figure.

Sunny sat down across from Allison and removed the sunglasses. Dark circles shrouded her eyes. "How is my daughter?"

"As well as can be expected. Why didn't you go to see her?"

"Because I doubt she would talk to me."

"You might be surprised."

Sunny didn't respond.

Allison waited through an awkward silence. Finally Allison said, "Is Maggie well represented?"

"Hank chose the lawyer," Sunny said with a heavy sigh, as though that explained everything.

"Why didn't you tell the police Desiree Moore was at your house the day Udele disappeared?"

"You don't mince words, do you?"

"Not when a child's future is at stake."

Sunny looked away. "Maggie told you about Desiree?"

"Yes."

Sunny shook her head. Allison felt sure she would deny the allegation, but instead she said, "I didn't know she knew."

Allison looked around, debating what to say next. Near them, two businessmen chatted over coffee. Somewhere behind them, a baby started to cry. Allison could hear the mother's attempts to comfort it. Allison felt removed from all of them. She'd almost forgotten what *normal* was. Right now, it was her and Sunny—and Allison wanted answers.

"What are you hiding, Sunny?"

When Sunny didn't respond, Allison said, "Don't you want to fight for Maggie?"

"She didn't do it."

"I know she didn't."

"Hank isn't convinced."

"So what? As long as you believe in her, that's what matters."

"You don't get it, Allison. He will destroy me."

"Why, Sunny? What does he have on you that could possibly be worth losing your daughter over?"

"He owns me, Allison. He rescued me from who I was and gave me a life. Respectability. Money. But the price is too high. I need time to think." She looked down at her hands. "And paint."

Confused, Allison said, "Paint? I thought you'd given that up."

Sunny met Allison's gaze with an intensity that startled her. "I paint under a different name now. I'm good, very good." Sunny tilted her head up, proudly. "I even have a small following. Hank doesn't know that."

"Does Maggie?"

Sunny looked confused. "Apparently. You said she saw Desiree at the house."

"Maggie said Desiree's your lover."

Sunny threw her head back and let out a despairing laugh. "Desiree Moore is not my lover. She was there to buy a painting. She'd been coming to the house to see the work in progress. I agreed to let her. After everything our family put her through, how could I say no?"

"Your family?"

"Maggie. Hank." Sunny paused. "Hank wasn't exactly friendly when the Moores came forward with those letters. He was rather...threatening. So how could I refuse Desiree's request?"

Allison considered this new bit of news. Maggie, having witnessed her mother's affairs in the past, assumed Desiree was her lover. It was the reason she didn't say anything. But there were still holes.

She said, "If you keep your artistic life separate, how did Desiree know?"

Sunny looked down at her hands, clasped before her, knuckles white. "I told her. In confidence. We knew each other from the kids' school."

Allison thought of an old saying her father had been fond of: "Trust is the mother of deceit." She'd always considered it a terrible mantra, but it rang so very true in this instance. "She asked to come to your house?"

Sunny nodded.

"Over a period of weeks?"

"Much longer. It can take a while to get a painting right."

"Did she ultimately buy it, Sunny?"

Sunny nodded. "For her entry hall."

Allison had been to the Moore home and hadn't noticed the painting in the foyer. There could be a logical explanation—the painting was being framed, Desiree had given it away as a gift—but this was one too many coincidences involving that family. She stood.

Sunny reached out and grabbed Allison's wrist. "You don't get it, do you? Hank knows about the child who ran away. Violet somebody-or-other. He knows, and he will use that information to hurt you if things get too out of hand. He wants this behind him. Maggie in a psych hospital...he won't see that as the worst of all outcomes." She tightened her grip on Allison's arm. "Don't interfere."

Too late. At the mention of Violet, Allison's stomach clenched. She hated that Hank McBride knew about Violet. It felt dirty, wrong—and Allison felt just as violated as she had when she first read that damn article. But it only strengthened Allison's determination to get to the bottom of this. McBride was a bully, plain and simple. She refused to be intimidated.

Allison said, "Don't you see, if Maggie is arrested, we all have more at stake than our reputations. Especially your daughter."

Sunny was silent for a moment. "I'm leaving. For a while, at least."

Allison was struck dumb. Leaving? "How can you go now? Maggie needs you."

"I'm no help to Maggie. I'm no help to anyone." Tears were streaming down Sunny's face, pooling in the lines around her mouth. Allison was struck by the ugliness of self-pity. A truly useless emotion.

Allison said, "Don't let Maggie take the fall for this. Help me find the real killer."

Sunny put her sunglasses back on and stood. "It's too late for that now."

Allison watched her leave. She considered her own family and realized that there were so many ways to be a motherless daughter. Illness. Death. And abandonment. Her. Violet. And now, Maggie. She felt the old raging grief come back to her and swallowed it down. Not now. Now she needed to find Kyle Moore.

Vaughn arrived home just as Mrs. T and Angela were trading shifts. "What are you here for now, Christopher?" Mrs. T said. "More biscuits?"

"Jamie awake?"

"What's wrong with you?" she said. "You look like you've seen a ghost."

"I need Jamie. Is he up?"

She nodded, looking concerned. Vaughn sprinted into Jamie's room. His twin looked up, surprised to see him.

"I need you to do something for me."

He didn't wait for Jamie to say anything on the monitor. He grabbed a piece of paper and a notebook and wrote something quickly. He put it on Jamie's bed, next to his hip, where Jamie could read it.

"That's the number for Lieutenant Helms. He's investigating the Feldman murder."

Jamie raised his eyebrows, questioningly.

"Jason called back. The pentagram at the scene was inverted, like you said. It was all stereotypical Satan stuff. The chalice. The markings. The blood. The inverted cross."

DONE BY SOMEONE WHO HAD READ THE RIGHT BOOKS.

They stared at each other, and Vaughn was sure they'd reached the same conclusion. "We've been asking a lot of people a lot of questions. If things get freaky, use that number for Helms. You can help Angela explain what we think has gone down."

BE CAREFUL.

"I will."

I LOVE YOU, YOU KNOW.

Vaughn said, "I love you, too," and left.

On the way to the Moores' house, Vaughn listened to Allison's messages. Clearly she had something to tell him, but she didn't say what. He tried her cell three times. No answer. He called her home phone and her office phone. Nothing. Where was she?

He half-expected to see her car at Desiree's house. But not only wasn't she there, neither was Desiree. Vaughn decided to head to Allison's house, then to First Impressions.

And if Allison was *still* M.I.A, he'd call Helms himself.

* * *

Allison pulled up to the address for Kyle Moore's business that she'd gotten off the Internet and stared at the street in front of her. Something wasn't right. She was familiar with Center City Philly, but this was not the business district, much less the neighborhood she'd expect for a burgeoning tech company.

Rundown row houses, their windows barred and stone stoops crumbling, stretched along one side of the street. Along the other side, the row houses were punctuated by an old church, its window sills blackened by a long-ago fire, a check-cashing shop, a boarded-up falafel takeout joint, and a windowless bar, its neon sign illuminating only the letters *B* and *R*. No sign advertised Kyle Moore's business, TECHNO, Inc.

The sky, the color of fresh bruises, was steadily darkening. Soon it would be night. The thought of being in this abandoned stretch of Philadelphia, alone, was unsettling. Allison double-checked the address against the black letters on one of the row houses. They matched. This was the official Philadelphia address for TECHNO, but how could that be? Allison wanted to ask someone, but the street was empty of cars and people. Only the pulsing sign for the bar showed any sign of life.

Her head was pounding and her nose was beginning to run. She searched for her migraine medicine. Finding none, she dry-swallowed two Excedrin, grabbed a handful of tissues and hoped for the best. Then she got out of the car. Thinking better of it, she crawled back into the front seat and opened the glove compartment. She pulled out two things Jason had bought for her long ago: a pocket knife and a can of pepper spray. "You never know who's lurking the streets," he'd said when he stored them in her car. "And you never know when you'll have an emergency." She sent a silent prayer of thanks for the small comfort these items gave her and tucked them both in her coat pocket.

Outside, a bitter wind was picking up. Litter swirled in tiny cyclones along the pocked pavement. Allison took a quick look around and walked to the building marked 2413—where the

TECHNO office was supposed to be. Like the other buildings along the row, this one had barred windows. She climbed the three steps to the front door and tried to see inside. No lights were on, though she could make out a short entry hall and steps leading to a second floor. The house appeared empty.

She rang the bell. Broken. She knocked. No answer. She tried the knob. Locked. Frustrated, she looked around for another entrance. She'd known it was unlikely Moore would be here, but she at least expected a secretary or a maintenance crew—someone who could help her get in touch with him. She didn't want to go through Desiree. She'd already shown too much of her hand to that woman. Direct confrontation was best, but Allison didn't have time to drive to the company's corporate headquarters in Virginia. She needed Moore's cell or home number or direct work line.

She eyed the bar two doors down. Maybe someone there could tell her something. Reassuring herself that she still had the knife and the spray, she hurried down the street and opened the bar's heavy front door. Once inside, she slid into the shadows.

The interior was dark and dank and smelled strongly of stale beer. She could make out a bar on one side. A few men sat on stools, watching with seeming disinterest what was happening at the other side of the room. One or two of the men glanced her way before turning back to the entertainment. Allison followed their gaze. There, on a makeshift stage, two young girls gyrated to an imaginary rhythm, their slim, boyish bodies completely nude. Allison felt ill. These girls couldn't have been more than fourteen or fifteen.

Nothing outside indicated that this place was a nude bar. She thought of Violet—and Sparky—and was pretty certain this was the type of establishment Sparky would have run. From the outside, it looked like a neighborhood bar, to throw off the cops, but inside...inside would be a special kind of entertainment. Though she wanted to scream, Allison tried to keep her breath even. She hated the thought of Violet working in a dump like this, being ogled by old men, her young body simply a thing to be judged and auctioned to the highest bidder. She hated the thought of these girls being made to live the same sort of life.

Allison scanned the room for another door. Sure enough, toward the back was a stairwell lit faintly by red light. Her nightmarish suspicions were confirmed.

These girls didn't just dance.

Allison thought of Moore at the restaurant with that teen. Maybe it was no coincidence he kept a property here. This place, right next door, offered easy pickings. For all she knew, he owned the bar and the row house registered to TECHNO. She looked around the bar. She wouldn't get anything out of these men. Even if they knew Kyle Moore, they would never admit to it.

Allison edged back toward the door, hoping to escape before anyone noticed her. She felt along the wall for the doorknob and pulled the heavy barrier open just wide enough to slip outside. Once there, she pressed her back against the building and closed her eyes for a second, letting the disgust and anger wash over her. She would call the police and let them know what was happening inside. The image of those girls, so many years and such potential ahead of them, flashed before her eyes, their faces replaced by Violet's. She needed to get on the road. But if the police could bust this place, something good would come out of her otherwise wasted side trip.

She opened her eyes and reached into her pocket for a tissue. At the same time, a hulking figure rounded the corner and came toward her, head bent over a lit cigarette. He reached the door of the bar, gave Allison a glance, and went inside. Her pulse pounding, Allison walked toward her car. She wanted out of this neighborhood.

She sneezed and wiped the tissue against her face. The sensitive skin around her mouth was already beginning to chap from the friction. She thought of Arnie Feldman, of Vaughn's description of the murder scene. He had had abrasions on his face, around his mouth. Sasha had said he was bound by duct tape, which also covered his mouth. What if those abrasions were caused when duct tape was ripped off repeatedly?

As though the murderer had been questioning Arnie and removing the tape to let him answer.

Allison opened her car door and got inside, quickly locking the doors. She started the ignition and pulled away from the curb. *Duct tape.* If the police were right and Maggie and Ethan were the killers, why would they question Arnie? They wouldn't. But someone with something to lose, someone who wanted to know whether Arnie had exposed his secrets, *would* question him. And torture him to get the information he needed.

The inverted cross, burned into Arnie's chest.

Not a satanic ritual. A very practical attempt to get Arnie to talk.

It was all adding up. The underage girl, Sunny's painting. Kyle Moore had access through Desiree. And if she could only prove a connection between Kyle and Arnie, she was sure she'd have motive, too.

Allison pushed down on the gas pedal. She needed to get to Lieutenant Helms. It was time to share her suspicions about Kyle Moore.

THIRTY-SIX

Allison didn't make it to police headquarters. On the way, her phone rang. It was a very distraught Desiree asking to meet her. Now.

"I need your advice," Desiree said. "I wasn't totally honest with you before. About Maggie. There's more to the story. It's Kyle. I don't know what to do about Kyle."

Allison's mind raced. This might just be the break they needed. She didn't completely trust Desiree, but the woman sounded desperate. She should send her right to the police. But what if the police didn't listen? Allison turned off the exit that would lead to her office building. She gave Desiree directions to First Impressions.

"How quickly can you get there?" Allison said.

"Twenty minutes."

"I'll be waiting."

After Desiree hung up, Allison pulled over to the curb and put her head against the back of the seat. Her temples throbbed. She thought of Maggie, alone in detention. Of her mother, alone in her own head. Of Jamie, trapped in a physical prison. And of her house, and how right it had felt a few days before, waking up to Jason.

She'd been a fool.

Allison dialed Jason's mobile number. He didn't pick up. Disappointed, she left a simple message. "I'm ready," she said. And then she pulled out onto the road and headed to her office.

* * *

Vaughn knocked on Allison's front door. No answer other than Brutus's menacing bark. He figured that, her car wasn't parked in the driveway or the garage. He called her cell phone again. No one picked up.

Desiree Moore missing.

Allison missing.

While under normal circumstances, those two facts would be merely a coincidence, this time he knew that wasn't the case.

He ran to his car, slammed it into reverse, and dialed the number for Lieutenant Helms. Then he called Jason.

Allison climbed the two floors to First Impressions. Once inside, she unlocked the front door and headed straight for her office, where she sat at her desk and cradled her aching head in her hands. The sniffling was now accompanied by aches and chills. She wrapped her coat tighter around her shivering body and willed herself to feel better. She needed her strength and mental clarity.

She was just picking up the phone to try Helms when there was a strong knock at the door. *Desiree, already?* Allison took a deep breath and rose to answer it.

Another knock.

"Coming!"

Allison swung open the door. It was Desiree, and she didn't wait for an invitation to come inside. She was dressed simply in black pants and a dark gray sweater. Her hair was pulled back in a severe ponytail, and her face was free of makeup. She may have been distraught before, but she was composed now.

"Are you alone?" Desiree said, closing the door.

"I am. Are you going to tell me what this is all about?"

Desiree nodded. "Can we sit?"

Allison led Desiree to the client room. Desiree carried a heavy duffel bag, which she placed on one of the chairs. It was the same bag she'd had at the art center.

The art center!

In a flash, Allison thought of the pottery tools. The double-handled wires Desiree had used to slice the top off of clay. Feldman's throat had been sliced by a wire. All along she'd been suspecting Kyle, but what if...what if it had been Desiree?

But why?

Why would Desiree kill Arnie? Allison gave the woman a second look. She noticed the sneakers and black leather gloves. Outside was chilly, but not gloves chilly. With sudden comprehension, she knew this was no social call. Her heart pounded against her ribcage.

Desiree said, "Sit." Her voice came out in a low growl.

Quickly, Allison moved toward the front door. She needed to get out of there. Before she made it ten feet, she felt Desiree on top of her, pushing her down. Allison's forehead hit the floor, hard, just as Desiree's knee slammed into her spine, knocking the wind out of her. Allison tried to twist around to take a swing at her, but her spine screamed in agony. Allison's eyes met Desiree's, but not before Allison saw the gun pointed directly at her skull.

"You're going to do exactly as I say, Allison. Beginning now."

Midge slammed her foot on the brake and turned into the parking lot in front of Allison's building. She parked next to Allison's Volvo, got out and locked her door. Kit was standing outside First Impressions looking sexy in an orange peplum jacket and skin-tight floral skirt. Not exactly the outfit she'd have chosen for an intervention.

Midge pointed toward Tori's minivan and Kit nodded, a huge scowl on her face. Kit had gone along with the idea reluctantly, but they needed to do this. For Allison. Allison might balk at first, but in the end, she'd be grateful to know how much they cared.

Kit teetered over on four-inch stilettos. Midge cringed. What was the woman thinking?

"Any day now," Kit said. "We're not goddamn detectives. And it's not like I don't have a life. I want to be home for CSI."

"We're almost ready," Midge said. "Diane will be here soon."

Tori walked over and joined them. "All set?"

Kit rolled her eyes. Midge gave her an encouraging smile.

"We do this with love in our hearts, ladies," Midge said. "Whatever is going on with Allison, we can help her. It's the least we can do."

"What the hell are you doing?" Allison said.

"What does it look like I'm doing?"

There was a noise at the front door, and Desiree climbed off her, keeping the gun firmly pointed at Allison. "Come in!" she yelled.

A second later, another figure walked inside and then closed and re-locked the door. Wiry frame, red hair, large mole on his face. Kyle Moore. He must've been waiting in the shadows outside the door the entire time. Allison cursed her own stupidity. She should have never fallen for Desiree's phone call.

"Did you get it?" he asked.

"Not yet," Desiree said. "Get up!" she commanded. Roughly, Desiree pulled Allison to her feet. Allison's head was a pulsing, throbbing mess. She didn't resist when Desiree led her back to the client room and pushed her into a chair.

With gloved hands, Desiree pulled a white envelope from inside her duffel bag. Carefully, she pulled out two pieces of paper. The first she put in front of Allison.

"Sign it."

Allison scanned the writing. It was a suicide note, full of remorse for belief in a felon and humiliation over her ruined career. It was short and powerful and, Allison hated to admit, almost believable.

She said, "No."

Desiree pistol-whipped her on the side of the head.

Through the searing pain and sudden haze, Allison managed, "You can go to hell. I'm not signing anything."

Desiree ignored her. She smoothed the second piece of paper—newsprint between her fingers, curling the edges purposefully. "It won't do to have this look too fresh, will it? Better to look worn, as though you'd fretted over it."

Allison didn't even have to ask. She knew the paper was the news feature that reporter had done, the one in which Catherine McBride called her a fraud. She knew, too, that if Desiree had her way and framed this as a suicide, Hank McBride would add to the story, using her death to buoy his own message about Maggie. She and Maggie would both lose.

Thoughts of Maggie fueled her resolve. They couldn't be allowed to get away with this. But what could she do? How could she distract them? Her head was pounding. Her spine screamed. She could barely think.

Desiree put the suicide note in front of Allison again. "Sign it. Now."

"Hurry," Kyle said. Unlike Desiree, he looked nervous. He held his gun uncertainly. Sweat beaded across his forehead. He was the weak link.

"No one will believe this, Desiree. We know you murdered Feldman and Udele. We know you had access to the McBride house, that Kyle was Arnie's client. And we've told the police already." She lied, but her only hope was to get them talking. Buy time until she could make a move.

"Arnie wasn't my attorney," Kyle said. Allison was surprised to hear a faint stutter. "He was Desiree's. This is all her fault."

Desiree came around behind Allison. She jerked Allison's head back by her hair, hard. Allison bit her lip against the tears welling in her eyes. She needed to think through the fog. *Damn it, Al! Focus!*

"Kyle has an addiction," Desiree was saying. "He's pathetic." She leaned down so that her mouth was against Allison's ear. "He likes to screw young girls." She straightened up. "Isn't that right, Kyle? You can't keep your pecker in your pants, and so here we are."

"Why are you protecting him?" Allison asked.

Desiree hit Allison's head with the butt of her gun again. Allison felt a sticky warmth trickle down the side of her face. The shock added to the cyclone in her skull.

Keep her talking, Al. She whispered, "You still love him."

"Shut up! I'm protecting Sarah and Megan. From scandal. That's what good mothers do."

And killing wouldn't cause a scandal? "That's why you killed Feldman. He was going to tell."

"The idiot suddenly got a conscience."

Kyle said, "That's because you told him too much. That was stupid—"

"Shut up! Do *not* blame me for your idiocy!" Desiree pointed at the table, at the documents that still sat, unsigned, in front of Allison. "Make her sign them, Kyle. Now!"

Kyle moved closer, his gun trained on Allison's face. Allison eyed the barrel, wishing she had paid more attention in self-defense class. She kept one hand on the table where Desiree could see it, but let the other one fall to her lap. Inch by inch, she maneuvered it toward her coat pocket. Kyle seemed weak, but she reminded herself of the devastation he and Desiree had wreaked on Feldman. She couldn't afford to underestimate them.

"Why Udele?" Allison said.

"Why not?" Desiree said.

"So the painting you bought from Sunny, all of those trips to the McBride house...you were simply looking for ways to frame Maggie. Udele was disposable, so you took her out. A great way to lead the authorities to the McBrides, in case the police weren't sniffing around them already."

The truth dawned on Allison in one flash of clarity. Desiree had had access to Maggie's bedroom, to things containing Maggie's fingerprints. She could have memorized security codes at the Feldman's. Her daughter Sarah might have even had a key from her days of visiting Ethan. And Udele...poor Udele would have let Desiree in the house willingly, a known and trusted acquaintance of Sunny's. The monstrosity of what the Moores had done—killing two innocent people, framing a child—was hard to comprehend. As was the hopelessness of her own situation in the hands of these psychos.

"Sign the damn note," Kyle said.

"No."

"Kyle! Make her!"

Kyle grabbed Allison's wrist and yanked her arm behind her back, a surprising show of strength for such a small man. Allison yelped. Kyle reached around and fingered her exposed throat.

"There are a lot of ways to commit suicide," Desiree said. "You could slit your wrists. You could blow your brains out. Or maybe you're some kind of masochist and—"

"Just sign the letter, bitch," Kyle hissed.

He looked up and said to Desiree, "We have to get out of here. Just shoot her. *I'll* sign the letter."

"We can't risk leaving anything behind, not even a handwriting sample."

"Then leave it unsigned."

"No. She needs to sign it, Kyle."

"Damn it!" Kyle punched Allison in the back. "Sign the letter."

Desiree sprang around the table and grabbed his arm.

"What are you doing? You can't leave bruises. I told you, no evidence of foul play. Only her head—it'll be blown to bits anyway."

While they argued, Allison reached into her pocket. She grabbed the pepper spray, covered in a wad of used tissues. She faked a sneeze, then pulled the spray out and aimed it at Kyle's eyes. He screamed when the spray made contact.

Before Desiree could react, Allison grabbed the gun from Kyle's hand and aimed it at his head. She hesitated for a second before slamming the butt of the gun against Kyle's temple. He looked momentarily surprised. She did it again. And again. Finally, he slid to the floor.

Allison turned to Desiree only to see that the woman had a gun pointed at Allison's head. A faint smile played on her lips.

"Drop it."

Allison glanced at Desiree, then down at Kyle. He was out—for now, anyway. But she would never be able to aim at Desiree and pull the trigger before Desiree got her first. And so she dropped the gun.

Desiree yanked Allison's arm. "We're going into your office. You will sit at your desk like a good girl and sign the paper."

Allison nodded, her mind racing for a way out.

Just then, there was a knock at the front door.

Desiree's grip tightened. "Are you expecting someone?"

Allison shook her head.

"Don't make a sound," Desiree hissed. "Or I *will* kill you right now."

THIRTY-SEVEN

Midge pounded on the door of First Impressions again. She was starting to feel angry, and that wasn't a good thing. Bad things happened when she got angry. Like Randolph, poor dear. She pounded again. Her good shoes hurt her feet, and she wanted to go home.

"I swear I heard voices," Diane said. "Allison and someone else."

"She's having an affair," Kit said. "Let the woman have a fucking affair."

"Shhh." Diane put her ear to the door. She motioned for Midge to come closer. "Do you hear anything?"

"Try the knob," Kit said. "Maybe it's unlocked."

Midge straightened her features into a look of stern yet nurturing concern. An intervention should be direct, no-nonsense. She hoped that Allison wasn't having an affair—it wouldn't do to find her in a compromising position. She grasped the knob. It was locked.

"Allison?" she yelled.

Suddenly there was a scream, followed by the sound of metal hitting the floor.

"Allison! We're coming!"

Kit screamed, "Break down the door!"

"We can't!"

"Oh yes we can," Tori said. "Stand back!"

Once, twice, three times, Tori pounded her body against the door. The third time, Midge heard a crack as the lock gave way.

"Together!" Tori screamed.

They all pushed at the same time. Midge's heart raced with the effort. When the door opened, Midge heard Allison scream "in here" from somewhere to their left.

Kit grabbed Midge's hand and they ran toward the sound of Allison's voice. In the doorway stood a woman holding a gun pointed at Allison's head. Allison's face was a collage of fresh bruises and blood. Her eyes looked slightly out of focus, as though she'd been drugged. Rage filled Midge. The nerve!

"Get away from her," Kit said.

"Move and I kill her," the woman said. She pulled Allison by the hair and shoved her toward the client room. "Get in there." She motioned for the women to go in first.

The woman ordered everyone to sit, but there were only four chairs. Midge stood behind Tori. She saw a man on the floor, slumped in a heap.

"Coming here was stupid," the woman said.

"Who the hell are you?" Kit said.

"That doesn't matter."

"Desiree Moore," Allison said. "The Main Line Murderer—"

Before she could finish, the woman slapped Allison across the face with the back of her hand. Her ring drew fresh blood. Midge's fist clenched around her purse strap.

Desiree sneered. "It's Allison who will have killed all of you, then herself. 'Image consultant goes postal.'"

Allison, her voice slurred, said, "No one will believe that." Her breath was uneven, blood trickled down her face and her hair was matted in crimson patches. Still, she said, "Don't...hurt anyone...and maybe the police—"

Desiree hit Allison again. Her head slammed backward with the impact.

Irate, Midge looked up and Kit caught her eye. Kit motioned subtly toward the metal waste can, which was next to Midge's leg. Then Kit, on the chair next to Allison and close to Desiree, started to cough. Desiree threw her a razor sharp look. The coughing turned to choking and for a moment Midge thought Kit really couldn't breathe. Kit caught her eye again and Midge understood what she wanted her to do.

Kit stood up, grabbed her throat, and started to convulse. She bumped into Desiree who lost her balance. Desiree screamed, "Sit down," but not before Midge had the waste can in her hand. And with all the anger she'd stored up since she'd found out about Randolph, she brought that can down on Desiree's head.

The blow didn't knock her out, but it bought enough time for Allison to push herself up and fall against her. The weapon spun from Desiree's hand and slid across the floor, toward Allison. She reached for it, fumbled, and finally grasped it in both hands. Holding the gun to Desiree's head, Allison stood up unsteadily. Kit pinned Desiree to the ground.

Allison kicked Desiree in the side with one pointed pump. "That's for Maggie." She kicked her again, almost falling over from the effort. "And that's for Violet, and all the girls like her."

Midge had no idea what she was talking about, but before she could ask, Kit looked at her sharply. "Call 9-1-1. Hurry."

Overwhelmed, Midge nodded. But when she looked up from the chaos in the room, Vaughn was standing in the hallway with two police officers in uniform.

THIRTY-EIGHT

The hospital room pulsed in and out of focus. Allison preferred the moments of pain and lucidity to the twilight-like dream state during which nightmarish scenes played out before her. Maggie at juvenile. The young girls dancing at the bar. The hatred in Desiree's eyes. And Violet. Always Violet.

She pulled the thin, white blanket around her to ward off the chill in the room and blinked against the darkness. How long had she been here? She couldn't say.

"You have a severe concussion and a terrible cold." It was a woman's voice. Allison turned her head, wincing at the pain, and saw her sister sitting by the window, her thin frame shrouded in their mother's wool coat.

"Faye."

"I'm giving Jason a break. He's been here round the clock."

"How did you know I was here?"

"Vaughn called me. One of his nurses is staying with Mom and Dad for the night."

Allison closed her eyes and then opened them, wanting to make sure this was not another dream. "Are they okay?"

Faye smiled, and warmth shone in her eyes. "They're fine. It's you everyone is worried about. Those people gave you a terrible head injury and a sprained back."

No one had to tell Allison about her back. She felt dull aches and spasms every time she moved. She smiled wanly. At least the pain meant she was alive. "I guess it's better than the alternative."

Faye looked thoughtful. After a moment she said, "I'm sorry for everything—"

"Don't."

"Please. It needs to be said, Allison. You've carried a burden of guilt with you for years. And I let you. In fact, I encouraged it. And then everything with Dr. Hom. I was wrong not to bring you in from the beginning. When I got the call that you'd almost been killed...well, I realize now how silly we've been. Our childhood still haunts us, Allison. We need to deal with that."

Allison turned her head away. She didn't want to have this conversation. Not now. Not ever.

But Faye continued. "Daddy was not a nice man. He still isn't, though the years have worn away the edges of his cruelty. He will never change. But sometimes you simply take what you get." She grabbed Allison's hand and squeezed gently. "The thing is, we let Daddy get in the way. We let him dictate how we felt about Mom, about ourselves. About each other. It's time to stop that. It's time to be sisters again."

Allison wanted that. How she wanted that. She could feel the tears flowing down her face. She would never truly get her mother back. And Faye was right, her father would never change. But she and Faye...they could be family to one another. They could give each other in adulthood what neither of them had received when they were young.

Allison whispered, "Nothing would make me happier."

Faye smiled. "We'll work the rest out when you leave this place." She sighed. "For now, rest. It's apparent you've had a busy few weeks."

Lieutenant Mark Helms didn't seem surprised to see Allison when she arrived at his office ten days later. He rose from his chair and gestured for her to take the seat opposite.

"You look better than you did the last time I saw you," he said. His mouth was set in a firm line, but his eyes danced with good humor.

"I feel better."

"Maggie is well?"

Allison nodded. She'd seen Maggie four times already since she'd left the hospital and expected more visits. It was clear that although the girl was attached to Brutus, it was Allison she came to see. The ordeal over Feldman and Udele, along with Sunny's disappearing act, had left Maggie wounded. But the kid was resilient. In time, she would heal and, Allison hoped, be her old oppositional self again.

In the meantime, Sunny had come back to town, although she'd left her husband. And Hank McBride was Hank McBride. His chances at achieving a Senate seat were slim, given all the bad publicity he'd received when everything came to light. The public disliked a man who didn't stand by his own. But he and Allison had developed a sort of truce based on a common nexus of self-interest: Allison wanted to see Maggie, and Hank was happy his daughter's name had been cleared.

"You heard about Jamie Vaughn?"

Allison nodded. That had been an unexpected delight. The police, impressed with Jamie's online detective work, had hired him to do contract work for the force. Vaughn was helping his brother set up a better office at home, but Allison knew it also meant Jamie would get back out into the world. It was about time.

Allison opened her briefcase and pulled out a bundle of papers, laying them out before the Lieutenant.

"I understand that Kyle didn't own that bar, but he knows the man who did. These were Violet's letters. They paint a picture, Lieutenant. And I suspect they may help in the case against the pimp Kyle Moore used to get his girls."

The Lieutenant looked them over, one by one, the expression on his face never changing. When he looked up, though, the good humor was gone. "Moore's pimp is not named Sparky. It's Roger. Roger Aubrey."

"But he could have aliases."

"He could. And there's something else. Moore described his contact as a severely deformed man, his face as...melted."

"As though by fire." Allison took a deep breath. *Sparky.* The fire Violet had set. After all these years. When Allison had walked into that bar, had seen those young girls, she'd known there was a connection. There was no good reason, other than Violet's descriptions and her own intuition.

After the Moores were arrested, Allison had told the police about the bar near TECHNO's business address, about the underage dancers. The Philadelphia police seemed unimpressed and said the girls were likely runaways and throwaways, a term Allison detested. Only Mark Helms seemed concerned, and Philadelphia wasn't his jurisdiction. But because of the Main Line murders—and the connection to his suspects' motive—he was able to set things in motion that she could not do on her own. Allison should have felt happy, vindicated even. But she felt only a vague sense of justice mixed with a profound sadness. Even if Roger Aubrey turned out to be Sparky, none of this would help Violet.

"You know, Allison, if this keeps one girl off the streets, that's something." The Lieutenant gave her a look of understanding and she smiled in appreciation. Of course he was right.

Helms leaned back in his chair. "So it's over now. The Moores are behind bars. Maggie is home. You can go back to making the Main Line look fabulous." His tone was kind, despite the gentle teasing in his words. This time, he wasn't looking at her with even a hint of dismissiveness. Just respect.

Allison rose. She *wished* it was over. "Not yet. I still have one piece of unfinished business. And it's the hardest piece of all."

THIRTY-NINE

Allison stared at the row house on East Berks Street in the Fishtown section of Philadelphia. The house looked like all its neighbors: brick front, white window trim, two window wells at ground level. Outside, a pink tricycle had been parked in front of a set of cement steps. That tricycle gave her pause.

"Are you sure you want to go in alone?" Jason said. He squeezed her hand and she squeezed back. He kissed her softly on the cheek.

"I'm sure."

It was a sunny May day and a light wind blew crumpled candy wrappers and bits of discarded paper across the sidewalk. Allison stepped into the street and then stopped, not quite mentally able to go forward. Her back hurt, the injuries she suffered when Desiree wrestled her to the floor nearly a month ago not quite healed.

Allison felt Jason's hand on her shoulder, and then he whispered in her ear, "You need this, Allison. Go."

And so she went. She walked across the street, between the cars parked along the sidewalk, and around the struggling tree that stood between her and John "Junior" Swann's house. When she got to the front door, she turned around. Jason stood on the sidewalk, right where she'd left him. He wore a Penn t-shirt, cargo shorts and a Phillies baseball cap. And those Tevas on his feet. But he was waving to her and smiling, and she took her cue and knocked.

* * *

The first thing that struck Allison about John Junior was his smile. It was Violet's smile, somehow at once generous and haunted. He had the same color eyes as Violet, too, and when he opened the door those eyes looked at her with a mixture of curiosity and suspicion.

"You a Jehovah?" he said.

"No." She had trouble pulling her gaze from his face long enough to answer.

He was completely bald, but had bushy, graying eyebrows and a neatly trimmed beard. In an instant, Allison decided he had a kind face, and she was glad. "I knew your daughter."

He stared at her for a long moment and then came out on the small stoop, closing the screen door behind him. "How'd you know Violet?"

"We...we worked together long ago. At the Meadows. My name is Allison Campbell."

He smiled then, a smile of recognition that held more warmth than Allison would have expected given the role the Meadows played in Violet's ultimate undoing. John Junior sat on the stoop and waved for Allison to sit next to him. She sank down onto the cool concrete and watched as Jason walked farther down the street, toward their car.

"What'd you come here for?" John Junior said, not unkindly.

Allison had practiced for this moment over and over for the past few weeks, ever since she'd decided to make the visit. But still, words failed her.

"She's dead, you know," he said.

"I was afraid of that."

"She was a pretty girl, that one."

"I know. And smart."

He smiled. "You were the one that filled her head with all that business about college and art, weren't you?"

"Maybe." Allison returned the smile. She said, "How did Violet die?" and held her breath, so scared of the answer.

John Junior spat on the sidewalk, wiped his mouth, and then looked at Allison, a wistful expression in his eyes. "I wasn't no good a dad to her, Miss. After her mom died, well, things got real bad. But I loved Violet. I always loved her."

He turned to look across the street, squinting against the sun. "She was in a car accident. Six years ago. Hit by a drunk driver." He shook his head. "Lasted an hour in the hospital. That was it."

Allison breathed. So all this time...she made it out of Philly. It wasn't AIDS or Sparky or a "joe" that did it. "Can I ask, what was her life like, before?"

He stood up and stretched. "Like the life of any young woman, I guess. Some schooling for art. A paying job. A man. I didn't have much contact with her. She lived in Colorado."

"Was she happy?"

John Junior turned to look at her, as though considering the question. Finally, he said, "Are any of us happy? I don't know. I think so." He nodded. "Yes, I think she had to have been very happy."

"She never contacted me. All those years ..."

"She was afraid, I think. Afraid to come back East. Afraid of her past. But I think she always intended to find you someday. She wanted you to be proud."

Allison wiped the tears from her eyes and stood. She'd gotten what she had come for. Violet hadn't died in the throes of poverty or at the hands of a pimp. She'd had a life. Hopefully, she knew love. Grateful for his time, for this comfort, she turned to go. But John Junior put his hand on her arm.

"Just a minute. I want to show you something, if you don't mind."

He disappeared into the house. Allison spotted Jason a half block down talking to a Hassidic man with long ear locks. Brutus was in the car, his great burly head hanging out the window. Up the street, two little girls walked a large mixed breed dog past an old woman who looked on from her perch on the stoop. Allison waited. She felt numb, filled with relief and an unrelenting sadness for Violet. In the end, Violet got the second chance she'd hoped for.

The front door opened and John Junior came back out, followed by two young girls. One had to be the owner of the Barbie tricycle. She was no more than three or four, with dark skin and tight ponytails tied with beaded elastic. The other girl was tall and thin. She had long, straight dark hair and delicate features. And she stared at Allison with Violet's eyes.

"The little one is Serena," John Junior said. "My neighbor's girl." Then he took the older girl by the hand gently and pulled her forward. "And this is Ally, my granddaughter. She lives with me since her mama passed on." He shrugged. "I guess maybe she's your namesake."

Allison smiled and Ally smiled back. She looked healthy—thin, like her mother—but healthy. All at once, Allison felt Violet's presence. The sulking girl in the nurse's office, the burgeoning artist in her office, the naïve street urchin in those early letters, and the very brave young woman who'd made it out alive.

"She's an artist like her mama, too," John Junior said. "Only nine years old and already taking fancy art classes, ain't that right?"

The child nodded.

The moment stood still for Allison. John Junior on the step, Jason a block away, waiting for her, and Violet there with them in the form of this little girl who shared Allison's name. In that second, everything in her life made sense.

"Thank you," she said to John Junior.

Their eyes met. John Junior smiled and then walked back inside, hand in hand with his granddaughter. Allison waved to Jason and headed back to the car.

READER'S DISCUSSION GUIDE

1. The story is set on the Philadelphia Main Line, a wealthy suburb not far from some of Philadelphia's most depressed neighborhoods. What role does setting play?

2. How does Allison's career choice reflect the themes of the book?

3. Family and family dynamics play an important role. Allison thinks about her own family and realizes "there are so many ways to be a motherless daughter. Illness. Death. And abandonment. Her. Violet. And now, Maggie." But the book is also about finding that nurturing from other sources. Can you think of where the characters developed maternal-type relationships with people to whom they are not related? How has that affected them?

4. One of the themes running throughout the story is change–the ability of people to change, to have a second chance. Are there times when characters had the opportunity to change and chose not to, for better or worse? How does this theme play into Arnie Feldman's murder?

5. Another consistent theme is image versus reality. How is this theme reflected in the characters? In the murders of Arnie and Udele? In the setting?

6. For Vaughn, the pain of seeing his brother is a constant reminder of his own past. How has Vaughn dealt with his youthful transgressions? How are Allison and Vaughn similar?

7. When Mia and Allison reconcile, Mia says, "maybe those of us who've touched the void and lived–and losing a child immerses you in the void, Allison, believe me–maybe we survivors need to protect ourselves from ever visiting its depths again." In what ways have

Mia's decisions–moving to the country, leaving her practice, even her relationship with Vaughn–reflected that need?

8. Allison accuses Jason of giving up on his dreams following the death of his sister. He responds by saying, "Wake up, Al. People don't come all neatly packaged. You've spent your whole adult life trying to force people into these tidy little boxes. Things don't work that way." What events in Allison's past may have led her to view the world this way? Does this change as the story progresses?

9. Maggie and Violet come from very different backgrounds, yet Allison sees similarities. How are the two girls alike? In what ways are they quite different?

10. Allison gives Violet *We the Living* by Ayn Rand to help with her insomnia. The book, and the very act of reading, helps to broaden Violet's world and her perspective. Why might Allison have chosen that book? What impact did books, and Allison's actions related to reading, have on Violet and Violet's choices?

WENDY TYSON

Wendy Tyson wrote her first story at age eight and it's been love ever since. When not writing, Wendy enjoys reading other people's novels, traveling, hiking, and playing hooky at the beach—and if she can combine all four, even better.

Originally from the Philadelphia area, Wendy has returned to her roots and lives there again with her husband, three kids and two muses, dogs Molly and Driggs. She and her husband are passionate organic gardeners and have turned their small urban lot into a micro farm. *Killer Image* is the first novel in the Allison Campbell mystery series.

Don't miss the 2nd Book in the Series

DEADLY ASSETS

Wendy Tyson

An Allison Campbell Mystery (#2)

An eccentric Italian heiress from the Finger Lakes. An eighteen-year-old pop star from Scranton, Pennsylvania. Allison Campbell's latest clients seem worlds apart in every respect, except one: Both women disappear on the same day. And Allison's colleague Vaughn is the last to have seen each.

Allison's search for a connection uncovers an intricate web of family secrets, corporate transgressions and an age-old rivalry that crosses continents. The closer Allison gets to the truth, the deadlier her quest becomes. All paths lead back to their sinister Finger Lakes estate and the suicide of a woman thirty years earlier. Allison soon realizes the lives of her clients and the safety of those closest to her aren't the only things at stake..

Available July 2014

Visit www.henerypress.com for details

Henery Press Mystery Books

Before you go...
Here are a few other mysteries
you might enjoy:

CIRCLE OF INFLUENCE

Annette Dashofy

A Zoe Chambers Mystery (#1)

Zoe Chambers, paramedic and deputy coroner in rural Pennsylvania's tight-knit Vance Township, has been privy to a number of local secrets over the years, some of them her own. But secrets become explosive when a dead body is found in the Township Board President's abandoned car.

As a January blizzard rages, Zoe and Police Chief Pete Adams launch a desperate search for the killer, even if it means uncovering secrets that could not only destroy Zoe and Pete, but also those closest to them.

Available at booksellers nationwide and online

Visit www.henerypress.com for details

MALICIOUS MASQUERADE

Alan Cupp

A Carter Mays PI Novel

Chicago PI Carter Mays is thrust into a perilous masquerade when local rich girl Cindy Bedford hires him. Turns out her fiancé failed to show up on their wedding day, the same day millions of dollars are stolen from her father's company. While Carter takes the case, Cindy's father tries to find him his own way. With nasty secrets, hidden finances, and a trail of revenge, it's soon apparent no one is who they say they are.

Carter searches for the truth, but the situation grows more volatile as panic collides with vulnerability. Broken relationships and blurred loyalties turn deadly, fueled by past offenses and present vendettas in a quest to reveal the truth behind the masks before no one, including Carter, gets out alive.

Available at booksellers nationwide and online

Visit www.henerypress.com for details

LOWCOUNTRY BOIL

Susan M. Boyer

A Liz Talbot Mystery (#1)

Private Investigator Liz Talbot is a modern Southern belle: she blesses hearts and takes names. She carries her Sig 9 in her Kate Spade handbag, and her golden retriever, Rhett, rides shotgun in her hybrid Escape. When her grandmother is murdered, Liz hightails it back to her South Carolina island home to find the killer.

She's fit to be tied when her police-chief brother shuts her out of the investigation, so she opens her own. Then her long-dead best friend pops in and things really get complicated. When more folks start turning up dead in this small seaside town, Liz must use more than just her wits and charm to keep her family safe, chase down clues from the hereafter, and catch a psychopath before he catches her.

Available at booksellers nationwide and online

Visit www.henerypress.com for details

DOUBLE WHAMMY

Gretchen Archer

A Davis Way Crime Caper (#1)

Davis Way thinks she's hit the jackpot when she lands a job as the fifth wheel on an elite security team at the fabulous Bellissimo Resort and Casino in Biloxi, Mississippi. But once there, she runs straight into her ex-ex husband, a rigged slot machine, her evil twin, and a trail of dead bodies. Davis learns the truth and it does not set her free—in fact, it lands her in the pokey.

Buried under a mistaken identity, unable to seek help from her family, her hot streak runs cold until her landlord Bradley Cole steps in. Make that her landlord, lawyer, and love interest. With his help, Davis must win this high stakes game before her luck runs out.

Available at booksellers nationwide and online

Visit www.henerypress.com for details

BOARD STIFF

Kendel Lynn

An Elliott Lisbon Mystery (#1)

As director of the Ballantyne Foundation on Sea Pine Island, SC, Elliott Lisbon scratches her detective itch by performing discreet inquiries for Foundation donors. Usually nothing more serious than retrieving a pilfered Pomeranian. Until Jane Hatting, Ballantyne board chair, is accused of murder. The Ballantyne's reputation tanks, Jane's headed to a jail cell, and Elliott's sexy ex is the new lieutenant in town.

Armed with moxie and her Mini Coop, Elliott uncovers a trail of blackmail schemes, gambling debts, illicit affairs, and investment scams. But the deeper she digs to clear Jane's name, the guiltier Jane looks. The closer she gets to the truth, the more treacherous her investigation becomes. With victims piling up faster than shells at a clambake, Elliott realizes she's next on the killer's list.

Available at booksellers nationwide and online

Visit www.henerypress.com for details

DINERS, DIVES & DEAD ENDS

Terri L. Austin

A Rose Strickland Mystery (#1)

As a struggling waitress and part-time college student, Rose Strickland's life is stalled in the slow lane. But when her close friend, Axton, disappears, Rose suddenly finds herself serving up more than hot coffee and flapjacks. Now she's hashing it out with sexy bad guys and scrambling to find clues in a race to save Axton before his time runs out.

With her anime-loving bestie, her septuagenarian boss, and a pair of IT wise men along for the ride, Rose discovers political corruption, illegal gambling, and shady corporations. She's gone from zero to sixty and quickly learns when you're speeding down the fast lane, it's easy to crash and burn.

Available at booksellers nationwide and online

Visit www.henerypress.com for details

ARTIFACT

Gigi Pandian

A Jaya Jones Treasure Hunt Mystery (#1)

Historian Jaya Jones discovers the secrets of a lost Indian treasure may be hidden in a Scottish legend from the days of the British Raj. But she's not the only one on the trail...

From San Francisco to London to the Highlands of Scotland, Jaya must evade a shadowy stalker as she follows hints from the hastily scrawled note of her dead lover to a remote archaeological dig. Helping her decipher the cryptic clues are her magician best friend, a devastatingly handsome art historian with something to hide, and a charming archaeologist running for his life.

Available at booksellers nationwide and online

Visit www.henerypress.com for details

THE AMBITIOUS CARD

John Gaspard

An Eli Marks Mystery (#1)

The life of a magician isn't all kiddie shows and card tricks. Sometimes it's murder. Especially when magician Eli Marks very publicly debunks a famed psychic, and said psychic ends up dead. The evidence, including a bloody King of Diamonds playing card (one from Eli's own Ambitious Card routine), directs the police right to Eli.

As more psychics are slain, and more King cards rise to the top, Eli can't escape suspicion. Things get really complicated when romance blooms with a beautiful psychic, and Eli discovers she's the next target for murder, and he's scheduled to die with her. Now Eli must use every trick he knows to keep them both alive and reveal the true killer.

Available at booksellers nationwide and online

Visit www.henerypress.com for details

FRONT PAGE FATALITY

LynDee Walker

A Nichelle Clarke Headlines in Heels Mystery (#1)

Crime reporter Nichelle Clarke's days can flip from macabre to comical with a beep of her police scanner. Then an ordinary accident story turns extraordinary when evidence goes missing, a prosecutor vanishes, and a sexy Mafia boss shows up with the headline tip of a lifetime.

As Nichelle gets closer to the truth, her story gets more dangerous. Armed with a notebook, a hunch, and her favorite stilettos, Nichelle races to splash these shady dealings across the front page before this deadline becomes her last.

Available at booksellers nationwide and online

Visit www.henerypress.com for details

PILLOW STALK

Diane Vallere

A Mad for Mod Mystery (#1)

Interior Decorator Madison Night has modeled her life after Doris Day's character in *Pillow Talk*, but when a killer targets women dressed like the bubbly actress, Madison's signature sixties style places her in the middle of a homicide investigation.

The local detective connects the new crimes to a twenty-year old cold case, and Madison's long-trusted contractor emerges as the leading suspect. As the body count piles up like a stack of plush pillows, Madison uncovers a Soviet spy, a campaign to destroy all Doris Day movies, and six minutes of film that will change her life forever.

Available at booksellers nationwide and online

Visit www.henerypress.com for details

FORGIVE & FORGET

Heather Ashby

Love in the Fleet (#1)

When Hallie McCabe meets Philip Johnston at a picnic, she is drawn to his integrity. He is a gentleman. But also an officer. From her ship. Aware of the code against fraternization between officers and enlisted, Hallie conceals her Navy status, hopeful she and her secret will stay hidden on their aircraft carrier until she can figure out a way for them to sail off into the sunset together.

Caught in an emotional firestorm, Hallie faces a future without the man she loves, a career-shattering secret from the past, and the burden of being the one person who can prevent a terrorist attack on the ship she has sworn to protect with her life.

CPSIA information can be obtained
at www.ICGtesting.com
Printed in the USA
LVOW01s1033100716
495761LV00017B/893/P